8 Cool Cats

The Underdogs

Alex Maister

Prologue

Professor Fishtail was tall for a cat. That was the first thing one would say about him as he stood on the school performance stage facing the packed audience of cats and kittens waiting to see their favourite band.

The professor, looking very businesslike from head to paw in his brightly coloured chequered vest with purple tie, wasn't wearing shoes. That's because Animalians generally don't like wearing them, preferring to walk the land as their ancestors once did.

Glancing around the school hall, the professor murmured a quiet *ahem*, clearing his throat as he adjusted his spectacles, his twitchy nose twitching three times before his mouth opened to speak into the microphone:

"So now, cats and kittens, the moment you have all been waiting for. It is my great pleasure to invite onto stage our much-loved, adored, highly talented Purrville High School band, performing tonight one of their all-time greatest hits: 'The Wheels on the Bus.' Please give it up for the super, amazing . . . Eight Cool Cats!"

The spontaneous eruption of a multitude of forepaws thudding together excitedly, accompanied by a loud chorus of cheers, was quite an ovation as the Eight Cool Cats stepped onto the stage, moving confidently to their instruments that lay waiting for them.

Kreamy Flatnose was first out, striding proudly to her chair to pick up her flute. She smiled and stroked her long blonde hair with one paw. A grin spread across her face as her lips met the flute.

Sylvest Treeclimber, a larger-than-life kitten with muscled arms and a navy-blue tank top adorned with a colourful, drawn-on bow tie, grabbed his bass guitar and strummed the strings. The sound resonated throughout the hall through the stacks of loudspeakers flanking the stage.

Drummer KT Wisewhisker settled in behind his kit of small drums and cymbals, brushes at the ends of his sticks to soften his rhythmic beating of the percussion set that had once belonged to his father.

Nearby stood Tinki Sweetlife, who picked up her electric lead guitar, wired into an amplifier. She looked at the band members and smiled. To her, they were her family. They meant the world to each other, and they all knew it.

Close by was Mimi Krusher, lifting her violin and bow. She gazed into the audience eagerly, searching for her mother, but couldn't make her out among the rows of seats packed with two hundred cats and kittens.

On the other side was Purrsteph Truelip, holding on to two small cymbals. She looked somewhat bored, but she knew she was going to have fun once they got going.

Next to her was Fangl Longback, taking his seat behind his electronic keyboard and switching it on. Like all Animalians, his fore-claws had been replaced by finger-like protrusions, but they remained sharp.

Finally, Doubler Wagtail. He strode to the front of the stage, where a microphone stood ready. He wore glasses with narrow rectangular frames perched on the end of his nose. He never actually seemed to look through the lenses, which left the other cats in the band wondering whether he needed to wear them. Either way, it made him look smart, which he was.

Doubler glanced at his bandmates and nodded. They nodded back, and on Doubler's count of four, they began to play one of their favourite nursery rhymes, "The Wheels on the Bus."

One could hear the collective purr of cats and kittens as they listened attentively to the music. This regular quarterly event was one of the high points of life in Purrville, a sizeable town that housed most of the Indigenous cat population in the great lands of Animalia. It was a day filled with music, laughter, and plenty of cheers and purrs—a day of musical entertainment for the whole cat community.

Animalians came from all walks of primitive animal life and had evolved into highly intelligent, fully conversant creatures. They behaved similarly to humans and generally got along with each other. This helped forge a long-running peace in Animalia, but that didn't mean everyone liked each other. Quite the opposite; it was more a case of putting up with each other and keeping mainly to their own kind.

With all eyes (and ears) on the Eight Cool Cats, this is where our story truly begins. Little did any of them know that not only was their music about to change, but so were their entire lives. They were about to go through a great musical revolution that would create a new musical landscape across Animalia forever.

This was also the last time they would innocently play a nursery rhyme the way they were doing at that moment in time, because our talented band of musical cats was not just any old bunch of eager kittens who thought they were already grown-up cats. There was much more to them than that. They were highly resilient, infinitely curious, and almost recklessly adventurous, and they didn't give up so easily on any challenge.

No, they didn't mind taking on obstacles that lay in their way. If the truth were known, they often thrived on adversity . . . which was part of why the Eight Cool Cats evolved into something so much greater than they could ever have imagined they'd become.

That said, as you'll soon find out, this feat took them far longer than they could have anticipated.

Quite some distance away was a place in Animalia completely different from Purrville. Like a powerful magnet, it attracted Animalians from all walks of life. Right at the precise moment the Eight Cool Cats were performing their favourite tune, a secret meeting was being held in the great city known as Birdheights—a city where everything was possible. Take, for instance, a poor tiger called Boreme Kildare, who went from struggling hotel doorkeeper to founder of a powerful business empire within a few short years.

This secret meeting turned out to be the catalyst for what was to come next and had a devastating impact on the Eight Cool Cats, Purrville, and even Birdheights itself.

What happened next has gone down as one of the great legends of Animalia; a story no one could quite believe . . . but was all so believable.

***

Historical Context – An Introduction to Purrville and Dogwood

Before we begin, it's important to explain the historical background of the world of cats and dogs living in Animalia's peaceful land, mostly in purrfect harmony. While uninterrupted peace was incredibly rare, it would be true to say that when one goes back hundreds of years, there had been no outright hostility, major conflicts, skirmishes, squabbles, or street fights for as long as anyone had known. Some moments could create tension, such as accidental stepping on tails, food-rationing, or suspected outbreaks of feline or canine disease. In fact, strange to say, sometimes Animalians from different groups even neared a state of friendship.

But beneath the calm surface veneer, things were a lot more complex than that.

Most canines lived in a town called Dogwood, which was reminiscent of an early 1900s American cowboy town. It was messy, as expected, since dogs weren't great at keeping things tidy.

In contrast, cats kept Purrville pristine, always immaculate and well-cared for.

These towns were separated by approximately twenty-six miles of beautiful, winding, pebbled road meandering through lush green hills and descending into fertile valleys, providing spectacular and idyllic countryside views.

The interesting thing is nobody lingered in this rural area; it was mainly an unpopulated space, meant solely for travelling from one point to another—a kind of no-dog/no-cat no-man's-land. It seemed odd that the countryside wasn't used for picnics or neighbourly gatherings, but such a thing didn't appeal to cats or dogs, mainly due to their proximity to each other. So, it remained a large expanse that was not used for anything other than passing through as briskly as possible. Over time, this became a generally agreed-upon, though unwritten rule, for cats and dogs.

Hence, this land has existed as a dividing line between the two towns and helped keep things separate. It could be considered a significant factor in why Dogwood and Purrville's inhabitants had lived side by side so happily.

That is not to say other creatures could not occasionally be spotted in the sprawling twenty-six miles of green, open space. These came mainly in the form of insects, including many that had never evolved from their original states of existence—more on that later. Having said that, there were creatures of a mythical nature (no world would be the same without them!), and throughout Animalian history, many tales were told of their existence, though none were ever found to be real (yet).

There was another theory that Animalian Professors of Biology and History liked to pursue: in this incredible world where cats got on reasonably well with dogs and dogs got on reasonably well with cats, it was because, in some strange way, they both complemented each other with their different talents and skills.

Cats were highly adept at innovation, creativity, and making things look much more manageable and better than almost anyone else could, partially because they were ridiculously well-organised and ultra-clean, which gave them an advantage.

Dogs, however, excelled at manual labour that demanded strength and effort, like digging up materials from the earth or working on rugged farms. Surprisingly, they even excelled at recreational activities in rugged terrain that required a strenuous amount of effort. Where little effort was needed, they found a way to make it more challenging than it was, and they became good at it.

For instance, dogs could spend hours sitting contentedly by the river fishing, often without catching anything. What was physical about that? Well, dogs didn't just sit lazily by the river; they preferred to cling to their fishing rods for hours or stand upright in the river and cast their line for an entire day . . . remaining calm and at peace whilst hardly twitching a muscle. Give a cat a fishing rod, and they would choose to plant it in the ground and fasten it so that it stood there by itself whilst the cat lay lazily on a sunbed or snoozed in a small tent nearby.

It wasn't even the prize of catching the fish that the dogs were after; it was more the pleasure of doing next to nothing other than hanging on securely to the rod. Besides, in this land, even the fish were bright, and they knew better than to bite onto some dangling fishing tackle suspended in the water and then be dragged up to the surface, only to be thrown back in!

Incidentally, it's important to note that all the animals in this world were devout plant eaters; eating meat was strictly forbidden, and any animal found to have done so was cast out of their local community and forced to wander the lands of Animalia as a dejected outcast, despised by all animals alike. Meat-eating had been banned for a long time, as who would eat another intelligent creature or even one who hadn't yet had the good fortune to become highly intelligent, when such an abundance of plants and fruits was readily available? Of course, every young Animalian was taught in school that many centuries ago, such cannibalistic behaviour was the norm and still was in a number of different worlds. The very thought could make young Animalian schoolkits and schoolpups physically ill, such was their distaste for meat.

So here we were: two disparate tribes of cats and dogs finding a way to coexist harmoniously next to each other, rarely mingling with one another, apart from a few notable exceptions.

This story is one of those notable exceptions . . .

CHAPTER 1

Nursery Rhymes

In Purrville, the Eight Cool Cats were well-known for producing smooth purring harmonies and catchy, melodic nursery rhymes. Their performances often had a soporific effect, sending some audience members off to sleep! But this was a good thing. As all parents know, getting offspring to sleep is one of the most complex parts of parenting. Thus, playing the hits of the Eight Cool Cats on their player devices became the "purrfect" way to ease their young kits into the land of sleep!

Dogs, however, couldn't stand them. The feline group's lilting strings and flutes had no bark, bang, or bite—everything a good doggy ditty demanded.

Nonetheless, the Eight Cool Cats were Purrville's pride. They regularly performed for adoring kittens and cats at the local school, where audiences purred along and drank in the music like warm milk. In Purrville, not loving nursery rhymes was practically a crime.

In contrast, it was almost "criminal" for any dog to be caught listening to cats singing nursery rhymes!

If the Eight Cool Cats had never had to perform on any stage other than Purrville High's, they would have been purrfectly happy. However, things changed dramatically when a major talent agent from the famous city of Birdheights dropped by unexpectedly at the school one day: the talent agent arrived with a potentially life-changing announcement to make. In front of a packed assembly hall, with all staff and students in attendance, the talent agent—or rather talent vulture—rambled on for ten minutes before declaring with a flourish:

"Good catizens of Purrville, you are hereby invited to put forward a band of cats to enter the contest! The pre-audition will commence at Birdheights seven days from today!"

The roof of Purrville High almost blew off; such was the power of the super-excited students' collective caterwauling! Then again, it was a makeshift roof and not that sturdy, intended as an awning for when the sky was pouring rain.

Meanwhile, over in Dogwood, the mood was somewhat different. The talent vulture had already been to Dogwood High and announced to a similarly packed assembly hall, only to be greeted with stunned silence.

This was unsurprising, given that there was no canine equivalent of the Eight Cool Cats in Dogwood. The music "scene," such as it was, could only be described as a dire dog's mess. And that was being kind. Dogwood's most popular songs entailed the constant loud banging of drums and a cacophony of howls and shouted lyrics that were barely comprehensible to even those listening attentively. Knowing what was being "sung" was hardly an issue for dogs, as the vibrations and thumping generally touched their souls.

Dogwood bands consisted mainly of dogs getting together randomly and spontaneously, bringing their instruments to what you might think of as "open mic nights," with a warning on the door to wear earplugs to counter the howls and deafening thudding of the drums.

So, with no recognised school band to put forward for the international band competition, the assembly hall was the quietest it had ever been as the students and staff gawped at each other in utter bewilderment.

However, there was one member of Dogwood High whose hackles were bristling with quiet, growling excitement: Ruffa Puffertwight, the drama teacher. His misguided ambitions and actions set the scene for what happened next.

Ruffa Puffertwight had been experiencing a depressing time trying to get his pups to deliver a likeable show on the Dogwood school stage that could be compared favourably to those put on by the Eight Cool Cats in Purrville. He had been attempting this for over nine years, and over a hundred different pups had come and gone through the band's line-up. Ruffa had managed to get his band to generate a lot of energy and passion, which pleased him, but it was just loud noise, with little harmony, despite its appeal to the base instincts of Dogwood's citizens. Ruffa wanted more, and he could see it was there; he couldn't quite get it sounding right.

There were good reasons for this dog dump of a situation that was not entirely Ruffa's fault. The Dogwood music scene had been on the decline for a long time, with the limited selection of songs being constantly repeated and fresh music not being created by those who had the potential to do so. For the previous nine seasons, most of the shows Ruffa had staged were the droopiest and most embarrassing dog flops one had ever witnessed in the history of Dogwood. In catspeak, they were nothing short of catastrophic!

Sadly, there were more performer pups on stage at the most recent show than in the actual audience. To make matters worse, it was only midway through the show that the occasional paw-claps began to be replaced by the sound of agitated dogs despondently howling at the stage. Some were even barking at the performers to help alleviate the pain of enduring the despotic noises from the incompetent performers.

Ruffa was standing to the side of the stage, watching the performance deteriorate yet again. He shook his head, muttering in another internal conversation caused by the stress that engulfed him. These conversations went something like this:

"Come on, come on, get your act together! This is another disaster we're witnessing yet again! Nothing but an embarrassment to you and everyone in this town. They're going to fire you for this musical outrage. You're on your last leg. Then you're done. How can you survive this awful gig? It's not the first terrible show you've staged . . .

"Hey, hey, how about not being so tough on yourself, you fool? After all, you're a natural, and we all know there's huge talent in Dogwood. It's hard to spot among these novice pups because something's missing. A spark! You know what you are? You're a late-blooming genius, and one day, all Animalia citizens will most loudly acknowledge how brilliant Ruffa Puffertwight is. I swear it to you!"

This was a kind of internal conflict between the two halves of a damaged self, or maybe it was simply Ruffa's way of addressing his problems.

"This is stupid—you dumb mutt . . . No, it's not too bad, Ruffa; it's quite a commendable idea you've come up with. Those fools don't realise how far you've gone with such talentless pups, nor what you can accomplish if you get smart."

Ruffa shook his head, nodded, then shook his head again.

Now, you may be wondering why dogs occasionally still bark in this land of walking and talking animals. It should be noted that cats can still be heard meowing to each other even though they're purrfectly capable of speaking eloquently. There is a very logical explanation.

Certain hereditary traits were complex for such creatures to alter, and they remained ingrained in their beings. This didn't apply to cats and dogs; it applied to all creatures walking this land and beyond. Their natural, ancestral habits resurfaced when they became annoyed, overexcited, or bored, and their primitive states returned.

In human creatures such as yourselves, it's like picking one's nose or scratching one's itch. You could be the composer or conductor of one of the greatest symphonies of all time, and assuredly, you'd still pick your nose occasionally or scratch an unmentionable part. One couldn't help it; such actions were embedded in one's genes. Deep down, certain essential traits remained in all creatures, and you cannot dismiss your animal elements. So, there you go.

Now, back to the dreary performance by the Dogwood Droopsters. It proved to be such a mega disappointment that they were rightly barked off stage by the few remaining hounds who had bothered to hang around to witness it. The poor headmaster, Professor Mucka Macka Barker, had taken off and gone home way before the show finished. He claimed a sudden onset of abdominal pain and was hoping he'd wake up the following day, having completely forgotten what had transpired.

At the end of the show, Ruffa stepped apologetically onto the stage.

"I'm sorry to you all for enduring those awful sounds. Certainly not their finest hour—"

"They have never had a finest hour!" some smart aleck canine yelled.

"—but I hope you still enjoyed the show in its unique, special way." Ruffa scratched himself somewhere unmentionable; those who noticed didn't blink. "I want to thank everyone who stayed until the end and endured this hideous noise."

As the lights came on, Ruffa scoured the audience, his best fake smile soon disappearing when he saw that the audience of fifty at the start of the show was now down to one.

"Bravo . . . to you," Ruffa said, extending his paw to the brave old dog sitting in row three. "Hopefully, our show tonight wasn't a total waste of time. I heard that the catering may have made up for it! Especially those luscious doggy biscuits that were kindly donated by Miss Nucker Buxom. They are one of a kind. A lot can be forgiven and accomplished by providing good food. I have taken this inspiration to heart—"

"The doggy biscuits possess more musical talent than your band combined!" the one audience member bellowed.

"Ah, well . . . okay . . . moving on, as is customary after ANY show, let me introduce the band. As you know, we only have a modest band of four because of tight budgets. The good news is we are recruiting additional members to make a bigger band of eight . . ."
"No, no, please, I beg you. Don't do that. Have pity. You can't inflict even MORE misery on our poor ears! Don't do it!"

Ruffa ignored the heckler and moved quickly on. "So, here they are." Ruffa pointed to each band member and called out their names. "On vocals, we have our hugely talented Rommy. Rommy is blessed with an angelic voice, and she's our lead guitar player. A big round of applause to the lovely, multi-talented Rommy."

The remaining audience member slowly paw-clapped, but his muted response demonstrated scant enthusiasm.

"Then, on trumpet, we have the lovely and most talented Smackie here. She's sure got a big pair of lungs, and what a beautiful noise she can make. Give it up for our own hugely talented trumpet player, Smackie."

This was met with silence.

"Over on guitars, we have Sniffer, who strums on bass. Sniffer is a truly talented performer. So, everyone, give it up for Sniffer. A team player if I've ever known one."

Once again, silence.

"Finally, we have our thunderous drummer, Moss. Moss knows how to bang out great beats and has been largely responsible for maintaining the band's rhythm. Give it up for Moss."

The remaining audience member got up and shuffled away, muttering something gruffly under his breath. Moss hit the drums and banged away despite not receiving any applause.

"Well, I, eh, we hope you come back again to listen to us play," Ruffa called out. "Thank you, and good night."

He was met with four young, dejected expressions when he turned to face the band. Ruffa had run out of motivational words. Instead, he rubbed his jaw ruefully and hunched his shoulders. In a moment of frustration and quite out of character, Moss kicked his drum kit over (as drummers often did) and stood up as the others looked on, surprised.

"I've always wanted to do that," said Moss before trudging off stage forlornly.

"I know how he feels," Rommy said, her head dropping as she slumped away to join Moss.

Sniffer and Smackie looked at each other, both thinking the same thing, and went to commiserate with their bandmates. But Smackie stopped suddenly and turned back to Ruffa.

"What did you mean, sir, when you said our band of four was going to be eight?"

"Huh?" Ruffa said, caught off guard. "Oh, that. Nothing. I . . . no, it was nothing. I don't know what I was thinking. Just fishing for something to say at the time."

"Oh, okay."

Ruffa watched Smackie and Sniffer leave the stage. Then his eyes started blinking rapidly, as they often did when mad ideas began forming.

"I wonder . . ."

***

Ruffa didn't sleep that night. Instead, he grabbed his favourite bag of Bite-Sized Doggie Bones (a delicious savoury snack) and sat in his favourite "thinking spot"—his hefty, old, battered-but-still-cosy armchair that his grandfather had left him. Ruffa had spent many hours, even whole days, sitting in this magnificent high-backed chair, trying to devise crafty ways of forming the most incredible band Dogwood High had ever produced. He sat in it now, repeatedly running through his latest clever plan to achieve musical immortality in his mind. A wry smile lit up his mischievous face, punctuated by his beady eyes.

"Oh yes," Ruffa softly growled to himself, "this is going to be it, Grandad. I'll make you so very proud."

Grandad Ruffa Senior Puffertwight and his grandson Ruffa could easily have been mistaken for identical twins if they had been born together. The resemblance was uncanny. The similarities didn't end there, for Ruffa was a chip off the old block when it came to opportunism and conniving. Ruffa learned everything about being that way from his grandad, which was probably understandable given how close those two were and how much time they had spent together in his younger days.

As a glorious Dogwood dawn shone through his window, lighting up the room, Ruffa felt that today would be different—a new day. And like on all new days, you never really knew what the day might bring!

But for Ruffa, the appearance of the talent vulture and his announcement of the significant new band competition had ignited the fresh spark he needed to get his imagination firing once again. Here was the opportunity he had been waiting for, one that would lead to creating a decent band capable of rivalling the Eight Cool Cats.

Ruffa had been doggedly trying to push through many talentless young pups, expecting a similar degree of competency and talent that wasn't there. There seemed to be no progression in terms of the music. But maybe in reality, and perhaps naturally, young pups preferred to go out and chase balls with their fellow artists. They were drawn more to experiencing the outdoors than to rehearsing day after day in an often rank-smelling, claustrophobic basement at school. This, in many ways, inhibited the rise of fresh talent and the exploration of fresh-sounding music. In this stale musical atmosphere, Ruffa was left to constantly churn out loud, grinding songs featuring your usual canine trials and tribulations, often with the worst lyrics.

The music produced an incessant howl, accompanied by the headache-wrenching THUD-THUD-THUD of dull percussion sounds. Despite this being the kind of music that usually appealed to dogs, the dreariness of the noise left a lot to be desired.

Ruffa had finally concluded that pursuing wider fame would prove hard to pull off!

However, whatever one might think of Ruffa, his hope, optimism, determination, and incredible drive to succeed could not be questioned. He would never give up because music was his single most obsessive passion. And no matter how hard he tried—and failed—to form a band decent enough to be called a band and labelled talented, Ruffa always believed that his dream would be realised one day.

He was also a wily opportunist, an ambitious rogue. So, while he was musing on the international band competition and how brilliant it would be if a band he had formed from such a motley crew of mutts could somehow be acclaimed as the finest band of its kind, he suddenly declared to himself out loud: "If only there were some way for my band to be as good and worthy as the Eight Cool Cats!"

And just like all ideas that emerge out of nowhere, so did the one that formed in Ruffa's mind just as the sun suddenly rose over the horizon, like the flick of a light switch.

It stopped his mind in its tracks. He instantly froze as the crazy idea that had hatched itself in his subconscious replayed over and over.

"Why, that's it. Of course . . ." Ruffa muttered softly. Then, a wry, sly smile creased his sly canine chops. "Ruffa, you mad old dog, you are a barking genius."

Now, it should be said here that one man's—or dog's—genius might be another man's lunacy, and the correct interpretation is up to everyone to decide. Still, whatever you may call it, Ruffa's "idea" was, without a doubt, utterly outrageous. Okay, someone must voice it for what it was—it was stark raving bonkers! Potentially doable, maybe, perhaps. But totally nuts!

However, if there was a wily dog who could pull it off, it was Ruffa Puffertwight. After all, he had devised some daft schemes in his past. However, none of them were quite as dog-hair-brained as this latest one! Or as ridiculously brilliant. As the saying goes, it's the crazy ones who come up with the best ideas.

Yep, it must be said that this bordered on lunacy!

So, what did Ruffa do next, you may ask?

For one thing, he didn't give his "genius" idea sufficient time for doubt. He was already fully committed to it; there was no going back. To prove it, he hot-pawed it to Dogwood High's Deputy Head Dog, Professor Bobby Barker-Bones, with the guarantee that his band would not only sail through the Superband audition but would also go on to win this most spectacular and heavily promoted competition that was catching everyone's attention across the land.

When the talent vulture arrived at the school and Ruffa heard, "You are invited to audition for a brand new International Superband competition," Ruffa knew he would be entering a band of some description; not doing so was not an option. But what kind of band would that be? He had no idea—until now.

And he knew that whatever he came up with had to be drastic because there was no way the current Dogwood Droopsters would win the audition, let alone make it through one song before being booed off stage. The disgrace and shame that would follow would most likely cost him his job. The Head of Dogwood might even ban music altogether (as he often threatened), given the endless years of disappointment the Droopsters brought upon the school. With no band to play for Dogwood's community, the Head might even shut down the impressive, expensively constructed Dogwood stage hall, which would have been agonisingly embarrassing for Ruffa, for his great-grandfather had donated the building to the local community, having been the wealthiest dog in his time— the leader of the pack.

"I can work this out . . . no, I WILL work this out! Because I am so blessed and so clever. The whole of Animalia will bow down to me out of respect and admiration the next time my dogs set foot on stage. I swear it. My band shall be admired as the best in all the land, and everyone will travel far and wide to hear them play. I have this big dream, which means big outcomes!"

But then came the other voice in his head. "Ruffa, you complete idiot, your band has failed repeatedly, and you're the worst band manager there ever was! How can you ever make anything out of this pack of talentless fools? You have zero chance!"

Ruffa stiffened his posture and continued to babble to himself.

"Nonsense. I have it all figured out! Wait and see. I'm going to make the impossible possible!"

CHAPTER 2

Some Bright Ideas

Grandad Ruffa Puffertwight Senior and his grandson Ruffa could easily have been mistaken for identical twins if they had been born together. The resemblance was uncanny. The similarities didn't end there, for Ruffa was a chip off the old block when it came to opportunism and conniving. Ruffa learned everything about being that way from his grandad, which was probably understandable given how close those two were and how much time they had spent together in his younger days.

As Ruffa chomped away rhythmically at his mini-Doggie Bones, wolfing them each down a pawful at a time, his mind filled with images of his beloved grandfather, Ruffa Senior, and the article he had read in that week's newspawper, *The Dogwood & Purrville Times*. This was a pawper published jointly to help save on printing and distribution costs. Nobody was sure whether it did, but it claimed it did, so this was good enough! (Well, the media was always right, wasn't it?) But it was also felt, by the two mayors of each community, that sharing the news of each other's achievements or successes would be good for the peace that existed between them and might even prove inspirational for one or the other.

But not Ruffa. He couldn't stand reading about the Eight Cool Cats every month and yet another "sensational show" they had put on in Purrville.

"Here they go again," Ruffa grumbled and growled as he pored over yet another glowing, mawkish review gushing about how fantastically and wonderfully talented these eight balls of feline fur were at singing and playing.

"Pah, gets on my nelly, I tell ya, Grandad," Ruffa moaned, gazing at the life-sized Ruffa Senior painting above the fireplace. His beady eyes—a family trait—stared intently ahead into the distance, and that same wry smile creased his face above his whiskery chin.

Ruffa had heard that the newspawper was often biased and had doubts that anyone went to the performances anymore. They simply assumed it would be another great show and regurgitated the same old line. Rumour had it that not everyone was a fan. A few honest reviewers had even privately stated that the music of the Eight Cool Cats was nothing more than a monotonous, high-pitched whine that could cause significant harm to one's ears.

If only he had kept the couple of copies in which such reviews had appeared, they would have delighted him to re-read whenever he felt miffed about the cats or life. Unfortunately, that particular edition had been scrapped, with all remaining copies suddenly disappearing from sale, and the entire newspawper was reprinted minus the bad reviews. No one knew who had sanctioned this outrageous censorship. The Purrville editors denied it despite repeated challenges by the Dogwood faction, who claimed foul play. Being cats, they merely purred their way out of it and provided their signature expression of innocence.

Ruffa even went so far as to check the nearby Dogwood landfill, where he rummaged through acres of dog garbage. But he was unsuccessful in finding any of the original copies. All he got out of it was horrible-smelling fur, a situation that, although not unusual, was sometimes not liked by dogs. It took several days to eliminate the foul smell. He was so embarrassed that he didn't emerge from his home for a week!

But that no longer mattered, and Ruffa concentrated on his dastardly plan to win the Superband competition. An idea that initially seemed too preposterous to take seriously, a dog-hair-brained scheme too ridiculous to implement, began to sound more appealing. The more he thought about it, the less idiotic it seemed.

"All I need to do is persuade the Eight Cool Cats to join my band!"

That would take some persuading, of course, but Ruffa was convinced that a cat and dog band where the talents of one would complement the musical talents of the other would create something entirely fresh and new. Together, they would produce a distinctive sound nobody had ever heard. It would be, in the words of cats, purrfect!

One small snag.

Such a merging of cats and dogs in a band was not permitted. There was a law banning such things. Dogwood and Purrville were only two of hundreds of towns and villages that each had a distinct musical culture, and preserving these traditions within their communities was essential. This wasn't intended as a form of discrimination; it was just the natural order of things and the way to protect the cultural heritage of diverse species by not blending them into some unrecognisable mess. Mother Nature had dictated it this way, so why should music be any different?

Only in Birdheights was there some wiggle room. In a handful of small, underground venues, any species could mix and form bands with any other species. These were officially illegal, but they were tolerated in the name of having a freer and more liberal society. In human terms, it was a kind of "swinging sixties," where most things were allowed as part of a movement towards granting greater freedom and individuality. Not that it went down all that well with local Birdheights residents, and some visitors who witnessed such aberrations were genuinely shocked when they saw and heard this fusion music being flaunted so openly. Many visitors returned to their homes and swore never to leave their villages and towns again because they were convinced that life in Birdheights went against all that was decent and true, and that their ancestors were correct not to mix species. Stay precisely where you belong in the name of the survival of your kind!

However, this was one of the main reasons the new International Superband music competition was proposed and approved by the local Birdheights council: so that bands from all over the land could come and play their own music and show how diversity came from promoting your own musical culture, not changing it. It wasn't a case of mixing it up; it showed the rich variety of differences in cultures and traditions that existed musically across the land.

But to return to Ruffa and his dog-hare-brained scheme. He faced two challenges. Not only was it not allowed to showcase a band of mixed species, but how would he ever persuade cats and dogs to perform together in one band?

There was no way. Not a chance. Never in a quintillion, zillion years would cats willingly play with dogs, and dogs willingly play with cats! Even if the Eight Cool Cats were supercool and agreed, there was no way his Dogwood Droopsters would go for it.

So, what was Ruffa thinking, even to attempt such a feat? How could he possibly achieve the impossible?

Ruffa chuckled to himself as the idea ran through his cunning mind for the hundredth time, and well, this is where one must take their hat off to the wily hound.

Firstly, Ruffa would disguise the Eight Cool Cats as dogs.

Secondly, the Eight Cool Cats would agree . . . because Ruffa would have kittienapped their mommies and only released them once the cats had performed with his Dogwood Droopsters!

Simple. In theory. What could possibly go wrong?

Ruffa chuckled to himself again . . . and again. It was by far the most fantastic, maddest idea he had ever come up with (which is saying something, for he had dreamt up many grand plans in his time).

Ruffa rubbed his paws together gleefully. "Oh, this is going to be soooo delicious!"

"You fool, Ruffa," Ruffa's other voice chimed in. "What are you thinking? You will make a dog's rear-end of all this nonsense!"

"Oh no, I won't. Be quiet at the back! Always trying to have your way, holding me back, and curbing my genius and outrageously inventive mind! I don't know where you came from. You're not a true Puffertwight! Go away!"

Of course, such dialogues with himself were nothing unusual. It was all part of the "planning process." The more confident he felt about any plan, the greater his conviction that it would work. It was simply Ruffa's way of growing his confidence, no matter how mad the plan might seem to others.

"So, it's decided then. I'm doing it."

He was in that kind of mood. Determined. Emboldened. And when he felt like this, he knew he had no option but to follow through with his decision. Otherwise, he would forever be the regretful dog who had chickened out.

[It should be acknowledged here that the expression "chickening out" was disrespectful to all chickens from Chicktown who had on many occasions proven themselves brave and courageous over the years. In general, though, everyone knew chickens disliked taking risks and were the most risk-averse

creatures in the land. Therefore, it was hardly a surprise that no chickens had signed up for the International Superband Competition, so in this instance, they had all chickened out. Or they didn't have a large enough talent pool at Chick High to pull a good enough band together.]

The other thought that had travelled around in his mind when coming to his decision was, "What did he have to lose by giving this a try?" He was already known as the worst performing arts teacher Dogwood High had ever had the misfortune to take on. He kept his pathetic and immensely underpaid job because nobody else wanted it.

It hadn't taken long for Ruffa to hatch his daring plan, and within a couple of days, he began making initial preparations. He knew time was not on his side, as the competition was only a few weeks away.

First step: tailor the costumes for each of the Eight Cool Cats, who would secretly be transformed into performing puppies. This could be implemented at a secret, reclusive private compound he had inherited from his uncle, which he hardly ever used. He spent an entire week doing this in preparation for what was to come. He didn't expect to get hold of all the cats for his new band, so he had to plan to customise the costumes to fit any of the cats he could get on board. Of course, Ruffa hadn't sewn anything in his life, so he enlisted the help of his good friend Bumples, the local tailor.

While Bumples got on with creating one-size-fits-all-type canine onesies that any cat could fit into, Ruffa replayed the most crucial aspect of his plan—the kit-napping of the cool cats' mommies. Taking them hostage was the only logical thing to do. The only enticement any loving kittens would need to accompany this outrageous scheme to produce a dog-cat Superband!

But how could he kittienap any of the mommies, let alone all eight of them?

That question was tormenting him, keeping him awake most nights that week. *There must be some way*, he thought. Then it came to him.

"Ha ha!" Ruffa exclaimed joyously. "I *am* a genius! It will be easy. I shall drive up to each of their homes in a homemade milk float and offer the mommies an entire year's supply of free milk if they answer three simple questions correctly. When they walk over to the float and taste the fresh, delicious milk I will give for free to the lucky winner, I will drop a sleeping potion into their milk, which will send them off to blissful sleep as they talk to me.

"I'll then bring them all back here to the compound and tie them up for safekeeping as my hostages! I shall point out to the Eight Cool Cats that their mommies will need rescuing, and the only way to rescue them is to sing for me and put on the best show of their lives! Ha ha! They will have no choice! It's purrfect! I love it!"

Now, on the face of it, this was instead a mean and terrible thing to consider doing, and Ruffa was not the pleasant furry creature you might have liked him to be. However, it wasn't so much that he was a naughty dog with poor characteristics or a mad hound who'd lost his mind and abandoned reason; he was desperately looking for a chance to shine in his job. This was Ruffa being determined to find a way to please Professor Barker, the often-grumpy headmaster of Dogwood High.

Poor Ruffa had no choice but to think far outside his comfort zone. He didn't realise how ludicrous and twisted this idea was and what a mess it would create for everyone involved. But hey-ho, it was Ruffa Puffertwight right down to a tee!

So, having devised his audacious plan, he realised it could work no matter how ridiculous it seemed. The next step was to build his milk float! Now, this was something he could do all by himself, as he had always been a dab hand at playing around with gadgets and all mechanical things.

CHAPTER 3

First Attempts Fail Most Often

It was a bright, sunny day when Ruffa took a deep breath, got into his customised dog-van milk float, and set off for Purrville. He covered the twenty-six-mile trip in under two hours, riding over caked mud with long stretches of pebbles that had embedded into the ground over the years. He kept a keen watch for anyone passing by who might have been suspicious of this odd-looking vehicle haphazardly trundling along and see through his clever disguise. Fortunately, the road was mostly deserted, with only a couple of vehicles heading in the opposite direction, giving him no attention at all.

When he arrived on the outskirts of Purrville, he unfolded a map that Grandad Ruffa Puffertwight Senior had kept hidden away in his secret box of knick-knacks (a family relic that had housed many such documents and scrolls from Ruffa Senior's long list of roguish endeavours and equally hare-brained money-making schemes). Ruffa's first stop was at a place called Small Tail End Close. This was where the mummy of one of the Eight Cool Cats lived in her house, along with her daughter.

He pulled up slowly outside a big house and studied the front door cautiously, for this was no ordinary cat home, and the well-respected feline who resided here was no ordinary creature.

This was the home of Mrs Dee Krusher, the main owner of the water station situated by the lake. The same station supplied all the fresh water to the towns of Purrville and Dogwood. Hence, she was doing extremely well with her business and had amassed a tidy fortune.

Purrville was a peaceful place, and nobody caused much trouble there. Crime was infrequent. Given Purrville's long and tranquil history, the very idea that a planned abduction could ever take place was, well, inconceivable.

It was such a safe town that the police chief, a rather elderly woman named Kitty Smallpaws, spent more time teaching small kittens how to apply make-up in her night-school classes than working in the police station. The fact was that the Purrville police station had been left mostly unattended for many years. Kitty was, after all, the only officer dealing with law enforcement in the town, and rarely was there much for her to do.

The last time anyone was detained in a police cell was a couple of decades ago, and some say the incarceration was nothing more than a public relations stunt. Mucky Bighead, the local town clown, had decided to steal the high school long-distance running trophy that Bealy Bubb had won thirty-five years earlier.

That had been at an auspicious international sports tournament, and Bealy had surprised everyone by crossing the line first. The fact that this was one of the rare cross-town events meant that Bealy's accomplishment made headlines for weeks across the land. So, when Mucky Bighead stole the trophy, he deeply embarrassed Purrville.

He only wanted to hang onto the trophy for a couple of days because he had been an excellent athlete in his youth and had always dreamt that he would win some kind of sports award. But as there were no international sports competitions when he was growing up, this opportunity had eluded him. Generally, cats weren't keen on running a sports day in Purrville anyway, so Mucky barely had the chance to demonstrate how good he was at sports.

A few days later, the trophy was safely returned to an otherwise empty sports award glass cabinet with more spiders than sporting awards, and Bealy, who admitted he hadn't taken it to keep, was made to spend a couple of nights in the police cell.

The odd thing was that he disappeared soon after his time in custody, and nobody ever saw or heard of him again. Many thought he was too ashamed to face anyone after he was officially classified as a convict. Poor Mucky had become the only living cat ex-convict after being released, and this stigma had caused him a great deal of strain. Not only was his athletic career over, but he was also unwanted by all those around him.

Of course, Ruffa was fully aware that Purrville's only police station was largely unused these days, and it had only one elderly feline police officer to oversee "crime" and keep the peace. Thus, should any mishap occur during "Operation Milk Float," Ruffa knew he would have enough time to make a clean getaway.

With this in mind, Ruffa was confident and bullish as he strolled up to Mrs Krusher's front door and pressed the doorbell. A handful of resident cats passed across the street and noted the dog standing at the door, a milk float parked by the roadside. Ruffa smiled and waved. None of the residents waved back. The fact that nobody bothered to take any notice of him and his makeshift float showed how little the residents of Purrville believed anything suspicious was taking place.

After all, dogs occasionally appeared in Purrville, making deliveries or collecting household or recycling items, so having a dog show up in Purrville while doing his business wasn't unusual. Especially at this time of the day, when the kittens were busy in school, and the cats were either in their offices in town, working at their homes, or conducting business from their home offices. It was pretty much a normal, quiet day. It was also sunny and hot, and cats were known not to be too fond of the blazing heat.

The doorbell chimed, and Ruffa waited patiently for someone to arrive at the front door. A few moments later, the door opened. It wasn't Mrs Krusher, but her short and chirpy daughter, Mimi. Ruffa just stood and stared because standing before him was none other than one of the Eight Cool Cats, whom he was going to emotionally blackmail and coerce into joining his new hybrid band!

"H—hello," Ruffa stammered, starstruck, as he beheld one of the well-known young felines in the flesh and fur. For her part, Mimi glared right into Ruffa's sad, droopy, dark eyes with a sense of annoyance at having been disturbed. She also found Ruffa's appearance rather creepy.

"Is—is this the home of Mrs Krusher of Purrville?" Ruffa continued to speak nervously.

"Who asks, may I know? Who are you? You're not expected, or my Mommy would have said something to me," Mimi replied in a huff.

"Me? Who am I? That's a good question," Ruffa answered as he suddenly remembered his lines. "Well, miss, I'm a member of Dogwood's official milk marketing board. We-we are running a special promotion designed for you, for our wonderful new milk-flavoured product. I mean, not you specifically; it's for all cats. It's a taste that all cats and kittens love. Is your mummy home?"

"What? There's a milk board for Dogwood? I didn't even know there was anything of that sort," Mimi replied briskly. "Only Purrville has a milk board, as far as I am aware. Are you pulling my tail?"

Ruffa shook his head demurely. He had been caught off guard, as he wasn't expecting a Cool Cat at the door. The youngsters were meant to all be in school.

"Forgive me for asking, aren't you supposed to be studying at school, kitten?"

"Maybe. Or maybe I'm not well. Got a cold or something. Don't call me kitten; you have no idea how old I am."

"I mean, this is a regular school day. All kit . . . eh, cats need to be at school. So do most pups. It's general rules, you know."

"Well, it may be for you, but I happen to have a proper excuse. I must stay home so my mummy can take me later to the doctor because I'm not feeling too well. Besides, what business is this of yours, anyway?"

"Oh, well . . . uhm . . . none, I suppose." Ruffa squirmed inside as his bravado act collapsed, and he had to improvise. "Ah, well, you see, miss, the Dogwood Milk Board is a new thing—only been going a few days due to numerous requests to create a professional milk standard for residents. We've been advised our standard is now close to purrfect, and we have the good fortune of having large amounts of fresh, delicious milk that Purrville's lovely residents will love.

"So, we thought it would be a good idea to come here with a promotional offer introducing our unique new flavour at a special rate since we are new as a milk board. This new milk flavour is chocolate-orange milk. Of course, this is not flavoured with real chocolate or orange, as both substances are known to make cats extremely sick, but as an artificial flavour, it provides a novelty for them. It's amazingly yummy. Care to try? If you don't believe me, why not taste it for yourself? You really ought to sample my heavenly concoction."

This caught Mimi's full attention. The thought of trying new chocolate-orange-flavoured milk and being one of the first kittens to taste it was a tempting offer, especially if it was not actually real chocolate, which was bad for cat health. Everyone knew that doing something taboo was nothing less than cool.

"What's your very special price?" Mimi asked, taking a step forward and sizing Ruffa up. She thought he seemed harmless enough. Dogs were generally well-behaved, even though they were messy and poorly dressed on most occasions. Especially the ones that showed up in Purrville, who were generally lowly workers who couldn't afford fancy clothes. For cats, a fancy set of threads was a must. No cat in their right mind would underdress on any occasion.

Ruffa carefully considered the best reply to Mimi's question.

"Why, nothing less than an entire year's free supply of delicious chocolate-orange milk flavour if you answer my three simple questions and sample a smidgeon of this altogether delicious milk. It's entirely free of charge, of course. First, please tell me your thoughts about its deliciously cold and refreshing flavour. Wait there a second!"

Ruffa then disappeared and headed towards his milk float. He opened the van door and fidgeted about for a few seconds. Moments later, he held an old, beaten-up video camera and returned to the Krusher residence, saying to Mimi, "I need to film you giving your answer as part of our amazing promotion."

"Oh gosh, that does sound special indeed. Will I be on TV?"

"Oh yes," Ruffa replied, lying through his teeth.

"I guess I might be able to give up a few minutes of my time, but you know I'm busy and sick, not feeling too well. Plus, I've got homework as well." She stepped away from the front door and followed Ruffa to the disguised milk float. She was still watching him closely with more than idle curiosity.

A thought suddenly crept into Ruffa's mind.

"Go on, now's your chance! Grab her! Grab her! What? No. Don't be crazy. You can't do that! You cannot abduct a kitten, no matter how easy it might seem. No way! I am not going to do anything so abhorrent. Taking a mummy is one thing, but attempting to kidnap a tiny, innocent kitten . . . that, sir, without question, will be seen as a heavily punishable crime. I would be locked up for a long time, no doubt about it . . . in one of the smelly, dark, bug-infested, overflowing prison cells of Dogwood. I'd be surrounded by a motley collection of petty thieves, lazy old hounds, and the homeless stragglers who, unfortunately, have nowhere else to go. It would be terrible."

Ruffa suddenly grabbed Mimi a little too hard by the shoulders. "Oh, I just remembered, kittens are prohibited from our promotions. You must be a grown-up to take part. If your mommy happens to be at home, she is of course welcome to try it, and if she enjoys the taste, she can share some of this delicious concoction with you later on in private."

Mimi did not for one moment like to be dog-handled by this mutt.

"Hey, take those dirty paws off me right now before I yell out to my mommy and tell her what you are doing, or call our police captain."

"I'm so sorry, young miss. I forget myself sometimes and my rough old paws. Do forgive me." Ruffa bowed courteously, which seemed to appease her, though she was disappointed not to be able to taste the chocolate-orange milk sample.

"I'll go inside and see if she wants to taste your milk," said Mimi, "but I hope, for your sake, it tastes good. She's used to the finer things in life, and you won't be able to fool her at all. She can be a hard one to please."

Ruffa looked around nervously as he became unsure about his plans. What he intended to do was illegal to begin with, and this wasn't going as well as expected. "It could just be a glitch," he said to himself, "and things will get better when the right cat answers the door. Get the mommies one by one on your side, and then you shall have the kittens eating out of your paws. After this, they will join your band."

Mimi turned and ran briskly into the house, shutting the door behind her. Ruffa stood idly by his milk float, patiently waiting for Mimi or her mother to emerge. Minutes elapsed, and then half an hour had vanished into thin air. After some more time had slipped by, Ruffa rang the doorbell, but there was no answer. Ruffa continued to wait. Now, some of the other cat residents began to look at Ruffa a little dubiously. Nobody had come out an hour later, so Ruffa left hastily with his tail stuck between his legs, wondering what had happened.

Mimi had decided not to return to the house because she had found her mother in the garden by the pool. Her mother was resting on a sunbed when Mimi excitedly told her about the milk float and the peculiar dog from the Dogwood Milk Marketing Board. Out of breath, she explained all about the special free marketing promotion and urged her mummy to try it. It was precisely as Ruffa had expected she would do.

"Don't be so *udderly* silly, dear," Mrs Krusher said, twisting the word to make a point. "There's no such thing as a milk marketing board in Dogwood, and no Dogwood offer has ever been for free, I promise you. This means there will be an inevitable catch or something fishy. I have no interest in getting up from my comfortable spot here to find out. I'm preoccupied with reading this wonderful book. After my short snooze, I plan to resume reading with continued interest. You are sure you didn't make this nonsense up?"

"I wouldn't, Mommy," said Mimi, offended that her mother didn't trust her judgement. "It's all purrfectly true, Mummy. I saw the milk float for myself, and this strange old dog at the door told me all about this new flavour. I don't think he was fibbing in the slightest. He genuinely was giving away chocolate-orange-flavoured milk . . ."

By now, she was out of breath and tired of asking her mommy to do anything for her. It wasn't even for her, she thought. What was the point?

"I've heard enough of this nonsense," said Mrs Krusher. "If there is such a silly milk board based in Dogwood, which I doubt, I don't want anything to do with them. You can tell that foolish mutt to shoo away and leave us cats and kittens alone. We already have plenty of milk, thank you very much. We strictly obtain our produce only from official sources."

"But, Mommy, I want to try it," Mimi pleaded. "I've never tasted chocolate-orange milk flavour before. It sounds so delicious."

Now, Mimi knew she was exhibiting a sound of defeat in her voice that indicated she had resigned herself to not sampling any of that exciting new flavour based on her mother's stringent views and lack of interest in anything beyond what she was already preoccupied with: reading, sunbathing, and snoozing while lying by the pool.

"No more talk of such foolish nonsense. I've said all I intend to," Mrs Krusher said defiantly, raising her voice. "Now, please, can you leave me alone, dear?"

Mimi unhappily eyed her mom as the older cat put her sunglasses back on and closed her eyes. Lying next to her was the latest novel by Purrville's most famous author, Willy Two Whiskers. Mimi knew that trying to convince her to pay even the smallest amount of attention to what she was proposing was pretty much hopeless. The sun, the pool, and good old author Willy had grabbed her full attention, which meant there was no hope of getting her to break away from that spell.

Mimi returned to the house and headed straight up the stairs and into her bedroom, where she turned on her television and began watching her favourite TV show.

She resolved to forget all about the milk float and Ruffa's tantalising promotional offer. Unlike her mum, she didn't like being exposed to the heat, so she didn't want to stay in the sun for too long. In a few hours, her mom would be taking her to the dentist for a routine checkup, and by then, Ruffa would have disappeared.

She thought there might be another time, but very soon, she had abandoned any interest in Ruffa and his free special offer and drifted back into her own little world.

CHAPTER 4

Milk Float

Ruffa was back in his milk float, starting to feel fed up with his "clever mission" to snatch all eight mommy cats of the popular Eight Cool Cats band.

"Looks like you may have miscalculated the whole thing, Ruffa Puffertwight. But how rude was it of them not to take any interest in my amazing free chocolate-orange milk flavour? It shows you that many cats in Purrville are simply spoiled and rotten. They enjoy too good a life, and this one takes the biscuit!"

As he meandered through Purrville, grumbling to himself, a welcoming burger bar called Wimplebuns caught his eye, prompting him to pull over. He hoped a snack might lift his spirits; he was incredibly hungry.

He parked at the fast-food bar and entered, licking his chops eagerly. To his surprise, one of the servers was a big old dog, not a cat as he was expecting. This was quite unusual since the number of dogs living and working in Purrville was similar to the number of cats doing similar in Dogwood—you could count them on one paw. In fact, he wasn't sure any cats had ever stayed in Dogwood for more than a short spell, and apart from a very odd-looking cat who wore an eye mask most of the time, he didn't think any of them had remained.

Most of the dogs in Dogwood called this stray cat "Stumbles" because he was often tripping over himself. They figured he was ancient and had been exiled from Purrville, which evoked a sense of pity among them. Stumbles hadn't been seen around for a while, leading to speculation that he might have ventured back to Purrville or gone elsewhere.

After studying the menu, Ruffa headed to the counter and ordered a spicy whale-sized wheat burger, which sounded just what he needed.

The big old dog, Tracker, greeted Ruffa with a warm, friendly smile. "Hello and welcome to Wimplebuns, friend. We don't get a lot of canines here. Most of our customers are cats, for obvious reasons. What can I get you?"

"Well, I'd settle for literally anything with plenty of protein, but whale-sized is even better—just whatever does the trick. How large is the burger?"

"Large enough, or we couldn't call it a whale-sized wheat burger," Tracker said with a grin. "It should leave you feeling suitably full and satisfied. Coming right up." Tracker entered the order into his till. "That will be seven and a half rings."

"Oh my, I forgot to bring rings along. I only have some cubes with me. Will you take Dogwood cubes for payment instead?"

"Sure, one ring is the equivalent of three cubes. If you have them, you'll need to give me twenty-one cubes for seven rings."

"That's a lot of cubes for a wheat burger, even if it's a whale-sized one, if I may say so. Do you take notes?" Ruffa asked. "I've got some nine-cube notes. If we have a deal, I'll give you two, making . . . uh . . . eighteen cubes divided by three is six rings."

"You're right. Eighteen cubes make six rings . . . which leaves you short by one ring, sir. Why don't you give me three of those notes, making twenty-seven cubes, and then I can give you your change in two rings, the equivalent of six cubes, as two rings are each worth three cubes. That's the best I can do to make things add up correctly. We're not a currency exchange shop, so I apologise that I can't pay you back in cubes. There happens to be one downtown. Feel free to pop back in if you prefer to change your cubes there."

"You're kidding me! Oh, whatever . . . I don't mind getting my change in rings from a fellow mutt; I'm hungry now. Just give me some food, please."

"As you wish, my good sir. A whale-sized wheat burger is coming right up for my new friend here, sir." Tracker took Ruffa's notes and gave him the corresponding change.

Tracker served the wheat burger with fries and a fresh, warm, frothy milk drink. Ruffa stared at the giant wheat burger with a big, broad smile. "Well, that is big, as you say! I reckon I can eat it all because I am hungry."

"Actually, friend, as you said you were hungry, I gave you a double stack for no extra charge, courtesy of one old dog helping another out. This milk is plain, but you can choose vanilla flavour, coffee, chocolate, strawberry, blueberry, raspberry, or chocomint. Would you like one of these, or are you fine with regular milk?"

"Oh, no thanks, I've plenty of that stuff already sitting in my float, and I happen to be well-versed in the varied milk flavours one can get," said Ruffa. "Tell you what, have you got plain old water for a thirsty dog like me? That will do me fine."

It was right about then that something extraordinary happened. Ruffa decided to tell Tracker about his great milk-float operation (leaving out some details) and how little interest he had received in giving away his fabulous milk when he previously attempted to do so at Mrs Krusher's home. Of course, he was lying about his true intentions, but he anticipated further resistance to his tempting milk offer and wanted to see what Tracker would advise, as he was a good-hearted mutt.

He told Tracker that his float was full of chocolate-orange milk, a delectable new flavour that Dogwood had concocted. Once word got around how good it tasted, it was likely to take Purrville by storm. But exactly how he was going to get cats hooked on this new flavour, especially those averse to purchasing produce directly from dogs, was another thing. This was currently his main concern and was troubling his mind.

"What you need to do," said Tracker with an air of quiet confidence, "is to serve your new chocolate-orange flavour milk warm, with some yummy plain biscuits.

You give these cats a free sample of your milk to get them hooked. Cats can't resist something for free if it sounds tasty to them; warming the milk makes it more desirable than serving it to them cold. You'll be sure to get them purring for more of it in no time at all."

Ruffa pondered this suggestion with great interest. He hadn't even considered warming the milk or accompanying it with biscuits.

"Uh-huh, hmm," Ruffa quietly muttered as the idea gelled more fully in his mind. "I do like it. Where will I find some of these plain biscuits, and how do I go about heating my milk? 'Cause my float is primarily a fridge; it's designed to store only cold milk in a large volume."

"Ah, well, I may be able to help you in both these instances," said Tracker. "I happen to have loads of plain biscuits sitting in the storeroom doing nothing in the back of my restaurant. I bought way too many the last time. If I don't move these items, they will soon expire and must be picked up and sent to the dump. That'll cost me even more.

"I usually keep biscuits in abundance for my customers, as I know they like plain biscuits. But business has been quieter than usual over the past few weeks, so I've an overabundance. Normally, giving away some extra freebies is one of the reasons I've been successful in Purrville. Cats love free stuff. This store I own personally. I don't only work here; it's mine! Not many dogs can say this in Purrville."

Tracker winked as Ruffa raised his eyebrows, impressed that he had been talking to the owner of the establishment, not just a hired mutt.

"I always prefer to sell my milk hot, just as my customers like it. I will also lend you a portable kettle if it helps you in achieving your objective. It runs on any standard plug-point if you can find one. You can also run it straight off your vehicle battery if you have one of those built-in power sockets sitting on your dash."

Ruffa's eyes lit up as he realised that now, finally, he would have an edge that might make this dastardly plan of his work.

"I—I don't know how to thank you for all your generous help, friend. You're a lifesaver!" he exclaimed. "I'm so pleased I stopped by and met a fellow mutt as kind and giving as you."

"You do need to return the kettle, though, as it's the only one I've got. I use it for making coffee for myself, which I like first thing in the morning when I open shop."

Ruffa nodded. It pleased him to have found a genuine friend in what he considered to be an alien, foreign environment, and for the first time in a long while, he broke out into a happy Ruffa smile.

He was so incredibly fortunate to have met Tracker, the owner of this rather hip vegan burger joint in Purrville. Tracker was accepted in Purrville, which meant some cats liked him, and he had found a way to blend in without feeling out of place.

What a lucky old dog Ruffa was. He had accidentally stumbled across an incredible role model who had taught him how to be a more intelligent dog when appealing to cats in their natural habitat.

You have to make them think you are giving them something they want—this was Tracker's little secret, Ruffa thought. His new friend knew all about cats and knew how to outsmart them by playing directly to their innermost desires. Ruffa felt reassured that he was finally on his way toward executing his masterful plan. His confidence began to return, and a rising, powerful sensation suddenly gripped him that things would go his way.

About a half-hour later, after Ruffa had enjoyed his meal, he was presented with a big, dusty sack of biscuits, which Tracker gave him free of charge. He also temporarily borrowed a compact, portable kettle. Ruffa tested it out in his float, using the dashboard charging socket to heat the milk while the engine was running. Ruffa thanked Tracker for his support and promised to return the kettle as soon as he possibly could.

CHAPTER 5

Second Attempt

The next home Ruffa chose to visit was Sylvest's. Like the Krusher house, Sylvest's home was situated on a quiet street, away from prying eyes.

"Just how I like it," Ruffa muttered as he enthusiastically rang the doorbell to the Treeclimber residence, hoping Sylvest would be at school just as all the Eight Cool Cats were supposed to be and that only Sylvest's mommy, Mrs Treeclimber, would be in.

Indeed, she was, and she stood at the door, eyeing Ruffa with suspicion as she wasn't fond of dogs at the best of times. Also, Ruffa had a stale odour about him, and she sure didn't like how he smelled. Cats, much like dogs, possessed a refined sense of smell. Unlike dogs, they detested unpleasant odours and preferred to be in places without pungent odours.

"Well, what do you want here, stranger? I'm not buying anything from someone I don't know who steps up to my door uninvited, let alone a dog," Mrs Treeclimber sniped, looking Ruffa up and down distastefully.

"Oh, no, you misunderstand my kind-hearted intentions, dear cat. I'm from the Milk Marketing Board of Dogwood, and we are giving away some lovely free hot chocolate-orange milk accompanied by the delicious plain biscuits we know you cats like. I thought you might like to try some," Ruffa wheedled, trying to capture her attention.

"You do, do you?" Mrs Treeclimber retorted. "How do I know you're not lying about this enticing offer? It sounds too good to be true, which in my book indicates it usually isn't." She added, "Especially when it's coming from a foul, smelly dog like you who turns up unexpectedly on my doorstep."

With a polite smile, Ruffa ignored her not-so-subtle rebuff about his integrity and personal hygiene and showed her the plate of biscuits that came with the milk. "The milk's here just by my float, Miss Cat. It's lovely, warm, chocolatey, orange-tasting milk. You are going to love it, friend. Care to try some of my sweetened milk and biscuits? 'Cause it's a superb treat."

Despite all her cat instincts telling her not to trust a canine stranger with a foul odour, Sylvest's mom couldn't resist Ruffa's enticing offer. It wasn't long before she stood by the milk float, slurping warm chocolate-orange milk and munching her way through plain biscuits. For a few seconds, she forgot her worries and allowed herself to indulge in this unique taste experience.

Then the unthinkable happened, and it was all over so quickly that she barely knew what was going on as the "cat-mat", so to speak, was pulled from under her!

Quick as a flash, Ruffa slid open the side door of the milk float and suddenly produced a plain white sack, which he pulled over Mrs Treeclimber's head. She tried briefly to resist him, but it was too late. A strange thing was happening to her at the same time. She was starting to feel very drowsy, slipping almost instantly into a state of unconsciousness. Within moments, Ruffa had successfully abducted her and tied her up securely in the back of his milk float.

The first foul deed of the day had been carried out successfully!

"One down, seven more to go!" Ruffa exclaimed as he drove the fake milk-float dog van to the house of his next victim. Ruffa's plan was starting to work like a dream.

This inspired deception continued throughout the rest of the day and well into the night. And luck was most certainly with him, for all seven mommies had been home alone.

By the end of the very long day, all the mommies except Mrs Krusher had been captured and securely tied up in the milk float. They could not wiggle themselves free, as they were all packed inside like sardines. Besides, they were all in a very deep sleep. One of Ruffa's rare talents was always being good at tying things up and ensuring everything was securely fastened. It seemed cats were proving to be no exception!

Ruffa knew he had to capture them all in one trip, otherwise suspicions might be raised, so he decided to give it another shot and attempt to abduct the last mommy on his hit list—Mrs Krusher.

Later that night, he returned to Mrs Krusher's home and pressed the doorbell. Luckily for him, Mrs Krusher answered the door this time, not her daughter, Mimi, who was probably tucked up in bed and getting ready to drift off to sleep.

"Er, Miss Cat, I hope you are having a pleasant evening?" Ruffa began. Mrs Krusher was already scowling, but Ruffa continued, undaunted. "You may have heard about me from your daughter, when I dropped by earlier, that there's a genuine treat in store for you and your wonderful family? Did she mention I'm offering free, delicious warm chocolate-orange milk as a taster? It's a truly delectable treat just for you. You have been specially selected to sample this product on such a fine evening. Would you care to experience it? It's free and accompanied by plain, delicious biscuits."

"No thanks, you're a rather strange-looking mutt. We're not interested in taking treats from any odd, foul-smelling, strange dog that turns up uninvited at our door. Didn't she mention when you came by earlier?" Mrs Krusher said disdainfully. "You know that there is no such thing as 'free.' Never, ever. There's always a price for everything on offer in this world. You folks should know something about that, as you look like a business hound. Either that, or you're plain stupid, and I certainly will not be enticed to sample something by someone with limited intelligence. So, no to your tasting whatever you have in your orange-chocolate-flavoured milk float."

Mrs Krusher's dismissive rebuke went right over Ruffa's head, and he continued his patter as if he hadn't heard anything Mimi's mother had said.

"Warm, free, chocolate-orange milk happens to be on offer for your taste buds, dear Miss Cat, and it comes courtesy of the Dogwood Milk Marketing Board, a newly formed organisation set up to provide better service with superior products. We are trying hard to show clever cats like yourself how delicious our products are and encourage them to purchase some. There are no strings attached. This is an opportunity, if I may be so bold as to say," Ruffa elaborated, producing in his paw a plate of delicious plain biscuits on a paper plate, "an opportunity of a lifetime to try something new. You can also receive a sample of these lovely plain biscuits, free of charge. How can you possibly ignore such a generous offer? Have you not a little curiosity?"

Mrs Krusher eyed the delectable biscuits and stared at Ruffa with mounting suspicion. Her sixth sense flagged that something was indeed wrong.

"How do I know this is genuine milk and not a bizarre, artificial concoction that is based on harmful, or even worse, banned ingredients that could lead to an awful sickness? Do you have a legitimate business contract with our preferred suppliers at Cowpatch Town? Because only Cowpatch Town is legally authorised to deliver genuine milk products to Purrville. I've heard of what some call fake milk being manufactured in places and sold illegally.

This is, without doubt, a criminal enterprise that must be stopped.

"We here in Purrville are cautious about where our milk comes from. I suggest you be gone, for I won't partake in unlicensed tastings unless you produce a genuine certificate of authenticity from Cowpatch Collective Dairies. Or as we call it, the CCD."

"Tell me, Miss Cat, do you not smell the superior quality of my produce? I assure you emphatically that it's as genuine as you and I are both standing here together talking to each other," Ruffa insisted without any sign of letting up. "My good friend Tracker tasted some and told me you cats would love it."

"Oh! Tracker, you say? You know Tracker? Why didn't you say so in the first place? He's about the only mutt who I can half-trust! We've been going to his place for years."

"Oh yes, Tracker and I, we go way back. We're old dogs, and we've known each other a long time. You can trust him, can't you? The biscuits I'm offering are straight from his restaurant, and many cats have eaten there and appreciated the quality of his food."

Now presented with this information, Mrs Krusher's demeanour completely changed, reassured by the news that Ruffa and Tracker were old buddies. Having always been a risk-taker, she accepted the glass from Ruffa, gave the warm milk a quick whiff with her nostrils, and gave way to a slight, pleasant smile.

She swirled the milk around in the cup while continuing to inspect it. Then, finally, nodded in acceptance. "Yes, I detect something quite refined present in this beverage . . . it smells like quality milk to me. But where, I must ask, is your official certificate? I'm no fool, you know. Surely Tracker would have told you about our rules, especially if you two are as good friends as you claim to be."

"Well then, Miss Cat, why don't you just try it and tell me whether you think it's up to your high standards? It's free of charge, so there is nothing to lose. It's not as if you're going to be poisoned by a good friend of Tracker's and have to discard one of your precious cat lives by sampling a few small sips of my fresh, lovely, warm chocolate-orange milk-flavoured drink made by tender paws with the most loving affection and care," said Ruffa. "I've devoted years of my life to purrfecting this drink, which means a lot to me."

As soon as he spoke his last words, Ruffa regretted them, sensing he had "let the cat out of the bag."

Mrs Krusher narrowed her eyes once more with suspicion, trying to work out how this strange-looking mutt standing before her could produce anything that was likely to taste good, especially not when it came to the provision of milk. What did dogs know about providing milk? By now, all she wanted to do was find a way to get rid of him, though the milk did look tantalisingly good. It also had a lovely fresh smell about it . . . so unlike Ruffa.

"I tell you what," said Mimi's mom, "I'll give it a tiny sip as you're here and trying to impress someone important like me. But only if I pay for it—that's my condition. I will get you change, and you shall take it from me as fair compensation. Then, I will give you my honest opinion. We'll strike a fair bargain between us; this is important. Would you like me to trust you, Mr . . . I didn't catch your name?"

"My name? It's . . . I'm . . . I'm called Friendly. I'm a friendly dog, so that's what everyone calls me. As you can see, I only want you to like my delicious, fresh milk, and I work exclusively for the Dogwood Milk Marketing Board. When I said I had a paw in it, I didn't mean I'd made it all by myself. I'm not skilled in that way! I mean, I handle the delivery. And some promotion. I'd be so very grateful if you gave it a try. It's a sample being tested on the market as we speak. I assure you that many have tasted it, and they are all fine and happy to have tried it. I've a van full of free tasting samples with proof of this."

As he said that, Ruffa pictured the tightly packed mommies bound and gagged inside his milk float, and his face revealed a vague, subdued smile!

"Well then, Mr Friendly Dog, I shall go inside and get you some change for your warm milk glass and biscuits. If there's anything, even the slightest bit peculiar, I assure you that you will not get away with it. You'll be in trouble, and I'll report you to the authorities. I promise you will be banned from returning to Purrville and purveying any further goods. Wait here, and we'll find out the truth shortly."

"Oh, come on, Miss Cat. Give this old dog a break and a chance to prove himself. I'm a gentle creature with no foul bone in my entire body. I'm a professional, I assure you."

Without uttering another word, Mrs Krusher returned to her house and left the front door ajar. This was a good indication for Ruffa, who knew she'd soon be back with small change to make her feel better, and then she would no doubt be excited to sample his lovely warm chocolate-orange milk creation. Ruffa waited quietly, squinting, knowing he was only moments away from completing his eighth "kittie-napping" of the day and making his way back home with gusto.

But he couldn't help muttering some unpleasant words to himself while he waited:

"You silly old rascal, Ruffa. It's not going to happen. She won't be back. Right now, she's calling the police as you stand here stupidly by the roadside." But then Ruffa let out a grin directed at nobody as he smacked his left cheek. "Of course she will be back, buffoon—the door remains wide open. She's coming back here just as she said she was. I know she is. Unlike you, she keeps her word."

Fortunately for him, Mrs Krusher did precisely that and came straight up to him with loose change held in her paw.

"I confess it's difficult to resist your warm and appealing-looking flavoured milk on a cool night like this, I do confess," Mrs Krusher mumbled as she handed over a couple of brass rings.

Now, under ordinary circumstances, netting a couple of brass rings as payment for one glass of milk and some free biscuits Ruffa hadn't paid for was a stupendous outcome for a hard-working dog who could get back home and exchange these for six green cubes. Such a notable prize would buy him an entire meal in Dogwood. But this wasn't Ruffa's true intention, and he wasn't really after the loose change. Besides, what were a few brass rings to him? They were nothing for a direct descendant of his noble dog lineage. His ancestors were used to far greater splendour than he could ever imagine.

Mrs Krusher reached out her paws to take the glass of warm milk, and Ruffa watched as if it were all happening in slow motion. The excitement and anticipation steadily built inside him, knowing the last of the Eight Cool Cat mommies was about to fall into his arms!

Unable to resist his generous offer, Mimi's mother lapsed into a state of sleep within a minute of drinking it. Just as with the other mommies, Ruffa quickly draped a white sack over her head, tied her up, and gently placed her into his wagon float as she became drowsy and succumbed to a heavy sleep. He had to shuffle the eight moms together as space was tight and prepared to high-tail it out of Purreville as quickly as his milk float could take him.

Ruffa knew the sleeping drug would start to wear off after a few hours and that he might find himself dealing with a bunch of furious mommies who would no doubt cause him no end of bother and make a heck of a din doing so that could potentially wake up the whole neighbourhood!

With the last mommy secure in the van, Ruffa started the engine and returned to Dogwood on the winding road. For the first time in what seemed like ages, Ruffa felt more confident that his carefully thought-out plan would work as he intended.

Ruffa and his Superband would soon be on the brink of fame and stardom. He could feel it in his bones that his moment for achieving greatness was imminent.

"You'll smash it to the distant stars; wait and see. It's going to work like a sweet dream. You're one lucky mutt, you old dog. You're going to get what you so richly deserve for your efforts. The sweet taste of success is coming your way."

Then he pondered briefly while driving, "But what if it doesn't go my way as I've planned? Oh, forget what-ifs from now on, Ruffa. Let's go with what's in it for me, 'cause it's all about to happen big time. Those who believe in themselves and crush those in their way succeed. Yeah!"

CHAPTER 6

Jumping Into Action!

On the night Ruffa kittienapped their mommies, the Eight Cool Cats slept as usual. After all, cats stay out late at night, so the fact that all eight of the Eight Cool Cats' mums were not home yet wasn't unusual. As active mommies, they usually disappeared for a late-night stroll, returning in the early morning. It was in their nature. Mommies liked to wander downtown to Purrville and visit one of their late-night hangouts, where they often played card games. Or they'd prowl about looking in awe at the streetlamps, the trees, and the nicely lit buildings, admiring how spotless and delightful everything around them was.

The husbands tended to stay home to care for their children, so the mommies could get out and enjoy a relaxing stroll around town. Mommies would often pass each other and wave as they crossed the street or took off in opposite directions. Rarely did they stop to talk at length, but sometimes, if they hadn't seen someone for a while, they'd exchange a few pleasantries and smile at each other. Then, they'd carry on with their wandering.

This was one of those peculiar things about cats, especially female cats, who liked to mooch and explore late at night. The husbands tended to put up with it because allowing their ladies a bit of space was preferable to being constantly nagged late into the evening.

However, the following day, none of the mommies of the Eight Cool Cats had returned, which immediately became a real worry for the young kittens and their dads. It wasn't long before the police captain's phone started ringing off the hook, as one call after another came in to report a missing mom.

Police Captain Kitty Smallpaws would usually brush off such occurrences. Still, something about this got her thinking, especially the call from Mrs Krusher's daughter, Mimi, who was clearly in a state of panic. What perturbed her the most was that all the moms came from the families of the Eight Cool Cats. Little did she know then that she was about to have her paws full of many mysteries that would be hard to figure out.

It was only at school later that morning that all eight of the Cool Cats began to realise the seriousness of the situation.

Purrsteph and Mimi stood outside geography class with grave expressions on their young faces when KT came running up to them. "Hey, have you seen your mommy around? Mine went out last night for her usual stroll, but hadn't returned when I woke up. Dad went looking, but there was no sign of her. We have no idea where she is, but deep inside, I sense something may have happened to her. I'm worried sick!"

Purrsteph responded to her concerns calmly, but it was apparent she, too, was agitated by the situation. She had a much more rigid view when dealing with such matters, always trying to behave and sound official and proper rather than descend into anything resembling panic. She acted as if she knew things others didn't, but she clearly had no idea!

"Mine vanished too," said Purrsteph, "or so it appears. I did wonder earlier this morning what might have happened. She even forgot to tuck me into bed last night, and she never misses that, no matter how late she goes out. Also, when she's back from hanging out with her chums, she always visits my room to check on me and gives me a little peck on my forehead. I miss her already, but it may be nothing."

"You baby," said Mimi, attempting to smile, but her attempt to look unconcerned was masking the anxiety everyone knew she was feeling. "Your mommy still tucks you into your bed? Well, I am wondering where mine is. I checked my mommy's bedroom late last night. She wasn't there. As we all know, she's a busy cat, so I thought maybe she was working late into the night in her study. You know she sometimes does that. She always has a lot going on. But I couldn't find her anywhere. She's gone; that's for sure."

"I think something peculiar is happening here," Sylvest said as he joined the corridor conversation. "How can all our mommies disappear at the same time? It's not possible. It's not like there was some big party everyone was invited to or another obvious reason we're unaware of. Don't you guys think it's weird?"

Kreamy then appeared, saying, "Yeah, mine is also missing, and our fridge is almost empty of food. If she doesn't return soon, who will restock our fridge and feed me? I'll be running out of breakfast, lunch, and supper!" Kreamy moaned, growing more fretful. "I'll have to ask my daddy to step in. Maybe he can do some of the stuff mommy usually does until she returns. I know he doesn't like to, but he might have to!"

"You can add my mom to the list!" said Fangl, stepping up to the gang. "Doesn't bother me much. I could grow to like it, to be honest. But I wonder what could be happening that made them all disappear so suddenly without informing us. Is it possible my mommy may be in trouble? They may all be in trouble, and we don't know it. Dreadful thoughts keep filling my mind!"

"Well, I didn't notice mine not being there." Doubler pondered as he spoke. "But thinking about it, she wasn't home this morning, so she's probably doing whatever the others are doing. It's most likely nothing to be concerned about. It's too much to be a coincidence; we shouldn't overthink it. I mean, mine hardly gets on her feet in the mornings on most days, so I don't usually notice when she's not there."

"Ah, this potentially explains a bunch of things. A mist is starting to clear up," Tinki mumbled as she joined the group.

"What do you mean, a mist is clearing up?" asked Doubler. "Are you now an expert weather forecaster or talking to us in riddles? Is this some profound insight you're having? If it is, you may want to share it with the rest of us."

"Well, I came across a strange note in an envelope that happened to be lying outside my front door this morning," continued Tinki. "When I started reading, I thought it must be a prank, as the handwriting was terrible. It was the kind of thing much younger kittens sometimes do to wind someone up. Whoever wrote this can't spell properly. I don't know any cats with such awful spelling; they should be embarrassed and ashamed."

She unfolded the note and slowly read it out loud, finding it hard to decipher, even though she had read it multiple times:

If any of you kitens wish to see your mommies agin, then 8 kool cats, you betr meyt me at Purrville stage 8 p.m. tonyte, and come alown or you vill be sorri. Disobay and yur mommies are goyn to graytlee raygret it. You vill never see dem again.

The kittens glanced at each other in confusion. Nobody had ever considered kittie-napping a possibility. Kittienapped, they all thought silently, but how was this possible? It simply didn't happen in Purrville.

Sylvest took the note and examined it for a few moments.

"This has to be some stupid joke. I mean, it's ridiculous. It's beyond a joke because it's not funny. And I agree, Tinki, this is by far the worst-written note I've ever read.

The writer cannot string two simple words together; the spelling is atrocious."

"But . . . what if it's real?" asked Fangl. "What if our mommies *are* in danger, and some nasty critter has somehow kittienapped them all? Maybe they're trapped in some awful place, locked up, thirsty and hungry, who knows where? Maybe whoever is behind these kittie-nappings is an evil monster. We will have to help them, won't we?"

Doubler shook his head at the thought of it. "I don't think so, Fangl. I mean, it's too early to think of such things. Clearly, a fool, an idiot, wrote this. And I suspect it wasn't one of our fellow cats. First, it's written in red. Cats prefer to write in black or blue; we don't like writing anything down in red, so it's obviously not written by one of our kind. I agree with the others; someone is playing a prank on us and doesn't like cats much."

"Ah, maybe whoever wrote this note saw all our moms out together last night. They followed them and saw them having a party," Tinki said optimistically. "Maybe they all went on holiday together on the spur of the moment."

"Don't be daft, Tinki. Our mummies would never do that without letting us know," Mimi said dismissively.

Fangl was deep in thought. He didn't appreciate Doubler's negative assessment, as it opened a range of possibilities they had never considered. Do cats have enemies? He had never heard of anyone openly disliking cats so much as to consider them to be their enemies. Everyone tended to get along with each other in

Animalia. It didn't matter where you were from. There were occasional disagreements between different species. Arguments occasionally broke out between neighbours but were usually resolved once the other parties came to their senses. A blatant contempt for another species was unheard of. How was it even possible?

Fangl decided to share his frustration openly. "Well, I tell you one thing, if I ever get my claws on whoever is behind this 'prank'—or worse, kittie-napping—I swear they'll pay for it dearly. I'll show them what cat justice is like! We cats don't easily forgive anyone who tries to intimidate us or our families. If this note is simply a prank, it's despicable to send such a thing to anyone."

"The bigger question is," said Kreamy, "what are we going to do? Do we do as the note says and go to the school stage tonight? Or what?"

"I think," said Sylvest, "let's wait and see if our mommies return this afternoon. If they're not back by 7 p.m., let's all gather at the school playground and then go to the stage to find out what the hell is happening. Because if they're not back today, something must be wrong."

"And let's not tell anyone about this note, not even our dads," Doubler added. "All agreed?"

"Agreed!" the cool cats said as one, for, as often before, they preferred to handle this potential crisis independently without seeking outside help.

7:30 p.m., School Playground.

Mimi Krusher was the last to arrive, running up to the other seven cool cats, a little out of breath.

"Hey, sorry I'm late. My dad was grilling me about mommy and where she might be and asking if I knew where she was. He was very anxious, so I told him all the mommies had gone away for a few days, a spur-of-the-moment holiday! He was angry that she hadn't told us, but then I said it was a surprise organised by KT's mom, and they didn't have time to tell us. He calmed down after that. I know. I lied, but I didn't know what else to say."

Everyone stared at Mimi, mouths open in surprise, as Mimi was not known for being quick-witted or thinking on her feet.

"Wow, Mimi," KT said quietly. "Go you. You did well."

"And you put your dad at ease, nice one," Purrsteph added.

Mimi smiled coyly. "Thank you."

"Well, now we're all here, are we ready for this?" Doubler said decisively.

"We're ready!" came the reply.

The Eight Cool Cats made their way quietly and cautiously to the Purrville stage, approaching it from the left-hand side of the audience seating area. The stage was silent and empty, not a cat to be heard or seen. They cast glances at the audience seating areas that surrounded them, and all appeared quiet here too, but it was getting dark, which immediately created a sense of foreboding.

"It all looks very spooky in this light," Kreamy whispered to no one as she shuddered. She glanced at the others and saw they were feeling the effect too.

They stood in a line in front of the stage for a few minutes, each looking to the sides and behind them, to check if they were alone. That appeared to be the case, and they were about to breathe a sigh of relief when KT noticed a small video player sitting alone on the stage on top of a small chair.

"That's odd," KT said, pointing to the camera, and took the steps up to the stage to investigate. Feeling nervous, KT ensured no one else was hiding in the wings and carefully picked up the camera.

"I think it's one of the newer models—one of the portable TV players that fits neatly in your paw. The chimps have been jumping up and down in excitement, claiming they're the best thing ever and will revolutionise entertainment on the go. I've never seen one so small before. Wait . . . I can see there's a tape inside."

The player was already on, and KT realised the video was set up and ready to play. He pressed what looked like the play button as the other cats quickly gathered around him. They all stared at the device as if in a silent communal trance, transfixed by the machine.

On the tiny screen, there was a dark room with what looked like eight white sacks on the floor, each sack containing "something" that was wriggling about inside.

"It can't be, surely?" Fangl muttered softly.

Then two very hairy arms came into view, and then the face, shrouded by a white mask that had two small slits for the eyes, small holes for the nose, and a mouth to breathe through. The hairy arms lifted the sack off each wriggling body, and all eight cats knew precisely what had happened to their mommies.

"I don't believe it; they *have* been kittienapped," Doubler said, eyes wide in disbelief.

The paw that had removed the sacks from their heads then pulled off some silver sticky tape from Mrs Krusher's mouth. She coughed spasmodically as she looked towards the camera. They could see she was about to burst into tears.

She cleared her throat and spoke frantically in a shrill voice that wasn't usual. "Help! We've all been kittienapped, and we're in big trouble . . . We need rescuing! HELP!"

The tape was then quickly pushed back over Mrs Krusher's mouth, though she did her best to resist and say some more, but it was too late. Her voice was now completely muffled, making it incomprehensible. She couldn't do much else as her hands were tied up, as were her legs. She tried her best to move, but only fell over and knocked some of the other mommies over like dominoes. They all hollered in pain.

"NOOO!" Kreamy wailed as tears fell from her eyes. "Our poor mommies! What is this monster doing?!"

Tinki put her arm around her gently. "It'll be okay, Kreamy. Don't worry. We'll get to the bottom of this."

A sudden gruff bark on the video camera made everyone jump. They all stared at the screen as the kittienapper's masked face appeared, looking right at them.

"That sounded like a . . ." Doubler said wistfully.

The kittienapper made several attempts to speak, as if trying to disguise their voice, but then gave up, and it was clear who the perpetrator was—a hairy canine, a dog!

"I don't believe it," Sylvest said, dumbstruck.

The dog said, "If any of you puny kittens wish to see your mommies home again, then you better listen to what I'm saying."

The kittens leant forward in unison towards the small screen in a state of total shock . . . which only grew worse when there came a loud clanging noise, and something toppled over onto the floor not far away. Then, a distant figure ran away, heading towards the back of the seating area.

Fangl turned in that direction and, without hesitation, ran across the stage and leapt off, darting down the audience aisle in pursuit of the mystery figure.

KT was still clutching the video camera. His bandmates turned their attention back to it. The recorded voice continued, though it was more like incoherent mumbling. It tried to sound calm, but everyone there could tell this kittienapper was uncomfortable giving instructions.

Finally, it uttered them clearly: "You shall meet me in the town hall in Dogwood at 1 a.m. tomorrow. Yes, 1 a.m. is a purrrfect time for early birds, and I want you to turn up alone. As cats, you'll be used to moving about in the late-night hours, so don't complain. We will meet up in a few hours. This gives you no time to alert anyone else to this situation without things becoming much worse than they already are. You have a few meagre hours to get to me so we can progress our discussions. Do you understand? If anyone other than you eight cats makes their way to Dogwood, then you will all be sorrrryyy indeed. So will all your mommies, who are in my possession and control. Their safety and well-being depend entirely on doing precisely as I say."

Fangl had tried to catch up with the fleeing figure, but he was too late. Whoever it was had vanished into the night. From a distance, Ruffa glared back from behind the tree he was hiding behind. Whoever had chased after him had taken off in the wrong direction, and that kitten was now out of sight. Ruffa let out a brief, sinister-sounding chuckle and was gone.

When the video ended, all the cool cats stared at each other, still in shock.

"It's unbelievable. It's a proper kittie-napping. Our mommies have been kittienapped! Why? Why them?" Purrsteph wailed.

"This is serious," said Mimi. "We need to inform Professor Fishtail immediately."

By now, all the kittens were looking tearful and frightened. They glanced awkwardly at each other, and most of them trembled at the thought of anything terrible happening to their mommies.

"Everybody—listen up! We all need to calm down and think this thing through," Tinki said commandingly, finding the courage to pull herself together before anyone else. "Have we forgotten who we are? We have the strength to handle any situation, no matter how challenging."

Taking heart from Tinki, Doubler perked up. "Tinki's right. And the first thing we need to do is find out what that dog's motive is. We must discover who this perpetrator is and what they want from us and our mommies. We need to focus before we all panic or lose control, and this matter is put into the unreliable paws of someone incompetent and less qualified to handle it than us."

Sylvest nodded. "I agree wholeheartedly. Only we can solve this crazy, mean situation and watch out for our mommies. Who else will care as much as we do and try as hard to help them?"

Kreamy suddenly burst into tears. "What is that beast going to do to them? I want my mommy back now. This is so unfair!"

Sylvest tried to be sympathetic, but he shared his anger instead. "We mustn't get emotional now. We have all got to be strong so we can stand up to whoever wants to do any harm to our mommies."

Fangl returned from his pursuit and shook his head as his seven bandmates turned to him eagerly. He rejoined them on the stage feeling just as miserable as they were. Their whole world had been shaken to its roots. Their lives had changed dramatically and in a way no one had ever imagined possible. What misfortune had befallen them? What cruelty was being dished out for no apparent reason? Who hated cats and kittens so much that they could do such a terrible thing? What did they want?

"Does anyone want to see it again?" asked KT.

Fangl shook his head.

Mimi patted Purrsteph gently on the shoulder. "Wherever they're being taken away to by this criminal, the evil creature wouldn't dare do anything to hurt a hair on any of our mommies; I'm sure of this. However, let's bring this matter to the attention of the proper authorities. Professor Fishtail is a good start, and he will most likely know what's best to do. Or we take it to the police captain; she's a decent cat. My mommy is a prominent figure in Purrville, and the professor and the mayor will act immediately to deal with this horrible situation."

"No, no, definitely not, we mustn't go to Professor Fishtail; that won't do us any good," Tinki objected strongly. "You think getting that old cat involved will help us . . . Well, I believe it won't. We have so little time between now and 1 a.m. tomorrow morning when we're supposed to be in Dogwood. The same goes for our silly old police chief. She barely manages a group of young kittens when she talks to them and gives them advice. I've sat there and listened. Believe me, her philosophy is to wait and see what happens next, doing as little as possible. It's her job."

Tinki was feeling increasingly frustrated. She broke out in a cold sweat, and a few tears began trickling down her face.

"We must leave here immediately. It'll be too late by the time Professor Fishtail arranges a parents' committee meeting on what he considers to be the appropriate action on short notice. Once gathered, he will try to obtain a majority vote from the parents' committee. Although it won't be hard, can you imagine how long this will take?

They tend to argue and debate about everything. They'll want to explore various options, and then someone's bound to disagree. That will delay things big time, and the clock is ticking away. It'll be tomorrow night before anything gets decided, and an entire day will have been wasted. What happens to them by then? Tell me."

Tinki's eyes widened with fear. "We mustn't delay in taking action. We've a single opportunity to try to fix this, which will otherwise pass us. We should try to deal with this matter ourselves and not waste time passing it to someone else."

Sylvest mulled over Tinki's remarks carefully, and he nodded in agreement. He raised his paw. "Count me in. We should handle this ourselves as the Eight Cool Cats. We can deal with this serious kittie-napping; we will be the rescue party. Tinki is usually right, as is Mimi. We cannot afford to behave like cowards. We shall show them we are not afraid."

"But," said Doubler, "who will come to rescue us if we fail and don't tell them what's going on?"

"We won't fail," KT replied.

The others nodded quietly, but it was obvious that not all of them were as confident as they were pretending to be.

"I'm not scared of any dog, or pack of dogs, who think they can get away with kittie-napping our most treasured mommies," said Mimi defiantly.

The rest were still unsure about taking this upon themselves. Sylvest then spoke up. "I think some of us are not quite as sure as you appear to be, Mimi, or as brilliant as

Doubler. Each of us, however, brings our own abilities with us. We know Doubler's the brainy one. Then there's KT, who nobody wants to mess with—KT's one of those cats from the hood. Then there's Fangl, who can fearlessly face up to anybody who dares to bother us and act bravely, and Tinki, who is always reliable with her detailed planning skills and knows what's best in any situation. Together, we are strong, and nobody will mess with us."

Sylvest continued, emboldened. "I can run the fastest and handle myself in a physical confrontation. Mimi is more than capable of convincing anyone to do what's necessary. And as for Purrsteph, she's not just a pretty face. I've watched how skilfully she can find her way out of a few strange situations, especially when she casts that gorgeous smile. Underneath her tender looks is a fierceness that can scare any mutt away . . . let's see what these fools can do if they think they will get away with messing with us!"

"Well, there's only one way to show them what we are capable of," said Fangl, trying to wrap things up. "We will head off tonight to ensure we arrive on time." The kittens all nodded in agreement. "Who knows what will happen if we don't turn up as instructed? Not that we're allowing ourselves to be pushed around by some unknown adversary, but for now, we'd better comply until we know what we're up against."

"But how exactly are we going to get to Dogwood at such a late hour without informing someone else of our urgent, sudden need to travel?" Kreamy queried. "None of us has access to a motorised vehicle."

Kreamy had listened to what the others had to say and agreed, but deep down, he felt it was far too much to turn themselves, the Eight Cool Cats, into heroic rescuers ready to take on an unknown enemy. After all, the kittens were nothing more than eagerly developing musical artists. They were fooling themselves if they thought they could attempt to rescue their mommies on their own, coming against one dog, maybe more!

"Hey, I've got an idea," said Doubler after a flash of inspiration. "You probably won't like it—but I know where they keep the keys to our school bus."

His seven cool friends gawped at him.

"I also know how to sneak into the school without being noticed and commandeer the bus for our important mission."

"Wait a second, Doubler! Are you proposing that we steal our school bus? Are you nuts? Besides, who's going to drive it?" Kreamy said, dismayed.

"Steal? We're not stealing anything; we're borrowing for a worthy cause. And as it turns out, I can drive the bus," KT said reassuringly. "It's easy."

The other seven cool cats stared at KT unconvinced.

"I'm not sure," Mimi said, shaking her head.

"Have you got real experience driving a large bus of any kind, or any vehicle with four or more wheels?" Kreamy asked dubiously.

"I've seen the bus driver do it *countless* times—it's a cinch. I've sat inside right up front and closely watched what the driver does when he takes us to and from school.

How hard can it be to turn the steering wheel to the left or right and to press down a few pedals with one's feet? Those buses are automatic, and almost any fool can drive them."

The others glanced at each other; their troubled faces registered different degrees of concern.

"Look, we can at least give it a try. Our land is full of those who don't have the guts to attempt things—yet it's said we have nine lives! What's there to lose? We have little choice but to deal with this situation, move swiftly, and not delay acting. Our mommies require our help *right now*, and we mustn't sit back doing nothing while they wait and hope to be rescued. Can we afford to be useless to them?"

"No," Tinki replied, "we can't be useless. We need to do this."

"We've got to step up to being *more* than kittens," KT added. "Tonight, we've all got to grow up. This is our defining moment!"

Kreamy felt obligated to articulate her deepest fears. "What if we fail and something horrible happens?"

"It won't. We are going to see this thing through and rescue our mommies. We will not fail in the moment of their greatest need," Fangl said, looking resolute.

"These horrid dogs don't know us," Sylvest added. "They're in for a big surprise!"

"Yeah, too right, they'll wish they had never messed with us!" KT said defiantly.

Mimi perked up. "Well, then." She grinned. "What do we call ourselves?"

Tinki looked perplexed. "We already have a name."

"That's for singing, right?" queried Purrsteph.

"I think it's for anything we want it to be," said Fangl.

"Yeah, you're right," added Sylvest. "When we're together, we're Eight Cool Cats."

"Then it's agreed. We are going to fix this."

Together as one, they raised their paws in the air. "MEOOOOOW!"

[Now, it's crucial at this stage to mention that it's wrong to steal any vehicle or anything, for that matter, and the kittens all knew this. Only their desperation to rescue their mommies drove them to do such a thing. Despite their intense desire to rescue them, this behaviour remains unacceptable. Stealing is stealing, no matter how justified it seems to someone. But nobody's purrfect!]

* * *

Following a few false starts, the Purrville High School bus left the school grounds with the Eight Cool Cats on board. KT was behind the wheel, and Fangl sat beside him for support, watching what lay ahead. After all, visibility outside Purrville was poor at night, and no streetlights were on the dirt track road to Dogwood.

"Guys, are we sure this is a great idea, taking our only school bus down this dangerous, bumpy path so late at night?" Kreamy murmured as she sat in the back seat close to Doubler. She was attempting to feed on his more positive vibes, for she was terrified. It was so dark outside, and it was so late at night.

Doubler looked at her. "Nothing ventured, nothing gained. We will return the school bus safely, in one piece. It will be returned just as it is. Nothing bad will happen."

"Okay, let's get things straight, my fellow felines," Fangl interjected. "We've borrowed the bus and'll be sure to return it before school starts tomorrow morning. Nobody here thinks our mommies' well-being isn't worth taking this risk for, and we have an excellent driver behind the wheel. Trust yourselves and stop worrying about what is going to happen. Far greater concerns are ahead of us, and we must handle things calmly."

"How can you always be so confident?" asked Purrsteph. "I'm starting to feel jealous."

"Because," Mimi replied, "Fangl knows we're invincible as the Eight Cool Cats."

"Yeah, she's right. Now let's relax. You may not realise it, but we're embarking on an incredible adventure. We leave Purrville as eight kittens, and we'll come back not just as heroes, but as the Eight Coolest Cats, and everyone will know our names!"

"Yeah, right," KT said, ensuring nobody could hear him. "What could possibly go wrong when we're so cool?"

CHAPTER 7

Late at Night

The bus made its way along the twisting road, illuminated solely by the moon's gentle glow. The night enveloped everything around them, offering only the faintest navigational guidance from the minuscule illumination of the moon and stars above.

Due to the poor visibility provided by the headlights, the Eight Cool Cats struggled to see more than a few feet ahead as they drove down the mostly pebbled track.

"I've got to be honest. I'm a little unsure about night driving," Purrsteph whimpered. "It can't be that safe to travel at this late hour. Nobody knows we're here."

"Oh, come on," said Mimi. "The road's empty, nobody's about. It's just about the safest it can be, day or night. The weather's purrfectly clear, and there's no chance of a raging storm. What could go wrong if we don't deviate from this route?"

"I keep hearing the same thing. You're only saying it to help me feel better. To be honest, it's terrifying. I'm quivering." Purrsteph appeared to be trembling to make her point.

"My daddy, as you know, is the brother of our dear police captain Kitty Smallpaws. I can tell you nothing ever happens on this road other than an occasional broken-down vehicle," said Sylvest, in an effort to reassure them that nothing terrible or unforeseen was likely to happen. "From what I've heard, problems are usually dealt with promptly if things go wrong."

"It's true," said Fangl, catching on to Sylvest's spirit of reassurance. "Nobody travels out at nighttime because it's completely unnecessary. There's not much traffic on this road during the daytime, so why would anyone drive at night? It's a safe road, not affected by the time of day one travels. Of course, night itself can be considered an unknown entity, in a way, but it's the same exact road, right?"

And right on cue . . . KRRANG! When startled, the school bus hit a massive bump on the road, and the entire vehicle jolted up in the air, like a cat on all fours! KT slammed on the brakes so hard he almost jammed the pedal, but the sudden action had the desired effect and brought the bus squealing to an abrupt, grinding halt.

Purrsteph wailed. "See what I mean!" Now she was quivering.

"Wow, I wasn't expecting that!" Fangl exclaimed. "Everyone okay?"

"NO!" Kreamy and Mimi exclaimed back.

"I'll go check it out," said Fangl, as the others gathered at the window to watch.

Fangl wasn't afraid to be outside the bus in the dead of night because, generally, he was a Cool Cat and not easily spooked. He skirted around the bus, but the darkness made it difficult to see what damage it had suffered. After carefully inspecting the bus, he ran to the rear. A few moments later, he returned on board, looking confused.

"I couldn't see anything on the road, nor exactly the damage, if any. It's too dark. I can only think we hit a rock on the road. Start her up, KT, let's see what happens. Claws crossed, everyone!"

KT turned the key, and after a few attempts, it roared back to life, and they continued their journey.

"It was probably a loose connection—all's fine now. We can fix it properly as soon as we return home."

"I once heard," said Doubler dolefully, staring out at the foreboding darkness, "an extraordinary tale about a giant green grog."

The others had no idea what Doubler was on about but decided not to say anything.

"It's a ghost," Doubler continued, "that has been said to haunt this particular road and any road that has the misfortune of running through this dense and foreboding forest."

"Oh great, thanks, Doubler, what are you trying to do to me! A grog?" Purrsteph mumbled her response as her feet shook some more. "It sounds hideous. What in the world is it? I thought this was the only road in this forest so what do you mean?"

"The only *known* road, but it's a big forest," Doubler remarked, looking increasingly unsure. He was beginning to regret mentioning it.

"Tell us, Doubler, please explain yourself," Kreamy said meekly.

"Uhm, it's just a kind of frog, I think, only a giant one. This creature looks like a pale white ghost. It's said that one can almost see through it; it's virtually transparent. Folks in Animalia, where there are such woods, call these forest creatures grogs. I'm sure it's harmless. Who ever heard of a cat-eating frog before?" Doubler said with a chuckle in an effort to allay any fears.

The silence in the party was only making matters worse.

"Come on, Doubler. You're not telling us the whole story, are you?" Tinki said in an accusing way.

"Yes, come on, spit it out, Doubler. You brought it up; you may as well tell us the truth!" Sylvest demanded.

"Okay, okay. I'm sorry I even mentioned it; I was only speaking out loud to myself. Anyway. I heard tell that it's been spotted frequently around the swamps, which I believe are close by, and this vile beast sticks out its tongue at its victim and then catches its food by wrapping the tongue around its prey. It then pulls the food into its mouth and swallows it whole due to its enormous size. One can see the victim slowly getting devoured in the grog as the poor creature slowly dissolves in its gigantic belly."

Doubler looked around the bus at his stunned and terrified bandmates. "Well, you did ask."

By now, Purrsteph really needed to wee and was squeezing her legs tightly together, desperately trying not to wet herself. Sylvest, who was nearby, did his best to comfort her, gently patting her on the shoulder.

"Don't worry. There are no swamps around here. Grogs are a dumb fairytale some of our mommies told us when we were small kittens, misbehaving. They thought getting us scared would help them discipline us. You know, 'Finish off your food, or the grog will come and eat you alive as well as your entire meal.'"

"What do you mean there isn't a swamp near here? Then what's that I see directly ahead? Looks like the start of a swamp in this thick forest," Tinki said, pointing her paw.

"Yeah, so what? It's nothing like you imagine; that's only a few trees clustered together and a bit of water," said Sylvest. "Try to pretend it isn't there. We'll get through this patch of trees in no time, and I promise nothing bad will happen."

"The last time someone said that, the whole bus catapulted into the air!" Mimi exclaimed sarcastically.

With emotions running high, it seemed everyone needed some quiet time, and a heavy silence descended quickly as the bus struggled along the pebbled road that extended into an ever-expanding thicket of trees that seemed to stretch all around the road and beyond.

It was a peaceful bus as it continued through the woods—until once again the bus slowed to a halt.

"Now what?" Mimi moaned.

"There's a large tree blocking the road," KT said grimly. "It must have come down in a storm."

"We haven't had any storms around here for months," Sylvest pointed out.

"Well, it's right there, lying across the road and completely blocking our path."

"Well, if all we face is a fallen tree," Mimi said, almost inaudibly. Then, a bit more loudly, "We ought to be able to move it out of the way and get on with our journey."

"I think not," KT replied. "It's massive. Even if all eight of us try to shift it together, it won't budge an inch."

The sighs were long and forlorn.

Two bright lights suddenly appeared from nowhere, shining directly at them from one side.

"Oh, no! It's the killer green grog!" Purrsteph cried in a quavering voice, turning a pale colour.

"I hope not," said Doubler, "but it could be! Its eyes are said to emit beams of shiny light pointed directly at its victim. It's most likely sizing up its prey. Any second now, it's going to stick its tongue out and swallow us inside its huge tummy and horribly and slowly devour us."

Doubler looked glumly out of the window, lost in thought. Moments later, a third light shone in at the front of the bus, then started swinging from side to side as if examining the vehicle. Then, it started closing in on them. It moved closer, looking to be in no hurry.

Everyone was doing their best to stay calm as the light appeared, controlled by a burly figure approaching them. The figure clasped the roving bright light with a giant paw.

They watched in silent terror, so quiet that they could hear each other's unsteady breathing.

Deciding to act, KT nervously turned the key to the ignition, hoping to start the bus and reverse it away from the potential threat. But he was also suffering from the shakes and couldn't turn the key properly or correctly engage his feet on the pedals. He gave up when he realised what it was that was approaching . . .

"Ugh," KT said with a sigh of relief. "It's just a dog."

"Hey there, I hope I didn't cause any of you any alarm," the dog said cheerily as he stepped aboard the bus. "But what are you foolish kittens doing here at this late hour? Isn't it way past your bedtime?"

"I think I'm going to faint," Purrsteph muttered as she slumped back into her seat.

Fangl cleared his throat. "Er-hem . . . nothing much, sir. We were just out and about . . . exploring as part of a . . . science project for school. Yes!"

"At this time? Don't you know that driving down these roads so late at night is unsafe? Don't they teach you anything in Purrville? Unpleasant things can happen to the unwary. I can tell you that strange creatures lurk about in these dark woods and aren't friendly."

"So, it is true; there are such things as big, fat, ugly, killer grogs?" Purrsteph whimpered. "I knew it!"

"No, no, Miss, they don't exist, I can assure you . . . But large swarms of tiny insects inhabit this part of the woods. Some are known to gnaw away at their victims with such ferocity that you might end up with bite marks across your entire body. You may think they're no more significant than a simple fly or moth; some appear pretty, like butterflies. However, you'd do well to remember that these creatures exist in a highly primitive state and have not evolved like us. They're untamed, and some like to bite anything they can find, much like all the ancient animals and other species that roamed Animalia millions of years ago. There are zillions of these nasty mosquito-like little insects to be found.

"I'm sorry," said the dog, switching off his torch, "I haven't even told you who I am . . . I'm Harold, chief of police in Dogwood. I was about to move that darn log off the road when I saw your bus coming this way. I decided to wait until you came to a stop so as not to frighten you. I didn't want to alarm anyone unnecessarily at this time of night."

"We were not alarmed, sir, and we thank you for your generous concern," Tinki said meekly as her fear dissipated and was replaced by curiosity. "We weren't sure what we were facing here out in the dark."

Harold laughed out loud, and it sounded like he was snorting at the same time. "I promise you, most tales and myths about grogs and giant hedgehogs called 'ghogs' are exactly that, just tall tales and made-up legends with no basis in fact."

The Cool Cats glanced at each other, somewhat relieved, and then started chortling along with Dogwood's chief of police, one by one.

"I bet you cats don't have that many visitors coming to your side of the woods from Dogwood, do you? Few of your or our kind like going up and down this road anymore. We keep to ourselves. What a pity that is. We might consider getting to know one another better and appreciating our similarities and differences, rather than dwelling negatively on them. I bet we all have far more in common than we think."

The cats silently nodded. Of course, no one believed a word Harold said about cats and dogs getting along. Everyone knew deep down that these two species were biologically far apart, and that, other than for a few occasional attempts at creating a neighbourly atmosphere between them, it was best to remain apart.

Doubler decided to move the conversation towards the purpose of their travels. "We don't normally visit such places by ourselves. Dogs don't come and visit us much either; you are right about this, Mr Police Chief. We rarely see more than a few of your kind in Purrville. A pawful of dogs has, for a short spell, lived with us in Purrville, although they tend to stick with their kind most of the time. There's the odd one who hangs around longer, such as the well-known owner of Wimplebuns. You probably have heard of him? He's quite famous back home. Can I ask you? Have you heard of any dogs visiting Purrville over the past few days? I think one may have done so not long ago."

Kreamy quickly caught on to what Doubler was attempting to do. "Yes, that's right, sir. This specific canine was driving a milk float and was a dog of sorts, not some other random creature."

"We may have got this all wrong," Tinki added. "It may have been a large, obese-looking cat, faintly resembling a dog, selling milk and ice cream from a van. But I've heard from others who swear it was a dog, without any shadow of a doubt. An unusual dog with distinct canine features."

Kreamy was about to speak when Sylvest cast her a dirty look that convinced her to remain quiet. Sylvest wanted to give the police chief a few moments to respond and hoped that his cloaked interrogation would elicit a helpful response. There was little point in regurgitating what they already knew; Sylvest was keen to hear what the police chief had to say. He could provide the cats with useful information.

This was starting to confuse Chief Harold, who couldn't quite figure out what these cats wanted from him. He still had no idea why they were travelling to Dogwood in the first place. Then, all the confusion faded, and he began to laugh out loud again. He couldn't help himself, as he found it quite amusing that they were all pumping him for information using a routine police tactic of turning the tables on the subject to facilitate the imparting of valuable information. After all, he was the one officially charged with asking questions here. Who did these cats think they were? He marvelled at their audacity.

"I have heard of a headteacher who goes by the name of Fishtail. I believe he drove about in a milk float some years ago, but it was quite a long time ago when I was a mere pup. He wasn't a headteacher in those days either—and some considered him to be a bit of an oddball. I suppose it most likely wasn't him. I doubt it. I can't imagine Fishtail turning himself back into being an ice-cream vendor to relive his youth unless he is facing a midlife crisis. I think he has by now gone way past his midlife point. He comes across as far too stuffy to moonlight as an ice-cream vendor while running his school. Dogs don't appreciate ice cream as much as cats do. Cats passionately love the taste of milk. Thinking about it, I've not seen Fishtail around these parts for many years, so it couldn't be him. Well, this is all a strange mystery to me as well."

"The one we are asking about was most definitely a dog, one with extremely hairy arms," Mimi said, "and we think we spotted him recently. He was large, like you, and much wider than a cat can ever be around his waist, even if one of us gets obese. This kind of body proportion is rare. Cats don't usually get that big, as being rather chunky is not something we like to be. Unlike many dogs known to sit about and eat and eat until they expand and grow larger and larger."

"Can you tell me, sir, how that log landed on the road?" asked Fangl, attempting to change the topic again. He wanted to focus their attention on the obstruction that was preventing them from attending an urgent meeting, which he certainly had no intention of missing.

Harold stared at them curiously, then he relaxed. "Oh, that log fell off my trailer earlier today. I was hauling it to Purrville with several more in my pickup, and this wooden rascal chose to fall off and roll right onto the middle of the road. I needed a short rest afterwards, so I drifted off to sleep. I got up just before you came. What a surprise! A whole busload of kittens appears to be lost in the woods."

Doubler seemed a little cross. "Cats, if you please, sir, not kittens, and we are in a band, which means the band itself has a name. We're the Eight Cool Cats; you might have heard of us. We are not lost; we are on our way to meet someone. So, this log hasn't been lying there for long. Could someone have travelled down this road before you came along and had your log fall off?"

"I don't think so. Not unless that individual had made the journey before early afternoon. Now I have a friendly suggestion. If you're patient and wait a while longer, I'll winch this annoying log back onto my pickup, and then you can be on your merry way. I do apologise for any inconvenience this may have caused. I'll do my utmost to help you get back on your way. Drive on this road carefully, as it's still dark outside, and you should not be out so late at night."

"We appreciate your concern, sir," said KT. "We promise to proceed with the utmost care."

Harold turned around and switched his torch back on. The beam shone as it pointed towards his pickup, which had a winch on it. "By the way," Harold said, facing them, "where exactly are you going?"

"We happen to have a good friend who lives in Dogwood," Purrsteph replied quickly. "It's for a special occasion. We know she will be there, but she doesn't know we're coming. It's going to be a surprise."

"Hmmm . . . I wonder who this could be. Never mind. I won't interfere with the business of pups and kittens and their little secrets. Some of these, I suppose, are well worth keeping, don't you agree? I like surprises myself. However, as the chief of police, I really ought to know where you're all heading and who you plan to visit in my town, especially as you are so young and I feel responsible for your safety. I tell you what. You don't need to elaborate on the reason for your visit; let's leave that aside. I'm merely interested in knowing where you're going if something unexpected happens. I enquire so I know possible issues before they arise."

"I see. You're feeling concerned that something may possibly happen." Purrsteph was trying to accommodate Harold's curiosity.

"Yes, that's it. You seem like friendly kittens who are going about their daily business and coming to visit someone in Dogwood aboard an official school bus. I'd still like to know a bit more about your intentions. Otherwise, I may be compelled to ask you who permitted you to take this bus on a road trip at this strange hour to Dogwood and what kind of documentation you have on you."

"Documentation? Sir, it's Mr Jumbo's girl, Mop," Purrsteph blurted, even though she had made the answer up. She then held her breath as Harold digested the information.

"Oh, little girl Mop, I know her. Jumbo, her father, happens to be a good friend of mine. We go back years. Odd thing, though, I was with Jumbo not long ago–a few days back. He didn't mention anything about cat visitors coming over. I'm sure he would have informed me if he had known."

"Yes, exactly. Mop wouldn't have told him the details because it's a secret. As I mentioned, Mop doesn't know we're on our way. She thinks we've been unable to attend her birthday due to our commitments, and she would not be too disappointed as she understands it's not easy for us to get here. However, we decided to surprise her."

"Oh, right," said Harold. "Don't worry, what you've told me won't go any further, I promise," he continued, before winking. "Right then, let's get this bus on the road!"

He descended the steps leading off the bus and hurried to the pickup. The cats felt immediate relief, but weren't confident that Harold was buying their story.

Harold carefully raised the log back onto the pickup using the winch. Then he drove his pickup to one side of the path.

KT managed to get the bus going the first time, having regained his nerve. Harold waved goodbye to them as they slowly drove past. They smiled at him and waved back nervously. Once they had passed, they collectively breathed a sigh of relief as they watched him disappear into the darkness behind them.

KT made sure he drove the bus even more slowly and carefully than before, as they continued their journey to Dogwood. The hills soon became steeper, and it was many more hours before daylight was due to break. Visibility remained poor.

Purrsteph looked troubled as she turned to Doubler. "You know, we could have told the police chief about that nasty mutt and his fake ice-cream van, which he was using as a kittie-napping vehicle. Harold seemed genuinely concerned about us, and I am sure he would have wanted to help get our mommies back."

"Oh gosh, no," Doubler replied. "If we had, who knows what may have happened to our mommies? We all agreed it's up to us to rescue them, and we mustn't rely on any adults who are only likely to make matters worse."

"How did you come up with Mop's birthday out of the blue? Have you ever even met Mop before?" Kreamy asked.

Purrsteph shook her head. "I read about her in the local paper a few weeks back. The dogizens of Dogwood voted her the most likely dog to succeed in business due to her abnormally high scores in school exams, and she even won the recent Dogwood High spelling bee competition."

"You did well, Purrsteph. That was a great bit of on-the-spot thinking!" Tinki said with a big smile.

They were about a mile or so further along when they found themselves staring at another set of bright lights directly ahead. This time, it appeared different, as a single low-level light beaming towards them, and then, somewhere behind it, a much bigger and far more intense light shining at them from a different height. It wasn't just a torchlight—it looked far too bright. It had the hallmarks of a bright stadium light that could brighten up a large area. It was apparent to all of them that neither of these lights could be headlights like they had seen coming from the pickup, so what were they?

As they approached the light source, they realised it was the ice-cream van. The significantly brighter light appeared from a stand fixed securely to the van's roof.

KT stopped the school bus before the milk float, blocking its path. There didn't seem to be anyone around. As they cautiously climbed out of the bus to take a closer look, they noticed the bright light from the top of the float starting to move about.

Ruffa stepped out before them, silhouetted by the bright light shining directly behind him. It somehow made him look like a pop star of sorts. As he took another few steps towards the Cool Cats, firmly rooted on the path, they recognised his familiar hairy arms and peered uncomfortably into his cold, calculating eyes.

"Hi there, kittens, or should I say, Eight Cool Cats. I've heard a lot about you. I am delighted you decided to join me on this wonderful night."

Naturally, none of the cats felt the slightest bit of delight to be there. His presence made them feel ill at ease. This was the despicable creature who had drugged and kittienapped their mommies.

"That's him," Mimi rasped to the others. "I'm sure I recognise him—he was the one who drove to our house."

"We're here to get our mommies back, so hand them over," Fangl said defiantly.

Ruffa chuckled menacingly. "Really? Is that what you want me to do? Just like that? Why would I do that when I have only just taken them? Tell me, how many of those famous lives are you willing to put at risk, Cool Cats, in trying to rescue them? All nine of your lives would end up being a hefty price tag. Nine times eight, it's uh . . . a heck of a lot of lives lost." Ruffa virtually spat out his words in a manner that was not too friendly.

"Are you the only dog involved, or are there others? You're behind this whole thing, aren't you?"

Fangl rushed past Ruffa towards the milk float and started sniffing around, half expecting to pick up the scent of their mommies inside. "Are they in here all tied up and gagged? You rotten canine!"

"You're off to jail for a very long time for what you've done," Doubler said, pointing angrily at their kittienapper. "How dare you think of doing such a terrible thing?"

Ruffa smirked, which was profoundly annoying, with his bellowing voice that carried more than a hint of malevolence. Even Ruffa was impressed with how sinister he was sounding!

The effect didn't last long. Moments later, Ruffa began coughing spasmodically and subsequently lost the sharp edge to his tone. Much sooner than expected, he shrivelled back into the sad, miserable creature he, deep down, knew he was. He glanced ashamedly at them, unsure, wounded, and desperate to find words to explain his irrational actions that were suddenly eluding him.

"We'll report you to the authorities. You're nothing but a lowlife, half-witted, numbskull villain," KT blasted at the miserable specimen of a mutt, who was rapidly losing his confidence. "You're in big trouble."

Ruffa then attempted to pull himself together, doing his best to crank out a few hollow laughs. But he was all spent by now; there was literally nothing left to give. Then he plucked up some remnants of his courage and stared at them with his beady eyes.

"You can attempt to do something in vain," he barked as he shrugged off their scathing criticism, "but then you'll never get to see your mommies alive and well again, not in a million years. How many lives do your mommies have left in their mature years, I wonder? I bet they have used more than a few to raise annoying little brats like you. Am I right? None of them seem like spring chickens."

It was the cats' turn to look at each other uncomfortably, and they each felt a sense of foreboding. Fear was steadily creeping into their every thought, and they were individually asking themselves, "How evil is this ugly mutt? What is he capable of doing to our precious mommies?" They were thinking hard about his open threats and began to consider the possibility that their mommies could well be in mortal danger.

"What made you snatch our mommies from Purrville?" Tinki asked reasonably. "None of this makes any sense. Why are you doing this? What do you want from us?"

"Ah, finally, someone has a clear head on their shoulders. Funny that you should ask me this question. Firstly, I invite you all to follow me to my private studio in Dogwood, where I will explain everything in more detail. Please don't look so stressed, dear kittens; this will work like a charm . . . for all of us. You do not yet appreciate it, but I have your best interests at heart and wish you nothing but good fortune."

The cats looked at each other, befuddled.

"You have a funny way of showing it, mister," said Kreamy.

Ruffa turned off the large spotlight perched on top of his ice-cream float to help calm things down. Then, he swiftly disassembled it and packed it inside his ice-cream float as the kittens watched him at work.

He was then holding a handheld flashlight as a replacement to see them more clearly by pointing the light beam at each of them. "Okay, folks. Let's get this show started. You'll all follow me to our destination. We shall proceed on foot after we park our vehicles nearby on the side of the road. We must ensure strangers do not easily spot them. After all, we don't want who knows who following us or trying to steal our vehicles whilst they're unattended."

"What about grogs?" a low voice whispered, and none of the kittens who heard it could tell who said those words.

The cats then glanced at one another, deeply confused by Ruffa's frequent changes of mood and tone of voice.

"There's a quaint layby a bit further down the road with a section with some high trees we can park behind. That's where we'll conceal the van and bus. It will avoid attracting unwanted attention."

"Wait a second. What if we don't comply with your demands?" Sylvest asked, although he wasn't sure he ought to challenge this nasty-sounding dog who had stolen their mommies—clearly a lunatic mutt leading them up some wild forest path to who knows where.

"Look. I've explained. It's simple. If you don't do as I ask, you can forget all about your mommies getting back to you safely. I fully expect you to make some effort here. At least for their sake. Why don't you nice little kittens behave yourselves, and let's be on our way."

"We should do what he says," Tinki proposed. "We must first find our mommies and ensure they are safe. It's the right thing to do."

Silently, the anxious, cool young cats climbed back onto their bus. KT sat in the driver's seat, started the bus, and followed Ruffa down to the layby. The two vehicles were parked behind many large trees off the roadside. The cats followed Ruffa down a narrow trail as he casually pointed the way, leading them to his mysterious destination.

"Oh, I hope there are no grogs in those woods." Kreamy squirmed as she squinted her eyes into the darkness that extended in almost every direction. "It feels creepy here."

"I promise you there are no grogs," Sylvest said. "That police chief has told us this—it's just a made-up story."

"Do you seriously believe everything a grown-up says?" Purrsteph asked. "You know how often they lie."

"Why would the police chief want to lie about things that lurk in the forest?" asked Fangl. "He didn't appear to be afraid. I don't think we're in any danger."

"I think the danger is walking right in front of us. Why would anyone lead us to a scary, unwelcoming place like this? Don't you all know dogs love to lie to anyone who bothers to listen?" Mimi said. "It's in their nature. They're not honest animals like us cats."

"I didn't realise that," Kreamy mumbled. "You know something? I do think we're getting pretty good at lying to ourselves. Are we turning bad?"

"You may have a point," Doubler remarked. "But it's not the same thing. We only lie because we have been forced on an important mission to save our mommies, and we are dealing with scoundrels who mean us and those we care for harm. Sometimes, one is forced to lie to protect oneself and those one cares for."

To this, they all nodded quietly as they blindly followed Ruffa into the thickest part of the forest . . . keeping themselves alert for any strange monsters that might come their way, just in case, because, after all, nothing is impossible!

CHAPTER 8

Band Aid

Doubler was the first to notice the large, crumbling shed up ahead—the very place Ruffa had been leading them to. It loomed dark and neglected, its timbers sagging with age.

Without a word, Ruffa produced a chain of rusty keys and began trying them individually. The first didn't fit. He glanced at the cats with a sheepish grin and tried another. Still no luck. By the fifth attempt, his forced cheer gave way to barely concealed exasperation. At last, after fumbling through nearly the entire ring, a key turned with a reluctant click.

He pushed down on the handle. The door creaked open, stiff from disuse. Stepping inside, Ruffa reached for a switch inside the frame and flicked it on.

A single naked bulb cast a dim, yellow glow over the grimy interior of the shed. At the far end stood a makeshift stage—little more than a jumble of old crates and battered boxes hastily reassembled into a platform. The cats filed in silently; their eyes fixed on the pitiful structure.

Ruffa flipped a switch, and a blue spotlight snapped on, bathing the stage in cool light. Somehow, it looked slightly less ridiculous.

He circled a few stray boxes near a rickety table, then leant over a console perched on another crate. He set something quietly in motion with several button presses and lever pulls.

"Ehrm, you'll find your costumes near the stage. Go try them on."

Sylvest had had enough. "What's this about? Are we supposed to get on that thing there and sing? Why are we here? And where are our mommies?"

"You told us you'd take us to our mommies," KT added. "I don't see them here in this dump."

Fangl was also having none of it. "You're kidding me. You bring us to this rundown, derelict building and direct us to a stage? Are you insane?"

"All shall be revealed in good time. Before we proceed, I want to know whether my efforts are in vain. I propose you try on your costumes and step onto that stage to ascertain this. This isn't it! It's just to give me an idea."

The cats stared blankly at each other.

"If I'm satisfied, I'll take you to the main compound. However, I must first know that you can make this work before I divulge my secrets and introduce you to my dogs. The worst thing is that I might make my dogs even more dejected if my plan doesn't work. I can't allow that to happen."

"WHAT PLAN?" Fangl shouted, having lost patience.

"Yes. What? Why? None of this makes sense," Purrsteph blurted, feeling increasingly uncomfortable. "Are you some kind of sick dog?"

"Excuse me," Doubler said. "But let's approach this rationally. Why are we here? We thought our mommies were being held captive inside, and you were going to lead us to them. That's why we followed you down this horrible path late at night. There's nobody here but us."

Now it was Ruffa's turn to look frustrated, and it was evident he was also losing his patience.

"Oh, no, that's not why I brought you here, foolish cats," he retorted. "I brought you here to show you what you need to do to earn the privilege of getting your mommies back. One must show patience; good things take time. I thought you cats were known for being very calm and collected. Take it easy for a second . . . and do as you're told."

"Give us one reason to trust you for one second!" Sylvest challenged Ruffa, deciding it was time to move on to the offensive. "Maybe it's our time to teach you a fine lesson, you dirty fiend."

Fangl didn't want Sylvest to take charge. He needed to assert his leadership, and he followed up with his verbal assault. "How about I land a few carefully targeted punches straight at your face? I can rearrange that stupid grin you keep mocking us with. Maybe it'll focus your attention on our demands."

"No, no, let's not resort to violence," Ruffa said, backing up slightly, his hands raised in mock surrender. "Because if you try anything . . . overtly aggressive toward me, I promise you—it won't end well. For any of us."

His eyes swept the group, voice dropping an octave, colder now. "You've got me all wrong. I'm not your enemy. In fact, . . . I may be the only friend you have left. But you must be patient."

He paused, letting the silence stretch, the tension settle in the room like dust. Then he sighed a long, theatrical breath, as if his burden was almost too heavy.

"Tomorrow," he said slowly, almost reverently, "ehrm, tomorrow will mark a turning point. There's to be a performance at Dogwood High. A very important one."

Ruffa stepped closer to the dim blue light, half-illuminated, like a prophet in half-shadow.

"Tomorrow, I hope—and pray—that you, my talented feline companions, will take your rightful place alongside my dogs. Not all at once. No. I will choose four of you. Four to stand on the Dogwood stage and show them what we're capable of. The rest of you will have to wait. But your time will come."

He tilted his head, eyes gleaming now with something between vision and mania.

"I have big plans," he whispered. "Much bigger than any of you can yet imagine."

Ruffa paused. He was met by stunned silence and furrowed brows.

"Are you out of your tiny mind? Are you suggesting we *perform* with your band of *dogs*?" Sylvest raved shrilly, dismayed. "We're the EIGHT COOL CATS, and we only perform together. It's in the name, dummy. We'd never perform at Dogwood High; we play our kind of music on our school stage because cats like what we sing. I want to make it purrfectly clear that we only perform together as a group of eight, never apart."

"Exactly," Tinki affirmed, joining the chorus of disapproval. "We're not dogs by any stretch of your peculiar imagination. We happen to be a band of eight very cool cats! Get that through that dumb mutt mind of yours. You mommy-kittienapper!"

"This old dog does not know what he's talking about. He has gone off his rocker," KT said contemptuously, shaking his head. "You've gone cuckoo, you know that? You're with the birds."

Astonishingly, this made Ruffa chuckle. "Oh, how little they know. I must forgive them for their ignorance," he muttered to himself.

"Well, he's doing a half-decent job in scaring the tail off me, so I would like to leave this place, please," pleaded Purrsteph. "I need some hugging and proper looking after by a cat who cares for me, like my mommy. I don't mind admitting I'm insecure, and I insist on having my mommy now."

"I want my mommy, TOO!" Kreamy wailed.

Then, they all blurted their message to Ruffa in unison: 'We want our mommies now!" They repeated this so often that Ruffa decided to cover his ears with his paws and wait for the tsunami of mommy-worshipping to subside.

"Enough!" Ruffa barked loudly. "I'm going to clarify things one more time. I want you dressed in your costumes to check whether you cats—doggies, can be a part of my dog band. I must see how you look and sound as a mutt. If you cannot pass this first test, this whole thing is over."

Doubler immediately saw an upside to Ruffa's demands. "If it's over, do we get our mommies back?"

"No! You . . . won't ever see them again. So, you have no choice but to do your best. Understand?" Ruffa looked truly agitated.

Mimi thought about Ruffa's insistence on checking them out in dog costumes while they were lying on stage. "Wait a moment, guys. Let's try to cool this down. It's getting too hot for anyone's liking." She stepped closer to Ruffa and stared him directly in the eyes.

"What harm could you possibly do to us and our mommies if we were not to comply with your bizarre wishes? We outnumber you here eight to one. There's one of you, and there are eight of us. We can be very mean if we want to. Look at you. You're old. You smell foul; your teeth look like they're all rotting. Wherever you've hidden our mommies, someone will soon find out where they are; they'll be returned safely to us. Right?

"You can't stash away eight mature—and we all know highly strung—mommy cats in any confinement for long, I can assure you of that. They'll find a way to escape. They'll climb the walls; they'll jump over fences. They'll get out. I think we ought to report you to the chief of police. He's the big dog we met earlier who looks scarier than you! Police

Chief Harold. He'll fix this in no time. You'll be sent off to jail because you're nothing but a lowlife criminal."

"You'll get locked up," Tinki added. "With any luck, they'll throw away the key forever, leaving you in a dark cell somewhere for the rest of your natural existence. Looking at you, it might not be for very long. At least you'll have some fine quality time to ponder all the horrible things you've done throughout your life. From what little we know of you, I bet there are many."

"Tinki's right," said Sylvest. "You're in heaps of trouble, buster, and you'll pay for it big time."

Ruffa stared at all of them, surprised. He wasn't expecting an all-out verbal assault from these kittens. How dare they pluck up the courage to challenge him? He was giving them the opportunity of a lifetime, and this was how they planned to thank him? Accusing him of being a criminal, attempting to degrade him by calling him a pathetic lowlife villain?

"I should show you what I can do. I should," Ruffa said, but he wasn't talking to them. He was once again talking to himself.

Then he began to chuckle.

"I told you, didn't I? They'd be something of a handful. I warned you. You've got your work cut out . . . turning these kittens into superstars."

"Who are you talking to?" Tinki asked. "Is there someone else here?"

"Yes, there is. There's me. I'm talking to all of you . . . of course."

Ruffa continued to chuckle. His chuckles grew louder, and he sounded even more annoying. It was like hearing a sinister, evil creature unleashing wicked laughter upon the world.

It was laughter that could only come from someone furious and possessed. Someone full of bitterness and filled with deep-seated hatred. Ruffa was now laughing so loudly that he had to lean over and spasmodically cough from all the exertion. Then it all stopped as if he'd run out of steam.

"You're all dumb kittens. You've got no idea who you are dealing with. Do you truly wish to test me? Try using those tiny, pea-sized minds of yours for just a second. Because once you make me angry, you've no idea what I'm capable of."

Ruffa startled them when, from nowhere, he produced a large knife. They all gasped in unison.

There was a hushed silence in the shed as they reflected on what kind of mad dog they were dealing with. It was clear Ruffa was insane and ought to be locked away permanently. But there he was, and who knew what such a mad dog could do or what danger they were in.

Ruffa turned and pulled out a trolley. A badly baked cake sat on top.

"Cake, anyone? I made it myself. A slice of cake, I find, makes all one's troubles go away. It brings a fresh perspective to life. I shall cut a slice for each of you."

The Eight Cool Cats sighed with relief. Poor Purrsteph had nearly wet herself. She crossed her legs, hoping that she could hold it in for a while longer.

Ruffa shook his head and put the knife beside the cake. "But first things first. Why don't you indulge me and try on those costumes? I want to see if we can pull this thing off. If we can, it will be so incredibly glorious for us all. You'll see how much hard work I have expended to make our dreams a reality."

He faced them squarely as he stood directly in front of the cake and cast what was the closest expression to a genuine smile he'd so far produced. His mouth widened beyond what any of them thought was possible, and he exposed some of his rotting teeth. He grinned like a Cheshire cat.

He grinned so hard that it hurt the sides of his mouth. He kept smiling, trying his utmost to appear friendly and likeable. He wanted them to think he was their mentor. A friend. He wanted them to believe he was one of them.

"Let's get this over with," Mimi sighed, deciding to move things forward. While the others stared in bewilderment, Mimi quietly made her way over to the costumes and carefully selected one, picking it up and holding it out in front of her. It had the silly face of a dumb-looking, wide-eyed puppy. It appeared to be the shape of an oversized coat, which she could easily slip into, considering that she had such a slim, petite frame. She zipped it up carefully, and Mimi was no longer there; she was a dog.

To her utter astonishment, it hugged her figure almost purrfectly. How was this even possible? Was it some strange coincidence that she had picked the correct size?

"I can't believe you are even considering this. I look like a dog!" Mimi tried to bark, but it sounded terrible. She barked several times and then started giggling. This broke the tension, and the others giggled as well. But then they all stopped.

"Okay, Mr Smarty Tail, I'll also try it on. I can't imagine I could look remotely like a dog," Kreamy murmured. "But I'm willing to try."

Intrigued, KT joined her and picked up one of the nearby dog costumes. "How are you going to fool anyone with these? Any half-wit will soon figure out we're not real dogs. You call this a clever disguise? It won't work, you foolish mutt; it's a complete waste of time."

Ruffa grinned some more, trying to hold this friendly pose he had adopted. "Ah, well, that's where you're wrong. Can I ask you to step back onto the stage for a moment? Stand somewhere in the middle. Pretend you are holding a musical instrument. Indulge me. You'll be pleasantly surprised."

Mimi looked towards Ruffa quizzically, wearing her dog costume. She turned around and took a few small steps as she climbed onto the creaky wooden stage that didn't feel solid under her feet. Mimi was hoping it would hold her weight. She made her way to the centre of the stage.

"I'd like you to stand still for a moment," Ruffa smirked. "KT, join her. Now everyone. Observe what happens next." Ruffa pulled a couple of levers and turned a few switches on a nearby console, and the next thing everyone noticed was that the stage was beginning to fade into darkness.

This terrified Mimi and KT, although KT did his best to hide his fear. He looked at Mimi, close to him, and reached out to reassure her with his paw on her shoulder.

After a few seconds, several blue and orange light strobes lit up and danced like ballerinas around the stage. It made the whole stage look dreamy and hypnotic as the lights played about.

"Oh my gosh!" Purrsteph almost shrieked. "It looks too real. It's hideous!"

Ruffa turned to his cake, carved out some slices, and began to hand a slice to each of the cats watching the spectacle. "It's all about getting into the right mindset. Animalians can believe almost anything if someone demonstrates enough conviction and makes it look real. So have some tasty, fresh cake, my friends; chew on it and enjoy the show."

Whether they liked it or not, they were each given their slice of cake, which they quietly munched on as they watched Mimi and KT on stage.

Sylvest turned to Fangl as he took a bite. "I hope this food isn't drugged." This made Fangl hesitate, but he noticed the others were all eating it and appeared to be satisfied. After all, they hadn't eaten for a while and were hungry. As if Ruffa could read their minds, he took a bite from the remaining cake. "There's nothing wrong with it; it tastes delicious."

Ruffa returned to the console, slowly brightening the stage lights so that the strobes were less distracting and made the two artists' presence more serene. The setting looked more natural now, and, surprisingly, Mimi and KT looked like pups rather than kittens.

Mimi stared back at her bandmates. Feeling slightly bored, she slowly danced to the loud, banging dog music that Ruffa played via his console.

"No way should this be possible," Fangl muttered, shaking his head because he couldn't quite believe his eyes. "What strange tricks of light are you playing on us? It can't be right. This is a freak of nature."

"Witness it for yourselves. This will be how the Eight Cool Cats can successfully transform themselves into eight cool dogs and appear credible in my band on any stage. Some brilliant lighting wizardry enhances these fabulous costumes. I only need four of you at a time on stage, and the four remaining cats remain backstage. They'll be on standby if I require replacements in the upcoming Superband Competition at Birdheights. I intend to win! After that, we go on tour."

Fangl looked dumbfounded. "Birdheights? Tour? What tour? What is he going on about? What Superband Competition? Someone needs to explain to us what's going on here. I heard something about a competition, but our headteacher, Professor Fishtail, doesn't believe in developing a competitive spirit against others. Each cat must look out for itself and ignore everyone else and the stuff they get up to; that's always been the right way."

Tinki stepped up. "Well, if you're going to try to pull off this crazy stunt, you silly mutt, you better come up with a cooler name."

"What do you suggest? If you have a better name in that head of yours, why don't you spell it out?"

"Sure, I will! How about W-E-A-R-E-N-O-T-D–O-G-S-W-E-A-R-E-C-A-T-S!" Tinki said, shouting the letters out.

Ruffa thought about the letters momentarily, strung them together to form words. Then he realised he was being had.

"No, seriously! Here's your one chance to suggest an alternative, and you mock me. Tell you what, we will keep it just as it is. I happen to like Dogwood Droopsters. It has a nice ring to it."

Ruffa's mind was already whirring as he started thinking about other possibilities just after he had spoken. "Maybe I could call it the Dogwood Dynamos, or even better . . . The Eight Hell Hounds. No, it's too scary—the Furry Friends—no, unlikely. The Magnificent Eight is too dramatic. No, the Rolling Bones. Too rumbling. No, the Super Tramps are too poor. I think I'll stick with the Dogwood Droopsters. Dogs like to be droopy; it's ideal."

Fangl suddenly got annoyed. "You have no imagination. All those suggestions are terrible. Dogwood Droopsters is the worst of the lot."

Sylvest grinned as he shook his head. "Fangl's right. None of them are any good. How about you call it the Eight Fakesters, or even better, the Dogwood Dumbsters? Does it need 'Dogwood' in it? How about calling it The Illusion?"

Ruffa realised Sylvest was also mocking him. "I'll consider your suggestions. But I won't change the name without integrating it into my carefully worked-out plan. Certainly not until we officially enter the competition or go on tour. First, we must win the Birdheights Superband Competition, or we will likely be disqualified for changing our name. I've entered us already as the Dogwood Droopsters, so the name remains."

"Now look, just wait a second!" Fangl cried out. "If you want us to help you succeed with this hare-brained scheme, you first need to take us to our mommies and prove your intentions were never to cause them harm. We ALL need to know they're purrfectly safe before we help you with this ridiculous idea. How do we know you're not just barking a pack of lies at us and treating us like a bunch of fools?"

"That's all in good time, my fluffy friends," Ruffa retorted, brushing off their wishes as if they didn't matter. "First things first. I had to ensure you kittens could pull off this stunt and successfully integrate with my band in disguise. You've passed the first test. The costumes work, and the lights can help to disguise any possible blemishes anyone spots when you appear on stage. The next step . . ."

"Oh, here we go," Tinki groaned, rolling her eyes.

"As I was saying, the next step is performing a low-key show on the Dogwood stage tomorrow night."

"*TOMORROW!*" the Eight Cool Cats exclaimed loudly in disbelief.

"That will be when we know whether my genius plan has a good chance of succeeding. After *that* and plenty of rehearsals, we will take this show to Birdheights to win the Superband Competition."

"But everyone in Purrville will start to worry about our mommies going missing as well as us. How do you plan to get away with this?" Kreamy openly challenged Ruffa.

"Easy," he replied. "The mommies will update the daddies and friends and tell them that their kittens are on a special holiday to stop anyone from getting too concerned. Nobody will ever know what you were up to."

"Now, stop this for a minute! What happens if this crazy idea of yours doesn't work, and we're found out to be cats pretending to be dogs because of your devious disguises?" a nervous Purrsteph queried defiantly. "You might think you can fool a few in the audience for seconds with these fancy lights and costume trickery, but it's going to be a different situation entirely for us to get up on a real stage and face a live audience. We'll need to entertain them for a prolonged period without being found out."

Mimi followed Purrsteph's logical train of thought and was impressed. "And what about when we walk in the corridors and set things up? Won't others notice who we really are and see through these flimsy costumes right away?"

"You kittens are worrying way too much. I do not doubt that this will work out. Do you know why? I believe in myself. Strangely, I believe in you and my dogs, too. I believe in musical integration. I believe in the art of talented fusion. And I believe in winning at almost any cost. My love of music and success are not in conflict; they will work together harmoniously for everyone's benefit. As for strutting about backstage, I have these branded hoodies which will cover us up, and nobody can tell you kittens apart from my pups."

There was a stunned silence in the ramshackle shack.

Ruffa shook his head. "Well, at least that's what I keep telling myself. I know I'm good at improvising, and what I'm talking about is the way to go." Ruffa slapped himself on the cheek. "Oh, shut up, Ruffa! Just shut up! You don't need to explain anything to these unbelievers. They will soon learn for themselves. All will be revealed."

At this point, he was doing all the talking, and it looked like he was deeply engaged in a conversation with himself. This further confounded the already mystified and perplexed Cool Cats, who had no idea what to make of him or this absurd scheme.

"Purrsteph makes a good point," Fangl challenged Ruffa. "What if your idea doesn't work out as you hope it will? What then happens to our mommies if we fail to fool the audience? What if we fail the audition? What if things go wrong? Will you let them go free then?"

"Yeah, what if?" Sylvest echoed.

This took Ruffa completely by surprise. They all looked at him with the same burning question in their curious minds.

Then they all said it together, "What if this fails?"

Ruffa gulped. He had not considered failure as a possible outcome when it came to pursuing his grandiose vision.

"It won't fail. It will work, and that's all I can say about it. Believe in yourselves. Believe in making what seems impossible possible. Without this, who are we?"

Doubler shook his head. "You're missing the point. How can we trust you? You're a devious scoundrel, and you intend to use us purely to achieve your gain. You're a fraudster, a trickster, a liar, a deceiver, a manipulator, and a debaser of all things right. This plan is so crazy, and besides, there may be a purrfectly logical reason that nature intended us not to sing together."

"Well said," KT chimed in. "What Doubler says sums it up purrfectly."

"It's right on the button," Mimi added.

"This is utterly hopeless," Ruffa complained to himself. "Why does nobody here understand that love for music and love for recognition and success require great sacrifice and determination as well as a ruthless streak? This is why the music scene remains unsophisticated. I'm a groundbreaker. I'm a true visionary."

Without any warning, Ruffa held his head down and began to sob. He slowly wiped his face with his greasy paw and turned away from them out of sheer embarrassment. He was bawling his eyes out and could no longer control the emotions he had bottled inside of him. Seeing a ruffian like him break down in tears and act like a fragile pup took the Cool Cats completely by surprise.

Eventually, he sputtered out a few words. "You think I'm nothing but a meanie; I'm not. For my entire life, I wanted to make something of my life, to be someone special. I am fed up with always feeling like a loser. It has to change."

The Eight Cool Cats looked at him in stunned silence. Ruffa sobbed some more, peeping out from behind his paws to gauge whether his sob-story "act" was working. Slowly, he pulled himself together, satisfied that the kittens were perplexed enough.

"You see, my super-gifted felines, my poor, untalented dogs, are just not at your level—well, they're not at any level. They're at zero. The harder they try to be good at their music, the worse they sound. It's not that they don't have tremendous potential—they all do. But something's missing. I've listened to bands from countless towns across the land and travelled there in disguise, pretending to be part of their audience. Everything sounds dull; there's so little life in the music. I know that music is about integration just as much as diversity. I'm convinced that you eight incredibly talented kittens can help me fix this. After all, you're the Eight Cool Cats, and you're already famous."

"I wouldn't go that far." Sylvest rebuffed the notion that they already enjoyed a level of celebrity. "I mean, we can carry a half-decent tune, and we know a bunch of groovy dance moves that other cats enjoy watching on stage when we sing our nursery rhymes. But this doesn't make us musical superstars by any stretch of the imagination. Apart from our local high school shows, nobody notices us beyond Purrville. Nursery rhymes don't appeal to different creatures and are most popular with cats. We cats have a particular liking for them. We tend to find these to be soothing. They're a peaceful way to listen to music, and we can relax as we reflect on their deeper meaning."

"You cats have so little idea what it feels like to be a nobody." Ruffa bowed his head again, hiding behind his mangy paws, peeping out to see what the cats would do next.

"Hey, friends," Kreamy said, motioning them to gather. "I need to be honest about how I feel. I've developed a tinge of pity for this ugly old mutt crying his eyes out before us. We have experienced many failures, and it's not a nice feeling. Maybe we should give it a try. If we fail tomorrow, we can add it to the string of failures we have already experienced. Besides, I don't think we have any other option if we want to save our mommies."

The Eight Cool Cats looked at each other, and then at the miserable kittie-napping hound.

"I guess you're right," said Doubler.

CHAPTER 9

Cats Meet Dogs

An hour later, the Eight Cool Cats were back on the bus with KT behind the wheel, cautiously following Ruffa to Dogwood as the sun rose from behind the rolling hills.

"I say, once we get there and see our moms, we overpower that fool dog," Fangl said grittily. "We shouldn't be doing what that ruffian wants. As soon as we see them, we force him down, tie him up, and then rescue them."

Doubler scratched his head, pondering the situation. "I agree, but we've made a devilish deal with that horrible mutt—I've forgotten his name. Did he tell us his name? I think he did."

"Yeah, Ruffian, wasn't it?" Fangl sneered.

"Yes, that's right," Doubler replied.

"No, it wasn't," KT said, looking in the rearview mirror. "It was Ruffa. What's up with you, Doubler? You never forget anything."

"I think I just want to block this Ruffa out of my mind," Doubler muttered. "I'm just trying to imagine myself singing and playing harmonica in a dog costume. I swear I'll sweat like a dog."

"That's the general idea, isn't it?" Sylvest grinned sardonically but quickly realised it was no time for humour as his bandmates stared back at him coldly.

Tinki added, "Don't forget, Kreamy convinced that old dog to give us one year's unlimited supply of fresh milk and cookies for each of us and our mommies at no extra charge if we put on a great performance on the Dogwood High stage. So . . ."

"Tinki! Really?" Purrsteph rasped. "You're thinking of the reward at a time like this?"

"Just saying. It's not *all* bad."

Mimi interjected, "But don't you guys see what's happening? We're making a deal with an unscrupulous kittienapper. How can we allow ourselves to go along with his deceitful plans? He's dishonest to the bone. There's a reason that bands don't mix, and he intends to create a monstrosity. That's what it will end up being. We're better than that, aren't we? We must retain our pride and dignity, be proud cats, not dogs."

Fangl had been listening intently but was now looking at things differently. "What if he's right, though? What if by combining our diverse talents with those of the Dogwood dogs, we manage to put on a show that can win this singing contest and change the whole musical landscape of Animalia?"

The others reflected on this quietly as Fangl continued. 'I mean, I can't stand the mangy mutt; none of us can.

However, sometimes, one needs to pursue desperate measures to get noticed in the entertainment space. Forming a band of cats and dogs is certainly way out there, but it's also brave. Something never done before."

Mimi didn't accept the proposition.

"Even if we were to win this mega contest, it wouldn't be us who get the recognition, would it? All the accolades go to the dogs, the Droopy, whatever. We'll be seen as one of the dogs. Part of their pack. And it's Ruffa who ends up being the ultimate winner; we end up with nothing."

Doubler reflected on this. "Then there's the shame of it, should anyone back home ever find out that we agreed to pretend to perform as dogs. We agreed to be on stage with them, all of us, together. Just imagine the looks we'd get! Nobody will care to look us in the eye without being sickened by what we have done. It's the ultimate insult."

"At least we'll have our mommies back," Kreamy said quietly, attempting to focus on the brighter side of things amidst all this talk of doom and gloom.

"Fortunately, we don't have any suitable jails in Purrville to be locked up in!" said KT half-jokingly. "Besides, kittens are never locked up; their families stringently discipline them. Even our parents behave in a civil and law-abiding manner all the time. Because when this venture fails—and it almost certainly will fail—the seriousness of this . . . what amounts to *fraud* basically . . . means someone *is* bound to get locked up! We have been forced into it so it's doubtful it will be us. It'll be that old fool and his renegade band of dimwits."

"I hope they don't lock us up," Kreamy muttered, complaining. "I hear the dog cells are always packed with misbehaving mutts. They lock them up for any old reason. It's as if they're being called to something higher. 'If you don't do some time, you don't know what's out of line' is the Dogwood motto, or so I've heard. They can easily accommodate the pack of Dogwood performers and that old mutt who thinks he's some closet genius. Dogs are far too uncivilised. We'd never tolerate such control over our kind. Such a desire to dish out punishment like it's part of growing up."

"If we don't speak up, though, we may be marked down as accomplices," Sylvest added. "We may have no choice but to blow the whistle and have these fools arrested. If we go along, we're just as bad, and doing so could land us in a Dogwood jail. We may end up in the Dogwood jail as part of a new integrated arrests experiment!"

This terrified the rest of the cats, but then Kreamy laughed.

"Ha ha." Kreamy couldn't help it. "You think the mayor of Dogwood, Mr Bigsnot, is likely to arrest any of his dogs for entering a band competition and lock them in jail because a bunch of cats had their feelings hurt and tried to rescue their mommies? Could Dogwood, or even Purrville, put up with the shame of having their star performers turn out to be cats and the cats be so gullible?

"Mayor Bigsnot would have to accept that his dogs couldn't put up a good enough band to win and needed the help of cats to pull it off. We'd be there to remind him.

He'd become the laughingstock of all Dogwood, and our mommies would be the fools in Purrville if any of us got locked up by Police Chief Harold. They'll bury this, turn a blind eye. Nobody will want to acknowledge a disaster of this size."

"How do you figure all this, Kreamy?" Purrsteph queried. "We're getting hurt, so why should we bear all the shame?"

"No, you're misunderstanding me. The shame will be on the mutts. Sure, our mommies were fools to succumb to that old dog, but that's not half as embarrassing as the fact that Dogwood needed cats to put on a decent performance.'

"So, what you're saying," said Purrsteph, trying to digest what Kreamy was getting at, "is that even though there's a risk that things can go wrong, if they do, nobody will want to know the truth, anyway?"

"Yeah!"

"My goodness, Kreamy, that's the smartest thing I've ever heard you say!"

"Well, I'm not just a cute-looking kitten."

"I agree," said Fangl. "I think we need to go along with it for now. Our risk isn't as great as we think. We mustn't fear doing what's needed. We are not afraid. We will go rescue our mommies."

"Agreed. This must be our number one priority," Purrsteph emphasised. "Even if it means going along with an imbecile lunatic, and we pretend that we're somebody else. We must ensure we don't get caught."

"Then we proceed with this performance tomorrow," Sylvest wanted to clarify for everyone's benefit. "Our top priority is to ensure that our mommies are released, and after that, KT, Fangl, and I will visit Ruffa and have a serious discussion with him about what will happen if he attempts anything else. We'll tell him exactly how this plays out, and he will listen."

"What are you going to tell him?" KT asked. "Make him an offer he cannot refuse?"

"Yeah, I will. I propose we all leave, or we'll expose Ruffa's band to Animalians at the competition, and everyone will know what a desperate fake he really is. If everyone knows, Dogwood will undoubtedly be up in arms."

"This is all such a mess. We're not meant to perform together, are we?" Tinki asked, frustrated. "It's not natural. Dogs are inferior to us cats."

"Every one of us will do our bit to make this rescue work." Doubler stepped up. "But let's not assume the dogs are talentless and part of Ruffa's misguided schemes. I guess they're just as much in the dark as we are. We're all being taken advantage of here by this egotistical mutt. I will not associate myself with putting any other species down."

"Okay, then. It's agreed. We'll go along with this for now and see how things unfold. Yes?"

"Agreed!" The Eight Cool Cats nodded to each other with resolve.

"Then we teach him a lesson on why he shouldn't mess with cats," Fangl said with a sly grin that everyone else replicated.

***

By the time the school bus reached the outskirts of Dogwood, the landscape had changed dramatically. Endless rows of grimy streets stretched before them, littered with rubbish spilling over pavements and choked alleyways. A foul stench clung to the air, thick and inescapable. When KT tried turning on the airflow inside the bus, it only worsened things, circulating the hideous odours straight into their sensitive noses.

After a long stretch down a bleak main road, the bus veered left into a narrow side alley that looked like a dead end. The cats exchanged uneasy glances as the alley narrowed, eventually tapering off at a broken, rusted gate. Oddly, the gate was already ajar. It was clear that someone from within had unlocked it. As the bus crawled through, the cats caught a flicker of movement at the edge of their vision—near the gate—but it vanished too quickly to identify. Whoever it was had already slipped away into the shadows.

The road beyond turned to a rough, mud-baked track. Stones jutted unpredictably, causing the bus to lurch and jolt as it navigated the uneven path. On either side, the dense forest rose thick with undergrowth and silence. It was clear now—this place was cut off, hidden from the rest of Dogwood.

Eventually, they reached their destination: a large, dilapidated wooden building that loomed in the clearing like a ghost from another time. Once majestic, it now sagged under the weight of decay, its weather-beaten boards and shattered windows betraying years of abandonment. This was Ruffa's home.

The cats stared in disbelief. Whatever grandeur this house once held had long since faded. It was little more than a collapsing shell, yet it stood on what had once been an impressive estate.

KT pulled the bus up beside Ruffa's milk float, parking awkwardly close—but it didn't matter; the exit door was on the other side. Trees pressed in tightly all around them, cloaking the grounds in shadow. This wasn't just a rundown house—it was a secluded compound, tucked away on private land, with several outbuildings scattered beyond view.

A strange quiet settled over the group as they stepped off the bus. They had entered another world that felt forgotten or deliberately hidden.

"I didn't know that Ruffa was a wealthy dog," Kreamy told Mimi.

"Size isn't everything, girl. It may be big, but I wouldn't want to live in this dump." Mimi shook her head as she studied the imposing building.

As they clambered out of the bus, the first thing they noticed, apart from the foul stench that pervaded the air, was that the entire compound seemed eerily quiet.

All they could hear were the occasional gusts of wind that came and went, with leaves in the trees fluttering away.

Then, out of the blue, the quiet was brutally interrupted by the harsh beat of loud drums banging away, the fierce blast of a trumpet, and the low thumps from an untuned bass guitar that reverberated wildly and sounded like someone was being strangled. These sounds were atrocious; all eight cats covered their ears with paws.

"Don't worry, folks. It's my musicians practising inside!" Ruffa shouted. "They're preparing for tomorrow."

"You call that practising?" KT grimaced as he tried to shout above the noise, his paws firmly over his ears.

They went through the creaking front door that Ruffa opened for them, and through a narrow corridor, they entered what appeared to be a living room.

As they entered, they could hear a female voice making loud, crying noises that sounded strangely melodic. The crying had an echo, which gave it a faintly musical quality.

The living room had been converted into a performance studio, with instruments and speakers scattered at one end. Wiring was everywhere on the ground, and none looked that safe. It was a sorry sight, including several ancient speakers that lay sideways across the floor, precariously stacked on each other. For a moment, it looked like one or two of them would topple over as they vibrated, but they managed to stay in place.

Sitting at the drums, they noticed a hairy, chubby, bespectacled dog furiously banging away with beat-up sticks. The dog was having a great time and wore a dirty yellow headband across his forehead. They couldn't work out whether that was for sweat or something else.

Next to him stood the bass guitar player—a slender, tall dog with a droopy beard and a big nose. His eyes bounced around the room as he tapped his feet and plucked his guitar. He wore a waistcoat with several missing buttons and stains that were unlikely to be removed.

On the far side was a rather stern-looking, chubby-faced, black female dog whose cheeks constantly expanded and contracted beyond what the cats thought possible as she wilfully forced air into her rusty trumpet. Between her puffs, she gasped for breath. She wore a tight, dirty white blouse that barely contained her large frame. She also wrapped around her chubby neck a yellow silk scarf with drawings of flowers. Her most noticeable feature was her bloated belly, which protruded from the bottom of her blouse. She had a bone stud in her navel.

In front of them stood the singer and lead guitar player, who appeared to be the youngest in the band. She was a handsome dog with greased-back hair and delicate cheekbones that made her look more like a male than a female. She glanced over, saw Ruffa enter with the cats, and stepped away from the mic. The other three dogs stopped playing their instruments as the room grew silent.

Just as someone was about to open their mouth, the strange scene grew even stranger as Doubler's mommy, Elsa, burst into the room carrying an old silver plate stacked with freshly made sandwiches! She had big ear guards on but appeared jovial as she headed directly towards the band.

"Lunch, children!" she called to the canines, then turned to see the cool cats and Ruffa by the door. "Oh, my goodness, me," she cried joyfully. "The children have finally arrived. They're here in the room—all of them!"

As soon as she spoke, the other mommies filed in behind her. They were all dressed in tatty-looking nighties, apart from Mimi's mum, who still wore the lovely dress she'd had on when she was abducted.

The surprise on the faces of the Eight Cool Cats was indescribable as the mommies sprinted up to them and hugged them individually. Tears streamed down the kittens' cheeks.

Ruffa quietly grinned as he watched this spectacle and stepped out of the way to avoid interrupting a magical moment of joy.

It was Fangl who was the first to pull himself together.

"Wait a second, what's going on here? I thought you had all been kittienapped by that nasty mutt and he had been starving and torturing you." Fangl had to pull back as his mommy tried to give him a bear hug. "Are you telling us you're here because you chose to be?"

Mrs Krusher, Mimi's mommy, was the first to reply. "Goodness gracious, no. We were all kittienapped, that is true. But you see that mutt Ruffa isn't who you think he is. He told us about his genius plans, and we sat quietly and listened. What a brilliant mind that dog has! We were so enamoured, and what a kind heart for an old dog. He has been looking after us, feeding and treating us with kindness and generosity. We've had buckets of delicious fresh milk, which always makes us happy. Since we've come here, all of us have felt so much better, and for the first time, I can honestly say I'm relaxed. In my heart, I want to be kind and help others who need our help. I know it's not like me at all! But what can I do? I've changed. We all have. Our special mission is to create the first superband in history—my child will be a part of it. I'm so excited!"

Mimi stared in shock at her mum. "She's right; it's not her at all."

Mrs Krusher leant down and tried to give her daughter another kiss when Mimi grabbed hold of her mother's face and tried to pull her skin off with sudden force.

"Ouchhhhh! You've got to stop that! It hurts. Have you gone crazy? What's gotten into you?" Mrs Krusher screeched in pain as she pulled away.

"It can't be real!" Mimi shouted at her mother. "Ruffa is without question the most evil and deluded mutt we've ever come across, and there is no way you can be so nice to him and that dreadful-sounding band he wants us to join."

"Now, my dear, what did I teach you about always having good manners?" Mrs Krusher replied curtly. She dared not get any closer to her daughter, who appeared to be distraught. "You'd better apologise to Mr Ruffa for making such a rude remark. Especially to a poor old mutt who has all our best interests at heart and has already given so much."

"Poor old mutt, did she speak those words?" KT said, more in shock than anything else. "They're not our mommies, but they look like them."

"I'm telling you, my dears, our darling Ruffa has been misunderstood. We've spent a lot of time with him since yesterday, and it's clear that he has invested much energy into transforming his band into something that can potentially win the biggest band competition anyone has known. I'm convinced, and so are the other mommies present, that Ruffa has hit upon the most brilliant idea to help create a historical moment in the history of our land. What he has in mind can—no, it will change all your lives in the most amazing ways."

"We didn't come here to help out that vile dog, Mrs Krusher," Doubler said, having heard enough. "We came here to rescue you. What has that beast done that has turned you into his devoted fan? You've been thoroughly brainwashed. It's like you've joined this cult led by a furious dog."

"See, didn't I tell you they wouldn't understand why I need to do this, Mrs Krusher?" Ruffa calmly explained. "Nobody here does. Greatness is a path one must travel alone. It's unfortunate. It took me weeks to convince my dogs to make room for these talented cats, and now I must persuade your kittens. We don't have weeks; there's no time at all."

"You are right, good friend," Mrs Krusher said, in full support of Ruffa. "I am so sorry for all this pain you are forced to carry inside you to attain our moment of greatness. It's not for any one of us; it's for all of them."

"*Good friend,*" Mimi blurted at her mother. "HE is not a good friend. He deceived you with his disguised milk float and took you by force. Then he blackmailed us into coming here by threatening our safety. Now he's trying to make us pretend we are dogs. And to what purpose? So he can make himself and those foolish pups over there famous by winning some strange singing contest that none of us have even heard of until today. What do we get?"

"Now wait a second here," the horn player, Smackie, cut in. "Who are you cats calling foolish pups here? 'Cause you're just eight talentless kittens as far as we dogs can tell. I've heard you kittens sing before, and the only thing it accomplished was sending me off to sleep before I could count to eight. Don't go around boasting we're nothing much as performers and try to elevate yourselves on pedestals 'cause you're a bunch of popular cats in Purrville. I won't tolerate such nonsense, nuh-uh. You are all talking cowturd as far as I can see."

"So, if I've got this straight, Mrs Krusher," Fangl butted in, "you are here voluntarily, and you think that what Ruffa is doing by creating a mixed band is smart, and it could even win this competition?"

"Yes," Mrs Krusher replied. "I do. You kittens are so young. Let me tell you something. You have to be destructive to be creative. If you follow all the dumb rules grown-ups make, you'll never be any better than or different from anyone else. I believe this. Rules are made to be broken. How else can one bring about change?"

Fangl looked at the mommies, completely confused. "So, you think we ought to be helping his band of dogs by livening up their music with our melodic tunes? Are we innovators in your mind?"

"Yes. Of course! This whole thing is a stupendously amazing idea." Mrs Krusher was starting to get even more excited. "Don't you see it?! This world is yours to conquer as you wish. But you need to be creative and find a different path from what has been done before. Discover new ways. This is such an incredible opportunity."

Fangl scratched his head. "Okay. So, what happens to all our mommies if we refuse to help this mutt?"

"I . . . I don't know," Mrs Krusher replied. "We haven't considered it possible because we feel it in our bones. You'll be willing to help once you see the light. We're all on the same team. Music knows no bounds; it's not species-specific and is for all of us. Ruffa is a genius coach."

KT had heard enough. "Look, Mrs Krusher, with all due respect, I think you have all lost your minds."

"My dear, I've not felt so happy for a long time. And I believe the same applies to the other ladies. It's Ruffa; he's been so charming. He makes you want to attempt the impossible. To try something exciting, to once again feel alive."

The other mommy cats nodded and grinned stupidly in agreement.

"Ruffa is playing with fire, and I would have thought you'd all understand as you're much older and wiser than us."

Mrs Krusher and the other mommies looked confused. Ruffa stepped forward as the mommies and the kittens eyed each other quizzically, each baffled by the other's views.

"I know this is all a lot to take in. Why don't you all get some rest? I've made comfortable bunk beds for you, and I think a few hours of lying down and getting some sleep will work wonders. We've got a big day coming up tomorrow. We'll be performing together for the first time and need some time earlier to rehearse. Mommies will take you to your room to tuck you into bed, and rehearsals shall commence in five hours. Follow them; they'll show you the way. Mommies, let your kittens rest."

The mommies silently nodded as the Eight Cool Cats quietly followed them down a long corridor.

"This is the strangest thing I've ever witnessed," Sylvest whispered to Fangl. "It's obvious our mommies have been brainwashed. Do you have any idea how?"

"Nope. They don't appear drugged or in a state of trauma. Ruffa hardly knows anything. I doubt he knows about the constitution of cats, so how can he manipulate them like this? No, this is something worse, I fear, but I have no idea what."

"Whatever trickery is being used, we must get to the bottom of it. After we're tucked into our beds, why don't we sneak away and investigate what's going on?"

"Count me in. I am not playing in some silly tin-pot band with these strange mutts until we get to the bottom of this crazy nonsense."

Tinki was right behind them, stepped up, and eyed them both. "Don't lose sight that what's happening here could be a blessing. I believe we're all about to embark on a new journey of discovery that will most likely make us all much wiser and successful."

"Oh, not you as well. Please shut it, Tinki," Sylvest retorted.

"Wait and see, boys. I believe I'm right." Tinki left them to continue whispering to each other.

It wasn't long before they reached the bedchamber, where a cosy bed awaited each of them. To their surprise, neatly folded pyjamas lay at the foot of every bed—each set thoughtfully made to adjust to different sizes. The sleeves were a bit long on little Doubler, and slightly too short on tall Sylvest, but overall, they fit well enough and felt wonderfully soft.

Each bed had a small curtain that could be drawn around it, giving the children privacy while they changed. Their mommies waited patiently, smiling as they listened to the quiet rustling behind the curtains. They were happy to know that their children were safe and well.

Once everyone had changed, the curtains were drawn back, and the mommies came forward to tuck them into bed gently. Each child was tucked in and given a soft kiss on the cheek. The room was calm and warm, filled with the peaceful stillness that only bedtime can bring.

"Goodnight, dears," the mommies said in unison, and then they quietly marched out, their footsteps soft and synchronised.

"How strange," Purrsteph whispered.

"Yeah, bizarre," Kreamy agreed. "I don't mind being mothered, but I want my real mommy back—not a robotic version."

"I think in a way it's beautiful," Tinki said softly. "I don't think she'd tell me off the way she is—she would just smile. I can get used to it."

"Oh, come on," Purrsteph muttered. "Something about it makes me want to throw up."

Then the lights dimmed slowly to black, leaving the room in silence and the soft sound of distant, mechanical humming.

No one spoke again. Sleep came eventually—but not without questions.

CHAPTER 10

Spellbound

Later that night, when the lights were off and the house had fallen silent, Sylvest quietly nudged Fangl awake. The two young toms slipped out of bed and dressed, wearing regular clothes over their pyjamas.

Tinki, always a light sleeper, stirred the moment she sensed movement. Blinking through the dark, she spotted the boys creeping toward the door. Curious and quietly alert, she waited until they had gone, quickly dressed, and slipped out to follow them.

Fangl took the lead, moving with deliberate care. He avoided obstacles and kept his steps light. Though lined with worn, shabby carpet, the corridors helped muffle their movements. Occasionally, he glanced back to check that Sylvest was close behind.

At one point, Sylvest paused beside a window. He peered out into the darkness, then gave a low, sharp cat whistle. Fangl froze, turned on his heel, and padded quickly back to where Sylvest stood, still and focused, eyes fixed on something outside.

"What is it?" Fangl asked. "Anything of interest?"

Fangl peered out of the window at a couple of buildings.

"Over there, look. That building has a bright light on the first floor. There's someone busy doing something inside, which looks a bit odd. I don't think it's Ruffa—I'm pretty sure he's sleeping in the main house somewhere."

Fangl started to get excited by the idea that they might be onto something. "Let's check it out. Maybe we can get to the bottom of what's been going on."

They moved cautiously down the corridor, their footsteps muffled by the worn carpet. As they reached a T-junction, they hooked a sharp right, trusting their instincts that this path would lead them to the main door—and, hopefully, a way out.

Sure enough, a thick wooden door stood at the end of the hallway. But as they approached, Fangl's optimism faded. The door was solidly shut, held fast by two hefty bolts, and the empty keyhole stared back at him.

Fangl quietly slid back both bolts with care, avoiding any loud clanks. Then, he clasped the handle and turned it slowly. It moved—but the door didn't budge.

"It's locked. Someone has sealed us in."

Sylvest scanned the area for a key. "Nothing here. Maybe it's locked from the outside."

"How can that be? The bolts were secured from the inside. But how do we get out?" Fangl muttered, frustration creeping into his voice. Being trapped was not part of the plan.

Then, from the shadows, a quiet voice broke the silence. "Perhaps I can help."

Startled, both boys spun around. Tinki stood just beyond the reach of the hallway's dim light, dressed like them—clothes hastily pulled on over her pyjamas.

"You gave us such a fright," Fangl said, narrowing his eyes with more than a hint of annoyance. "Please don't go sneaking up on us like that, or you might cost me an entire life next time."

"I didn't mean to. I think I can help get that door open for you. I want to help if I can. I hate the feeling I'm useless."

"Nobody's useless here," chimed in Sylvest. "We're a team. We're the Eight Cool Cats, the number one band in Purrville."

"That's right," added Fangl. "We're a brilliant team. The best in Purrville. Of course, it helps that we're the only band in Purrville—but we'll keep that little detail to ourselves."

"Well. Shall I see if I can sort this problem out?"

Without waiting for an answer, Tinki waved the boys aside and approached the door. She pulled a hairpin from her furry head and inserted it into the keyhole with practised ease. It bent and twisted under her nimble paws. A moment later, she retrieved a second pin, sliding it in beside the first, adjusting both until they clicked into a promising position.

With a few delicate twists and careful listening, she heard a soft, satisfying click. A grin spread across her face.

"I may have done it." Tinki's eyes sparkled with pride. "We're in! I mean . . . we're out!"

She grabbed the handle and pushed down firmly. The heavy door groaned open, revealing the night beyond.

Fangl and Sylvest exchanged impressed looks.

Then Fangl's expression sobered. "Maybe you ought to go back to bed. If you go out there with us, it could be dangerous, and I wouldn't want you to be in any trouble."

Tinki shook her head, disappointed but determined. "You're not going to get rid of me so easily. No way. I'm going with you. I don't care how risky it is. All our mommies are in terrible danger, and they need our help. The way they've been behaving . . . It's so unnatural."

Sylvest nodded slowly. "She makes a good point."

With quiet determination, the three cats stepped outside into the cool night air. They crept across the open yard, heading toward a distant building where a light glowed in an upper window. They slowed as they approached, staring at the illuminated floor above.

It wasn't easy to see what was happening inside from the ground. But something was going on up there—and it was waiting for them.

Before Fangl could get another word out, Tinki had already leapt onto the broad tree trunk. With nimble paws, she reached for a branch and began climbing, quickly vanishing into the canopy's shadow.

"Wait a second!" hissed Fangl, springing after her. "We're coming with you!"

Sylvest followed close behind. Neither of the boys was fond of heights, but pride wouldn't let them admit it—not to Tinki, not now. They gritted their teeth and climbed.

The night was still, and every creak of bark or rustle of leaves seemed magnified. They knew they had to move carefully, quietly. Any sudden noise could give away their position—and alert the mysterious figure they had glimpsed earlier through the first-floor window.

Fangl struggled more than the others. He misjudged a step, grabbing a weak branch that snapped loudly beneath his weight. The sudden crack split the silence like a whip.

"Shh! Keep it down, fool!" Sylvest snapped in a harsh whisper, his annoyance barely restrained.

They froze, breath held. When no movement came from the window, they continued their ascent, inching along a thick branch that curved toward the side of the building.

Tinki crept forward first, edging carefully along the bough. She stopped when her eyes found the window.

She stared.

For a moment, she didn't say a word—just blinked in disbelief.

"No," she finally murmured. "No, it can't be. What's one of those doing here?"

Sylvest leant in beside her. "What is it?"

"A crocodile," she whispered. "From Swamptown. They rarely come inland."

Sylvest squinted through the glass. An enormous dark-green crocodile paced slowly across the floor inside the well-lit room. Thick spectacles perched awkwardly on his snout, and he held a peculiar object in one claw.

"That's a big one," Sylvest muttered. "And what's he got there? Is that a . . . chain?"

Unbeknownst to them, the crocodile's name was Herbert. He was from Swamptown, temporarily residing in this strange old building—a quiet retreat, far from the wetlands.

Fangl crept forward for a better view, edging along the same branch until he was almost nose-to-ear with Sylvest. Feeling crowded, Sylvest leant instinctively toward Tinki, who shuffled farther along the branch.

But the branch was thinning.

And bending.

A sharp crack rang out—louder than before.

Sylvest instinctively shot his paws upward and grabbed a branch above. Fangl slipped, yelping under his breath as smaller twigs scratched at his fur. As he tumbled, he managed to hook one arm around Sylvest's waist.

Tinki was not so lucky.

The branch beneath her snapped entirely, sending her plummeting, but with lightning reflexes, she caught hold of a lower limb and clung tightly, her heart pounding in her ears.

None dared scream, though every instinct screamed at them to do just that.

Inside, Herbert had heard the noise. His snout tilted. He turned toward the window.

He took a few slow steps forward and eased it open, poking his broad head outside. His yellow eyes scanned the moonlit garden, narrowing as he focused on the nearest tree.

Just then, something moved—not outside, but behind him.

Herbert turned sharply.

There, standing ten feet away, was Mrs Krusher.

Her eyes were glassy. Her stance was vacant. Something was wrong.

Very wrong.

Without a word, Herbert raised his clawed hand. A golden chain dangled from it, attached to a gleaming pocket watch. Slowly, deliberately, he let it sway from side to side.

The polished surface caught the light with every pass.

Back and forth.

Back and forth.

Mrs Krusher didn't blink.

Herbert's voice was slow and silken inside the room, his words dripping with coaxing intent.

"Relaaaxxx . . . That's it, dear Mrs Krusher. You're already so calm. So very calm. There's no need to trouble your pretty mind with anything . . . trivial. Only listen to me now."

He smiled—wide, reptilian, and cold.

"Why don't you settle back onto that ever-so-comfortable sofa behind you? Yes, that's it. Let's continue our pleasant little chat. Such a peaceful evening, don't you agree?"

Mrs Krusher moved like someone underwater, her motions slow and dreamy. Her eyes never left the golden stopwatch as it swung rhythmically in the crocodile's claw.

"You're having a wonderful time," Herbert continued, the watch catching the light with each arc. "And your dear friend Ruffa—what a marvel he is. Bringing such an incredible opportunity to those darling kittens. To the entire Cool Cats community! What a glorious service this is to the feline world. Just imagine how proud they'll all be when your kittens sing their little hearts out and win."

He leant slightly closer.

"Tell me, dear . . . how do you feel about all this?"

Mrs Krusher dabbed at her glistening eyes with one paw, never blinking.

"I . . . I feel so wonderful!" she exclaimed, her voice unnaturally cheerful. "Simply marvellous and completely at ease. Ruffa is a superstar—a dog of unmatched talent. A genius! Just imagine the future he's shaping for our kittens. For everyone! How lucky we are!"

"Yes," Herbert purred, "precisely."

Outside the window, hidden among the branches, the three young cats clung to the tree, watching, listening, stunned.

They couldn't hear every word but saw the golden stopwatch swing and Mrs Krusher's unblinking, glassy gaze.

Tinki, still perched on a lower branch, strained to whisper. "What's going on? I can't see anything from here."

Sylvest didn't want to say it. But she deserved to know. "It's Mrs Krusher. She's in there . . . with that crocodile."

"What? Why is she talking to that hideous thing?"

"I think . . . he's hypnotising her. Look at that watch. I'm pretty sure he's working with Ruffa." Sylvest glanced at Fangl, looking for confirmation.

Fangl nodded grimly. "I think you're right. That golden watch must be how he's doing it. I've heard of this thing but never seen it before."

Tinki gripped the branch tightly. "But why would a crocodile work with Ruffa? What could a dog possibly offer him? There isn't even a swamp anywhere near Dogwood!"

"Maybe Ruffa promised him something," Fangl said. "Like a home. Acceptance. Some place to belong."

Tinki frowned. "That's hardly a great deal. This town's not exactly paradise."

"We shouldn't hang around," Sylvest whispered. "We've already made too much noise."

He began to climb down, fluid and quiet. As he passed Tinki, he reached out a paw to help her off the branch. She clutched it gratefully and followed. Fangl brought up the rear, dropping the last few feet and landing with a muted thud.

Once all three were on solid ground again, they exchanged bewildered looks under the pale moonlight.

"What now?" Tinki asked. "We should expose that croc. The more we learn, the less I want anything to do with this 'competition.' Something's very wrong."

She paused, then added, "And there's one more thing."

"What's that?" asked Fangl.

"Our mommies are in danger. You saw what's happening. And we're the only ones who know. If we don't act, who will?"

Sylvest's brow furrowed. "She's right. But I don't think the dog band's to blame. They're probably just playing along with whatever Ruffa tells them. Maybe they're hypnotised too."

Fangl wasn't keen on hanging around debating. "We've seen enough. We need to get back now. If they find out we've been snooping, we'll be watched, restricted. Ruffa isn't playing games. If he catches on, he'll make sure we can't move an inch without his say-so."

The others nodded in agreement.

Silently, they crept back toward the building, hugging the shadows.

Once inside, they changed back into their pyjamas, climbed into their bunk beds, and pulled the covers up high. Their hearts were still racing.

But they said nothing more.

Whatever tomorrow held, it would begin with secrets . . . and the heavy weight of truth.

It was just as well they had returned when they did. The bedroom door creaked open only a few minutes later, and Ruffa poked his head inside. His eyes swept slowly across the room, studying each bed in turn. Every one of them appeared to be occupied. Satisfied, he lingered for a moment longer . . . then quietly shut the door.

Ruffa slowly shut the door and returned to the main stage room. Herbert was pacing up and down, looking decidedly nervous. He had run to the house, and he was out of breath. Ruffa could see that something was bothering him.

"It wasn't them, Herb. All of them are tucked up in bed and sound asleep," Ruffa said.

"Oh, good. But I swore someone was lurking outside when I was working on the big cats. I'd keep a close eye on them. Those kittens are much trickier than you think. If you don't, they may find a way to get the upper paw."

"Oh, I intend to watch them like a hawk. But I can't lock them all up in their cages, or they will never follow my plans. When it comes down to it, it's their talents that we're making the most of."

"I can see whether I can hypnotise them for you as well. Makes life easier."

"No, that's a terrible idea. There's no way they will sing and play their very best if they've been hypnotised and can't remember who they are. I need the Eight Cool Cats, not a bunch of mindless zombies."

"Well, that's fair enough. But you may not have much choice if these kittens and their mommies get onto us. Individually, I have no trouble handling a bunch of kittens. Collectively, they could prove a real pain."

"Don't worry about them. Just keep the mommies smiling and let me look after these furry kittens. This is going to go well; I'm certain of it. We are doing something truly remarkable here. Amazing!"

"The good thing about you, Ruffa, is that you don't need to be subjected to hypnosis to believe in anything you set your mind to. You're brilliant at convincing yourself o anything you want to. I'd say it's your greatest strength. Just don't let it flip around into a weakness. That's all I ask."

"Thanks, I'll take that as a compliment. I don't do flips; I deal with the cards I'm given. With a few small, carefully calculated enhancements, of course."

Ruffa and Herbert settled into a couple of armchairs and enjoyed a few late-night drinks as they reminisced about their past lives and laughed off previous mishaps. Ruffa wanted to regale Herbert with his exploits in days gone by, which were, in truth, not all that exciting. And in his mind, the best was yet to come.

Fortunately for Ruffa, Herbert was well-practised in the art of selective hearing. He'd long since learned to endure Ruffa's rambling monologues—equal parts self-praise, conspiracy, and delusion—with a patient, reptilian stillness. To Herbert, it was just another occupational hazard of being a semi-professional hypnotist.

"You can brainwash the world," he said, "but it's a lot harder to brainwash yourself . . . unless you're Ruffa."

Herbert was a cynic by nature—dry, detached, and amused by the foolishness of others—but he rarely showed it. Unlike Ruffa, whose insecurities leaked like steam from a cracked kettle, Herbert knew how to seal his doubts safely.

The night passed without further events. In a long, dimly lit room at the back of Herbert's building lay the eight mommies, each curled up in oversized bunk beds. They snored softly in unison, tucked beneath thick blankets, their faces frozen in identical expressions of smug, glazed-over bliss. It would have been comical if it weren't so eerie.

Their contentment, of course, was no accident. It was the work of the great Herbert—Swamptown's most infamous hypnotist. In his heyday, creatures would queue down the muddy lanes to have their worries wiped away by the swing of his golden stopwatch.

For a while, it worked wonders. Even the Swamptown police chief, Flappo Wacker, had been a regular client. Under Herbert's spell, Flappo felt calm, focused, and unusually generous. That is, until the morning he snapped out of it and discovered that all his jail cells were empty— and the town's crocodiles had been giggling behind his back while they ran riot.

Herbert was promptly exiled from Swamptown and banned for life. He never looked back.

Some in Dogwood had raised eyebrows when a crocodile took up residence in their quiet, dog-run town, but Ruffa's compound was secluded, and everyone already thought Ruffa was a bit . . . off. Few questioned it.

As it turned out, Ruffa and Herbert had met years earlier, during one of Ruffa's lowest points. Ruffa, the black sheep of a wealthy Dogwood family, had disappointed everyone who had ever placed hope in him. On a soul-searching trip to Swamptown—rumoured to be more of a self-pity tour— he'd heard whispers of a hypnotist who could "fix broken minds." Intrigued and desperate, he met Herbert.

Their initial sessions quickly turned into lengthy chats. Ruffa saw in Herbert a quiet intelligence and an unthreatening calm; Herbert saw in Ruffa . . . opportunity. Over time, the dog made repeated visits, and when Herbert was forced to leave Swamptown, Ruffa offered him a place to stay.

They lived alone, unbothered by family or responsibility, and their friendship—odd though it was—grew solid. It was convenient, quiet, and mutually beneficial.

Then came the Great Dogwood Talent Competition.

Ruffa, ever the dreamer with questionable ethics, decided to assemble a superband that would win the contest and take the region by storm. But first, he needed control—not just of the kittens, but of their ever-watchful mommies. That was when he remembered Herbert's gift.

Ruffa laid out his plan. He needed influence, obedience, and smooth compliance from all parties involved. Herbert, flattered by the faith placed in his talents, agreed. Hypnotising mommies? Easy. Kittens? A challenge—but one Herbert was eager to attempt.

The best part? Ruffa offered him a proper role in the band—as stage manager for the post-victory tour, a gig that promised adventure and endless new creatures to "experiment" on.

Herbert was sold.

He'd always wanted to travel, and now, thanks to Ruffa's scheme, he could see the world and test the limits of his hypnosis on a much broader population.

Control for Ruffa—a new playground for Herbert.

And the mommies? Well . . . they wouldn't remember a thing.

CHAPTER 11

Reformed

The following day passed in a blur of rehearsals and instructions. Before they knew it, the newly formed superband—cats and dogs together—stood assembled on the makeshift stage in Ruffa's living room, rehearsing the songs they'd soon perform live at Dogwood High School.

Kreamy, Purrsteph, Mimi, and Tinki represented the girls. The boys were KT, Fangl, Sylvest, and Doubler. Across the room stood their dog band counterparts—Moss, Rommy, Sniffer, and Smackie—curious and slightly amused as they watched the cats sweating under layers of thick stagewear.

Each of the Eight Cool Cats had been issued a dog costume. Now fully suited up, they looked more like furry impostors than performers. The heavy material itched and clung, making them flustered and faint. But they said nothing—for now.

At least Ruffa had relaxed one rule: they could leave their hoods off during rehearsals. It was a small mercy which meant the dogs could see their real feline faces instead of the fake dog masks that came with the costumes.

Then, without warning, Herbert arrived.

He emerged as if conjured from thin air, striding forward with a polished cane in one claw and an air of self-importance wrapped around him like a second suit. He wore a freshly pressed dark ensemble, a colourful walking stick in hand, and a black top hat perched confidently on his head. Tinted sunglasses obscured his eyes. He looked less like a stage manager and more like an over-decorated aristocrat on parade.

The cats gawped—most had never laid eyes on the crocodile before. This was the creature from the window. And now he was here.

Ruffa, grinning at the sight of his co-conspirator, stepped forward.

"Everyone," he announced grandly, "meet your new Happiness Group Manager—Herbert! He'll help you work out the details of your performance and handle day-to-day organisation."

He raised his voice a little. "I'm the strategy guy—the big picture. I sit at the top. Herbert, however, will be in the thick of things—rehearsals, logistics, scheduling. And while I'll be seen as the official showrunner"—he puffed up slightly—"our success will owe much to Herbert's . . . unique talents."

He gestured with mock humility. "Over to you, my friend."

Herbert stepped forward, baring a wide, toothy crocodile smile. He tapped his colourful cane lightly against the floor and bowed his head exaggeratedly.

"Thank you, Ruffa, for that most elegant introduction," he drawled. "Greetings, all. I am Herbert. I will be leading the practical running of this fine show."

He tilted his hat, lips curling in a polished grin. "The brilliance of Ruffa's planning utterly inspires me. He has wisely entrusted me with preparing you for your grand debut. So, let us work together . . . and make something truly unforgettable."

His cane tapped once more. The room was silent. The cats exchanged uncertain glances.

Something about that smile didn't quite sit right.

Rommy felt a prickle of suspicion the moment Herbert stepped into view. She had never formally met the crocodile but she knew he lived in one of the other buildings on Ruffa's compound—and something about him had always unsettled her. "I thought Herbert was the caretaker here—I didn't realise he had proper musical experience. Tell me Herbert, what have you done previously?"

Herbert smiled, but this one was a little more crooked. "Plenty of things. A heck of a lot, if you must ask. I'm all about bringing happiness and joy."

"I'm listening. You have my full attention."

"Well, hmm. I always sing in the bathtub, and of course when I swim in the swamp. I have a terrific karaoke voice which comes into its own in confined spaces such as caves. Would you like to hear me sing?"

"No, croc," said Smackie, butting in. "We don't care about your singing abilities if you're going to manage us. What Rommy means is, what experience do you have in managing bands? Did you manage bands, and where did you come from?"

"Yeah," Rommy added. "Who did you manage before us? That's what I want to know. It's an important question."

"Well, I used to manage the New Year's Eve party choir performances in Swamptown. Nine crocodiles sang a cappella. Their most famous song choice was well-known; I bet you've heard of it."

"I haven't heard any crocodile songs before," Rommy said. "Do enlighten us."

"Nor I," added Smackie. "I don't much go for a cappella music either; we're musicians, in case you haven't noticed. We like tunes, and I love the sound of the wind. You know, making music with wind instruments. Trumpets, horns, saxophones, flutes. That's why I like to blow music."

"Well, the song is called 'I Love You My Sweet, I'll Eat You Alive,' and it was written by the tremendous singer Araba Swonky . . . You may remember her. She was the most famous crocodile who ever existed in Swamptown. Many years ago, there was an international singing competition, and she won it outright with her other brilliant song, 'Life's All About Rolling Around.' Well, my crocs sang it every year, and it brought the house down. They had to rebuild it a few weeks later, but that was no big deal."

"Look, folks, this is all very interesting," Ruffa interjected, starting to get annoyed by the line of questioning. "But all you need to know is that I trust Herbert implicitly, and he will manage all your future performances with his utmost dedication. So enough of these petty questions. Let's get on with it."

"Before we do," Herbert began, "I should just add that I do happen to play the flute."

The cats and dogs looked surprised.

"One second, I'll be back to prove it. I keep a stack of them because I love chewing on them afterwards." Herbert ran to the back of the room and came back with a small flute in his claws. Ruffa rolled his eyes.

Herbert tapped his colourful walking stick against the floor, then carefully set it aside with the reverence of someone handling a sacred relic. With thick claws and surprising delicacy, he raised the flute to his wide crocodile mouth.

The room fell silent. The cats and dogs stared, unsure whether to laugh or duck for cover.

Then he played.

A gentle, mournful tune filled the room—light, fluttering notes that floated through the air like smoke. It was . . . unexpectedly good. Beautiful, even. The group was dumbfounded.

And just like that, he stopped.

Herbert lowered the flute, blinking rapidly. His sunglasses had slid slightly down his snout, revealing moist eyes.

"I'm sorry," he said, voice thick with emotion. "That . . . that took me back."

He sighed deeply, placing a claw on his chest.

"My Mudder taught me to play this beautiful instrument as a hatchling. She always dreamt I'd become a professional flautist. Join a big band. Tour the world." He shook his head wistfully. "But alas, there are few opportunities for a flute player in an a cappella group. I couldn't sing a note. Not even a hum. So . . . my dream was dashed."

He looked around, sniffed, and added with a dramatic pause, "I mostly just played alone. For her. My dear Mudder. She loved to listen."

A long silence followed.

Then—*clap clap clap.*

Everyone turned. It was Smackie.

Realising all eyes were on her, she stopped abruptly and cleared her throat. "What? That wasn't bad! Give the croc his due. Ruffa says he's good, and now we've seen he's at least got some talent. Might as well give him a shot. How could he possibly be worse than what we've already been through?"

Sniffer smirked. "It's gonna take a miracle to squeeze a decent song out of the twelve of us. A big one."

"Eight," Ruffa corrected, stepping in with his usual authority. "There will only be eight artists on stage. I shall designate four as reserves—four cats, four dogs. We'll rotate performers depending on the songs. Nobody in the audience will know—we'll drop the curtain, swap you out, and pretend nothing happened."

He gave a wink.

"Smoke, mirrors, and costume hoods. Showbiz, my friends."

"You see, dear kittens . . ."

"We're cats!" Mimi yelled. "Why do they keep on calling us kittens? It gets so annoying!"

"Sorry, *cats* . . . I figured you guys might be unable to go through the entire performance, not like how we do it. We usually play for hours. It's going to be tough, working with us dogs. We expect a lot of stamina and energy. And we know how to play our music with pace."

All the dogs grinned and nodded.

"Okay then," Ruffa continued, "dogs and cats-pretending-to-be-dogs, how about we rehearse as true professionals? I have three songs lined up for tonight, and I want them all to sound amazing for the show at Dogwood High."

Herbert put the flute in his mouth one more time and quickly blew it. Then he went over and picked up his stick. "Our esteemed leader, Ruffa, will hand out the lyrics and music sheets. I want you to take a few minutes to study them before we commence our rehearsal."

Ruffa shuffled through a stack of papers, licking his paw before handing out sheets like a self-important lecturer. "Here we are," he said, distributing lyric sheets and music notations. "We'll all rehearse together, and tomorrow night I'll select the final four cats for the live performance."

Everyone took a sheet. Some squinted; some mouthed the words silently. Even the cats—still simmering under their thick, itchy costumes—began reading through the lyrics with mild interest.

Purrsteph was just about to comment when Herbert suddenly raised a claw to his lips.

"Shhh."

It was dramatic. Too dramatic.

Purrsteph raised an eyebrow but held her tongue.

Then, the rehearsal kicked into gear.

They began slowly, tentatively, stumbling over the first few bars. But as they progressed through the songs, something curious happened. The usual dog-heavy percussion—loud, chaotic, and relentlessly barky—had been softened. The rhythm now followed a gentler tempo, and the melodies curved to accommodate feline voices.

It sounded . . . almost good.

The dogs glanced at one another in surprise. The cats were equally startled—but tried to hide it.

When they took their first break, even Ruffa looked less tense. He served refreshments—cups of squash and a mountain of suspiciously well-decorated cupcakes—and for a moment, he resembled less an authoritarian band leader and more an overworked school assistant.

Tinki bit into a cupcake and turned to Smackie, who stood beside her, licking icing off her paw. "Who wrote these songs, anyway?"

Smackie glanced around before lowering her voice. "I'm not supposed to say, but it was Moss. He's been writing for ages. No one ever took him seriously—until you lot showed up. With cats on board, we needed something more . . . tuneful."

"I like it," Tinki said. "Do you think the audience will?"

"Don't worry, gal." Smackie grinned. "There's still going to be plenty of thumping. Moss wouldn't dare put on a show without a few big bangs. It's tradition."

The rehearsal continued for another three hours. When it finally wound down, the musicians collapsed onto a mix of stools and battered armchairs. The cats sat apart from the dogs, exhausted and overheated, silently questioning everything.

In the corner, Ruffa and Herbert huddled in whispered conversation.

Then, Doubler stood up and marched across the room, straight toward them.

"I have a crucial question," he announced, squaring up to them.

Ruffa blinked. "Uh . . . go on?"

Doubler gestured to his oversized dog costume. "The rehearsal's going fine, I guess—but we're sweating in these things. How do you expect us to wear these under full stage lighting? What if someone needs to scratch their face? Or use the toilet facilities?"

Ruffa looked to Herbert to respond.

Herbert straightened his sunglasses. "Stage fans. I've already arranged them. Giant whirring propeller fans on either side of the stage. They'll keep you cool. Trust me—I've considered every detail."

"What kind of fans?" Doubler asked. "Cheering fans? Screaming dogs?"

Herbert frowned. "No, the mechanical kind. Cool air. Spinning blades. Honestly."

He tapped his temple with a claw. "This croc head? Not just for show. I might add that there's a brain here—massively underrated."

Doubler wasn't laughing. "If this goes wrong, I want your word that our mommies will be freed."

By now, Tinki and Kreamy had joined him, eyes narrowed, waiting for a serious answer.

Herbert rolled his eyes and raised his voice slightly. "You must stop being so negative! This is exactly why I was brought in—to bring positivity! Your performance will be brilliant. You are all hugely talented, even if this is your first time. It's . . . mind-blowing, honestly."

Doubler, caught off guard, gave a hesitant nod, then turned and walked back to his armchair in silence. Tinki opened her mouth to speak, but Kreamy pulled her back.

When they returned, Purrsteph looked up. "What was that about?"

"Nothing much," Doubler replied, frowning. "I was looking for some reassurance."

"Did you find any?"

"Sort of. Herbert thinks we're incredible. Apparently, we're going to dazzle everyone. No pressure."

Kreamy grimaced. "I hate this costume. It's so tight, I can barely breathe. My tail is practically folded in half."

"We all hate it," Fangl added from across the room. "It's like dressing up in a furry oven."

"I guess we just play along for now," Tinki whispered.

Sylvest nodded. "Until we have a plan. We've got to focus on freeing our mommies. That's the only thing that matters. I mean, do any of us care about the show?"

"I do," Mimi said softly.

"So do I," added Kreamy.

"As do I," Doubler said quietly.

Tinki looked around. "We may hate how this all started—but when I step on that stage, I'm not just Tinki anymore. I'm a musician."

Kreamy nodded. "Yeah. Me too."

Sylvest sighed. "Fine. We'll give the show everything we've got. But if the audience doesn't like it, we pull the plug. From that point on, we go full rescue mode."

Fangl stood up. "We'll talk after the show. I've been thinking a lot, and I've got some ideas."

They all fell silent.

Then, as if a collective decision had been made without words, they returned to the stage and resumed their final run-through.

Two hours later, Ruffa raised a paw.

"Alright, boys and girls, that's enough for tonight. This rehearsal went better than I ever imagined. Congratulations to you all."

He gave a theatrical bow and swept out of the room.

The Eight Cool Cats and the Dogwood Droopsters exchanged glances, shrugged, and shuffled offstage in silence, heading back to their bunks—hot, tired, and filled with questions about the day ahead.

* * *

Some eighteen hours later, they were back on the road, crammed into a beat-up school bus provided by Dogwood High, rumbling toward the venue. This was the official Dogwood High School bus, but it looked more like it had survived a riot. Torn seats, graffiti-splattered walls, and rubbish littered the floor from front to back.

The Eight Cool Cats, all suited up in their thick, stuffy costumes, were visibly uncomfortable. The bus offered little relief—no airflow, padding, or dignity.

Ruffa was at the wheel, eyes fixed on the road with forced determination, while Herbert lounged in the front seat beside him, leaning in close to whisper something under his breath.

At the back, Mimi glanced sideways at Moss, who was hunched over a crumpled paper bag, stuffing biscuits into his mouth like he hadn't eaten in days. He caught her looking, paused mid-chew, and flashed her a grin.

That was when Mimi noticed: several of his teeth were missing, replaced by shiny, ill-fitting silver dentures that caught the light most alarmingly.

"What do you want, cat?"

"Nothing much." Mimi felt more than a little uncomfortable.

"If it's nothing, why are you staring at me?"

"No reason. I was feeling a little peckish . . . and I should be. I've been so nervous. I ate only two cupcakes since our rehearsals yesterday, and we haven't eaten much today with all the extra rehearsals. I'm sorry."

Moss eyed Mimi some more and then grinned. To Mimi's surprise, he handed her his bag of biscuits. "Go on, take one or two. Have whatever you want. Don't be put off. They taste fine."

Mimi reached into the crinkled, transparent bag. Without a word, she took one biscuit and returned the rest to Moss. Then, with slow precision, she guided the biscuit up to the small hole in her mask and took a careful bite.

The crunch was oddly satisfying.

She chewed thoughtfully. It was surprisingly tasty—sweet, crumbly, with just enough flavour to lift her spirits. Without hesitation, she finished the rest, licking a few crumbs off her paw as she leant back in her seat.

"Tastes nice, doesn't it?" Moss smiled as he spoke. "You cats think we eat any rubbish, but we have some of the best cooks in the land. They may be messy, but they sure can cook. This comes from the best bakery in Dogwood. And you know who owns it? My dad. He's been running it for more than thirty years. He sure knows how to bake a cake or anything."

"Please don't tell me it's something horrible that will make me want to be sick. What's in it?"

"Flavoured marshmallows with finely sliced hazelnuts—one of my favourites. Performing makes me hungry, so I've got to stock up on good grub before I get onto that stage. 'Fill your belly before you climb onto that stage, boy,' my pappy used to tell me, and he was right. You know, my pappy, he also played in the school band before my time, and his pappy before that. Playing music has also been a family tradition, as has his baking. I plan to take over from him when he's old and retires."

"My family isn't musically inclined or into baking," Mimi said. "My mummy was always into business. But I don't like business dealings. I enjoy playing my cello, and sometimes I sing too, but I'm not the lead singer. That's KT, and sometimes Tinki joins. She's got a beautiful high voice—it's dreamlike."

"You cats don't sound too bad, if I'm sincere," Moss said, glancing at Mimi. "Today sounded better than we ever played. I wasn't sure about Ruffa until today, but he's onto something. You can't blame the guy for having to disguise you all. He doesn't make the rules."

"Yeah, when we play, we play from our hearts." Mimi smiled as she looked at Moss with an interest that hadn't been there before. "We're alike in a few ways. We're ordinary, and our parents control our lives. Everything has already been planned."

Moss nodded. "I've never played with cats before. But I tell you what, I'll play with you cats anytime."

"Well, a lot is riding on this show. Ruffa's counting on it being a big hit. Do you think we can seriously get into this competition?"

"If things don't go well tonight, I think it's over. Ruffa can't afford to lose. He has put everything into it. Rumour has it that the entire compound was put up as collateral so he could invest in this band and its competitors. If he fails, he may lose everything."

"Oh, gosh!" Mimi exclaimed. "I just wish he were a bit nicer to everyone. He can be mean."

"Oh, don't be fooled by the old mutt. He's not as bad as you think. The problem with him is that he always aims for the moon, and not everyone has the chance to become a superstar and live out their dreams. I mean, for most of us, we've got to do what our parents and the community expect us to."

"I know exactly what you mean. But sometimes one likes to dream of other possibilities. I never imagined something like this could happen. If I weren't worried about our mommies, I could even enjoy this experience."

"For us mutts, this band means everything. If you took my music away, I'd be depressed. My family doesn't have much money; they don't even have a social class, and they sure aren't in charge of anything or anyone either. They're nobodies in music or anything artistic. My dad's a well-respected baker—he chose a professional career. In food circles, I may be allowed to feel a little special occasionally, but the band makes me feel my life is meaningful."

"I agree." Mimi considered Moss's perspective. "I feel that way, too."

"You want some more of these?" Moss offered.

Mimi shook her head, but then she changed her mind. "Oh, okay. One more will be great. They're delightful. If you've got one to spare, that is?"

"Of course." Moss handed her the bag again. "Take as many as you'd like. I've got another bag stashed in my room at home. I'll be chomping on that later. And my dad's bakery is full of these goodies."

Fangl and Sylvest sat side by side at the back of the bus, heads close together as they whispered in hushed tones. A few seats away, KT leant slightly in their direction, pretending to look out the window, while secretly straining to catch every word.

"What's your plan? Share it with me," Sylvest whispered.

"Don't mention this to anyone yet. If this fails tonight, there is only one way out of this kittie-napping and blackmail that we're being subjected to. We must retrieve the keys for the bus, then take our mommies back and bring them home safely. It's the only option left before something even worse happens."

Sylvest was surprised. "How is that going to happen? They don't even want to leave the compound. That croc has them under his hypnotic spell. I'm no hypnotist, and I've no idea how to undo it."

"We're not asking for their permission. We gather the troops and take them back by force if we must. No ifs, ands, or buts about it—we must rescue them and take them back home. We take our mommies straight to Headmaster Fishtail and tell him all that has happened. He will contact the mayor, and then we can sort this mess out properly. We can't leave them here with that mutt and his croc partner. Who knows what Ruffa and Herbert may do? Ruffa's insane, and the croc is out of his prehistoric skull."

KT had managed to pick up most of the conversation, and he didn't like the sound of it. "Who hypnotised them? Herbert?"

Fangl motioned to KT to remain quiet. "Let's not get into this right now, but that croc Herbert is a skilled hypnotist who has our mommies under a spell. Who knows how long this thing lasts, or what permanent damage it will likely inflict on them? We're out of our depth here. We need to take them away and return home, and hope that the sickness they're suffering will start to wear off. For now, we play along. Don't do anything rash."

KT looked visibly upset. "You found out all this about Herbert and our mommies, and you didn't tell the rest of us what was happening. Who decided to put you in charge of our rescue mission? Don't we have a say in how things should be handled?"

"Keep it down, KT, or we'll all suffer."

KT couldn't understand why everyone seemed so afraid of Ruffa and Herbert. As far as he was concerned, he could take them both on easily, if it came to it. Still, he chose to keep that thought to himself, for now. The situation had grown more complicated by the day, especially with the mothers now seemingly part of the Ruffa fan club. That changed everything.

KT no longer knew what the most sensible move was. If something truly sinister was happening—hypnosis, manipulation, or worse—then maybe it was better someone like Fangl had taken the lead. Though he'd never say it aloud, KT admired Fangl's steady leadership and trusted his judgement without question.

But even so, KT believed the kittens wouldn't get far without him. He was the most pragmatic of the lot, willing to make hard decisions and act when others hesitated. They needed someone less idealistic than Fangl. Someone willing to do what the rest of them wouldn't dare consider. They needed him.

If it ever came to a real fight, who else could handle two self-obsessed lunatics like Ruffa and Herbert? Sylvest, flashy as ever, was all talk and, in KT's opinion, far too timid to stand up to a crocodile with a tail like a wrecking ball. Fangl might be the brains, but KT was the brawn—the one who did.

And now more than ever, he knew he had to stay close to them. The moment for action was drawing near. He could feel it. And when that time came, they'd need more than a plan.

They'd need him.

CHAPTER 12

Dogwood Show

As the Eight Cool Cats piled out of the bus, their oversized Dogwood Droopsters hoodies swaying with every step, they caught their first glimpse of the back of the sprawling brick building that housed the school stage. The bus had driven them straight into the staff car park, where a few scattered vehicles were already parked near the entrance. Still, the lot felt oddly deserted—too early for the crowds to arrive.

The show was still an hour and a half away. Many audience members lived far outside the town centre; for some, the journey into Dogwood could take over thirty minutes. Though the town centre was densely populated and full of activity, dogs didn't tend to live there. They preferred open spaces—fields, gardens, and places where they could roam freely without concrete underfoot.

Dogwood itself was better known for its warehousing and goods transport. The centre was dominated by large depots and storage facilities—solid, functional, and deeply uncharming. Most buildings were tall and blocky, lined with rows of grimy windows that seemed permanently smudged with soot and time.

A side door creaked open as the newly reformed superband approached the building. It was being held ajar by a burly guard dog with long, twirly whiskers and an unimpressed stare. This was the first real test: could the kittens pull off their disguise?

Fortunately, Herbert had provided them with a crash course in how to walk like they belonged. Heads down, just enough to appear aloof. Shoulders back, steps confident— almost swaggering. The look of minor celebrity disinterest. They just had to look like dogs who'd done this a hundred times before.

And it worked like a charm.

The Eight Cool Cats and their four genuine dog bandmates strode briskly past the guard, who barely glanced at them. They entered the corridor and went to a stairwell where concrete steps rose steeply to the first floor.

At the top, Herbert was waiting. He gave them a nod and gestured toward a massive set of double doors that opened onto the auditorium's upper level—the circle.

Stepping inside, the group came to a halt.

Below them stretched the vast belly of the theatre. Over a hundred rows of seats fanned out in the stalls, all leading to the edge of a generous stage bathed in warm light. From this height, the space looked enormous—imposing, even— the kind of room where secrets got swallowed or shouted to the back wall.

The Cool Cats stood in silence, absorbing the scale of it. This wasn't just another rehearsal.

This was the real thing.

Kreamy turned to Purrsteph and couldn't help but mention the obvious, "Why is their auditorium so much better than ours?" Purrsteph had no response to offer and just shrugged. "I can't believe we will play in front of so many dogs. Now I'm scared."

As if he'd been listening in, Herbert suddenly stepped forward, his polished cane tapping lightly on the floor.

"I'd better take you down to the dressing rooms," he said, eyes scanning the group. "You'll find clean water and a chance to freshen up. You've got one hour until curtain. We'll collect you and lead you to the stage when the time comes. So be ready. Understood?"

They all nodded, though an uneasy tension passed silently between them. The nerves were creeping in.

A few minutes later, the group found themselves in a surprisingly well-appointed dressing room. Each performer had their own mirror, table, and chair. The dogs were automatically directed to one side of the room, the cats to the other—as if it had been planned down to the last detail.

A modest spread of good-quality cosmetics and a jug of fresh water sat on each dressing table beside a clean glass. The musicians poured themselves drinks, gulping the cool water gratefully after hours in their suffocating costumes.

Then the door creaked open.

A tall, elegant dog entered, closing the door quietly behind her. She wore a flowing chiffon dress over a crisp white garment, and her bright pink lips contrasted sharply with her glossy black nose. Her thick, exaggerated eyelashes seemed to flutter toward whomever she faced.

The cats froze. They yanked their dog masks back on in a heartbeat and stood at attention.

"Hello, darlings," she cooed. "Don't fret—it's only me, Nippy. One of Ruffa's oldest friends. And don't worry, your secret is safe with me."

Her voice was smooth and theatrical, each word carefully chosen.

"I know exactly what's going on here," she continued. "Once you step through that door behind me, your masks must be on—securely. But in here, you can breathe. Be yourselves. Cats, dogs—whatever you are."

There was a pause, then she smiled. "This is all so very exciting. History in the making, wouldn't you agree? No one's ever heard of a band made up of creatures from such . . . diverse backgrounds. If it sounds as good as I think it will, well—this could be truly revolutionary."

At her reassurance, the cats wasted no time pulling off their headgear, their fur matted and damp beneath the costumes. With a chorus of sighs, they flopped back into their chairs, drinking more water and taking deep breaths of unfiltered air.

Then, almost instinctively, they began to apply make-up—carefully, quietly, as they always did before a show. It was part ritual, part armour.

No one said it out loud, but each of them felt it:

This wasn't just another performance.

This was something else entirely.

Kreamy was the one to ask the obvious, dumb question that was on everyone else's lips. "If we're wearing hideous masks, why are we applying make-up to our faces? It doesn't make sense."

"Course it doesn't," Tinki replied in a hushed tone so the dogs nearby couldn't pick up on what she was saying. "At the end of the session, though, we may choose to reveal who we are, and everyone will be amazed to see that the Eight Cool Cats are in their presence and can play so well. We need to look good for that special moment."

Moss looked towards them. The dogs had heard some of the conversation. Sniffer whispered to him, "That lot of artists seem a bit dumb. Do they seriously think Ruffa will let them reveal their true selves? Do they know what a thousand hounds would do to them if they did?"

Smackie clipped Sniffer on the back of his head. "Do not mention such things. They may hear you, and it'll frighten the life out of them. We'll end up getting into even more trouble."

Rommy came up close, trying to keep the conversation private from the cats. "Who cares what we say? Ruffa's so far up his backside, he isn't paying much attention to what we think. He depends on us to do what's *needed* and sounds *good*, and we will, and so will the cats."

Smackie shook her head. "Don't think you have what it takes to get us through this. We can play with a house of dogs, but playing in Birdheights in this big competition is something else. Rehearsals were good and tight, though.

Moss's stuff has a neat new sound. My guess is they're going to lap it up; you wait and see.

"But you know, boys and girls, success brings its own set of problems with it. Don't ever forget, there's no easy life for hard-working musicians. It's all toil and sweat—that's what musicians end up with."

"You're kidding," Sniffer said. "That's only because in Dogwood, opportunities are limited. Attaining wider success is a problem I'd like to have."

"Now hush, and save that precious energy of yours for singing," Smackie whispered sharply to Sniffer, her tone just short of a growl.

"What do you think those mutts are going on about?" Tinki asked Sylvest, who was at the table beside her.

"Who knows—and honestly, I don't care," Sylvest muttered, staring into the mirror. "Let's finish this experiment and do what we must." He adjusted his mask slightly and grinned at his reflection.

KT stood and stepped beside him, leaning in until their faces nearly touched the glass.

"Like what you see, my friend?" he said dryly. "Good. Now try backing it up with a half-decent performance—because a lot is riding on this."

"Don't we know it!" Tinki exclaimed.

An hour later, the auditorium was packed wall to wall with eager dogs, many of whom had travelled far and wide for the occasion. Despite the lukewarm reception the Droopsters had received at their last few outings, tonight's performance buzzed with expectation. Rumour had it that a major talent scout from Birdheights was in attendance—someone with real influence over who might be selected for the prestigious Superband Competition that had everyone talking.

This was more than just another local concert for the town of Dogwood. It was a chance—perhaps the only chance—to earn wider recognition for their talents. The locals had turned out in force, barking in support, tails wagging with pride and curiosity. Say what you will about dogs, but their loyalty is second to none when it comes to backing their own.

Dogs were never known for their quiet restraint. The auditorium buzzed with energetic chatter, excited yips, and the occasional howl as the crowd settled in. But as the house lights began to dim and the stage slowly lit up, a hush began to ripple across the room. All eyes turned forward, where the band's instruments now stood gleaming beneath soft spotlights.

A moment later, Ruffa strolled casually onto the stage, his tail flicking with carefully controlled confidence. He approached the lone microphone perched on a pedestal and paused, taking in the scene before him.

The auditorium was full—packed.

For a breathless moment, Ruffa felt a rare swell of elation. This was it. His moment. Before him sat a packed house, here to witness what he believed to be his most incredible creation: a brand new style of music, performed by a band like no other. He couldn't remember the last time he'd seen this many dogs turn up for anything he'd organised. Maybe never.

He approached the mic, cleared his throat dramatically, and coughed. Loudly. Repeatedly. Almost comically.

It was his way of burning off nerves.

The crowd chuckled softly, but the laughter faded fast. Two ushers stationed at the sides of the hall immediately turned their steely gazes on the audience. One of them leant in toward a boisterous young mutt still yammering away with his two friends and pointed a stern paw at him.

The message was clear: silence now. The show was about to begin.

"You don't shut it now; I am throwing you out."

The pup soon shut up.

"Well, folks," Ruffa said, stepping into the spotlight with practised charm, "I'm delighted to be here with you tonight to present this brand new superband show we've put together just for you. One that I think you're going to love."

He paused for effect, scanning the audience, then pressed on.

"We've doubled the size of the band tonight. That's right—eight talented dogs will be performing live on this stage. And as we all know . . . more is always better."

A ripple of anticipation stirred across the crowd.

"So, without further delay . . . here they come! Give them a warm, wild, Dogwood welcome—use your paws, voices, and howls! Let them hear it!"

The audience exploded with applause. Barking, howling, whistling, tail-thumping—a chaotic symphony of doggy enthusiasm.

From the left wing of the stage, the band began to emerge.

First came the original Dogwood Droopsters—Rommy, Smackie, Moss, and Sniffer. Each wore an expression somewhere between forced confidence and genuine terror. Though seasoned performers, they'd never played for a crowd this size—or this loud. And their past shows had ended with more walkouts than encores.

As they made their way toward their instruments, Smackie leant over to Moss and whispered nervously, "We better not mess this up. You see how many crazy dogs we've got out there? This is either gonna be amazing . . . or a total disaster."

Moss just gave a slow nod. He remembered the jeers, the early exits, the harsh reviews. Tonight felt different—but whether that was good or bad, he couldn't yet tell.

Then came the second wave.

Four of the disguised Cool Cats—Mimi, Kreamy, Fangl, and Doubler—stepped into the light, their paws trembling inside their too-warm dog suits. The din from the crowd rose even louder, a sea of wagging tails and waving paws.

Mimi scanned the auditorium, trying not to panic at the noise surrounded her. Kreamy squinted through her mask, heart hammering in her chest. Fangl appeared calm but sweat soaked through his costume. And poor Doubler was practically shaking, his glasses fogging up inside the mask. He stumbled on his second step, and only Fangl's quick grab kept him upright.

But then something remarkable happened.

The howls grew louder. The crowd kept cheering.

And not a single dog seemed suspicious.

The disguises were working!

Mimi blinked in disbelief. Kreamy felt her breath start to steady. Fangl allowed himself the faintest smile. And Doubler finally exhaled. The ruse was holding. They were getting away with it.

Backstage, the remaining four cats stayed suited up, ready if needed. Everything had been rehearsed, and Ruffa and Herbert planned it to the second. Roles were locked in. Rommy would play guitar and handle vocals alongside Mimi—a late and surprising change made at Herbert's insistence. Kreamy was on lead guitar, Sniffer and Doubler on bass, Moss on drums—now surrounded by an even bigger set-up of toms and cymbals to satisfy the audience's thirst for noise. Fangl held a flute. Smackie, gripping a trumpet like it might explode, stood ready at the brass mic.

Then Ruffa stepped back to the centre of the stage and cleared his throat loudly into the microphone twice—just in case anyone had forgotten who was in charge.

"Some of you already know," he began, "tonight is no ordinary night."

A hush settled again.

"We have a very special guest among us," Ruffa said, puffing up slightly. "Straight from Birdheights . . . the legendary chief talent scout himself!"

Gasps rippled through the audience.

"There he is!" Ruffa pointed with theatrical flair.

All eyes turned to the front row where, straddling two reinforced seats with his massive wings draped around him, sat the unmistakable figure of Ikabin Bokasquawk. A real vulture—not just metaphorically—dressed in a long charcoal cloak, an oversized notepad in one talon, and a razor-sharp pencil in the other.

He wasn't looking up. He was scribbling furiously.

"Tonight," Ruffa boomed, "we aim to make history. We'll blow Ikabin's feathers right off and prove that Dogwood has the best band in Animalia!"

The crowd erupted again—howling, barking, stamping.

Up front, Ikabin slowly raised his head. Around him, dogs barked and howled, waved their paws, and stuck out their tongues in celebration.

The vulture blinked.

"Well," he muttered, barely audible beneath the din, "we'll *see* about that."

Judging by his expression, he made a quick note on his pad—something short, sharp, and not entirely complimentary.

Ruffa lingered in the spotlight, soaking in the roaring crowd, the lights, the electricity in the air. But then, without warning, a sudden burst of ferocious drumming shattered the moment.

It had begun.

He gave a subtle nod and quietly slipped offstage as the spotlight shifted to the performers. His part was done. Now it was all up to them.

"This is it, old boy," Ruffa whispered backstage, a wild blend of nerves, hope, and swagger surging through him. "This is your night."

The music erupted like a thunderclap—an unrelenting barrage of cymbal crashes and primal drumbeats from Moss, followed by fierce, jagged guitar screeches and a blaring trumpet blast that pierced the air. It was chaotic, loud, and intense, and the sound hit the audience like a shockwave.

It was impossible not to feel it in your chest.

Then Rommy stepped forward to the mic and barked out the opening lyrics. His voice rode the noise like a surfer on a tidal wave, perfectly timed with the frenzied jamming behind him. Somehow, it worked. The chaos became rhythm. The crowd went wild. The giant speakers on either side of the stage throbbed with the band's pulsing beat, shaking the walls.

And then—just as quickly as it had begun—the storm stopped.

A single note rang out from Fangl's keyboard, long and sustained, gliding through the silence like a whisper in a cathedral.

Mimi stepped up to the mic.

Her high and pure voice emerged so softly it barely rose above a murmur—but every creature in the room leant forward to catch it. The tone was delicate, almost ethereal, and her lyrics unfolded with a warmth that wrapped around the audience like a blanket. It was gentle, melodic, and intimate.

Rommy joined her, not with words, but with a low, steady hum that filled the space between her verses. Together, they created something strange and beautiful—an unexpected duet, equal parts bold and tender.

The audience didn't know what to make of it.

They didn't have to.

They were spellbound.

Then—CRASH! Cymbals. Drums. Thunder again.

The song surged back to life. Rommy's voice soared, full of grit and fire. Guitars shredded behind him, basslines thumping like a racing heartbeat. And just as suddenly silence. Only the delicate plucking of the lead guitar remained, twinkling like stars in a dark sky.

Fangl raised his flute. A lilting, trembling note joined the melody.

Mimi returned, her voice weaving through the music like thread through fabric. Rommy's hum followed her, soft and grounding.

They had built a masterpiece of contrasts—raw and refined, fierce and fragile, power and poise. The crowd had never heard anything like it. Not from dogs. Not from anyone.

The song ended.

The following silence felt suspended in midair, like the entire auditorium held its breath.

And then the explosion came—applause, barking, howling, stamping, whistles. Dogs leapt into the air. Some hugged each other. Others just stared at the stage in disbelief.

In the front row, Ikabin Bokasquawk was furiously scribbling into his oversized notebook, wings fidgeting as he glanced around at the pandemonium. His expression was neutral, but his eyes gave him away. He was impressed—visibly so.

The performance didn't let up. One song after another delivered the same wild blend of energy and elegance. The band captivated the crowd for an hour, building a set that moved seamlessly between madness and melody.

The audience erupted in a full standing ovation when the final chord rang out. Every creature was on its feet, cheering, howling, whistling, and clapping.

The band moved to the edge of the stage and bowed. Again, Fangl had to grab Doubler as the poor kitten nearly tripped into the crowd. He recovered quickly, offering a small wave as the lights dimmed.

The applause followed them offstage.

Backstage, Ruffa and Herbert were already ushering them down the corridor, their pace brisk and full of adrenaline. When they reached the dressing room, Ruffa slammed the door shut and locked it with a click.

The cats tore off their masks, gasping in lungfuls of air, their fur matted and damp with sweat. The others helped them shed the heavy costumes.

"That's just for a breather, kittens," Ruffa said quickly. "You'll need to suit up again when it's time to leave. Just a moment to catch your breath."

Rommy and Smackie clapped their paws in excitement. The whole room buzzed with giddy disbelief.

Ruffa turned to Herbert, his eyes gleaming. "What did I say, Herb? What did I say?! That was astounding!"

Herbert gave a low, croaky chuckle and raised a claw for a fist bump. "We rocked the house. I mean—rocked it! That was historic. We may have just rewritten the book on animal music."

"We smashed it, boss!" Moss exclaimed, still beaming. He turned to the others—Rommy, Smackie, even the cats—and gave them a solemn nod of respect. "Music like it's never been done before."

For a moment, the room went quiet. Everyone could feel it.

They had done something significant.

And somehow, against all odds, the Cool Cats and the Dogwood Droopsters had pulled it off together.

"How was it for you?" KT asked Fangl, his voice laced with a teasing sarcasm.

Fangl gave a half-shrug, trying to sound unfazed but not quite managing. "Yeah, cool," he said. "Too bad you couldn't be with us, though. It would've been cooler if all twelve of us had sung together. That would've been a real blast."

Before KT could respond, Ruffa—still riding the high of the performance—drifted into their conversation, arms behind his back, rocking on his heels.

"Don't you worry, kittens," he said, flashing his usual smug grin. "You'll all get your moment. I've got plenty more shows planned, and every one of you will get a chance to play on stage. Big things are coming!" He gave a wink and strolled off, humming to himself.

Doubler stared after him, brow furrowed.

"Did he just say what I think he said?" he asked quietly.

The other cats turned to him, their post-show glow dimming slightly.

"More shows?" Purrsteph echoed. "That wasn't the deal."

Doubler nodded grimly. "Exactly. And that's the problem. We may have just stumbled into two of the worst possible outcomes tonight."

"What do you mean . . . worst?" she asked, her voice cautious.

He glanced around to ensure no dogs were within earshot, then leant in. "Think about it. If we'd bombed, Ruffa would've had to choose between letting us go and cutting his losses or pushing a flailing band while trying to maintain control of our moms. And he knows—it would've collapsed sooner or later. His little con would've run out of steam."

Sylvest nodded slowly. "Yeah. A total failure would've been obvious. He wouldn't have had the energy to keep pretending for long."

"Exactly," Doubler said. "But now? We succeeded. We blew the roof off. And that gives Ruffa everything he needs to justify dragging this out . . . indefinitely. More rehearsals. More shows. More lies. And more control over our moms."

A heavy silence fell over them.

Tinki looked up. "So instead of ending the nightmare . . . we might've just made it stronger."

No one argued. Moments ago, the room was filled with post-show exhilaration, but now it buzzed with the uncomfortable thrum of reality setting back in.

"Well, you're making it sound like losing would've been the better option, Doubler," Sylvest said, tilting his head. "I'm glad it went the way it did. I don't like losing. Never have."

Doubler's frown deepened. "Yeah, well . . . sometimes losing means freedom. Sometimes a flop sets you free. But winning? Winning ties you to the thing that made you win. Don't you see? Now we're a real prospect. We've got a shot at the Superband Competition. Maybe even at winning it. And that means Ruffa will do everything he can to keep us under his thumb."

The others absorbed this with a growing sense of unease.

Then, unexpectedly, Moss spoke up, his voice slow and thoughtful. "You don't need to worry about being captives, dear cats. This thing you're fearing—it's built into the arrangement. Because, let's face it, dogs and cats don't get along. Not really. We don't think alike or act alike, and we don't dream the same. This thing we're doing. It won't last. It can't."

Smackie nodded. "He's right. This is temporary at best. One day, it'll fall apart—whether Ruffa wants it to or not. We're not built to blend forever."

As if summoned by their doubts, Ruffa strode in from the corridor, his tail swaying lightly. Herbert followed close behind, eyes scanning the group like a chess master sizing up the next move.

"Now, now," Ruffa said, spreading his arms wide in mock offence. "What gloomy talk is this? Cats, dogs—you were brilliant tonight. Spectacular. I'm asking you to consider what's next: the Superband Competition. If we enter and win, we'll be famous. If we don't, well . . . we gave it our best. No harm done."

Rommy crossed her arms. "And what happens if we do win?"

Ruffa smiled. "Then we make history. And with fame and success come opportunities. Incentives. Peace. I've worked with all kinds of creatures. Let me tell you—winning has a wonderful way of aligning everyone's interests."

"But what about our mommies?" Kreamy interjected. 'Let's not pretend we're all free here. They're still under your spell."

Herbert stepped forward, his voice buttery and falsely warm. "Your mothers will be your greatest fans, no matter what happens. They'll cheer for you from the front row, tears in their eyes. Win or lose, they'll be proud. Mommies are the most loyal fans in all of Animalia."

Then Mimi, quiet until now, stepped forward and met Herbert's gaze directly. Her voice was sharp and clear.

"They're only loyal because you've hypnotised them."

The room fell utterly silent.

Even the humming of the fluorescent lights above seemed to pause. Herbert blinked once, slowly. Ruffa's confident smirk faltered.

Someone had said it out loud for the first time since the plan had begun.

And no one dared to move.

"Me? Hypnotise them?" Herbert said with an exaggerated scoff. "Don't be so silly. I talk to them. Help them see sense. Offer . . . clarity."

Mimi's glare didn't waver.

Ruffa stepped forward, his tail flicking with agitation. "Look, everybody," he said, his voice more strained now, "in just a few minutes, you're all going to step back out there and play one final song. Together. Your fans are already howling out there. They're waiting for you. And I promise I won't ask for anything more if we don't win the Superband Competition. If by some miracle we win . . . I'll be the happiest mutt in the land! Either way, we all sit down and decide what comes next after tonight.

"You may think I'm controlling or obsessed—but maybe I'm just a strong, positive force for change. And this. This could change everything."

Mimi folded her arms, not buying a single syllable. "You keep trying to sound sane. Reasonable. But do you know what I've learned about creatures like you, Ruffa?

The ones who preach about *positive change?* They're the ones who twist truth into a leash. The ones who smile while they take control. You talk a good game, but I don't trust you. Not one inch. And aside from Herbert, I doubt anyone here does either—not even your loyal little mutts."

Herbert blinked. "Who says I trust him?" he replied, surprisingly candid. "I trust no one. I'm a solo croc, and I always have been. But right now—at this precise moment—we're onto a good thing. Wouldn't you agree?" He pointed a thick claw at Ruffa. "And like it or not, that dog made it happen. Not you, not me. Him."

The room went still. Even the cats stared at Herbert, floored by the blunt honesty.

Before anyone could respond, there was a loud knock at the door. A muffled voice called through:

"Curtains back up in five! Be ready. The house is going wild out here—I've never heard anything like it!"

Ruffa turned to face the room, his eyes wide, paws raised in a gesture that was half-pleading, half-prayer.

"I can't make you do anything," he said quietly. "Not anymore. Your talent has put you in charge. So here it is. We go out there and chase the adventure together . . . or walk away. Right here. Right now. What do you say?"

Silence.

The air was thick with uncertainty. No one wanted to answer. Not yet. The room was heavy with a truth they were all trying to make peace with—something terrible had brought them here, yes . . . but something incredible might come of it too.

None of them had ever been part of anything this strange . . . or potentially meaningful.

And deep down, each one of them felt the same electric tug—a whisper in the bones. Destiny is watching.

Could they walk away now?

CHAPTER 13

Paws to Vote

Mimi, tucked up in her bunk, was the first to stir. She yawned, pressed a paw to her mouth, and instinctively licked it. The faint taste of chocolate-orange milk still clung to her fur—a reminder of last night's indulgence. She blinked a few times and slowly sat upright. The others were still fast asleep.

At the far end of the room, KT was snoring with the force of a motorbike, which made her wince. She shook her head and climbed out of bed in her pyjamas.

What had they done last night?

They'd gone along with Ruffa's absurd scheme. Worn, itchy dog costumes. Played music on stage for a crowd of barking mutts. And now . . . they were floating. Elated. Confused. Maybe even famous?

The memory of Ruffa's gloating announcement returned to her in full force. After the show, he had revealed that Ikabin Bokasquawk—the fabled music scout from Birdheights—had pulled him aside. The vulture's exact words: "I'd be cuckoo not to let those musicians audition."

Which meant they were in. They were actually in.

In a matter of days, they'd be travelling to Birdheights for formal auditions, and if that went well, the Superband Competition itself—held at the legendary Central Park Arena—awaited them in less than a month.

Mimi's head swam.

She tried not to panic as she tiptoed to Doubler's bunk and gently nudged him. He stirred and blinked blearily behind his crooked glasses.

"It's too early," he mumbled. "Let me sleep. Last night was exhausting."

"Don't be silly," Mimi said. "It's morning. If we're doing this, we ought to practise."

Doubler groaned. "Practise? Ugh. Honestly, I want to go home."

Mimi cocked her head. "You don't want to be in the Superband Competition? Travel to Birdheights? Play on the biggest stage in the entire land?"

Doubler sat up with a faraway look in his eyes. "Truthfully, I've been tossing and turning all night. At first, I thought it was a bad dream—we were trapped in Dogwood, forced to wear those ridiculous outfits, bossed around by a megalomaniac mutt and a hypnotising crocodile. But nope. It's real. All of it. And I still can't believe we're acting like this is normal."

"But maybe . . . it's not all bad," Mimi said quietly.

Kreamy had just woken up and padded over to join them. "There's something to be said for upside-down adventures," she added thoughtfully.

Doubler gave a slight shrug. "Maybe. But it still feels like a trap."

Kreamy nodded. "I know what you mean. But remember the audience last night? They were howling for more. It was electric. I've never felt anything like it."

"It was also terrifying," Doubler murmured. "Do we have to do it again?"

"What do you mean, do it again?" Kreamy frowned. "We pulled it off once. Of course, we can do it again."

"Think about it," Doubler said. "We played in front of a hall packed with dogs while pretending to be dogs. We're being used—manipulated—by a showboating dog and his creepy croc accomplice. We're not even allowed to be ourselves. That's not a band. That's a circus."

Kreamy tried to sound upbeat. "Our mommies know we're here, right? They'll be proud."

"Will they?" Doubler whispered, his voice catching. 'Or are they just under Herbert's hypnosis, cheering like zombies? And when they snap out of it, will they think we're heroes . . . or fools? What would your mum say if she found out her daughter was parading around in a dog suit to impress a bunch of mutts?"

By now, the others had gathered, drawn by the heated voices.

KT stepped forward and raised a paw. "I'd like to say something."

All eyes turned to him.

"Not all of us were on stage, but we still felt it. The buzz. The music. It was real. I've never felt so alive. I want to be up there next time. I don't care where or for whom. We have something special—and I'm not giving that up."

"Born to perform, are we?" Sylvest muttered, unimpressed. "We've been tricked into helping a delusional mutt chase his fantasy. We're not stars. We're prisoners."

Fangl now stood up, riled. "So, what do you suggest, Sylvest? That we storm out of here, kidnap our moms, and run? Hide in a ditch until the coast is clear? Yes, we're being used—but maybe we can use this, too. See new places. Do something bold? This might be our only chance."

Kreamy was torn. "It is dangerous," she admitted. "Someone could get hurt."

"Exactly," said Purrsteph sharply. "We can't pretend this is a school play anymore. It's an abduction."

Doubler slumped. "We're the victims: us and our moms. If the dogs ever find out we're not one of them . . . it won't end with applause. It'll end with us in a landfill."

Kreamy gagged. "That's disgusting."

"Do they even have rubbish collectors in Dogwood?" Tinki asked. "I thought the trash just piled up till it decayed."

Fangl frowned. "They must collect it . . . eventually."

KT scoffed. "You are suddenly an expert in Dogwood law? Maybe we're not even protected under it. For all we know, we're considered rogue strays."

Sylvest had had enough. "Let's stop kidding ourselves. We're in danger. We've been conned. I say we take the bus and bring our moms home. Today."

"Then let's vote," Doubler suggested solemnly.

A hush fell.

Nobody knew what the correct answer was. Not yet.

"Okay, well, everyone who wants to carry on and proceed to Birdheights on Monday for the audition, hold up your paws. Remember—if you raise your paw, we postpone any plan to rescue our mommies."

"Does raising our paw mean we want to perform? Are you raising your paw?" asked Kreamy.

Doubler immediately dropped his paw. "No, I was just demonstrating how to do it." He raised it again. "See? Like this. Raise your paw high if you want to continue with the competition." Then he lowered it again. "You must keep your paw down if you don't want to go on. Everyone's got that? It's not hard to figure out. So—paws up if you're in."

Sylvest kept both paws planted on the ground and scowled. "Don't be foolish. This whole enterprise stinks— from the moment Ruffa kittienapped our mommies. Don't raise your paws if you've got any sense."

Fangl was the first to defy Sylvest. He raised his paw slowly. Doubler and the others stared at him in surprise but stayed silent. They all respected each other's right to choose.

Kreamy hesitated, then raised her paw too.

"Kreamy, you'd better think carefully about this," Doubler warned. "It's wrong to be pushed into something under such shady circumstances."

"Then what circumstances are acceptable?" Mimi cut in. "When was the thing we're doing never meant to be allowed? Look, I don't like it either. None of us do. But how is that better if we plan to take off with our mommies, who won't even come with us willingly right now?

"And let's not pretend this whole thing isn't thrilling or that we're not curious. Despite all the underpawed tactics Ruffa's used, we'd be cowards to back down now. Sometimes, good things come from bad situations—it's how life rolls."

Mimi raised her paw. "So—I'm in, for what it's worth. That doesn't mean I like Ruffa or that slithery croc with mind control. But I do like making music."

KT glanced around at the others. "I agree with Mimi. Let's not pull out just yet. I want to see Birdheights for myself. We can still figure out how to rescue our mommies if necessary. It takes more courage not to run."

He raised his paw.

Now, three cats—Fangl, Mimi, and KT—had paws in the air.

"Well then," Doubler said flatly. "Three in favour. Are the rest standing against? Or is there another fool among us?"

He stopped mid-sentence when he saw another paw rise—slowly, reluctantly. It was Tinki.

"Why, Tinki?" asked Sylvest.

"I didn't get to go on stage. Why should I miss out on the biggest audience I'll ever see just because a few of us fear a mutt and a lunatic croc? I want to know what it feels like to be famous. Just once."

The others looked around—some confused, some resigned. Four paws were now up. Fangl, Mimi, KT, and Tinki were in favour; Doubler, Sylvest, Purrsteph, and Kreamy were against.

"So, what now?" Doubler asked. "It's a draw."

"We either need another paw to go up," he said, "or someone to put theirs down. We must break this deadlock."

Tinki raised her paw a little higher.

"Do you want to go through with Ruffa's whole plan that badly?" asked Kreamy.

"I just want a decision," said Tinki. "I can't stand not knowing which way we're going."

Kreamy looked at her, disappointed. "So you're voting to follow a brainwashing mutt just to resolve indecision?"

"Yes. At least then we know what's happening."

A moment passed. Then everyone nodded. Decision made. The competition would continue. They weren't pulling out.

There was something about cats—they rarely fought over decisions. Not because they didn't enjoy a good scrap, but because curiosity always won. They had to know what would happen next. It was part of who they were.

And yes, curiosity had a reputation for danger. It wasn't called a killer for nothing.

But still, despite all the red flags, all Eight Cool Cats had to admit it.

They wanted to see where Ruffa's plan would lead.

For now, they were in.

CHAPTER 14

Transformed

Early the following morning, long before the others had stirred, Fangl and Sylvest quietly slipped away from the group. They had agreed the night before that they needed answers, and the biggest question on their minds was what had happened to their school bus. Without it, any chance of a clean escape would be near impossible.

Rain lashed down again, heavier than the night before, drumming against the roofs and splattering into puddles. But luck was with them. Hanging by the entrance to one of the storage buildings were two oversized waterproof jackets—dog-sized but usable. They pulled them over their clothing. Not only would they shield them from the weather, but they also disguised them just enough to blend into the wider compound.

They moved in silence, ears twitching with every echo and creak. The compound was vast and oddly quiet at this hour. Most other animals were asleep or inside, and the steady rainfall muffled their movements.

They prowled the perimeter for nearly an hour, checking each building they passed. Their paws grew heavier with clinging mud, and even the rainproof coats weren't enough to keep the wet from seeping into their legs and tails. Despite their best efforts, they couldn't find even a glimpse of the bus.

"This is pointless," Fangl muttered, shaking water from his ears. "The rain's getting heavier, and we won't find it this way. It could be anywhere."

Sylvest snorted. "Come on. We're not giving up just because of a little rain. I thought you were made of sterner stuff."

"It's not just the rain. We'll be in trouble if we get caught. Ruffa's not going to pat us on the back for snooping."

But Sylvest was already pointing towards a partly hidden structure beyond Herbert's residence. It sat half-concealed behind a rise in the ground and some overgrown hedges, looking more like a depot than a house.

"That looks promising," Sylvest said. "Big enough to hide something. Let's check it out."

As they trudged towards it, the feeling crept over them that they weren't alone. They paused often, glancing behind them. Still nothing. Just trees and the hiss of rain. But the prickling sense of being followed refused to go away.

When they rounded the far side of the building, they ducked into a narrow alcove beneath a ledge. Curtains hung behind the window above them, drawn tight. There hidden from view, they waited—and listened.

Then came the unmistakable sound of footsteps squelching through wet grass and mud. Slosh. Slap. Closer. Then, a pause.

From the gloom, a soggy shape stepped into view, huddled beneath a third oversized raincoat. Fangl and Sylvest instinctively tensed—then relaxed just enough to hiss in unison: "Doubler!"

The poor cat leapt nearly a foot in the air and landed with two loud squelches in the mud. "Don't do that!" he squeaked. "You nearly scared my fur off!"

"Why are you following us?" Sylvest snapped, peering at him from under the brim of his soggy hood.

"I thought you were running away!" Doubler confessed, slipping into the alcove, now crammed with three dripping cats. "You've both been acting strange. I thought maybe . . . I don't know . . . that you were trying to ditch the rest of us. Ruffa only needs four of us on stage, right? If two of you slipped away, he'd still have spares."

Sylvest gave him a gentle pat on the shoulder. "Don't be daft. We're not deserters. We're just looking for something."

Doubler narrowed his eyes. "What?"

"Our school bus," Fangl said plainly. "If it's here, we want to find it. Knowing where it is might matter later."

"Well," he offered, "I'd bet Ruffa hid it somewhere harder to access. Maybe beyond the tree line—where the forest gets thick."

Sylvest nodded toward another building just beyond a cluster of towering trees. "That one there," he said. "All those branches partly hide it. Could be just the front edge we're seeing."

Fangl adjusted his coat and turned to Doubler. "You're soaked. You should've fastened that thing up better."

Doubler shrugged. "Doesn't matter. We don't have time to worry about wet fur. They'll realise we're missing soon so let's not waste any more of it."

With that, the three cats pressed on towards the thicket

The tree canopy grew dense overhead, dimming the morning light. The rain eased to a fine mist as they moved deeper, the thick leaves above shielding them. The ground turned softer beneath their paws, the air more humid. And then—CRACK! A lightning bolt slashed across the sky lighting the forest in an eerie blue flash.

All three cats jumped.

"Yikes," muttered Fangl, shaking it off. "Let's keep going."

A narrow, winding path appeared ahead, almost completely overgrown but still visible. Moss-covered rocks and twisted tree roots bordered it, and partway down the trail, a massive, rotting tree trunk blocked their way.

They climbed over it one by one, silent now, each alert The air had shifted. They were getting close to something They could feel it.

And somewhere beyond that veil of trees and the curtain of rain, something was waiting.

"There's no way Ruffa could have driven the school bus down this path with that old tree trunk in the way," Doubler whispered, peering over the mossy log.

"Maybe not directly," Sylvest replied, crouching beside him. "But look—" He pointed to the mud just beyond the tree. Even though the rain had washed much of it away, faint tyre tracks curved off the main path and around the obstacle. "Something heavy came through here. Recently."

Fangl scrambled over first, his paws sinking into the slick earth with a squelch. "Well, let's see where it leads. No turning back now."

They pressed forward. At the end of the path, the trees began to thin, revealing a clearing none had noticed before. A derelict building stood half-sunken into the weeds and shadow, more broken down than the ones they'd been living and rehearsing in. Its walls sagged inward, streaked with mildew and peeling paint. The roof looked like it might collapse in the stiff wind.

The rain was easing. A dim shaft of sunlight broke through the thick canopy, dappling the clearing in golden patches. The trio felt a flicker of hope for the first time since they'd left. No one seemed to be around.

They crept forward, rounding the corner of the building in silence. There were no windows on this side— just rusted siding and crumbling bricks. But on the far side, they found something else entirely.

A wide opening—part garage, part tunnel—led directly into the structure. An old, cracked road sloped down into the entrance, and though weeds had overtaken much of it, the three cats could see the wide tyre tracks in the soft earth.

And then—a voice.

It drifted out from within the shadows of the building. A tuneless, croaky warble, accompanied by the slap of a wet paintbrush.

The three of them froze and looked up.

There it was.

The school bus.

Parked halfway inside, with its back end visible. But it no longer looked the way it had. Its bright yellow body was now covered in long, streaky patches of deep green and dull grey. And standing beside it—humming to himself, daintily dipping a brush into a bucket of paint—was Herbert.

"That's our bus!" Fangl hissed, loud enough to earn him a swift slap from Sylvest, who clamped a paw over his mouth. "What is that creepy croc doing?! He's ruining it!"

"He's trying to destroy it!" Doubler added, a little too loudly. And that did it.

Herbert's head snapped around.

"Who goes there?" he barked, dropping his brush. The crocodile took several lumbering steps toward the opening. "I heard that! Someone's lurking! Come out at once!"

The three cats ducked behind the corner, hearts pounding. They didn't dare move. They didn't dare breathe.

"I know you're out there!" Herbert growled, sniffing the damp air uselessly. "I hate snoops. If I find out who's sneaking around, there'll be trouble. Big trouble. You don't want to cross a croc."

He sniffed again, but the fresh rain had washed away useful scents. His nose crinkled in frustration, and a fat droplet plopped on his head. With a muttered grumble,

Herbert turned back and disappeared into the gloom of the building.

The three cats stood frozen for several long moments, the rain drizzling around them again.

When they were sure the coast was clear, they crept away, stepping softly, not speaking until they'd reached the safety of the path behind them.

Once out of earshot, their silence broke.

"What is he doing to our bus?" KT cried, his voice echoing through the trees.

"I don't know," Fangl said, still shaken. "Repainting it. Rebranding it. Hiding it. Who knows what Ruffa's plan is?"

"At least now we know where it is," said Sylvest, brightening. "That's something. That's more than we had yesterday."

Fangl and Doubler stared at him, unsure if he was being serious.

Sylvest grinned. "Think about it! We know where the exit vehicle is parked if we ever need to run for it."

"Just one teeny problem with that," Fangl replied dryly. "We'd need the key."

Doubler's whiskers twitched. Slowly, a smug grin spread across his face.

"What's so funny?" Fangl asked, narrowing his eyes.

"I may have seen where Ruffa keeps his keys," Doubler said, tapping his chin. "There's a cupboard under the stairs in his house. I've spotted him slipping down there a few times—always glancing over his shoulder first. I don't think it's even locked."

Sylvest's ears perked up. "Are you serious?"

Doubler nodded. "Serious as a thunderclap."

Sylvest clapped him on the back. "Well, that settles it. We've just stumbled onto the beginning of our escape plan."

Fangl glanced between them. "Don't forget—we agreed to see how the audition goes before anything else. If things go badly, we run. But for now . . . we wait."

They all nodded, still trying to get their heads around what was going on. Carefully, quietly, they climbed back over the fallen tree trunk and returned to the compound—muddy and drenched, with a better understanding of what was going on.

***

Meanwhile, back in Purrville, a few cats started showing concern. Police Chief Kitty Smallpaws sat at her desk, tail twitching anxiously. Something wasn't right. Questions had begun trickling—curious neighbours, concerned classmates, and the odd worried mother or two. All were asking the same thing. And more troubling still—where were their mommies?

With a sharp flick of her paw, Chief Smallpaws picked up the receiver and dialled the number for Professor Fishtail. If anyone knew anything, it would be the slightly scatterbrained, deeply opinionated headmaster of Purrville Academy.

The line clicked.

"Well, I've been meaning to call you myself," came the professor's voice in a fluster. "I'm very concerned—our school bus is missing!"

Kitty blinked. "The school bus?"

"Yes!" he exclaimed. "Gone! Vanished from the car park. And not a whisker of those kittens in sight!"

Kitty's eyes narrowed. "Hmmm. That is concerning," she said, now fully alert. "The kittens and the bus missing? This is beginning to look suspicious. What if—heaven forbid—they've been abducted?"

Professor Fishtail gasped, then sighed. "Well, that would be dreadful. But yes—yes, I think it's a good idea for you to investigate. I've got enough on my paws running this school. And if the kids and their mothers are in trouble . . . well, that's a disaster."

Kitty nodded grimly. "Leave it with me, professor. I'll start immediately by checking their homes and speaking with the mothers. If anything underpawed is going on, I'll sniff it out."

There was a pause on the line. Then Professor Fishtail cleared his throat.

"There is, of course, another possibility," he said slowly. "The Superband Competition. It's happening soon in Birdheights, and . . . well . . . perhaps the kittens decided to enter. Sneakily."

Kitty frowned. "I thought we'd agreed the school wouldn't be participating."

"We did," Fishtail replied. "But silly kittens do silly things. And if they somehow convinced their mothers to go along with it . . ."

Kitty cut him off. "I find that very hard to believe. Their mommies are model citizens. They'd never support such a covert stunt. Not without telling a soul."

"Hmm. Perhaps you're right," the professor admitted. "Still. I'd rather not find out they've skipped to Birdheights to chase fame and fortune without a meow of permission."

"They'd better not have," Kitty growled. "Missing classes is one thing. Deceiving the whole town? That's quite another."

"I'll trust you to get to the bottom of this," said Fishtail.

"You can count on me," said Kitty. "Leave it to Purrville's finest."

The call ended.

Kitty leant back in her chair and mulled over her next steps, paw absentmindedly swirling the jug of warm milk on her desk. Something didn't sit right. If this were an act of mischief, it was unusually elaborate. Too many kittens. Too many moms. Too clean a disappearance.

She downed her milk, grabbed her coat and badge, and headed out the door.

First stop: the kittens' homes.

She'd find them if they were sick in bed or playing hide-and-seek under the furniture—and they'd have some serious explaining to do.

And if not?

Then something more profound and darker was afoot in Purrville.

CHAPTER 15

Finding the Magic

In the days that followed, the compound pulsed with restless energy. The Eight Cool Cats poured themselves into long rehearsals, sharpening the songs they hoped to showcase at the audition. Each kitten took turns playing with the Dogwood Droopsters, the idea being that Ruffa and Herbert would eventually select the most potent combination and perfect setlist.

But something was missing.

Despite their efforts, no one could deny it—the magic of that first impromptu audition, the one that had left jaws hanging and even made the vulture tap her talons, had somehow slipped through their paws. The rhythm wasn't quite right. The energy didn't flow. Notes clashed. Spirits flagged.

Rommy finally broke the silence during a break, flopping back on a pillow with a sigh. "What's gone wrong? Was it a fluke? A one-off?" She looked around at the others. "What happened to us? We've lost our wow factor!"

A hush settled over the room. No one had an answer. They all felt it. The sparkle they once had—the raw, unfiltered joy—had been buried under Ruffa's misdirection and endless repetition.

During their rare breaks, the Cool Cats were granted limited time with their mommies, who, though sweet as ever, seemed wrapped in a strange, docile fog. The kittens tried to act normal, but the disquiet always lingered. These weren't their usual mommies, not as they should be. Something was . . . off.

The gossip would begin by nightfall when they returned to their cramped quarters. Whispered chats circled through the dark like moths to a dim bulb. They spoke freely about their odd canine bandmates, trying to make sense of their strange quirks and even stranger habits. But the tone shifted when the topic inevitably turned to Ruffa and Herbert. None of the kittens had anything good to say about the so-called *management*.

Why would they? Ruffa spent most rehearsals standing stiffly at the back, muttering vague encouragements like, "Carry on—it'll come together eventually," as if saying it often enough would make it accurate. Meanwhile, Herbert was rarely seen, claiming to be busy "behind the scenes," although no one knew what that meant.

It didn't take long before doubts began to fester. How had a clueless old dog like Ruffa even landed the role of stage manager? What sort of deranged audition board would have handed him a clipboard and said, "Yes, you're the one to lead our young musicians to greatness?"

And yet, for all his cluelessness, Ruffa had been the first to spot the bizarre potential in blending canine and feline talents. For better or worse, he had brought them together.

By Sunday morning, Rommy had had enough. She finally mustered the nerve to confront the dog directly. "Where's Herbert?" she asked Ruffa point-blank. "We haven't seen him in days. Isn't he meant to be helping us prepare for this?"

Before Ruffa could answer, the crocodile strolled in, looking unusually perky and positively glowing with self-satisfaction.

"Good morning, my talented troops!" Herbert beamed, showing off every one of his shiny teeth.

"Where were you?" Smackie asked coldly. "We expected some help. You know—coaching, direction, leadership . . . any of those words ringing a bell?"

Herbert chuckled. "Oh, no need to fret, my friends. I've been watching you the whole time—on camera." He pointed up to a tiny device mounted high in the corner. "And listening in, too. Very enlightening."

Smackie narrowed her eyes. "What are you even talking about?"

But Herbert merely grinned and offered no further explanation.

"Well then," Rommy said, trying to keep things on track, "since this is our final rehearsal, we need to make it count. Agreed?"

Fangl leant towards Sylvest in a quiet corner and whispered, "These mutts don't know the first thing about

music. Ruffa disappears for days and then turns up wit
nothing helpful to say. And their idea of a catchy tune i
probably a pack howl to the moon."

Sylvest gave a subtle nod, saying nothing. The trut
was too frustrating to argue over.

KT, however, had reached his limit. "Maybe it's time w
stopped waiting for them to guide us. Let's talk directly t
the dogs in the band. We've got to figure out what work
for us. Right now, we're not even close to being in sync."

"What was that?" Ruffa snapped, suddenly alert.

"Nothing!" KT answered quickly. "Just saying hov
grateful we are for your infinite wisdom and unmatche
leadership. We couldn't do this without you."

Ruffa gave a satisfied grunt, but Moss had overhear
everything, and his expression made it clear he hadn't bee
fooled.

He stepped closer to Doubler and whispered, "Let's sto
pretending. We must do it on our terms if we want to pla
like a real band. Music isn't about orders—it's about heart.

Moss then padded over to his drum kit and bega
tapping a slow, pulsing rhythm—steady and soft, lik
a heartbeat. Without a word, he summoned the other
forward.

One by one, the cats and dogs gathered around him
drawn in by the quiet conviction in his playing. Mos
looked up, his voice firm and unwavering.

"They think we're just pawns in their little dream
But we are not weak—not unless we choose to be. We'v
been brought together for their ambition, but we take tha

purpose back now. We make it our own. Because we are the music. And we are more alike than different."

The room fell still. This wasn't the same Moss they'd known—the quiet drummer content to stay out of the spotlight. This was someone else entirely—a leader.

Fangl blinked. *It's always the quiet ones,* he thought. *They're not silent because they don't know what's going on. They're silent because they're listening harder than everyone else.*

"You'll see," Sniffer said quietly, standing beside him. "When Moss speaks, it's time to listen."

No one objected. The band picked up their instruments and followed Moss's rhythm, one by one. A slow groove emerged, then quickened, then softened again. The dogs played with earthy boldness. The cats added shimmer and flair. And somewhere in the middle—against all odds—it started to sound . . . good.

Sniffer broke off mid-song just long enough to say, "This is how we win. Not by following orders—but by feeling it. Together."

Fangl grinned. "Then we'll play from the heart—and let the soul do the rest."

Off in the distance, Ruffa and Herbert watched from behind a pillar.

"What are they doing?" Ruffa asked, frowning.

Herbert tilted his head. "Looks like . . . bonding. Cross-species unity or something equally alarming."

Ruffa squinted at the group, then shrugged. "Well, whatever it is, it's working. Our master strategy of complete indifference seems to be paying off."

Herbert chuckled. "A genius tactic. Confuse them with neglect, and they figure it out themselves."

As the music grew more confident, Ruffa's tail began to wag. Even Herbert clapped along, his claws tapping the beat.

"Now that's more like it," Herbert said.

"You see that?" Ruffa puffed. "We did that!"

"Yes, yes," Herbert added proudly. "We're masterminding the coolest, droopiest band in Animalia."

"Don't get carried away," Ruffa grumbled. "We've still got an audition to win."

"Don't worry," Herbert replied. "We crocs don't get carried away. We lie low and wait for the right moment. We're swamp dwellers. We keep our tummies close to the ground."

In their minds, Ruffa and Herbert believed they were the visionaries behind everything.

The rest of the evening passed in a kind of musical trance. The band rehearsed until their paws ached and their eyes drooped. As dawn approached, the music grew slower and more introspective until it finally faded into silence.

Herbert arranged for a hearty meal and warm drinks. The cats were met by their mommies, who gently led them to their beds. Strangely quiet, the mommies barely spoke— but the kittens chalked it up to the lateness of the hour.

Tomorrow was the audition.

And something in the air told them—everything was about to change.

***

Later that evening, Tinki and Purrsteph sat sulking in the cats' shared bedroom, their whiskers drooping and tails curled protectively around their paws.

"What's wrong with you two?" Kreamy asked, eyeing them curiously. "You look like you've each thrown away many lives."

Tinki sniffled and blinked back a tear, but one managed to escape, trickling down her fur before getting trapped in the thick fluff of her cheek. She rubbed it away with the back of her paw, visibly irritated by the ticklish sensation.

"She's upset because our mommies couldn't come with us to the audition," Purrsteph explained gently.

"I know," said Kreamy, trying to console them. "But Ruffa was pretty clear—he said there's no room on the bus."

It wasn't just the cats who felt disappointed. The dogs in the band had hoped to bring their friends and relatives along too, but the decree had been absolute: no entourage, no exceptions. This trip was strictly for band members only.

Nearby, Fangl leant toward Sylvest with a worried look. "What do you think our bus will look like now?" he muttered. "That reckless croc's been tinkering away at it all week. I've got a terrible feeling it'll be a horror show on wheels."

Sylvest sighed. "Why didn't they just leave it alone and mess with their Dogwood High bus? I don't understand why they had to butcher our lovely ride. How are we going to explain this to Professor Fishtail?"

The two brooded over the matter in hushed tones until sleep finally claimed them.

Barely half-past eight the next morning, all Eight Cool Cats were yanked from their beds and ushered to get ready by their ever-smiling, ever-dazed mommies. By half-past nine, they stood outside the compound's main building, bleary-eyed and dazed, joined by the four canine bandmates.

Around them sprawled a jumbled sea of luggage—boxes of instruments, costumes, lighting rigs, and one oversized crate marked "Canine Facial Obscuration Console: DO NOT TAMPER." No one had anticipated how much equipment the "Dogwood Droopsters" now required to function.

In the distance came the throaty rumble of a vehicle.

"Right on time," Ruffa beamed, bouncing on the balls of his paws.

Not far off, the eight mommies huddled together in vibrant jumpers that read "Dogwood Droopsters" in bold lettering. The kittens waved at them awkwardly, while the mommies cheered and fluttered miniature flags with exaggerated pride.

Then the bus came into view.

The Cool Cats froze, their eyes widening in disbelief. As the vehicle trundled into the clearing, its engine emitted an unsettling groan, as if it too objected to the makeover it had suffered. With a sputter and a wheeze, it rolled to a halt and fell silent, as though glad its torment was finally over.

The once-charming school bus had been transformed into a two-storey contraption. The top level looked hurriedly slapped together with scraps and salvaged bits of metal, wobbling slightly as it settled. Painted in a garish deep blue, the words DOGWOOD DROOPSTERS were emblazoned in chunky white letters on both sides.

The mommies clapped again, waving their flags with comical enthusiasm.

The band members, however, were less impressed. Not a word was spoken, but the silent stares said everything: Is that thing even roadworthy?

Ruffa beamed with pride, bouncing down the final step like a game-show host unveiling a grand prize.

"That croc's a genius," he announced, clapping his paws together. "You can't have a superband without a super brand—and branding is everything, kittens and pups! You've been wondering what Herbert's been tinkering with all week, haven't you? Feast your eyes on his masterpiece!"

Herbert emerged moments later from behind the bus with a self-satisfied grin and a paint-smudged tail. His tired eyes sparkled with pride.

"Oh, it was nothing," Herbert said, brushing off invisible praise with the back of a scaly claw. "Just a little late-night carpentry, some on-the-go paintwork, and a minor reconfiguration of your transport infrastructure. Nothing any decent croc couldn't handle."

None of the young performers looked convinced.

The cats stared at the towering vehicle, their ears twitching uncertainly. Dogwood Droopsters glared down at them in blaring white font, a name that still made zero sense to them, especially since none of the "Droopsters" had been involved in naming it.

"We had a beautiful school bus," Fangl whispered to Sylvest. "Now we have . . . this."

"I don't know whether to climb aboard or file a health and safety report," Sylvest muttered.

Ruffa clapped his paws again. "Let me explain how this will work! The top deck is the dogs' domain—Dogwood's doghouse, if you will. Cats on the lower deck, along with our precious instruments and props. Everyone pulls their weight. That means everyone. Except, of course, the mommies. Mommies, feel free to keep waving."

The mommies, grinning like prize-winning sunflowers, waved their little flags even harder.

With weary sighs, the cats and dogs began hauling their boxes and bags aboard the peculiar bus. It creaked and groaned under the weight of each new item, as though mourning its former, simpler life as a perfectly ordinary school bus.

Inside, the décor took a stranger turn. The driver's seat was plush and extravagantly upholstered in purple velvet. Above it hung a framed photo of Herbert lounging poolside in oversized sunglasses, with two pink fuzzy dice dangling from the rearview mirror and a green candy dispenser on the dash, filled to the brim with his favourite fizzy mint tablets.

"Nice set-up," Sniffer said dryly as he climbed aboard. "Must be good to be the boss."

"Speak for yourself," said Smackie, grimly eyeing Herbert's holiday photo. "If I had to drive this thing staring at that face, I'd park us off a cliff."

"I don't get to go on holidays," Moss muttered behind them. "But maybe if we win this ridiculous competition, we'll get more than a bus ride to nowhere."

"More likely another week of forced rehearsals and powdered milk," Smackie replied.

Rommy followed them onboard, still chipper despite the grumbling. "We're heading to Birdheights," she reminded them. "That has to count for something."

"Oh yes," Smackie snapped. "It is another chapter in the ongoing tale of how we got roped into Ruffa and Herbert's half-baked experiment. If lucky, we'll be remembered as the first musical act to be manipulated, underpaid, and forced to ride a collapsible tin can into the unknown."

"Such drama," Rommy sighed, shaking her head. "One way or another, we're playing. And when we play, we shine. That's what matters."

Smackie said nothing, but her eyes remained fixed on the garish lettering painted across the bus's flanks. Dogwood Droopsters. The name said nothing about them. And yet, for now, it was the name the world would see.

She climbed aboard, biting her tongue. The road to Birdheights awaited—and with it, whatever strange, glittering future might follow.

Smackie didn't appreciate Rommy's gratitude for what little they had.

"They've done a good job of brainwashing us into accepting a meagre life. It's not just the cats' mommies under some dumb spell."

"Watch your language, Smackie," Rommy replied curtly, shaking her head. "I'm going along with this endeavour, just like you. But we've got to aim to win this competition. That's all that counts. When we do win, it must be us who get recognised. We're the artists. We are the ones making the music. They can't take that away. We're the ones on stage."

"You said it like it is real," Sniffer muttered, half-impressed, half-doubtful.

"Uh-huh. Us and a bunch of cats pretending to be like us will make it all even more legitimate," Smackie scoffed, her voice rising. "We have secrets, Rommy. And those secrets often make us do what the ones in charge tell us. We're part of a dumb experiment hatched in the warped minds of two lazy, self-appointed leaders. If we try to fend for ourselves, we risk losing everything. So we stay. We accept the crumbs they throw our way. And we're told to be thankful."

Rommy fell silent. She knew better than to argue further. Smackie wasn't the sort to back down, and part of what she said stung with uncomfortable truth.

Meanwhile, the dogs had to pass through the cramped lower deck to reach the stairs. The cats' section wasn't exactly spacious—four narrow bunk beds clustered on each side with barely enough room to squeeze past. Everyone was careful not to knock over the gear or upset the delicate balance of already-stacked instruments.

Rommy noted the shaded windows downstairs. Of course—they were to keep the cats' identities hidden. The whole masquerade depended on it. She also spotted a single toilet tucked at the back of the lower floor and frowned. If that were the only one, the dogs would need to descend every time they needed a break. Not ideal.

Sniffer reached the top of the stairs first. He gave an excited whistle, followed by a long, triumphant howl.

"Yowza! It sure is nicer up here, folks. Check this crib out!"

The other dogs trundled up after him, their heads ducking instinctively—the makeshift second level offered just enough space for crawling or stooping, but not much more.

Still, it had its charms. The floor was littered with plush cushions of various patterns, a large red mini-fridge buzzed cheerily at the far end, and next to it sat a tiny but fully functional pinball machine, bolted to the floor.

"This is nice," Rommy admitted, her eyes lighting up.

"I like it too," Sniffer said, flopping onto the cushions and stretching out with a satisfied groan. "I'm gonna have a quick nap. All this heavy lifting has made me tired."

"'Heavy lifting'?" Smackie's voice came sharp as claws. "You fool. You picked up one bag. One. And now you're stretched out like you just climbed a mountain. Meanwhile, those so-called lightweight cats are lugging the rest of the gear. You're an embarrassment to your kind."

"Shut up, girl," Sniffer growled, not in the mood for a lecture. "I can rest if I want. We've worked our tails off rehearsing this week. And nowhere in the band contract does it say we're baggage handlers. We're artists! We need a professional porter with a strong back and a respectful attitude."

"A porter!" Smackie spluttered, eyes bulging. "We ain't on our way to a five-star hotel with sun loungers and catnip cocktails! This is a working tour, genius. We do what needs doing."

"I say get that lazy croc to carry," Sniffer muttered, curling deeper into the cushions. "He's got the muscle. I've got delicate paws designed for plucking guitar strings, not for hurling luggage around. I'm a musician, not a roadie."

"You guys are way too much," Moss said, shaking his head as he turned back towards the stairs. "I'm going to help the others. Maybe we can salvage some dignity for this band. Right now, we look like a pack of lazy, pampered hounds."

And with that, Moss disappeared back down the stairs, his drumsticks tucked into his belt, ready to lend a paw—while Sniffer snored gently behind him, dreaming of someone else doing the hard work.

Smackie chose to follow Moss, shaking her head several times in frustration, but not before casting one last dirty look at Sniffer.

Sniffer shrugged off her disgust and stretched out fully on the cushions. Dogs were used to being criticised; they could take it.

Rommy soon followed her, leaving Sniffer alone. He didn't mind.

"This has to be the life," he murmured, letting out a contented sigh.

But as soon as his eyes closed, a flicker of doubt jolted through him like a paw to a live wire. With a reluctant groan, he sprang upright, glanced around guiltily, and dragged himself to his feet. He knew he'd never hear the end of it otherwise.

Grumbling under his breath, he descended the stairs.

Fifteen minutes later, all the luggage had been loaded. The cats were settled into their cramped bunk beds downstairs, and the dogs had returned to their upstairs haven and were now lounging comfortably. Moss noticed that, unlike the shaded windows on the lower level, the upstairs windows had simple dark blue curtains. At the moment, they were tied back with neat red ropes, letting light pour in.

The bus engine rumbled to life.

From their bunk beds, the Cool Cats watched their mommies, still waving enthusiastically with blank expressions and small triangular flags. The bus's front door remained open for a final moment as Ruffa grinned and returned the wave. From upstairs, Rommy peered down through the window at the strange scene below.

He narrowed his eyes. Something wasn't right.

The mommies were chanting. Their lips moved in perfect unison, but the bus engine drowned out the words. Their arms waved like clockwork toys, and their eyes were glassy and distant.

Rommy stepped back and slumped onto a cushion.

"What's on your mind, brother?" Moss asked.

"If these mommies are meant to be our cheerleaders," Rommy said slowly, "why aren't they coming along?"

"You're kidding me, right?" Moss raised a brow. "They're not cheerleaders. They're . . . drones. Herbert turned them into docile little puppets. You know that, right? Those mommies are in a trance. They've been brainwashed to make sure the kittens fall in line."

Rommy frowned. "Maybe that's true. But I think . . . deep down . . . the mommies want to be part of this. They're proud of their kittens. And we're a team, aren't we? A real superband. Dogs and cats performing together. It's special."

Moss folded his arms and leant back.

"Tell me this, Rommy. If you're forced to do something . . . can you honestly say it's what you want to do?"

Rommy thought about that.

"We're performers," he said at last. "We live to be on stage. We endure obstacles. We push through. That's what passion does—it pulls you forward."

"Fair." Moss nodded. "But what if they took your mommies and brainwashed them? Would you still be pushing forward?"

Rommy hesitated.

Smackie cut in, tired of the philosophical back-and-forth. "Let's not get tangled up in questions that have no answers. We're here to audition. We sound good. We work well together. Let's keep it simple."

Rommy gave a slow nod. "She's right. We've come this far."

"No," Moss replied, his voice low but firm. "That's exactly what they want us to think—it's all too complicated to question. But how you do something matters just as much as what you do. Ask yourself three things: Why am I doing this? How am I doing it? And what am I getting out of it? If you only focus on the what, you've already lost your way."

Sniffer, still catching his breath from earlier exertion, chimed in.

"Alright then. Why are we doing it? Because we want to win the competition. How are we doing it? With a brilliant band—unusual, yeah, but it works. And what do we get? Fame. For us. For Dogwood. For proving that we're the best."

"You left something out," Moss said, narrowing his eyes. "You skipped the part where the cats' mommies were abducted, where their identities are hidden. Where the band lies to the audience, pretending to be all dogs. That's not ambition. That's deception."

"They're getting something out of it," Sniffer argued. "We all are."

"No, they're not," Moss replied. "The cats downstairs? They get no credit. No recognition. No truth. If we win, they'll still be pretending to be someone else. How is that fair?"

"Life's never been fair," Smackie said bitterly. "We're used to it. We suck it up. That's how it goes."

"But it's wrong," Moss said. "And that makes what we're doing wrong. There comes a time when you've got to stand for something. Or else you're just part of the problem."

Rommy gave him a weary smirk. "There he goes again—Moss and his moral code. We let you rant because you're a good drummer, but never happy. You don't like Ruffa. You don't like Herbert. You don't like the competition. You don't even like the cats. Or us."

"Who says I don't like you?" Moss replied calmly. "I just don't agree with everything you believe. I'm here because I love making music. But I won't lie to myself about what's going on."

A heavy pause fell.

Then came the sound of Ruffa's paws climbing the stairs. A moment later, his head popped up over the top step, his tongue lolling out with delight.

"This is so exciting!" he yipped. "We're finally on the road! Come on, gang—group howl!"

The dogs let out a thunderous, unified howl. All except Moss, who made the motion but didn't utter a sound.

He just stared ahead, his eyes filled not with excitement but with something far heavier.

***

Birdheights was a fair distance away. Much farther than the journey between Purrville and Dogwood. It would take them almost eight hours, and most of the trip was on a single, long, winding road. Knowing it would be a lengthy ride, it wasn't long before the dogs raided the refrigerator while the cats snoozed quietly in their bunk beds.

As the bus chugged merrily along, Ruffa and Herbert sat at the front, deep in conversation. The road was quiet, and they were determined to reach Birdheights by mid-afternoon. They needed to begin setting up at seven that evening, and at their current pace, they'd arrive somewhere between four and five.

Their audition was scheduled for eight, giving them a decent buffer to settle in and run sound checks. The performance would take place not in Birdheights proper, but in a smaller village about half an hour outside the city. This village hosted the preliminary auditions in an open-air venue with a modest stage and a few hundred seats. While the Superband Competition would be held in a sprawling arena in a valley near Birdheights, today's event was humbler. The arena, they had heard, could seat nearly fifty thousand creatures of all shapes and sizes. It even had a string of high balconies, offering birds a soaring, top-down view of the stage, with special elevators for those lacking wings.

Although the band was eager to glimpse Birdheights, they wouldn't get one unless they made it through the audition. That stung a little. They were curious about the great city they'd only ever heard about in passing tales and magazine cuttings. Birdheights was the fabled capital of modern Animalia—a shimmering skyline of towers, neon signs, and dazzling spectacles. But none of the band members had ever set paw, claw, or tail there. Visitors to Purrville or Dogwood who claimed to have seen it described it as a marvel, though oddly, they never said, "You must go." It remained a mythic dream: absolute enough to believe in, distant enough to doubt.

The audition stage was in the heart of the village and cordoned off to keep out eager onlookers. Although hundreds of locals were expected to loiter around, hoping to catch a glimpse or overhear a riff or chorus, only judges and performers were permitted close access. A cloth canopy was stretched across the top of the stage to protect performers from the weather, but the audience would remain exposed to the elements.

Each band had twenty minutes to unload and set up their gear, and ten to fifteen minutes to perform. None of them knew that only four bands would audition per day over a week. Of the roughly thirty bands scheduled, just eight would be chosen to advance to the Superband Competition. From there, only two would walk away victorious: one runner-up and one ultimate winner who would gain fame across Animalia.

They also didn't know who the judges were. Perched quietly in the back rows would be three birds: a formidable eagle, a chatty swallow, and a wizened pigeon who—

despite being half the eagle's size—seemed to act as though he were in charge. The eagle had to sit across two chairs due to his sheer width, while the pigeon peered out from beneath his cap with keen, watchful eyes.

At around four o'clock, the Dogwood Droopsters' bus pulled into the village.

The view from the windows was, frankly, underwhelming. This wasn't the mighty Birdheights they'd been daydreaming about. It looked just like any other small town. Dusty roads. A smattering of trees. A couple of crooked rooftops.

Nothing spectacular.

Still, they had come this far.

Getting over their initial disappointment, Ruffa, Herbert, and the mixed cat-dog band began unloading their gear and made their way toward the dressing hut— an old, somewhat shabby structure just behind the stage. It wasn't much, but it would have to do.

"Can you believe it?" Purrsteph moaned. "We come all this way and end up in a dump like this. How pathetic is that?"

Kreamy was the first to agree. "You said it. We've been swindled by smooth-talking, smart-beaked birds from the Birdheights megalopolis. For all we know, this could be one big scam. Ruffa might've been conned too—and as for Herbert, he wouldn't know the difference between a concert hall and a compost heap. We're being managed by the two dumbest Animalians to ever walk on four legs."

Doubler gave her a sharp look. "Careful, Kreamy. You never know who's listening."

"Let her speak her mind," KT interjected. "If they want to make such a spectacle of this competition, the least they could do is make it feel like something special. First impressions matter."

"I think it's all part of the test," Fangl mused aloud. "They're deliberately underwhelming us. Maybe they want to see how we handle disappointment and adapt."

"That's giving a lot of credit to a bunch of high-flying, fluffed-up birds," Tinki replied, frowning. "I doubt they're that clever."

"Enough jabbering," Mimi snapped. "Let's just get on with it. We either get in or we don't. One way or another, we'll find out soon enough."

With that, silence fell. No one had anything more to say. The reality of the moment had begun to settle in.

CHAPTER 16

Audition

The evening air hung heavy with anticipation. At exactly 6:30 p.m., the time had come. This was it: their first real test.

Eight band members stepped forward, summoned at last to take the stage. Dressed head to paw in their elaborate canine disguises, the Cool Cats looked almost unrecognisable—even to one another. Kreamy, KT, Doubler, and Sylvest remained behind and were excluded from the line-up.

None of the four seemed particularly bothered. The eight-hour slog had drained them, and the uninspiring venue—hardly the glamour of Birdheights—had already dulled their spirits. The stage was plain, the seats sparse, and the judges seated so far back they were more shadow than substance. The whole set-up felt less like a shot at stardom and more like an obscure school recital.

Still, those selected to perform began to rally as they picked up their instruments. Across the open-air arena, three birds sat perched in the back row, holding notepads in their claws—watchful, unreadable.

Fangl leant toward Smackie and muttered, "Those must be the three in charge. Our fate lies in their puny claws."

"Don't be fooled by tiny frames and fluffy feathers," Sniffer whispered back. "Power doesn't always dress loudly."

Moss gave a quiet nod. "The good ones—the pure-hearted—don't chase the spotlight. It's the schemers who climb fastest. Those with no regard for others always find a way to the top. And that's when things go wrong."

Rommy, who'd been listening intently, spoke up. "Maybe these three judges are different. Maybe they're musicians, just like us. Who knows? Perhaps they still care about the music."

"I wouldn't count on it," Moss said, his tone sombre. "Wisdom doesn't always follow authority. And power rarely walks hand in hand with competence."

Rommy sighed. "There you go again, Moss. You always turn a song into a sermon."

"Hey boys," Smackie cut in, adjusting her mic, "we're here to play, not debate the meaning of Animalian life."

Offstage, Ruffa was absorbed by his equipment. He was flashing buttons like a grumpy stagehand.

"Alright then," said Moss, stepping forward and beginning to play. "Let's see what we can do."

***

Their exhaustive rehearsals had been harsh, and the results showed they had paid off. The eight-piece dog-ca band slipped effortlessly into a rhythmic, melodic groove. Rommy and KT proved a dynamic female duet, pouring their hearts into every line. The energy soared as the song progressed, layering the trademark Dogwood noise with moments of absolute musical finesse—those subtle, feline touches adding polish and poise beneath the barking bravado.

Moss held it together with steady, driving drums, his performance rising to the moment with pulsing intensity and skilful restraint.

They played two songs. And then, just like that, a paw signal from the shadows told them to wrap it up.

Even Ruffa was caught off guard.

The band bowed collectively toward the judges—still half-obscured in the gloom of the back row—and quickly exited the stage.

And that was it. Over. Gone in a blur of lights and nerves and barely enough time to register what had happened.

The drums were too heavy to carry, but two burly roadies materialised from nowhere to lift them off stage with impressive ease, taking the lighting rig with them. A new group was already waiting in the wings—three sleek-looking tigers, each with a guitar strapped over their shoulder.

Fangl blinked at the sight of them. "All guitars? That's . . . odd."

What the Dogwood Droopsters didn't realise was that, during their performance, hundreds of curious locals and visitors had clustered behind the outer walls of the cordoned area. They strained to hear—just a fragment of music, a hint of magic.

And somewhere in the crowd, a young squirrel tugged his mum's sleeve, eyes wide, overcome with emotion.

"Wow! These guys are so great! I love them!" he cried, tears of joy clinging to his whiskers.

That moment passed unnoticed by the band.

As the crowd grew too large, a squad of no-nonsense security apes swept in to disperse it. By the time the tigers struck their first chord, the audience had been ushered well back.

The Droopsters heard the tiger trio's faint strumming and howling vocals from the changing room. The sound was raw and powerful—just three voices and three guitars, yet it filled the space in a way that made some of the Cool Cats uneasy.

On the bus, with gear reloaded and exhaustion setting in, Fangl turned to Sylvest, who was slumped in his seat.

"I think that was pathetic," he muttered. "All these rehearsals . . . and for what? We didn't even get to finish our set. It felt like a letdown from start to finish. That gloomy little village, that disinterested panel of birds . . . and that stage? We've got better back home. It's like we were set up to fail."

"Our stage is better," Sniffer agreed sleepily as he padded down the stairs to the loo.

Sylvest didn't look up. "It was just an audition," he said flatly, then closed his eyes.

Fangl didn't reply. The silence that followed was heavy.

"You know what, kittens," Rommy said quietly, "life's often like that. When you think something amazing's about to happen, reality gives you a good smack between the eyes. Nothing turns out how you imagine. Ask for too much, and most of the time, you'll end up disappointed."

No one responded. The comment hung in the air. It was hard to tell whether Rommy was being cynical or wise—but Moss, for one, was quietly impressed. That sort of philosophy usually came from his corner.

None of them knew that the auditions had been deliberately kept low-key. The entire Superband Competition had only been dreamt up by the wise council of birds a month earlier. Their attention was fixed on preparing the grand arena in Birdheights, and they had gone out of their way to avoid fanfare at this early stage. The less attention, the better—for now. It was still a work in progress; the last thing they needed was chaos.

By the time the bus reached the outskirts of Dogwood, only Herbert remained awake—and fortunately, he was at the wheel. Ruffa was dozing beside him, snoring loudly, head slumped against the window as the streetlights flickered past.

CHAPTER 17

Outcome

When the band returned to Dogwood late that night, weariness clung to them like a second coat. They stumbled into bed one by one and were soon fast asleep—except for Mimi.

She lay with her eyes closed, willing herself to drift off, but a niggling thought kept tugging at her mind. Why hadn't their mommies come out to greet them? After all the build-up, the bus journey, the audition, and the late return, it felt strange—unsettling, even—that no excited hugs or worried meows had welcomed them home. But it wasn't a thought she wanted to pursue, not now. Eventually, sleep crept in and pulled her under.

The next time Mimi opened her eyes, the room was still dark, but something was off. Hovering directly above her face was a small plate with a freshly baked apple pie on it.

"Good morning, my sweet one," her mother chirped, eyes gleaming in the low light. "Look what I've brought you. Still warm, just how you like it!"

Startled, Mimi sat up slowly. She blinked around the room. A similar scene was unfolding in every bunk—each kitten being greeted by their mommy with an identical apple pie and the same unnervingly cheerful expression.

For a moment, it felt more like a dream. Or maybe a bizarre nightmare.

Then the door opened, spilling hallway light into the room, and Herbert walked in, all smiles.

The mommies gently nudged their children out of bed as Ruffa appeared behind Herbert, pushing a trolley clinking with glasses.

"Thirsty, anyone?" Ruffa bellowed. "Freshly squeezed orange juice! Or perhaps a hot cup of tea with some delicious biscuits? We're spoiling you today."

Kreamy rubbed her eyes. "What . . . is this? Breakfast . . . applause?"

"Is this your attempt to make us feel we did well?" Doubler asked flatly, suspicious of Ruffa's rare generosity.

"Not at all!" Ruffa declared. "This is what you deserve! You were all fabulous yesterday. I'm proud of every last whisker and paw."

Purrsteph narrowed her eyes. "This is getting creepier by the minute. One moment we're nobodies, the next we're treated like royalty. You'd think this mutt was our doting uncle."

"We are a family," Herbert said, as if reading her thoughts. "A mixed-up, marvellously talented family. And I'm confident we'll hear back from the noble judges soon. Today or tomorrow, I expect. I can already taste the announcement—we'll go to Birdheights for the final stage. The tallest buildings, the brightest lights. Names up in the sky."

"You mean our names," Ruffa added, puffing up. "But none of it will happen without dedication. So, eat up, rest well, and be prepared to work harder than ever."

Kreamy was already munching on her pie. "These taste amazing," she admitted, mouth full.

"Alright," said KT, licking crumbs from her paw. "Then explain this—why are our mommies acting even weirder than before we left? What are you doing to them?"

"Everyone in this compound stays here of their own free will," Herbert said, the smile never leaving his face. "And I'll tell you the secret to the apple pie—it's family."

There was a collective blink.

"My cousin, Michelangelo—Mikey Angels, as he's known in Swamptown—is the top chef in our region. Culinary legend. This pie? One of his signature creations. He's joined us on this journey. Lucky, right?"

"This croc used to run the finest restaurant in Swamptown. Five Crocodile Tails," Herbert added proudly, puffing out his chest. "That's a big deal."

"Croc Tails?" Purrsteph frowned. "Is that like Camel Humps but for food?"

"Oh, please," Herbert sniffed. "Camel Humps are just for beverages—entirely pedestrian. A Croc Tail is a badge of honour. One means excellent. Two means unforgettable. Three? That's transcendence."

Tinki scratched her head. "So, three Croc Tails means top of the pile?"

"Near enough, though we don't pile cuisine," Herbert corrected smugly. "Let's just say Mikey Angels is Animalia's closest thing to a food deity. And this delightful band of fur and fury—you deserve the best."

The cats exchanged looks. None of them could tell whether they were being treated . . . or tamed.

The Eight Cool Cats were unaware of a figure quietly lurking behind the scenes: Mikey Angels, the croc chef responsible for their apple pies, had a distant but notable connection to Birdheights. His path had once crossed—indirectly—with that of Boreme Kildare, the wealthiest merchant in the city. Although they didn't know each other personally, Kildare had long been a friend of Herbert's father. And when the old croc passed away, Kildare began watching Mikey's culinary rise with interest.

It was Kildare who had secretly financed Mikey's Swamptown restaurant. Mikey never knew where the generous support had come from. But it was no coincidence. Kildare had plans in motion—plans that reached far beyond the kitchen.

Back in the bedroom, Fangl had heard enough pie praise and culinary boasting.

"You've done nothing but use us," he snapped, glaring at Herbert. "First by taking our mommies, and now you try to blackmail us with sweet treats and compliments, like we've never tasted anything half-decent. Spare me."

Sylvest sat upright in bed, brushing crumbs from his chest. "I agree with Fangl, but let's see what the day brings, alright? Everyone needs to relax a little."

Fangl looked at Sylvest with a disappointed look. It felt like a betrayal, as if their concerns were being swept aside with a shrug and a pie crust.

Most of the cats finished eating silently, too emotionally weary to argue further. The mommies hovered nearby, smiling wide, unsettling smiles, like cheerful puppets caught mid-performance. It was disconcerting—there was something not quite right in the way they beamed at their children, and the Eight Cool Cats could feel it in their fur. Their mommies were still missing . . . something—something vital, something real.

Fangl placed his unfinished pie on the bedside table with quiet disgust. No one said anything more. Speaking out would only reopen the wound they all shared: helplessness. Their mommies were here—but not here—and everyone knew Herbert had something to do with it. And so, their silence thickened.

From the doorway, Herbert smirked at Ruffa, the knowing, smug grin only a crocodile could pull off convincingly. This was a game to them—a strategy. And the cats? Just the pieces they moved around the board. Their trump card had been the mommies, turned into enchanted buffers to keep the kittens in line. And it worked—brilliantly.

The rest of the day passed uneventfully. The Eight Cool Cats and their four dog bandmates rehearsed several new songs they might use in the Superband Competition—if they made it that far. Despite the tension, the music kept them anchored.

It wasn't until just before lunch the following day that something changed. A phone rang somewhere in the hallway. Ruffa, who had been dozing near the door, suddenly sprang to life and bolted toward the receiver with astonishing speed.

No one was visible in the corridor, but a few curious heads peeked out. The cats and dogs watched Ruffa's ears perk up and his tail wag like a metronome on overdrive.

"Yes, sir. We'll all be there, as you say," he said briskly. "Every single dog will be present and ready. All twelve of us, sir. You can count on us."

There was a pause. The faint squawk of a surprised voice on the other end could be heard.

"Twelve?" it crackled.

Ruffa's response came smoothly. "Eight play, and four are on backup. That's how we roll, sir. Full of energy. Full of talent. Sir, we intend to win."

Another pause. Ruffa's tail gave a hopeful twitch.

"Very good," the distant voice replied. "We'll make room for them. They may need to share accommodations, but that can be arranged. We'll stay within budget."

Ruffa nodded eagerly, though no one could see. "That's perfect. We'll be there on Sunday afternoon. Just before the big day. Thank you. We can't wait to make music history."

As soon as the line went dead, Ruffa turned and sprinted down the hall like an excited puppy. He burst into the rehearsal room with a wide grin nearly splitting his face.

"Well then," he announced, breathless with triumph, "we did it! We're in the finals! We're going to Birdheights!"

A stunned silence followed. The band stared at him, mouths open. Had they heard right? Was he telling the truth?

Surely, he wasn't lying about this. It felt too big. Too real.

The weight hit them all at once: they were going to the big city, and they were finalists in the Superband Competition. It was happening.

Ruffa, seeing their shocked expressions, softened his tone. "As a reward, you get the afternoon off. Enjoy yourselves—but don't leave the compound. We've got serious work ahead starting tomorrow."

The news was still sinking in. The Eight Cool Cats and the Dogwood Droopsters had made it through. One more step, and they'd be standing in the biggest spotlight Animalia had ever built.

But even as joy spread, a few flickers of unease remained. Nobody knew who was moving the pieces in this game or how high the stakes might go.

A short while later, Kreamy was enjoying a brisk stroll with Purrsteph when something caught their eyes— movement in the trees at the compound's northernmost edge.

They rarely ventured so far. Everyone knew that part of the grounds was strictly off-limits. But curiosity tugged at their paws, and before long, they found themselves wandering toward the trees, unaware that someone was already watching them.

That someone was a wiry dog named Snoop—true to his name, a nosy part-time photographer from Dogwood. Most of his photos were blurry disasters that never made it into the Dogwood Daily Pawper, but Snoop was persistent. And today, he was hunting a story.

He had heard whispers that Ruffa was secretly training a band for the Superband Competition inside his old compound—rumours strange enough to warrant a snoop. So, Snoop had spent the last two days lurking just beyond the boundary fence, crouched in tall grass and dodging thorny branches, waiting for something worth snapping.

The rumour about giant grogs living on the property had kept most curious animals away. Ruffa himself had probably spread it, knowing it would deter nosy neighbours. But Snoop didn't buy into fairy tales. Grogs were just bedtime nonsense. What he did believe in was getting a scoop.

So, when two cats suddenly appeared from the brush, Snoop's eyes widened.

"Cats?" he whispered, startled. "What are cats doing in there?"

He fumbled for his clunky old camera and zoomed in, confirming what he'd seen. He started snapping quickly, heart thumping. The camera made its usual wheezing click-chunk noises, but the two felines—Kreamy and Purrsteph—were deep in conversation and didn't notice.

"This is huge," he whispered, tail twitching with excitement. "A Snoop-scoop! Might even get front page..."

Meanwhile, Kreamy and Purrsteph wandered through the clearing.

"You hear that?" Kreamy said suddenly, freezing mid-step. A twig had snapped somewhere behind the trees.

Purrsteph squinted into the trees. "Maybe it's one of them grogs."

"Oh, don't start that again!" Kreamy hissed, swatting the air in annoyance.

Purrsteph giggled. "You're too easy to spook."

Now hidden behind a bush, Snoop crouched lower and accidentally dropped his camera lens into a muddy patch. He didn't notice. All his focus was on the cats, who were far too close for comfort.

"Where are we going exactly?" asked Purrsteph, watching the forest grow denser ahead.

"Don't you ever wonder what's beyond that tree line?" said Kreamy. "We never go this far. Don't you want to know why?"

"I do wonder. But I also don't want to get into trouble. We could run into anyone out here—a guard dog, or worse, Herbert. It's not safe."

"I know, I know," Kreamy muttered, ears twitching. "But it still feels like there's something they don't want us to see."

She turned back toward the compound. "Come on, scaredy cat," she teased. "I'll escort you back safe and sound."

Purrsteph shot one last glance toward the trees before following. "You know what gets to me?" she said quietly. "We keep relying on our mommies, but right now . . . they're the ones who need us. They're not themselves, Kreamy. Ruffa's using them—Herbert's done something. He's got them under some spell."

Kreamy frowned. "Even if that's true, what can we do?"

Purrsteph didn't hesitate. "We find out how it works. Maybe we can break it."

Kreamy blinked. "And then what? We march home and pretend none of this ever happened?"

"I don't know," Purrsteph said, her voice strained. "All I know is that I miss my real mommy. She might've been bossy and a bit loopy, but this version of her. This . . . smiling, pie-baking stranger? I want her back."

Kreamy nodded slowly. "Alright. Then let's start by looking around. I'd rather poke around Herbert's house than tiptoe around grog-infested woods."

They altered course, cutting through a line of shrubs toward Herbert's wooden cottage. As they neared it, a low sound caught their ears—chanting.

They crept along the side of the building, hugging the wall. The chanting grew louder, though still muffled.

"It's the mommies," Kreamy whispered.

"But what are they saying?" Purrsteph whispered back. "Is it . . . mommies-talk?"

They reached a half-open window and crouched below it, ears pricked, hearts racing.

Inside, the hypnotised voices of their mommies murmured strange rhythmic phrases in unison.

Kreamy and Purrsteph exchanged a look.

Something very odd was happening. And it was only beginning to unravel.

"It's coming from in there," Kreamy whispered to Purrsteph.

They crouched beneath the window's edge, the chanting growing clearer now with every passing breeze. Purrsteph cautiously edged forward and peered up, but her view was obstructed by a white net curtain that fluttered in the wind like a ghostly veil.

"What can you see?" Kreamy whispered, flapping with nervous excitement.

"Shhh. Keep your voice down or they'll hear us."

"I want to see too," Kreamy said, trying to sneak around Purrsteph, who gently yanked her back down.

"Not yet. I'm not quite in the right position. I'll slide the curtain just enough for a better look. We can't hang around hoping for another gust."

"Let me do it!" Kreamy insisted. "I can do it better. I'm quieter."

"No, you'll get us spotted. You're bound to squeal when you see your mommy. You're too . . . excitable," Purrsteph was baiting her.

"I'm not immature!" Kreamy hissed. "You're just bossy."

"Shhh. Do you want to give us away?" Purrsteph's nerves were fraying.

Kreamy, realising the stakes, clamped her mouth shut. As much as she longed to peek, she didn't want to ruin their chance or get caught.

Another gust of wind came, pushing the net curtain inward, and Purrsteph seized the opportunity. She rose slowly, drew the curtain aside with a careful paw, and took a sharp breath.

Inside, the room resembled a strange classroom. Their mommies were seated behind tiny desks, zombie-like, staring ahead with empty smiles. An enormous stopwatch hung on a blackboard—not drawn but real and embedded. Its hands spun wildly while the board itself shifted side to side like some hypnotic pendulum.

Scrawled in thick chalk were the phrases:

We are mommies.

We love our kittens.

And the chanting—low, eerie—came in rhythm with the motion of the stopwatch.

"We are mommies. We are mommies. We are mommies . . ."

Herbert stood to the side like a schoolmaster.

"Now, now, mommies," he purred. "Remember your inspiration. Who do you obey?"

The mommies responded in eerie unison: "You are the one we obey, Herbert. You are our spirit guide. We follow you anywhere and everywhere—we obey."

Purrsteph ducked down and signalled for Kreamy to retreat. They crawled away in silence, not daring to speak until the safety of a distant tree line embraced them.

Once hidden, Kreamy finally whispered, "I think I know how to stop them."

"How?"

"It's the stopwatch," Kreamy said. "It's what's keeping them in the trance. The writing on the board helps too, probably, but I think the stopwatch is the key. Without it, the spell might wear off."

Purrsteph thought carefully. "You might be right. When we remove it, the rhythm will break. The cycle will stop."

"But how do we do that without them noticing?"

"Come on," said Purrsteph. "Let's walk back. I'll explain."

As they returned toward the compound, Purrsteph whispered her plan. "We can't do it yet. If we break the spell now, it'll be too obvious. Herbert will know instantly. He'll search for the stopwatch. And if the spell isn't completely broken, our mommies might still side with him—they'll think he's their guide."

"And we could get caught," Kreamy muttered, ears twitching.

"Exactly. We need to wait—strike when it matters most. Probably after the competition. That'll give us time to prepare, to figure out how to hide the stopwatch . . . and where to run if it goes wrong."

Kreamy scowled but nodded reluctantly. She didn't like waiting. Every moment they delayed, their mommies were being fed that twisted mantra. But she knew Purrsteph was right. Timing was everything.

Still, a small voice in her wondered if Purrsteph's patience came from somewhere else. Was she less worried because, deep down, she liked being in charge and free from her mommy's constant fussing?

The next few days passed uneventfully. The Eight Cool Cats and their dog counterparts rehearsed diligently. But now, there was a quiet, urgent hope behind every chord they played and lyric they sang.

A hope that when the curtain finally rose in Birdheights, it wouldn't just be for finding purpose—it would be for freedom.

***

Meanwhile, Snoop returned to his tiny pad and darkroom, buzzing with excitement as he developed the negatives from his photos in Ruffa's forest. He squinted at the damp prints, each clipped to a wire, swaying slightly above a humming radiator. Most of the images were disappointingly blurry, but one stood out.

Clear as day: two cats. Cats. And they were inside Ruffa's compound.

"This is it," Snoop muttered. "A Snoop-scoop!"

Clutching the photo like a golden ticket, Snoop raced off to visit Brawl, the bulldog editor of the *Dogwood Times*. But Brawl wasn't known for his warmth or interest in flaky leads.

"There's no story here, you foolish mutt! Get out!" Brawl bellowed, barely glancing at the print before bursting into a barking laugh.

Snoop, tail dragging, turned to leave, humiliated.

But Brawl relented with a grunt. "Wait. I'll tell you what you can do. Get yourself down to the Superband Competition. Take some decent snaps of our Dogwood Droopsters. If they're any good, I might run one or two. Then, maybe—maybe—I'll hear more about your mysterious forest felines."

Snoop nodded slowly and slunk off. The bark had been worse than the bite . . . but only just.

Back home, he stared at the photo again. Maybe the cats were just strays. Or maybe Ruffa was up to something shady—but so what? The competition was only two days away, and he had nothing to show for his sneaking except soggy paws and a sore back. It wasn't like Ruffa's place was heavily guarded—it was falling apart. You could stumble into it by accident.

And so, with his confidence low and his prospects lower, Snoop decided not to return. "Forget it," he told himself. "It's just cats. Probably cleaning food and milk. No one cares."

He tossed the print onto a pile of rejects and sighed. Even the rain wouldn't let up.

A few days later, drenched to the bone, Snoop finally managed to snap a few more shots. Brawl rejected them all.

And now? Now he was being sent to Birdheights— with no pay guaranteed—to chase a bunch of noisy pups hoping to become stars.

He'd sleep in his old jalopy, couldn't afford a room, not with prices sky-high during the festival. He didn't expect to sell anything. Not unless the Dogwood Droopsters pulled off a miracle.

"Come on, Snoop," he muttered. "You've hit rock bottom. Might as well keep digging."

But if Snoop had returned to the forest . . . if he'd just pressed a little further . . .

He would've uncovered a big story that landed him on the front page.

A once-in-a-lifetime scoop.

The day before the Superband Competition, the band woke early and gathered all their gear at the compound entrance. A familiar bus pulled in—but to everyone's surprise, it wasn't Herbert at the wheel.

It was Ruffa.

Herbert wasn't feeling well and had asked Ruffa to take over. The band shrugged it off, loaded the bus, and clambered aboard to settle into their usual spots.

But before buckling up, they heard violent retching from the rear toilet.

"What's going on with that croc?" Doubler grimaced. "Are we travelling four hours with a sick Herbert in the facilities?"

The cats shared a collective frown.

A few moments later, Herbert emerged, green around the gills, wiping his snout with a grubby handkerchief before sneezing into it with such force it made the walls shake. Wordlessly, he climbed the stairs to the upper deck, his feet heavy on the steps. The cats stared after him until he vanished.

The road ahead would be over four hours before reaching the hills. And from there, still another hour to Birdheights.

Ruffa may have taken the wheel with a steadier paw this time . . .

But this journey?

This journey was not going to go smoothly.

Not at all.

CHAPTER 18

Bumpy Paths

After Herbert had slopped miserably back upstairs, still green from his ordeal in the toilet, a sudden bang jolted everyone on board.

The bus lurched violently, then shuddered to a halt.

A collective scream rang out as it became clear what had happened: the bus had swerved off the road and come to a stop with its front wheels pressed against the edge of the bridge, mere inches from the crash barrier. Beyond that? A hundred-foot drop into a ravine filled with jagged rocks and roaring water.

There was silence. Shock hung in the air like mist.

Ruffa slowly peeled his paw off the steering wheel. For a few seconds, he just sat there, eyes wide, breath held. Then he opened the door and stepped down with trembling legs. The first thing he saw was the sheer drop just ahead of him.

One slip and he'd be gone—smashed against the rocks like a dropped plate.

He gasped, the cold air slicing into his lungs. For a moment, he froze. The rain had begun to spit. Then, the sound of scrambling paws behind him snapped him out of it. Cats and dogs had rushed to the front to see what was happening.

Ruffa turned, his voice small and tight. "I . . . I ought to back us up. We're far too close to the edge."

He climbed back in and tried the ignition.

Nothing. Not even a wheeze.

"The battery's dead," he muttered. "Or maybe worse."

Herbert had crept downstairs and joined him. "Tank empty or something?"

"No. Worse. We're stalled on the edge of a ravine, Herb," Ruffa said through gritted teeth. "We nearly went over. The crash barrier saved us. Barely."

Herbert turned paler than a croc should ever be. "Oh, dear. Oh, dear. Oh, dear . . ."

"I need to check the engine," Ruffa said. "Maybe it's a disconnected cable. Or a loose fuse. Whatever it is, we need to fix it fast. Don't let anyone off this bus. If they step off wrong . . ."

"I get it," Herbert said, nodding nervously. "I'll keep them back."

Sylvest, pressed against the window, had seen enough to realise the actual danger. The view down into the ravine made his stomach twist. He didn't say a word, but the colour drained from his face.

Outside, the rain had turned heavy—buckets of it pounding down, making the narrow ledge slick with runoff. Ruffa stepped out into it, squinting through the downpour.

"Of course," he muttered. "Why not make it harder?"

He started his perilous sideways shuffle along the bus's flank, keeping as close to the metal as possible. The barrier beside him seemed to shrink with every step, and the ravine yawned wider. The rain made the ledge feel like ice beneath his paws. One wrong move—one slight misjudgment—and he'd be nothing but a memory.

Inside, everyone was dead quiet. The bus was perfectly still. A single squeak or shift might send it tilting over.

Ruffa scraped his claws along the window for balance. Each grip felt like it could give way at any moment. His legs trembled—not just from fear, but from effort—one foot, then the other. The drop beside him gaped, hungry.

He reached the back window and glanced in—two feline faces staring right back at him. Sylvest and Fangl.

Ruffa jolted at the sight, startled just enough to lose his footing.

His left foot slipped.

His body jolted sideways.

The world spun for half a second.

He caught the window's edge with both paws.

Time stopped.

Rain thundered down.

Then—inch by inch—he steadied himself. He clenched his jaw, dug his claws in harder, and breathed deeply.

Sylvest was frozen, eyes wide. Fangl looked like he was about to punch through the glass to help.

Ruffa didn't speak at first. He just nodded once, then resumed his crawl, each step a fight against fear and gravity. Every step was a gamble.

Whatever was wrong with the engine, it had to be fixed.

Because if he didn't, there'd be no competition. No glory. No winning. Nothing.

"What are you playing at? Get back to safety!" Herbert shouted. His voice was muffled but urgent through the rain-lashed glass.

Fangl and Sylvest pressed their faces against the window, unable to process the sight of Ruffa, who shuffled along the crumbling ledge. With each step he took, he appeared more reckless than the last.

"This is madness," Fangl muttered. "What is he trying to prove?"

Rain splattered on the windows relentlessly. Ruffa was shouting something, but the storm drowned out his voice.

"What did he say?" asked Fangl.

"Couldn't make it out. Something about the engine maybe? Whatever it was—this isn't safe," Sylvest replied grimly.

Sylvest raised his paw and mimed falling, then sternly shook his head through the window—a warning, a plea.

Ruffa glanced at him and gave a frustrated nod, his eye briefly filled with fear, then stubbornness.

He pressed on.

Suddenly, a blast of noise shattered the rain's rhythm.

A car horn.

The sound cut through the air like a knife.

Ruffa flinched—his paws slipped. He lurched toward the edge, claws scrambling for purchase.

"Ruffa!" Sylvest shouted.

In a flash, Sylvest shoved the window wider and reached out. His paw shot forward and grabbed Ruffa's wrist just in time.

Ruffa dangled for a terrifying moment, his feet skidding against the edge of the ledge. But Sylvest held firm. Ruffa gasped, blinked, and hauled himself upright with a snarl of frustration.

Once Ruffa found his footing, Sylvest let go.

Herbert stood behind the wheel at the front of the bus, looking pleased with himself. "So . . . it's not the battery," he said, mostly to himself. "That means it's mechanical."

Ruffa's ears twitched. *Herbert. You idiot.*

Still shaking, Ruffa continued along the side of the bus until he finally reached the back. He leapt off the ledge, his feet splashing into a shallow puddle. His relief lasted all of two seconds.

Two blinding headlights flared to life.

Ruffa threw a paw up, shielding his eyes. The sound of a large engine rumbled closer.

A wide pickup truck skidded to a halt, and a heavyset bull stepped out with surprising grace. He was broad-shouldered and wore a rain-slicker too small for his chest, which bulged beneath it.

"Hey there, good buddy," the bull called out as he trotted through the rain. "Everything alright? I wouldn't park that way. Looks like a recipe for disaster."

Ruffa was soaked, scowling, and not in the mood.

"I didn't park this way!" he snapped. "The bus lost control. We skidded. Now the engine's dead. We've got a competition to reach and no way to get there."

The bull's large ears twitched, but he kept his tone calm. "Sounds rough—name's Obbo. Heard a horn and figured I'd check in. I thought you were sightseeing for a second, but the weather's way too nasty for that."

Ruffa forced a thin smile. "Appreciate it. Thanks. Do you—by any chance—know anything about engines?"

Obbo shook his head. "Sadly, no. I'm more of a musician than a mechanic. Violinist. I'm on my way to Birdheights too, for the Superband Competition. I had a few last-minute errands, so I told my band to go ahead."

Ruffa's ears perked up slightly, but he kept his suspicion hidden. *Another competitor. Great.*

"Oh," he said flatly. "Well. Don't let us stop you."

"Wasn't planning to," Obbo replied with a smile. "You look like you've got it under control. Good luck out there."

And with that, Obbo turned and walked casually back to his truck.

Ruffa watched him go, teeth clenched. Useless. All that muscle and not a drop of help. But even more than that, Ruffa hated that this bull—this violinist—had caught him mid-crisis. It made him feel small.

Still, Obbo hadn't lingered to gloat. That was something.

The rain picked up again as Ruffa turned his attention to the bus's back panel.

He was cold. Soaked. Exhausted.

But he had to fix this.

Because the competition was tomorrow.

And they weren't going to win it by tumbling into a ravine.

As the three stood under the sheeting rain, exchanging strained pleasantries, Ruffa's gaze wandered behind them—and froze.

The back window of the bus had been slid open.

To his surprise and slight annoyance, KT and Moss had climbed out and landed safely on the muddy roadside. Their hind paws were caked in grime, but they were grinning—utterly unaware that Ruffa had nearly died climbing along the bridge ledge like a hero in a disaster movie.

Obbo blinked, still unfazed by the downpour soaking his shaggy hide. His calm eyes studied the newcomers.

"Hi, friend," said Moss, extending a paw. "I'm Moss. This cat here is KT. We're kind of . . . badly stuck. Our ride's gone kaput."

Obbo nodded with a warm grunt. "So I gathered. Your other buddy over there"—he gestured toward Ruffa with a tilt of his thick neck—"he's got a lot of bark."

KT smiled. "You're a musician too, right? You look the part. I bet you sing bass or something rich like that."

"Nah, no singing for me," chuckled Obbo. "I'm with the Blasting Bald Bulls. They call us the Big Bs. I'm the violinist."

Moss raised his eyebrows. "A violinist? That's unusual. Classy though."

"Thanks," said Obbo with a proud nod. "Rest of the band's already at Birdheights. I'm running late, so if you're all okay, I'd best—"

"You should go," Ruffa cut in, his voice edged with impatience. "You're no help here. We'll figure this out without you."

Obbo narrowed his eyes slightly. "Well now . . . no need to be so full of yourself, pal. I was trying to help."

An awkward silence followed. Moss glanced at KT, shifting uncomfortably in the wet gravel. The rain was thickening, and with the skies darkening fast, they knew they didn't have long before nightfall—and zero visibility.

KT stepped forward. "Hey, Obbo—mind if I ask for a little favour before you go?"

The bull looked at him curiously. "What's that, friend?"

"We need to move the bus back from the ledge. It's too risky to try to get everyone out through the back. You wouldn't happen to have any rope in your pickup, would you? Maybe help us pull it back?"

Obbo turned slowly to examine the vehicle. It was tilted ever so slightly forward, one of the rear tyres barely a whisker from the broken edge of the bridge. Beyond that there was only air and a hundred-foot drop into the rocky ravine below.

He took a breath, glanced again at Ruffa, then looked back at KT and Moss. These two were musicians. Real ones. And they didn't deserve to die because of some overconfident mutt playing at manager.

He gave a slow nod.

"Yeah, I've got rope," he said. "And you"—he looked at KT with a faint smile—"you play guitar, don't you? I can always tell a guitarist."

KT beamed. "You got it. Moss is on drums."

Obbo slung an arm around Moss's shoulder. "Always had a soft spot for guitarists and drummers. Alright, let's save your band."

They followed him to the back of his pickup, where he yanked open the rear. Obbo pulled out a thick coil of rope and slung it over his broad shoulder like it weighed nothing. Then he handed KT a metal hook and passed Moss a wrench.

"Let's get this show back on the road," he said with a wink.

And with that, the rain poured harder—but for the first time since the bus had stopped, hope came with it.

Ruffa kept a close eye on the operation as KT and Moss worked quickly to fix the rope to the back of the bus and then onto the front hook of Obbo's pickup. The rope strained in the rain as it was drawn taut, glistening like a snake stretched across the road.

KT clambered back into the bus through the open rear window, his paws slipping slightly on the wet frame. With a squelch, he landed inside and darted past Herbert, who blinked in confusion and muttered, "Where's the fire?"

KT ignored him, hopping into the driver's seat and placing his paw on the gearstick. He slipped the gear into neutral.

He paused for a moment, eyeing the dashboard. It was still baffling—why had the horn worked if the engine was truly dead? Battery fault? Or something tampered with? He didn't have time to unravel it now.

Outside, Obbo gunned his engine. The pickup's tyres spun wildly at first, flinging mud in every direction. The rain made the ground slick, but the bull didn't ease off. With a grunt of determination and the deep roar of the engine, the pickup finally gained traction, and the bus lurched backwards.

A groan came from the frame as metal shifted under pressure. The barrier gave a low creak but held. The bus moved just a few feet—enough to shift its rear safely away from the deadly edge of the bridge.

The band members erupted in relieved murmurs. One or two even let out a nervous cheer.

Obbo cut the engine and hopped out, hooves splashing into the soft ground. He made his way over to Moss with a cheerful nod and slapped him a hoof-paw high-five.

"That's all I can do for you, pals," Obbo said, tossing his soaked mane out of his face. "Time for me to disappear before someone else gets stuck in this mess."

"You're a hero." Moss grinned. "Seriously. Thank you, Obbo."

"You hang on to the rope and tools for now," Obbo added. "Return 'em when we meet again in Birdheights."

"Much appreciated, my brother," said Moss, clasping Obbo's hoof sincerely.

With that, Obbo returned to his pickup, gave them one last wave, and trundled off into the misty twilight.

Back on the bus, everyone gradually returned to their seats. The mood had shifted—indeed, there was relief, but anxiety lingered like fog on the windows.

Grumpy and damp, Herbert muttered loudly enough for the others to hear, "Stupid bull. Typical. Thick-skulled, slow-witted—no use to anyone. Took off and left us stranded."

KT's ears twitched. He turned slowly to face Herbert. "You're wrong. He did more for us than you have since we left Dogwood. He left the tools. He'll send help. And at least he didn't nearly kill Ruffa by honking like an idiot while someone was hanging off a ledge."

Moss gave an approving nod. "I second that. Obbo came through. But unless a miracle happens, we're stuck here overnight."

"No!" Ruffa exploded. He stood up, stamping his paw. "I am not letting this band miss the Superband Competition. We are not sitting here until tomorrow like soggy marshmallows. Even if we must walk to Birdheights through the night!"

The cats all turned to stare at him.

"Walk?" Kreamy gasped, her fur standing on end. "Through the forest? With grogs out there? Are you out of your doggy mind?!"

"Grog-schmog," muttered Smackie, appearing at the foot of the stairs, casually flicking her tail. "I say we chill out. Help's coming. Pour a nice drink and kick back."

"There are no cold drinks!" snapped Doubler. "The fridge is dead. No power, no fizz, no nothing. This is the end of civilised society as we know it."

Just then, a wild flurry of motion from the back of the bus caught everyone's attention.

"LIGHTS!" Herbert yelled. "LIGHTS COMING THIS WAY!"

Everyone rushed to the rear window, fur pressed against the glass, ears twitching with anticipation.

A deep growl of an engine rose over the rain, and then they saw it.

A hulking shape emerged through the mist. A massive truck, with headlights blazing, was slowly grinding toward them.

A heavy-duty loading platform jutted out the back like a tongue ready to scoop up a stranded beast.

Sylvest exhaled. "Either that's a rescue . . . or it's the grogs coming to finish us off."

No one responded.

All eyes were glued to the truck as it drew closer. It slowed . . . and stopped.

Then the door opened.

And a shadow climbed down.

Out stepped two very bulky, thickly coated bears, each the size of a small delivery truck and carrying the quiet confidence of animals who'd pulled more than their share of heavy machinery from ditches and disasters. Their fur was soaked from the earlier rain, and their expressions were gruff but not unfriendly.

Inside the bus, Herbert's crocodile eyes lit up with glee. He bounded off the steps like a wet green cannonball and scurried toward the bears, tail swinging like a wrecking ball. The cats and dogs on board stayed frozen for a beat. These bears were giant creatures you didn't want to cross paths with in the middle of a dark forest. Were they dangerous?

But then, to everyone's amazement, Herbert began chatting them up with a flurry of animated gestures and tail wags. The bears introduced themselves as Hammo and Quacker, and soon they were roaring with laughter. Their booming guffaws rattled the glass panels of the bus and made a few nervous kittens jump. Whatever they were saying, Herbert seemed to be getting along with them just fine.

Hammo and Quacker wasted no time. They gave the back of the bus a good once-over, inspecting the engine with thick-fingered precision. After a few murmured exchanges and deep frowns, they delivered their verdict: this wasn't a roadside fix. The bus needed a proper repair—garage-level repair.

Using the rope Obbo had left behind, the bears hauled the bus safely onto a metal ramp attached to their beast of a truck. With the front wheels lifted off the ground and secured, the school bus—still wearing its peeling Purrville High School stripes under Ruffa's glittery makeover—was now getting towed to Birdheights.

KT, seated at the wheel, steered cautiously as instructed. Herbert stood beside him, occasionally jabbing his claw out the window and barking corrections. Ruffa sat slumped in the passenger seat, sullen and quiet. The rest of the cats were stretched out in the lower cabin, dozing or murmuring. Upstairs, the dogs observed with their noses pressed to the glass, watching the winding road ahead turn to twilight.

Night fell on them soon enough, and the stars began to shimmer above.

"Well," Herbert said with a deep sigh, "at least we'll get there tonight. The bus can be fixed tomorrow, and we can focus on what we came here for—to make musical history."

Ruffa didn't answer immediately. He stared out into the dark with tired eyes, his voice a low growl when he finally spoke. "This isn't a good idea. Everything's been going wrong. I've got a feeling tomorrow's going to be worse."

Herbert scoffed. "Always the doomsayer. Don't worry, you old scoundrel. Want me to hypnotise you into optimism?"

Ruffa turned sharply. "No! No way. Don't even suggest that. Look—do you not see the problem here?"

Herbert blinked innocently.

Ruffa leant in and urgently whispered, "That bull saw the cats. Now these bears have seen them too. What happens if someone at the Competition asks questions? What if someone connects the dots and realises we've got cats in our dog band? You think that'll fly?"

Herbert raised his scaly brows, then waved a claw dismissively. "We explain to them that the cats work as our support. They're roadies. Maybe even cheerleaders. They can excitedly jump up and down if we win!"

"Cheerleaders? Have you gone insane?" Ruffa groaned.

"Well, they're not exactly glamorous, I give you that," Herbert admitted. "Okay, forget that. But we'll say they're here as part of our crew. They lug about our gear. They fetch snacks. They brush our fur before gigs. The normal stuff."

"They look way too clever to be your flunkies," Ruffa muttered.

Herbert patted him gently on the shoulder, still smiling. "Look, I know things seem wild now. But it's going to work out. Trust me. It's not our fault the bus is ancient. We're doing the best we can."

Then, letting out a crocodilian yawn so wide it showed every tooth in his snout, Herbert slumped across the front-row seats and closed his eyes.

Within moments, he was snoring peacefully, one leg twitching, as if dreaming of swaying pompoms and shiny trophies.

Ruffa watched him for a long, silent beat.

He didn't trust the road ahead.

And he certainly didn't trust sleep.

***

The sky had turned nearly pitch-black by the time they reached the outskirts of Birdheights. What met their eyes silenced every cat and dog on board.

This was no ordinary town. No simple city.

Before them shimmered the grandest, most awe-inspiring metropolis in the entire land—a place spoken of in hushed whispers and wide-eyed stories. This was Birdheights.

It wasn't just a city of birds, though the skies were thick with them. It was the living, breathing heart of the Animalian world: a place where species of every shape, feather, fur, and scale had gathered from across the continent. From the highest flyers to the lowest burrowers, from jungle dwellers to arctic roamers, Birdheights was home to them.

Here, opportunity could be found even for those who had little hope of striking it lucky. Fresh ideas were hatched. Legends began in back alleys. It was a city that exuded energy, where miracles and follies lived side by side. It was where fortunes were made, dreams realised, and destinies rewritten—every hour, every day.

It was a city of extremes: the richest mansions perched beside the scruffiest nests. The loudest voices were often from the smallest creatures. The boldest ambitions often belonged to the most foolish. But here, at last, anything was possible.

Birdheights wasn't merely a destination. It was the very idea of becoming more than what you were.

And now, with tired paws and muddied feet, the Eight Cool Cats, Ruffa, Herbert, and the rest of the Dogwood Droopsters had arrived at its gates.

The city of dreams was waiting.

And the real adventure was only beginning.

CHAPTER 19

Birdheights

Sniffer was the first to notice the glimmering lights in the distance.

He sat silently near the back of the bus, gently strumming his electric bass guitar. It wasn't plugged in, so the sound was barely audible—just the faint hum of strings reverberating through wood and bone. Still, he could feel it. Music had always stirred something inside him, even when he didn't feel like talking, especially when he needed something to believe in.

He hadn't said much since the bus had broken down earlier that day. Not that anyone expected him to. Sniffer wasn't one to share feelings or moan about setbacks. He preferred to live inside his thoughts, letting his music speak.

It wasn't that he didn't enjoy being part of the band—he did, mostly. But sometimes, late at night or on long, silent rides like this, he wondered what had possessed him. All this noise, this spectacle, this shouting into the wind. Was it the creation of music? Or was it chaos with a sinister rhythm?

The bass, he could handle. A low thrum. A heartbeat. Something solid beneath the madness. But the drums were another story—especially Moss on a roll, or worse, Smackie on her trumpet. And when Rommy turned the volume up to eleven on his lead guitar? Well . . . let's say Sniffer had contemplated stuffing cotton in his ears more than once.

Sometimes it felt like standing too close to a volcano just before it blew—thunder, heat, and molten racket. Not that Sniffer had ever experienced a volcano firsthand, but he had read about them. The legendary Mount Molt, long dormant, still smouldered at the far edge of Animalia. They said it had erupted so violently aeons ago that it had wiped out entire species. Some even whispered that strange, prehistoric creatures still lurked inside its hidden chambers, though Sniffer doubted that. More likely, it was just a good story to keep reckless creatures from climbing to the top.

He was half-lost in thought, his claws gently plucking strings, when something flickered in the corner of his vision. He sat upright. Ahead—just beyond the subsequent rise—was a skyline awash with golden light, a horizon pulsing with energy.

Birdheights.

The bus crested the hill, and suddenly, the sprawling city revealed itself like a stage curtain drawn back for the grandest of shows. It was luminous, breathtaking. Towers rose in glittering rows, wrapped in neon vines and blinking signs, some climbing over ninety floors high.

Lights stretched as far as the eye could see. It was more than a city—it was a living constellation that had fallen to earth.

Sniffer blinked. He hadn't known what to expect, but it wasn't this.

Others were rising down the bus aisle to get a better look. The cats and dogs pressed their faces to the windows one by one, eyes wide, ears twitching.

"This . . ." said Ruffa, breath catching. "This is the city of dreams."

"We're in the right place, then." Herbert grinned, his reptilian eyes gleaming as he leant over KT's shoulder at the front, watching the road ahead.

Hammo, the truck-driving bear, glanced in the rearview mirror and saw the excitement ripple through the cabin behind him. He chuckled to himself. It was a low-grizzly rumble.

"First-timers for sure," he muttered.

Quacker, his co-driver, nodded knowingly. "They think they've discovered paradise."

Hammo huffed. "They've found something different, alright. But Birdheights isn't just lights and dreams. It's got sharp teeth. This city can devour you alive."

The truck stopped beside a darkened building in the city's heart. Towering around them were steel giants—offices, apartments, entertainment halls—flashing with colours pulsing like veins at night. But the garage before them was silent, pitch-black, and seemingly closed for the day.

A newer, sleeker bus waited by the kerb outside, humming softly as though barely suppressing a yawn. Its glossy panels glinted under the city lights, and cool air sighed from its vents in regular rhythm. It looked far more impressive than the beaten-up school bus they'd arrived in—clean, spacious, and suspiciously well-maintained.

Hammo and Quacker climbed down from their truck and softly knocked on the rusted garage door. Moments later, a small side hatch creaked open, and two more bears emerged, nodding silently as they helped the travellers transfer their gear to the new bus.

"Your transport awaits," Hammo said, gesturing to the new vehicle. "It'll take you to your accommodation."

The band slowly filed off the broken-down bus, dragging their feet and stifling yawns. The long journey had drained them, even if Birdheights' dazzling skyline had given them a momentary lift.

"Good luck, musicians!" Quacker called out, tipping an invisible hat. Then he and Hammo climbed back into the truck and vanished into the night, towing the school bus behind them toward the now-illuminated garage.

On board the sleek replacement bus stood a thin, hunched crow with oversized spectacles and an impossibly crumpled beak. His feathers were patchy and greying, and he held a suspiciously soggy hanky in one claw.

"Welcome, welcome, welcome," the crow croaked in a voice as strained as his posture. "I'm Ook. A pleasure Welcome. Again."

He sniffled loudly and sneezed into the hanky with such force that it made the overhead lights flicker.

"Apologies," Ook muttered. "Just a cold. Harmless. Comes and goes. Don't mind me."

As the bus pulled away from the garage, it nearly collided with a half-naked orangutan pushing a squeaky, overloaded shopping trolley. The orangutan roared, beat his chest theatrically, and snarled at the bus, flashing a row of broken, jagged teeth. Ook responded by honking twice, loud and flat.

"Another filthy vagrant," he muttered under his breath, sniffing again. "They're everywhere. Wanderers. Came here, each with their dreams, and found nothing but hunger. Now they haunt the streets. Shadows of the Animalians, they once were. No homes. No hope. Just bitterness, regret, and muttered curses."

Fangl and Sylvest exchanged uneasy glances.

This wasn't what they had expected.

Birdheights was supposed to be a place of wonder and success, where bright-eyed hopefuls rose to fame, fortune, or something close to it. But here was a bitter truth growling from a trash heap.

Kreamy stared out the window at the orangutan, her ears drooping.

"Maybe we could help him," she whispered to Purrsteph. "Give him bread, or something to eat . . ."

"Don't be ridiculous," Purrsteph snapped. "He'll knock you flat, rob you blind, and be gone before you blink. That kind of Animalian? They're beasts, Kreamy. You don't throw kindness at a growl."

"Oh, stop," Mimi said from nearby. "You're scaring her. He's just a beggar—nothing more. Life's cruel sometimes, that's all. Some fall harder than others. Doesn't mean they're monsters."

"I agree," Kreamy murmured, tears welling in her eyes. "It's not right. No one should be left to fall apart on the streets. Not after they've lived a full life. No one deserves that."

"We don't know what he did," Purrsteph replied, folding her arms. "Maybe he earned this fate that life has bestowed on him. We can't always assume the worst things happen only to the best creatures."

"But that's exactly the point," Kreamy said. "We don't know. So maybe the least we can do is to treat him like he's still someone."

The bus rolled on.

Minutes later, they pulled up in front of the Highlands Hotel—a towering edifice of metal and glass that seemed to lean into the clouds. With fifty stories or more, its height was dizzying. Giant neon letters buzzed above the doorway, and a rotating glass entrance shimmered like a portal to another world.

A tall, rail-thin ape in a red waistcoat approached with a polished trolley. He looked half asleep but extended a courteous paw as he prepared to collect their luggage.

Then came the flamingo.

She glided across the pavement in a billowy electric-blue dress, smiling at each of them as they exited the bus. Her neck curved elegantly, and she balanced on one leg with the poise of a streetlight.

Ruffa narrowed his eyes. Something about her was off—not suspicious exactly, but oddly theatrical. He watched her closely as she offered cheerful greetings, her voice light but unshakably precise.

No one said anything for a moment. The city lights glimmered around them. The night had swallowed the sun, and Birdheights loomed tall and strange.

The band had arrived.

But whether they had stepped into a dream or something much more complicated remained to be seen.

"Welcome, cats and dog friends, to Birdheights," said the flamingo in a voice as high-pitched as her neck was long. "My name is Lizzalee."

She beamed brightly—until her gaze swept across the group and her expression faltered. It was clear there were far more cats than dogs. Her thin pink eyebrow lifted slightly. She said nothing . . . but noted it.

Then, finally, the remaining dogs emerged, and Lizzalee's shoulders relaxed.

With Herbert behind him, Ruffa strolled down the steps and gave her a winning grin.

"Ignore the cats," Ruffa said casually. "They're merely our assistants. Very loyal. Very eager. They care for our every need."

Lizzalee tilted her head, unconvinced. "I have eight dogs called the Dogwood Droopsters in my records, and I've booked four rooms for the band, plus one for the manager. Where shall I direct your assistants? And . . . where are the other four dogs?"

Ruffa froze. Herbert jumped in, grinning. "They'll be along shortly. Got held up. You know how it is. As for our assistants, well, they can bunk together. Cats like that sort of thing—sleeping in packs. They love it."

"That won't be possible," Lizzalee said crisply. "This hotel has a maximum occupancy of two per room. And only two beds per room. We're a highly reputable establishment. I can try to arrange extra rooms for your assistants, but any additions will come at a charge. That goes beyond the current booking."

Ruffa frowned. "What do you mean, charge us extra? I was assured that accommodation was complimentary for the band and anyone else we deemed essential."

"That's incorrect, sir," said Lizzalee coolly. "Only four rooms were reserved for the band. Anything beyond that—including these 'assistants'—must be paid for out of pocket. And as for the crocodile . . ." She eyed Herbert uneasily. "Many hotels in Birdheights have hygiene restrictions on crocodilians. But . . . as you're with the Superband Competition, I may be able to make an exception."

"I beg your pardon," Ruffa snapped. "Herbert and I each require our rooms. One for the manager, one for the musical director. It's non-negotiable."

Lizzalee glanced at her clipboard. "You may share one of the four reserved rooms, or I can move you into an upgraded suite together. I can stretch the budget that far. But your assistants' rooms will have to be handled separately."

Herbert leant in close to Ruffa. "Don't make a fuss," he whispered. "We're both tired. I can tell you're ready to snap. Let's sort it. We can pay from the slush fund."

Ruffa squinted. "What slush fund?"

"I put a little aside," Herbert replied under his breath. "In case of emergencies. This counts. Don't worry—we can cover the extra rooms."

"You might've mentioned that earlier. I handle the accounts, remember?"

"Yes, yes," said Herbert breezily. "You're absolutely right. I just forgot in the chaos. We've had quite a journey."

Herbert turned to Lizzalee. "We'll take four extra rooms for the cats. Two per room. I'll pay in credits."

Lizzalee gave a curt nod. "Very well. But what about the missing four dogs?"

Ruffa and Herbert froze.

"They're following behind," Moss said quickly. "Got delayed. We'll sort their rooms when they arrive."

"Yes, yes," Ruffa echoed. "Busy day, logistics nightmare. Bands, eh?" He flashed the most charming smile he could muster.

Lizzalee paused, then nodded. "Very well." She turned and glided off toward the reception desk.

"Phew, too close," muttered Herbert.

"Nice save, Moss," Ruffa added, patting him on the back.

The group waited while Ook, their sneezy escort, helped the hotel porter unload their gear. Ook gave it his best effort, but every third movement was punctuated by a forceful sneeze that nearly sent him tumbling. The porter ape, wide-shouldered and calm, handled it all with ease.

"Lots of stuff," he grunted, wheeling the trolley toward the reception.

A short while later, Lizzalee returned and handed Ruffa and Herbert some room keys.

"All arranged. You'll find your rooms on the twelfth and thirteenth floors."

Within half an hour, everyone was tucked away in their assigned accommodations. Clothes were unpacked, musical instruments stowed, and the bus journey's aches became unpleasant memories.

Before retreating to his room, Herbert made one final announcement.

"Up at eight sharp. Hotel breakfast—don't lose out on a free meal. Then it's straight to the venue for signing in and set-up. Big day tomorrow!"

Despite the uncertainty of check-in, the discomfort of their travel, and the confusion over crocodile hygiene issues, the band felt a buzz of excitement. Tomorrow, their dreams might finally take flight.

And with that thought warming their hearts, one by one, they drifted off to sleep—cats and dogs alike—dreaming of lights, crowds, applause . . . and the thrill of the stage.

CHAPTER 20

All on Stage

The morning light broke over Birdheights with a subtle glow of golden promise. Inside the Highlands Hotel, every cat and dog in the group woke with the same thought echoing in their minds:

This is it. The big day has finally arrived.

They were no longer just hopeful travellers. They were contestants in the prestigious Superband Competition, preparing to play their finest set of songs in front of a massive audience—tens of thousands of Animalians strong. By the end of the day, they'd either walk away victorious . . . or return to Dogwood empty-pawed.

Ruffa stood by the window in his hotel room, gazing out across the sparkling skyline of Birdheights. His tail flicked with anticipation. He thought about everything it had taken to get here—the rules he'd bent, the lines he'd crossed, the risky deals he'd struck. And yet, here they were. Here he was. On the cusp of proving to all Animalians that a mixed band of dogs and cats could outperform any single-species act in the land.

They wouldn't be recognised as both cats and dogs, of course. On paper, they were the Dogwood Droopsters—a dog band, plain and simple. But Ruffa had made his peace with that compromise. Success was what mattered. Recognition would follow. Eventually.

"I'll show them," he whispered to his reflection in the window. "I'll prove what this band is made of. And they'll declare me a genius—the genius. I'll be on top of the land!"

There was nothing quite like the loyal self-confidence of a mutt on a mission. And Ruffa, for all his schemes and shortcuts, had one unwavering belief: he was destined for greatness.

Of course, he wasn't the only one with such a lofty opinion of himself.

"You know what you are, Ruffa?" Herbert had said the night before, just before falling asleep. "You're a genius."

And Herbert, naturally, considered himself one too. After all, as he liked to remind Ruffa, only a genius could spot another genius.

"There are so few of us," Herbert would say, nodding sagely. "We understand the sacrifices. The sleepless nights. The extra mile. The rules we must bend to get the job done. Doubters? Pfft. Let them doubt. That's the burden of genius—we endure their ignorance . . . until we prove we were right all along."

Genius, Herbert believed, always came with a price.

But oh, how sweet the reward would be.

***

The next morning, the Dogwood Droopsters, the Eight Cool Cats, Ruffa, and Herbert assembled in the grand café of the Highlands Hotel. A vast, gleaming buffet stretched the room's length—laden with colourful fruits, finely cut vegetables, aromatic leaves, berries, seeds, and dishes none of them could name, let alone pronounce. Everything was fresh, vibrant, and bursting with flavour. The smells alone could send even the weariest performer into culinary bliss.

For a while, the past days—broken buses, near-death ledges, and stressful disguises—melted away. The cats tucked in with gusto, their faces alight with giddy satisfaction. Laughter broke out as they sampled exotic fruits and made friendly guesses about what they might be. The whole crew relaxed for the first time in what felt like forever. It didn't matter that the fate of their secret band hung in the balance.

To other hotel guests, this odd little group could have been anything—schoolmates on a city trip, theatre lovers, backpacking eccentrics. Nobody paid them the slightest attention. In Birdheights, it was normal to see mixed gatherings in public. Nobody imagined that this collection of cheerful cats and casual dogs was, in fact, a band. Such a thing wouldn't even occur to them. Mixed-species bands were not permitted. It simply wasn't done.

The competition itself was run under the watchful eyes of the Three Wise Birds, a mysterious trio of senior judges who held complete authority. They had overseen the auditions and now stood as the sole arbiters of victory. There was no audience vote, no second chances. The audience could cheer, whoop, and weep—but their opinions were decorative at best. The decision lay entirely with the judges.

Nobody questioned this. Not in Birdheights. Here, authority was rarely challenged. It was expected, even appreciated, that decisions came from above.

After breakfast and after the final belongings were gathered, the group placed their luggage in a secure hotel storage room. The band's bus—shining from a quick morning polish—stood ready outside, with their instruments and outfits already loaded. Lizzalee oversaw the final preparations, tipping the two large apes who handled the heavy lifting with credits.

Inside the official Superband transport, Ruffa's cats and dogs settled into the rear seats, sharing jokes and stories with surprising ease. Herbert and Ruffa sat closer to the front, speaking in hushed tones.

"It's good they're getting along so well," Herbert whispered, glancing back at the others.

"Yes," Ruffa replied slowly, "but let's not allow ourselves to get carried away. A little harmony can prove useful. If they show too much kindness, they'll start thinking for themselves, which can be problematic. One voice can challenge authority. Many voices . . . well, that's a whole lot worse."

Herbert turned to look at him, impressed. For all Ruffa's swagger and flamboyant foolishness, there were brief but brilliant moments when he spoke like a seasoned tactician. Herbert felt a warm surge of pride. He had chosen his partner well.

The group sat in awe as the bus reached the outskirts of the competition arena. The venue was colossal—an architectural marvel shaped like a sprawling shell, its silver spines reaching skyward like a chorus of trumpets. Electronic gates slid open with a low hiss, and the bus rolled forward into the restricted artist entrance.

They pulled up to a sleek landing bay sealed off from the public. A team of formidable apes in crisp red uniforms marched out in perfect formation. The Superband Competition Crew—strong, silent, and intensely efficient—boarded the bus after the band had disembarked and swiftly began unloading their gear.

Moss squinted as the apes moved past him, hoisting amps and cases like feathers. "Huh," he muttered to Rommy. "So, if you're born an ape in Birdheights, you end up with all the lifting jobs."

Rommy didn't even blink. "I don't care who does what," she said under her breath. "I came here to play. And to win."

Moss glanced sideways at her. There was something in her tone—some private urgency he didn't quite understand. For a moment, he wondered if Rommy wasn't just eager for the stage . . . but for the finish line. She just wanted this over. Whatever it was, getting to know this city wasn't for her.

And now, at last, the time had come.

An hour later, in the backstage changing room, the Eight Cool Cats were busy donning their elaborate dog costumes, transforming again into the Dogwood Droopsters. The process, once awkward and time-consuming, was now second nature. Every tail attachment, every snout tuck, every patch of fur had its proper place.

The mood was focused, but tense—this was no ordinary rehearsal. This was the day of their performance.

There was a sudden knock. Herbert crept over and checked the eyehole. It was Ruffa. He opened the door.

"There's been a tiny change of plans," Ruffa announced, his eyes gleaming. "And by tiny, I mean massive. We're going out as twelve."

Herbert blinked. "Twelve? What are you talking about? We've only ever practised as eight—maybe nine at most. We didn't bring twelve instruments. Are you sure this is wise?"

Ruffa waved a paw dismissively. "Don't worry about it. I double-checked the rules, and there's no cap on numbers. I just watched a performance by thirty chirping squirrels. Thirty! And they were dreadful. We can shine as twelve if that bunch can crowd a stage and squawk for five minutes."

Herbert scratched his scaly chin. "Still, it's a major shift. No rehearsal time, no arrangement—"

"They all know the songs. They've practised the harmonies. They've bonded. This is going to work."

Ruffa stepped forward and began issuing instructions like a general.

"Here's the new line-up:

— Doubler and Rommy on main vocals.

— KT won't play drums; instead, he'll do backing vocals alongside Sylvest.

— Moss covers percussion on the full kit.

— Kreamy on flute, Smackie blasting trumpet.

— Purrsteph on cymbals.

— Rommy and Tinki on lead guitars.

— Sniffer and Sylvest on bass guitars.

— Mimi plays violin."

Tinki's ears perked up in alarm. "Wait, I don't get to sing? I thought I was singing lead on 'Stomp the Storm!'"

"You're needed on lead guitar," Ruffa said firmly. "That's final. We need balance."

Purrsteph crossed her arms. "And I'm relegated to just cymbals? No vocals? That's not fair."

"This isn't about fairness," Ruffa barked. "It's about strategy. This is the only way we can make twelve work on stage. Not everyone gets their preference. I'm not looking for feedback—I'm looking for obedience. Herbert agrees with me. Don't you, Herbert?"

Herbert, caught off guard, gave a reluctant nod. "Well . . . I suppose. I mean, yes. This could potentially work. It's all a bit risky, but if you're sure . . ."

"I'm absolutely certain of it," Ruffa declared. "This is our single best shot. No band like ours has ever played on this stage. You want to become legends? Then you must follow my lead."

Purrsteph muttered, "More like a chaotic orchestra than a cohesive band."

Ruffa's ears twitched. "It'll be the best-sounding chaos these judges have experienced on stage."

But Moss wasn't convinced either. He leant toward Smackie. "Twelve on stage? This isn't bold. It's more like reckless. One wrong note, and we'll sound like a marching band crashing into a brick wall."

"I know," Smackie muttered. "It's sheer madness. And we've worked far too hard to rely on a wild gamble."

"I said—no more discussion," Ruffa growled. "This is going to happen the way I say it is."

The room fell into heavy silence.

Herbert cleared his throat. "Let's just do what he says. Maybe it'll surprise us in a good way. We've worked too hard to unravel now."

Reluctantly, everyone nodded and began finishing their preparations. Some tightened strings, others wiped nervous sweat from their fur. No one spoke. The air was thick with tension, anticipation, and fear.

Moments later, a knock came at the dressing room door. A voice called, "Dogwood Droopsters, please report to the stage entrance."

Twelve hearts beat faster in unison.

It was time.

The twelve Dogwood Droopsters marched steadily down the long corridors toward the main stage exit. The cats had their hoodies pulled low, the Dogwood emblem stitched boldly across their backs. No one could see their true identities beneath the disguises. A flurry of roadie had already finished setting up their equipment on stage, including Ruffa's gleaming light show console.

Then, cheers erupted. Wild applause burst from all directions as the audience caught sight of the band stepping into the light.

It was early afternoon. The sun shone from a clear blue sky, casting a golden glow across the stadium. Ten bands had been shortlisted for the Superband Competition, and this crowd had gathered to witness something incredible.

Upon a grand balcony were present the same three judges who had been at the audition: the elegant swallow, the broad-shouldered eagle, and the wise old pigeon with his persistent cough. They were closer to the stage this time, their bright ceremonial robes glinting in the sunlight.

The band didn't know that the pigeon was none other than Muffat Flapwell, Deputy Mayor of Birdheights—and the architect of the competition they were about to compete in. Muffat had held office for over a decade, far longer than most mayors dared. His grand idea was to launch the Superband Competition in the first place.

Beside him sat Buck Cloudwings, towering and regal. As chief of police, Buck had earned the city's respect through firm but fair leadership. Muffat and Buck formed a political powerhouse—Muffat wrote the laws, and Buck made sure they stuck.

Completing the trio was Ilga Finetuning, the swallow. Once a celebrated singer in Birdheights' premier flying cabaret, Ilga had transformed into a nightlife mogul, owning the three most popular venues on the downtown strip.

These three weren't just judges. They were Birdheights royalty. Sharp-eared, sharp-eyed, and not easily impressed.

A recent article in The Birdheights Bugle had stirred up quite a storm. It argued that the competition might inadvertently encourage "cross-mixing" of species in bands, potentially eroding long-standing traditions of musical purity. It warned that such mixing could undermine the cultural heritage built up in villages across the land. The piece had been controversial, and within days, it was retracted. Unsold papers were pulled from newsstands right across the city.

The Council of Wise Birds released a carefully worded statement: while cross-species bands remained banned, the issue was one of "cultural protection," not of committing any offence. Birdheights, they said, had to uphold each species' right to preserve its identity, not risk dissolving this in a hideous melting pot.

Still, tensions lingered. Birdheights was, after all, a city built on difference, thriving precisely because of its diversity. Species lived side by side. Traditions interwove. This paradox—diversity celebrated, yet rigidly compartmentalised—gave the city its unusual pulse.

Meanwhile, another rumour buzzed under the surface: the entire Superband Competition was said to be secretly bankrolled by Boreme Kildare, the wealthiest merchant in the city—a tiger with claws in every pie. Though few spoke ill of him openly, most feared him privately. Deals with Boreme rarely came without strings. Or teeth.

And so, into this simmering atmosphere walked the Dogwood Droopsters. All twelve took a deep breath as they stepped onto the vast stage. Before them stood a sea of faces—a hundred thousand eyes, it seemed, fixed on their every move.

They froze for a beat. Nobody had played a show this size before.

Moss was already perched behind his drum kit, twitching with excitement.

"Pssst," he hissed. "Snap out of it, guys! Plug up—showtime!"

The others sprang into action. Instruments were slung over shoulders, cables connected, and amps checked. Ruffa switched on his glimmering console, scanning his light board with a sharp eye.

Doubler and Rommy took centre stage, gripping their microphones. KT and Sylvest stepped up behind them as backup singers.

Kreamy closed her eyes, drew a long breath, and raised her flute to moist lips. A delicate, lilting melody floated into the air, clear and pure. It lifted on the wind, drawing the crowd into a willing hush. Then came Mimi's violin, weaving a softer harmony around Kreamy's tune like a silk ribbon.

Ruffa couldn't help smiling. Magic. Pure magic.

Then, Sylvest moved.

He bent down, slung a spare bass guitar over his shoulder, and joined the line. Ruffa's jaw tightened. This wasn't part of the plan. No, no, no! That guitar was for emergencies—string breaks, not spontaneous solos!

His hands danced over his light board as he tried to keep his cool, his inner monologue spiralling: *Why's he doing this? It'll throw off the whole arrangement!*

But before Ruffa could signal a correction, the music erupted. Four guitars struck up in unison and were in purrfect sync. Moss hammered on the drums, driving the tempo relentlessly forward. Rommy and Doubler leant into the rhythm, voices rising, joining effortlessly with the beat.

Fangl layered in dreamy keyboard chords, setting a shimmering tone behind the melody. Sniffer and Sylvest strummed their bass guitars in tandem, locking into the groove.

KT and Sylvest leant in as the chorus hit, harmonising on their backup mics. KT gave Sylvest a quick wink.

They sounded like a dream.

A dream on steroids.

And in the crowd, something stirred—whispers, claps, paws, and wings tapping in time. The energy began to shift.

The Dogwood Droopsters were no longer a dozen anonymous figures in costumes.

They were a musical force.

And they had just begun.

The music had come alive—truly alive—and the crowd was sheer electricity. Fans howled, whistled, and danced to the notes soaring from the stage. The sound was truly staggering—polished yet raw, full of power and heart

Even the judges—stoic as they were—leant forward, eyes wide, utterly mesmerised.

Not one of them could believe what they were witnessing. Twelve anonymous dogs from Dogwood? Producing this?

The set moved seamlessly into their second number—an aching, soul-stirring ballad about loss, memory, and rediscovery. Ruffa himself had written it, though few would have guessed such heartfelt emotion had poured from him. The audience quieted, swaying gently, many humming along with the chorus.

Then came their third and final song—an instant anthem. As the beat dropped, the crowd rose to their feet—paws clapping, wings flapping, tails thumping the air. The voices of ten thousand creatures joined in as the chorus rang out, echoing across the great expanse of the arena.

It was a moment beyond music.

On stage, the twelve Dogwood Droopsters gave it everything they had. Every note, every beat, every breath—it all poured out of them like wildfire and magic.

Who would have guessed that twelve dogs (technically four dogs and eight very sweaty, disguised cats) could unleash a performance like this? They weren't just performing—they were setting the place alight.

As the final chord reverberated into silence, the band members bowed in unison, deeply and proudly. The roar of the crowd hit them like a tidal wave. Moss let out a cheer from behind his drums. Even he, gruff and grounded as ever, couldn't resist grinning at the sea of love washing over them.

It felt unavoidable—almost inevitable—that they'd just stolen the show. A few bands remained on the roster, but it was hard to conceive that any act could top this.

Backstage, Ruffa and Herbert watched the scene unfold, their mouths agape and their eyes and ears soaking in the moment.

"Did . . . did our band do that?" Herbert murmured, almost afraid to believe it.

Ruffa puffed out his chest. "Come now, my dear Herb, haven't I been saying it all along? We've just made Animalian history. No one will forget this day. We're going home as champions, mark my words."

The band made their way offstage, walking on air. The Eight Cool Cats broke into a sprint the moment they hit the corridor, desperate to escape the stuffy, sweltering dog costumes. The bright lights and roaring crowd had left them drenched in sweat, and cats hated to sweat.

When they were inside the dressing room, water bottles were guzzled down in a hurry. Costumes were flung onto tabletops without any thought. The cats then collapsed into comfy chairs, gasping, smiling, laughing— giddy with delight.

Herbert burst in behind them, panting, his scaly face streaked with tears of joy.

"You were . . . you were magnificent!" he bellowed, voice cracking with pride. "Brilliant! Beautiful! Superstars!

I swear, we're going to win this competition. Ruffa thinks so too. You did it. You all did it!"

The cats and dogs looked at one another, dazed with joy, too breathless to speak. They'd done the impossible. They'd stormed the stage at Birdheights, won over a crowd of thousands, and played the most incredible set of their lives.

For a moment, none of them wanted to move or do anything.

Then, one by one, they nodded.

Yes. This was it. This very moment would be remembered forever. The day they'd played not just with instruments, but with their hearts. The day they'd become a band in the truest sense of the word.

No matter what happened next, they knew they had already won.

CHAPTER 21

What Happens Next

A few minutes later, a loud and frantic knock rattled the dressing room door.

"Let me in! Let me in!" came the unmistakable rasp. "It's me!"

Inside, Herbert sprang into action. "Password?"

"Oh, for fleas' sake—Grog Bog!"

"Repeat it. Did you say Ghog Bog?"

"No—Grog Bog! Grog Bog! Now open the blasted door!"

Herbert finally unlocked it, peering out with theatrical caution. "Sorry," he mumbled as Ruffa shoved his way in, flustered. "Can't be too careful. The cats are out of costume."

"Thought you'd know me by now," Ruffa huffed, tail twitching in irritation as Herbert relocked the door behind him.

But Ruffa raised a dramatic paw just as the Eight Cool Cats were stretching, towelling off, and pulling off the last remnants of their disguises.

"No! Stop! Don't take anything else off. Get back into costume. Now!"

They all froze, stunned.

"Are you serious?" Purrsteph blurted, halfway through peeling off her hoodie. "I'm drenched. I reek. This fur's not meant to be sealed in dog suits all day."

"I need to breathe before I expire!" cried Kreamy. "I'm two gulps of hot air away from fainting. And for what? For performing another lie?"

Ruffa sucked in a deep breath, trying his utmost not to lose it. "Listen. The judges might call back the top acts—maybe the top two or three—for one final performance. A song of their choice or a reprise. It's not yet confirmed, but it's a possibility. You're leading, but not by much. This last round could be it."

"We've already given everything we've got," Purrsteph muttered. "And nobody knows who we are. It's our triumphant moment, and we're invisible. Feels like we're being robbed of our very identities."

"That's exactly what it is," said Kreamy. "We're not allowed to be proud of who we are."

Rommy stood, her voice low but assertive. "They should appreciate who we are, how we came together to create this, and that this mix of cats and dogs made something so special."

Ruffa's ears were starting to twitch. He could sense the growing unity between them, which alarmed him. His carefully conceived plan, built on a devious structure of silence and secrecy, was slowly disappearing.

"You don't understand what's at stake," he growled. "If you reveal yourselves now, you'll be disqualified. The judges will tear up your score sheets and toss them like confetti. We'll be humiliated. I'll be ruined. Herbert too. And you, when you go back to Purrville, how do you explain this? That you helped deceive an entire city. Do you think they'll call you heroes? They'll call you liars. Sellouts. You'll destroy the Eight Cool Cats legacy. All because you couldn't sweat for five more minutes."

Silence fell. The Cool Cats huddled.

Then KT stepped forward.

"No, brothers and sisters, don't fall for it. I'll tell you what this is about." He jabbed a paw toward Ruffa. "They don't care about music. Or us. Or truth. They care about one thing—the win. They want their names in lights, on the back of our sweat and talent. They didn't do the practice. They didn't haul instruments in the rain. They didn't sleep on the school bus!"

"We did this," said Mimi quietly. "Not them."

"We're not your stooges, Ruffa," KT said. "And you know what? We're done. We're going home."

Ruffa's face turned a dangerous shade of scarlet. His voice cracked with fury. "I spent weeks planning this. I put in everything—time, credits, my reputation. And now you're telling me it means nothing?"

"Hey!" Herbert cut in. "What about my contribution? We may not have played on stage, but we produced this act. We gave you the training space, the equipment, the tour bus—"

"You mean our school bus?" Tinki interrupted dryly, raising an eyebrow.

Herbert faltered. "Well . . . yes, but it was used effectively."

"I slept on a peanut shell," Sniffer added.

"I had to use a trumpet case as a pillow," muttered Smackie.

"You see?" KT said, rounding back on Ruffa and Herbert. "This band isn't about lights, lies, or pretending to be something we're not. We've earned this. If we perform again, we'll do it our way. As us. Or not at all."

A long pause followed. Ruffa looked cornered. Herbert looked like he was mentally calculating how many credits he had left.

Finally, Rommy stepped forward again. "We might go back on. We're not sure yet. But if we do . . . we will do it as who we are. No more pretending."

And with that, she turned her back on them both. One by one, the other cats followed.

Ruffa stared at the door as it clicked shut again behind him.

Herbert exhaled. "Well . . . that went well."

Ruffa slumped onto a nearby stool, burying his head in his paws.

"We might've just lost the Superband Competition."

Herbert nodded solemnly. Then he looked up.

"Or . . . we might've helped change Animalia."

Herbert stepped up beside Ruffa and gently patted his shoulder. He gave him a slight, reassuring wink, trying to ease the simmering tension in the room. Ruffa, still seething, gave the faintest nod back.

"Look, folks," Herbert said, his voice calm and measured. "Let's all take a breather. Fine—get out of the costumes. Relax for a moment. But please . . . don't spoil this over some noble ideal. A lot is riding on this. For all of us."

And with that, the two slinked out of the dressing room, turning back once to glance at the Cool Cats and Droopsters—still exhausted, still conflicted.

A few long hours passed.

The twelve musicians sprawled around the room, slowly untangling their nerves. Costumes were half hung over chairs. Empty bottles of water stood like weary sentinels. They'd even discovered a crumpled packet of biscuits near the sink and were now nibbling through the last few crumbs like survivors after a storm.

Then, just when it felt like the day might finally be over, the door creaked open—and in shuffled Herbert and Ruffa.

They looked wrecked. Drained. Limp-tailed and bleary-eyed. Ruffa dragged his feet like a ghost, and Herbert—eyes fixed on the biscuits—snatched the last one without a word and stuffed it in his mouth.

They stood silently for a beat. Then Ruffa spoke.

"I didn't appreciate the way you treated us earlier. You hurt me. You hurt Herbert. And I want you to understand something clearly: we are broke. Completely broke."

He paused for effect.

"We used every last credit we had to set this up—the rehearsal space, the school bus—yes, your school bus," he added with a half-hearted smirk, "and the best gear we could afford. We even paid the Superband Competition entrance fee out of our own pockets. None of this came free. Nothing does."

Herbert nodded, chewing. "He's right. We gave you the tools. The ride. The opportunity. And now we've got nothing left but a biscuit I had to wrestle from a chair cushion."

"You went off to sulk," KT said bluntly. "You both look like you're about to be arrested. What's going on?"

"What about our mommies?" Kreamy suddenly demanded. "Are they safe?"

"They're fine," Herbert said quickly. "They acted of their own free will. You've seen it with your own eyes."

"They're alone in that Dogwood compound you call home," Fangl said, crossing his arms. "You sure they're not worried sick about us?"

"They're not alone," Herbert assured him. "My cousin's with them. A lovely croc. He's a great cook! They'll be eating well. Probably having second helpings right now."

"That's not the point," KT growled. "You've brainwashed them and hypnotised them. And now you want us to go back on stage for what? So, you can squeeze one more tune out of us and walk away with the glory?"

Herbert raised his hands, palms open. "Look—I know you're angry. I would be too. But we'll wait and see what happens next. Great things take time. No masterpiece was ever rushed."

And then—rap rap rap! A sharp knock came at the door.

Herbert perked up. He trotted to the door, tail wagging slightly, and pressed an ear against it.

"Uh-huh . . . right . . . Okay, got it."

Everyone leant forward as Herbert turned around, his face unreadable.

Then he broke into a grin—a broad, lopsided crocodile grin that threatened to split his face in two.

"Well, excellent news!" he beamed. "You're down to the final two. They want you back on stage in a little while. You've got another chance to impress the judges. We're not done yet!"

"Does this mean we'll be in second place even if we don't win?" Sniffer asked cautiously. "That's something at least."

Ruffa straightened up, brushing his fur as he stood up straighter than ever before. "No! It means we're meant to win. Second place isn't acceptable for a band with your immense talent. I can feel it in my whiskers and all over my hide. We're meant to triumph."

But Kreamy sat slumped in a corner, her eyes glassy. "I just miss my mommy. I wish she were here. I don't care about any competition. I want to go home."

Ruffa knelt beside her, softer now. "She'd be proud of you, Kreamy. So proud. And you will see her soon. Just one more performance. Let's finish this."

He and Herbert left the room, leaving the band to prepare.

But as they slipped through the door, Fangl leant in toward Sylvest.

"I don't care what happens tonight," he whispered. "After this madness, I'm returning to Dogwood to get our mommies out. I don't trust those two farther than I can flick a flea. They've lied enough."

Sylvest gave a firm nod. "When this last song's over, we're gone. It's the only plan that makes sense."

Once filled with instruments and ambition, the room now echoed with silence and something else: resolve.

CHAPTER 22

Unexpected

Within half an hour, they were back on the main stage. The sun had begun to set, dipping low behind the horizon, casting long shadows across the grand arena. The light was softer now, fading. A few dark grey clouds drifted in overhead.

"I hope it doesn't rain," KT muttered to Moss, glancing at the gathering gloom. Moss was already perched behind his drum kit, adjusting his sticks.

"I think the stage has a cover," Moss replied, nodding toward the roof. "There's a canopy that rolls out if it rains. See that groove up there? That's where it comes from."

Smackie squinted. "That's kind of cool. I wish we had one over our garden—I could sit outside even in a downpour."

"Hardly any point," Moss said dryly. "Your garden's a cluttered shoebox. And I thought your family was moving into an apartment?"

"It's got a balcony," Smackie snapped back, slightly offended. "Besides, it's not decided yet. My parents are still dithering."

The banter faded as a hush fell over the crowd. The audience hadn't left their seats—in fact, no one had moved—but the mood had shifted—eerily quiet, charged with suspense. It was as if everyone present knew that the defining moment of the competition had come. This wasn't planned—it was unexpected, making it more tense.

Unknown to the band, the three tigers had already returned to the stage earlier. They unleashed a bold new number filled with electrifying strumming and emboldened it with their charismatic vocals. Their performance was nothing short of magnetic. Even the judges nodded along with their sharp timing and infectious rhythm.

Yet despite the tigers' surge in popularity, the Dogwood Droopsters still hung onto the edge. Barely.

Doubler and Rommy stood side by side, conferring with each other in hushed tones. They chose to perform a new song they hadn't picked earlier—a haunting ballad of love, loss, and finally letting go.

It told the story of two turtles, deeply in love but tragically out of time. The female had fallen gravely ill and was being returned to the sea, where she was destined to live out her final hours. Her body was weakening; the water would soon claim her.

But she would not be truly gone in the legends passed down among their kind. She would wait below, in the deep places. Waiting for her love.

Her mate followed her into the waves, swimming as far as he could. But when he saw her begin to sink slowly and steadily, something inside him faltered. He knew with aching certainty that evolution had changed them. Their kind no longer had the stamina to stay submerged for long. Their love, timeless though it felt, was still bound by mortal limitations.

He watched her descend into the deep, a flicker of green against the blackening sea, until she disappeared altogether.

The song was slow, solemn, and heartbreakingly beautiful. The drums grew softer with each verse, mimicking the slow fading of her heartbeat. The guitars strummed at half-time, stretching every note into something long and longing. The flute returned, mournful and pure, weaving gently through the verses like waves across the surface.

Doubler and Rommy sang in gentle harmony, their voices aching with sorrow. It was a love story not about triumph or reunion, but about goodbye—about the one who had to stay behind.

As the song reached its final verse, the cymbals clashed like a sudden storm, marking the moment of parting. The following silence was filled by a ceremonial trumpet, which rose from the background to replace the flute. Its lonely cry traced the male turtle's return to the surface—alone, broken, but alive.

He looked back one final time at the depths and knew she was gone. Forever.

The final note rang out into the twilight air. And for a moment, there was nothing but stillness.

By now, most of the audience was in tears. Faces were streaked with moisture, and creatures from every corner of

Animalia wiped their eyes with paws, claws, pads, wings, and feet.

There was a moment of heavy, reverent silence when the song concluded. Then came the sound of soft applause—fragile at first, like the fluttering of wings—and it slowly swelled into a full-throated roar of appreciation. The audience rose to their feet, their clapping growing louder and more unified. It was a standing ovation that came from admiration and being deeply, truly moved.

Even the judges were no longer composed. On their lofty balcony, all three birds wept openly. Ilga Finetuning dabbed her silk robe with a handkerchief. Buck Cloudwings, ever the stoic eagle, blinked away tears with trembling eyes. And Muffat Flapwell sobbed so loudly that sniffles and honks replaced his usual cough. They clapped with every ounce of respect in their wings and acknowledged a performance that had transcended the competition.

Backstage, Ruffa stood beside Herbert in stunned silence. He didn't even try to hide the tears in his eyes.

"That was the most beautiful song I've ever heard," Ruffa murmured hoarsely. "I can't bear to hear such tragedy again . . . but I must. Because it says so much about everything, don't you think?"

Herbert remained silent. He gave no reply, whether he was moved, overwhelmed, or simply stunned. He stared at the stage as if something enormous had just shifted.

On stage, the performers bowed deeply. The moment had emboldened them. They had given something of themselves, and the world had taken notice.

Kreamy, already breathless, suddenly broke. She gasped for air; her costume mask was suffocating her. Without thinking, she reached up and frantically tore it off, gulping in the cool evening air. Tears streamed freely down her cheeks. Whether it was the heartbreak of the song, the weight of the deception, or both, she couldn't say. It didn't matter. It all spilt out in that one moment.

The others barely had time to react.

Just then, a blinding flash lit the stage.

Snap!

A camera flash went off directly in front of them. And there, poised like a hawk who had been circling for days, was Snoop. He stood at the foot of the stage, wide-eyed and triumphant. He'd been waiting for this—this. One of the Eight Cool Cats had pulled off her disguise right in front of a full house. And he had caught it.

Not just a scoop. The scoop. Proof that the Dogwood Droopsters were not an all-dog band at all. Proof of a deception that could rock the entire Superband Competition.

He clicked away as if his life depended on it—one shot, two, three, four—before the lights began to dim and the curtains swept closed. His heart was thundering. This was it. The photo of a lifetime. A scandal. A revelation. The kind of story that could change everything.

"Why'd you do that, you fool?!" Smackie hissed, rushing to Kreamy and trying to shield her face from view.

Purrsteph and Mimi bolted forward, desperately helping to slip the mask back on before anyone else caught sight. But it was too late.

Snoop had his shot.

And he knew exactly what he was going to do with this trophy.

"No one can know who you guys are," Smackie whispered urgently. "If they were to find out, we'd lose this competition. We've got to keep this our secret, alright?"

"I . . . I'm so sorry," Kreamy sobbed, her voice cracking as she broke down. "I couldn't breathe under that mask. I needed air. I was about to suffocate."

"It's okay," Mimi said gently, wrapping a comforting paw around her. "I don't think anyone noticed in the moment. We should be safe."

"Maybe . . . but I've got some bad news," Sylvest said grimly. "That photographer? He was right at the edge of the stage. I'm pretty sure he captured the moment. He was snapping away like a lunatic."

Rommy looked unsettled. "Something tells me he was waiting for that exact second. Like he knew it was going to happen. If that photo gets out . . . we're toast."

At that moment, Ruffa sprinted up, panting and flushed, nearly tripping over cables as he bolted toward them. He just managed to keep his footing.

"Have you all lost your minds?!" he hissed. "Cover it up— now! Get her to the dressing room. No one leaves until I say it's safe. Herbert stays with you. We're this close to winning, and you choose to pull something like this now?"

"Calm down, Ruffa," Sylvest replied firmly, stepping in before things heated up. "She couldn't breathe. What did you want her to do—pass out right here on stage?"

Three cats hurried Kreamy away, pulling her hoodie over her and shielding her face. In minutes, they were all back in the dressing room, the door shut behind them, Herbert posted at the entrance like a bodyguard.

Inside, the Eight Cool Cats sat in exhausted silence as they peeled off their masks. Bottles of water were passed around like life preservers. No one spoke at first—they were too drained.

"I get it," Moss said finally, breaking the silence. "These costumes are unbearable. And hiding who you are—that's not easy. Kreamy did what she had to do. I'm sorry management hasn't treated you better."

"That doesn't excuse the risk," muttered Sniffer. "We've all got something to lose here. One selfish move and this whole thing could blow up in our faces."

The conversation faded again into stillness. Fatigue and stress had drained them. They waited, eyes flicking to the door, unsure what the next knock would bring.

About half an hour later, Herbert walked up to the door, unlocking it with a click. He glanced back at the group.

"I'm going to check what's going on out there. Try to find Ruffa. No one leaves this room. Not until it's completely safe. Got it?"

They nodded silently.

Just as Herbert turned to leave, the door opened, and Ruffa stepped in, his expression unusually heavy. He shut the door behind him with a soft click and stood facing them, his eyes slightly glazed. Something wasn't right.

"I've got bad news," he began, then quickly added, "and some good news too."

"What's the good news?" Rommy asked. "We could use some cheer before the doom and gloom hits."

"I'd rather hear the bad news first," KT muttered. "Might as well get the pain over with."

Ruffa ignored the request. "The good news is—we're still in. We haven't been disqualified. We still might win."

A beat of hope flickered through the room.

"Okay," KT said cautiously. "Then . . . what's the bad news?"

"The judges couldn't agree on a winner," Ruffa said with a sigh. "They think both final acts were equally strong. So, they've postponed the final decision until tomorrow morning. They'll decide in private. No audience. And there's a chance they'll ask both bands to perform again—one last song. Something new."

"What?" Herbert blurted out. "You're kidding. How can it be a draw with three judges? Can't two out of three make a final decision?"

Ruffa shook his head. "Each judge has three options— vote for, against, or abstain. One abstained. The other two were split. So, technically . . . it's a tie."

Doubler groaned. "I don't think I can do it again. We already gave everything we had. They've no idea what it takes to walk on that stage."

"I want to go home," Kreamy said quietly. "I don't like it here anymore."

"We all want to go home," Tinki added. "The dogs should go back to Dogwood. We cats want to return to Purrville. With our mommies. This . . . whatever this was—it's over. We're done."

Purrsteph nodded in agreement with Tinki. "It's not just about our mommies anymore. This whole situation—it's got too much. The pressure, the deception . . . I'm amazed we've made it this far without buckling under."

"It's one more day," Ruffa pleaded, his voice strained. "Maybe not even an entire day! Just a morning and we'll have the final verdict. Please, my fellow musicians—you mustn't give up on us now. We're so close. Stay strong, stay united. If you give up now, you fail each other."

"He's right," Herbert added.

"The judges don't need to bring us back again," Tinki pointed out, clearly frustrated. "There won't even be an audience! Something fishy is going on here."

Doubler shook his head. "Who's to say they'll be fair? This whole thing feels rigged. Maybe the delay's intended to disqualify us without anyone ridiculing the judges for it."

"Oh, come on," Ruffa snapped. "Don't be so negative. I haven't seen any rigging or foul play. I should be able to tell."

"That's rich," KT muttered. "You haven't seen a lot of things. Like the photographer who was ten feet from the stage. The one who probably now has a picture proving we're not even dogs. Maybe the judges already know. Maybe they're stalling until they figure out what to do with us."

"No, no, no!" Ruffa barked, stamping his paw. "You do deserve to win. All of you were incredible out there. Cats, dogs—it doesn't matter. Mixing with you was the best decision. You've got to hang in there a little while longer. One more night. We can win!"

The others fell silent. They didn't argue. They didn't doubt Ruffa's belief. But the truth was, none of them cared anymore. They were too tired, too drained, too sick of the lies. The competition had become a burden rather than a dream. They just wanted to go home.

Still, a single major issue loomed larger than any competition outcome: this was Snoop, the photographer.

One flash of his camera, one snapped moment—all it might take to unravel everything they'd worked so hard for. Fangl sat in silence, staring at the floor, reflecting on it. He could see it in the others, too—the resignation, the quiet despair. They all felt it in their bones. They were pawns, pushed and pulled in a game they hadn't signed up to play.

They had been made captives to Ruffa's ambition. An ambition that didn't seem to know any moral limits. Ruffa would do anything to get what he wanted—and Herbert, loyal to the end, backed him at every turn. The Eight Cool Cats had been dragged into a twisted game where success came at the price of their freedom, their honesty, even their families.

Fangl was done with it. Win or lose, he knew the moment the final curtain fell, they were leaving this madness behind.

Before departing the arena, the band quietly packed away their instruments and stowed their gear. The roadies, now familiar with the Droopsters' elaborate set-up, handled the drums and Ruffa's prized lighting console with care. Ruffa gave them a weary nod—he had no energy left to micromanage. Tomorrow would bring what it would bring.

About thirty minutes later, the band boarded the transport back to the hotel. Lizzalee, their escort, was waiting at the steps, clipboard in paw, and guided them aboard with her usual calm efficiency.

She gave them a long look once they were seated. The group looked completely spent. Dogs slouched in their seats. Cats curled up in silence. The exhaustion was visible—palpable even. Lizzalee tilted her head. If she hadn't known better, she'd have sworn the cats were part of the band.

Funny, she thought. *The way they walk and carry themselves, they don't act like a support crew.*

And another thing. Weren't there supposed to be four dogs? So, where had the other eight come from on stage?

But Lizzalee was no investigator. Her job was simple: get the band to and from the venue safely, make sure their needs were met, and keep everything moving on schedule. If something strange was going on, it wasn't her business to uncover it. She'd dealt with far worse personalities as a tour escort. This band, odd as they were, was polite and respectful.

So, she let the questions slide. She didn't need answers—that was not her remit. If the judges or organisers wanted to dig deeper, let them. Lizzalee would focus on doing her job.

She turned back to the front, checked her clipboard one last time, and called out: "Back at the hotel in ten, everyone. You've all done wonderfully today. Rest well—you've earned it."

The van hummed along the darkening roads, carrying twelve exhausted souls, each silently wondering what the morning would bring.

CHAPTER 23

Creature Comforts

While the final rounds of the Superband Competition played out under the sparkling stage lights of Birdheights, Police Chief Kitty Smallpaws was making her quiet rounds in the sleepy town of Purrville.

House by house, she knocked on doors—eight in total—expecting to find at least one of the Eight Cool Cats or their mothers. But each door remained unanswered.

Only at the seventh house did someone appear: a weary-looking tabby tom with a newspaper tucked under one arm and a steaming mug in his paw. He blinked at her from the doorstep, confused by her concern.

"Haven't seen my daughter or the missus in days," he admitted with a shrug. "But you know cats. They go off and do their own thing. Probably bonding or shopping. Mommies and daughters need their little adventures."

With a lazy wave, he closed the door in her face.

Kitty Smallpaws stood frozen for a moment. A chill trickled down her spine. Something didn't feel right. The voices on the answering machines—her own and Professor Fishtail's—had sounded distressed. And now this? Eight mothers and eight kittens gone. No school bus. No notice. No explanation.

Her whiskers twitched. That uneasy feeling in the pit of her stomach was quickly blooming into full-blown dread.

Just then, her phone buzzed loudly.

"What is it?" she barked into it. "I'm in the middle of something important. Is this urgent?"

It was Agatha Whiteclaw.

Of all the cats in Purrville, Agatha was famously independent. She barely trusted the council, let alone the police. If she was calling, it had to be serious.

"My cooker's caught fire!" Agatha screeched, her voice panicked and shaky. "I tried putting water on it, but now it's spread to the cupboards! My sitting chair has caught alight too—I can't put it out! It's burning—everything's burning!"

"Call the fire brigade," Kitty said automatically.

"I did! Three times! They're not answering! I think the fire chief's asleep again. Please, Kitty, I don't want to lose my house!"

Kitty winced. Fire Chief Wiggly Woods was known for his . . . excessive love of naps. Not even the fire bell could stir him when he was out cold.

"I'm on my way, Agatha," she said firmly. "Stay out of the kitchen. Close the door behind you."

"What door?" Agatha asked—but Kitty had already hung up and sprinted toward the fire station.

She hated turning her attention away from the missing cats. Everything about it felt wrong. Professor Fishtail had been right to worry about the missing school bus. The more Kitty thought about it, the more the dots connected troublingly.

But Agatha was in immediate danger. A house fire could be a tragedy in minutes.

First, the fire, she told herself. *Then the mystery.*

And yet, even as she raced down the main road, she couldn't push the deeper fears from her mind.

What if this wasn't just a case of a rebellious batch of kittens sneaking off to Birdheights to enter the competition against the elders' advice?

She had warned them about that place.

Birdheights was too flashy, too proud, and far too permissive for the humble values of Purrville. It was a city of shiny distractions and shady dealings. Worse still, it was the playground of Boreme Kildare—the sleek, sharp-toothed tiger merchant who always got what he wanted no matter who got hurt.

Kitty had taken several trips to Birdheights over the years, none of which had left her with fond memories. She had pleaded with the elders to steer Purrville away from the place.

"It will corrupt their innocent minds," she had told them bluntly. "No good comes from dealing with Birdheights."

But now the school bus was missing. The Eight Cool Cats were nowhere to be found. Their mothers, too. And Kitty Smallpaws couldn't shake the growing sense that something bigger, darker was happening just out of view.

Maybe it was just a teenage kitten rebellion.

Or maybe . . . it was something else entirely.

For now, she focused on what she could fix. She had a house to save. A fire to put out. A sleepy fire chief to shake awake—hard.

But once that was done?

Kitty Smallpaws would find out exactly what was going on. And if anyone had taken her kittens—or their mothers—against their will, well . . .

There'd be no sleep in Purrville tonight.

***

When the transport finally pulled up outside the hotel, the Eight Cool Cats breathed a sigh of relief. *At last*, they thought. Soon they'd be tucked up in warm beds with fluffy pillows and dreams of going home. Just one more day, and they'd be back with their mommies—just one more day.

Lizzalee disembarked first and turned to the group. "Wait here for a moment, please. I need to check something with reception before we go in," she said briskly, then disappeared into the hotel lobby.

Ruffa and Herbert remained outside, eyeing their band like two overworked managers unsure whether to offer them praise or apologies. The performers were exhausted.

The day had physically drained them, emotionally, and spiritually as well. But despite it all, they'd exceeded every expectation and played their hearts out on stage.

"What's going on now?" Mimi asked, glancing nervously at Herbert.

Herbert shrugged, looking as befuddled as she was. "I think . . . she's checking out the bookings? Making sure we've still got rooms for another night?" he guessed, without offering much conviction.

"We just want a bed," Purrsteph whimpered. "Is this too much to ask? A nice, cosy bed."

Fangl and Sylvest were whispering again. "Everything about this feels off," Fangl muttered. "Always one more hiccup. Always something else."

"This is what happens when amateurs run the show," Smackie said, folding her arms and glaring toward the hotel. "We should be asleep already. Instead, we're loitering like abandoned alley cats while some overworked admin figure sorts out who gets to use a toilet."

Moss sighed. "At this point, nothing surprises me anymore. This whole thing's been run like a soggy biscuit. And those two"—he nodded toward Ruffa and Herbert—"couldn't manage a band of wind-up toys."

The "few minutes" stretched painfully on. Finally, Lizzalee reappeared, running, clutching hotel passes in her paws. But instead of handing them to the group, she went straight to Ruffa and Herbert and pulled them aside, speaking in a hushed, urgent tone.

Herbert's face darkened. He shook his head repeatedly, his scowl deepening with every word. Ruffa's brow furrowed, and his tail twitched irritably.

Then Herbert blurted, loud enough for all to hear: "Tell them yourself. This is ridiculous. I'm filing an official complaint first thing tomorrow morning. We're being sabotaged by judge interference. Someone better fix this."

Ruffa and Lizzalee finally turned back to the waiting band, most of whom now slumped on the kerb, barely upright.

Ruffa cleared his throat. "We've . . . encountered a small problem. But there's a simple solution, I promise."

The cats groaned.

"Due to an administrative mix-up, our extra hotel bookings were cancelled. There are only three rooms left. Two for the dogs, one for Herbert and me. The rest of you . . . Well, we'll have to improvise."

Lizzalee looked ready to melt into the pavement. She hadn't said a word yet. She didn't want to be the messenger, and she certainly didn't want to be the target.

Ruffa pushed on. "Luckily, the upper deck of our fabulous tour bus is still available. It's surprisingly comfortable. I usually reserve it for top talent, but I'll allow the cats to stay for one night."

"'Top talent,' huh?" Purrsteph snapped. "And what exactly are we? Backup dancers?"

"This is absurd," KT said. "There are other hotels in this city. Why can't we book somewhere else?"

"Because we can't afford it!" Herbert snapped, finally breaking. "We're out of credits. Spent everything on your transport, your instruments, your rehearsals, your extra snacks—"

"Our school bus," Tinki reminded him.

Herbert ignored her. "We've barely got enough left to fix the bus for the ride home. If we splash what's left on more hotel rooms, we risk being stranded here. And I think we all want to get home tomorrow."

"We do," Tinki admitted. "But that doesn't make any of this okay. We've been tricked, manipulated, lied to—and now we're sleeping in a cramped bus because you ran out of money?"

"Let's not make a scene here," Ruffa said, glancing nervously at Lizzalee. "She's with the organisers. We need her cooperation. One more day, everyone. Just one."

"One more disaster, you mean," said Kreamy quietly. There was a new steel in her voice, something no one had quite heard from her before.

"This better be the final hiccup, Ruffa," KT growled, jabbing a paw toward him. "Because if anything else goes wrong, you won't have a band left to mismanage. Even your loyal mutts are on the verge of quitting."

Ruffa looked visibly shaken. His bluster deflated, replaced by weary desperation. "Please. We're almost there. One more night. Then it's over."

He turned to Lizzalee. "Give the passes to the dogs. Take them to their rooms. I'll handle the cats' sleeping arrangements."

Lizzalee nodded, still avoiding eye contact with the performers. She began handing out keycards with quiet efficiency.

As the dogs filed into the hotel individually, the Eight Cool Cats stood off to the side, tails drooping. The exhaustion in their eyes said it all.

One more night.

Just one more.

But somehow, it felt like the longest night of their lives was still ahead.

Lizzalee had no interest in being caught in the middle of another tense exchange, so the moment she had the excuse, she whisked the dogs away. With a polite smile and quick pawwork, she handed out the few remaining room passes and led them toward the hotel entrance.

Rommy glanced back as they walked. He lowered his voice to Smackie beside him.

"This feels wrong. Doesn't it? The cats keep getting a raw deal. No matter what they do."

Smackie gave a resigned sigh. "We've got no choice but to play with what we have. This is about getting through the competition."

But Moss wasn't pleased at all. His tail twitched irritably.

"This won't do. They've worked as hard as we have—even harder, perhaps—and they're being treated like they're nothing more than backup. It's disgusting."

"Shhh!" hissed Sniffer, shooting Moss a sharp look. "Keep your voice down. The last thing we need is Ruffa overhearing and throwing a fit. We need to finish this thing first, then talk."

Lizzalee didn't hear every word, but she could feel the shift in the air. The way the dogs were talking. The way they kept glancing back. They weren't happy—and they had good reason.

Trying to defuse the tension, she addressed them gently. "Don't worry. The tour bus is in the garage—it's warm, dry, and better than it used to be. I've handed the keys to your manager, and he'll make sure the cats get settled in safely."

She looked at each of them, a touch more thoughtful now.

"In some ways, your cat support staff reminds me of myself. We do the background work—quiet, important things. And it often goes unseen. But it matters. It always matters. Once you're all in your rooms, I'll see if I can help get them situated, too. Everyone deserves a little dignity. Don't you agree?"

There were small nods all around. Lizzalee smiled faintly. "Even if they don't sing or play, talent takes many forms."

Rommy nodded slowly, more to himself than to her. Smackie looked away. The group was too tired to speak up, but appreciated the sentiment.

Still, something was off.

Smackie muttered, "We'll be fortunate if this band ever makes it to morning."

Back by the garage doors, Ruffa was already scheming. He could feel it—resentment, bubbling beneath the surface.

The cats were ready to revolt. This could fall apart in front of his eyes.

He turned to face them. "I know this isn't how it's meant to be. I didn't plan for things to go this way. But we're so close. You've worked too hard to throw it all away now."

"That's easy for you to say," KT snapped, his fur bristling. "You're not the one being shoved into a stuffy tour bus because of your poor planning. That 'monstrosity' was our school bus—and I wouldn't board it again if you paid me in goldfish."

"Then take the keys," Ruffa said, handing them over quickly. "Decide for yourselves. I'm not trying to control you. I want this to end well for all of us."

They had reached the garage. Ruffa fumbled with the lock, swinging the door open with a loud clatter. Fluorescent lights flickered overhead.

There it was—their old bus. But cleaner. Sleeker. Tidied up and scrubbed down to something almost . . . respectable—a strange symbol of everything that had happened.

"See?" Ruffa said, attempting a grin. "It's ready. One more night. One more day. Then we go home. Birdheights will be behind us."

Nobody answered. The cats filed in, saying nothing. One by one, they made their way up the stairs to the top deck of the refurbished bus.

For most, it was their first time seeing where the dogs had been sleeping. The difference was stark—lush cushions, smooth panelling, a panoramic window with blackout shades, even a mini-fridge. It was a world away from the cluttered compartment below where they'd been crammed during rehearsals.

Sylvest thought grimly, *So, this was where Herbert had been putting all his effort.* While they had been shoved in the back, sweating and starving, this was where the pampering happened.

None of them said a word, but they didn't need to. The plush silence said it all.

Ruffa waved at them vaguely from the stairwell, then disappeared into the night.

The door clanked shut behind him.

And for a moment, all was still.

But inside each of them, a storm was beginning to build.

* * *

Upstairs on the plush top deck of the bus, the gentle rise and fall of sleepy breathing meant that calm had taken over. Most of the cats, worn out beyond words, had drifted into an uneasy slumber—tails twitching, ears occasionally flicking as they dreamt of things they wouldn't remember in the morning.

But Fangl was still wide awake.

He sat beside the narrow window, his eyes scanning the shadows of the now-dark garage. The overhead lights had gone off earlier, probably set on a timer. The building had returned to silence, lit only by the soft glow of moonlight filtering in through dusty panes.

He exhaled slowly.

So many thoughts swirled in his head—about their mothers, the deception they'd endured, the fact that they were sleeping in what had once been their school bus, now dressed up in soft cushions and cosmetic comfort to hide the truth of their journey.

Below them, in the hotel's gravel lot, Ruffa and Herbert had stood in the dimness exchanging quiet conspiracies and hollow reassurances.

Now they were gone, vanished into the night, no doubt still plotting how to wring one more performance out of a band that had already given everything it had. Fangl could almost hear Ruffa's voice echoing in the back of his mind: "We are going to win!"—as if saying it loud enough could make it accurate.

Fangl didn't believe in declarations like that anymore.

He believed in family. In the strength of truth. And in getting home.

He pulled the curtain across the window and settled on the edge of a cushion that smelled faintly of lemons and stage make-up.

Just before closing his eyes, he whispered into the quiet: "One more song. One more sunrise. Then this ends."

Then, finally, he too surrendered to sleep.

CHAPTER 24

Diggout

Moss and Sniffer had ended up sharing a hotel room.

No sooner had Sniffer kicked off his boots and flopped back onto his bed than Moss winced and grabbed his nose. A foul odour wafted across the narrow gap between the twin beds like an invisible fog of doom.

"Phew!" Moss muttered under his breath, debating whether to speak up. "Do me a favour and rinse those paws in the shower before you lie down. They stink!"

Sniffer grinned lazily, assuming it was just a bit of teasing—until he saw the dead seriousness on Moss's face. Still, he shrugged and rolled over, deciding to ignore him. Within seconds, he was snoring, utterly unfazed.

Moss said nothing more. Instead, he quietly grabbed the room key and slipped out the door. Sleep was impossible tonight. Far too many thoughts entered his mind, which he couldn't shake off, no matter how hard he tried.

Outside, the air was cooler, calmer. But Moss's mind remained troubled.

He wasn't happy with it. Not just the set-up, but the endless lies, and how Ruffa and Herbert manipulated the kittens into joining their band of misfits. And why did everyone keep calling them kittens? They weren't kittens anymore. They were young cats—growing, evolving, still mischievous but capable, creative, and brimming with potential. They were musicians, every bit as talented as the dogs. The fusion of cat and dog created musical magic that no one had ever expected.

But look at how far they had got. Did that make it right? Why did it still feel so wrong?

The more he thought about it, the more he wondered if Ruffa and Herbert had run out of credits. Could they be that broke? Or was it just another excuse, another layer in their pyramid of lies? Were they overspending or simply being stingy . . . or worse, hiding something?

But what disturbed him most—the part he couldn't ignore—was what had been done to the mommies.

The brainwashing.

The hypnotic suggestion had taken away their free will. On the surface, they looked happy, supportive, and smiling as they waved flags and cheered from the stands. But Moss could see the truth behind their glassy eyes. That happiness wasn't theirs. It had been programmed. Stolen. Replaced.

Even if temporary, it was so very wrong.

Moss had never been one to cause a stir. He was the quiet type—the steady rhythm behind the chaos. But lately, the rhythm had gone offbeat. Everything felt wrong.

Fake. He didn't want to perform again. Not like this. Not tomorrow. Not when everything was built on deception.

Why had Birdheights—the most modern, diverse, celebrated metropolis in the entire land—allowed such rigid, outdated rules to govern its so-called progressive competition?

Wasn't this the city where one's dreams could come true? Where new ideas flourished?

Then why the fear of change?

Moss didn't need to ask. He already knew the answer. Deep down, they all did.

It was a fear of chaos. Fear of evolution. Fear of dogs and cats, side by side, making something greater than either could achieve alone—fear of what that meant for the old order.

Old prejudices die hard, even in Birdheights.

The Dogwood Droopsters had created something extraordinary. The music they played together had power—real power—but the system wasn't ready for it.

And maybe . . . maybe Ruffa wasn't either.

Moss had to admit that Ruffa's ambition was staggering. Maybe even admirable. Perhaps that kind of vision could only come from someone without barriers. He'd often wondered if geniuses were troubled beings who saw the world differently and refused to abide by the rules. Was Ruffa a genius, or just an opportunist who got lucky this one time with a wild idea?

Either way, Moss couldn't sit still. Not tonight.

He needed a distraction. Something to drown out the thoughts that were eating away inside. He remembered Rocko—the gruff old biker dog who used to hang around the music scene—and the club he'd once recommended. It had been a couple of years.

Maybe he'd head there now. Catch up with Rocko. Maybe hear some real music from the heart, not some grand illusion.

He turned down a side street, paws in his pockets, the soft thrum of the city at night surrounding him.

It was time to clear his head.

Moss ambled through the lively heart of Birdheights, weaving between late-night wanderers and neon-lit market stalls until he finally found the place he was looking for. After a few friendly directions from passing Animalians, he came to a narrow alley, tucked away behind a bakery and a noodle shop. There, beneath a flickering blue-and-pink neon sign, was The Diggout—a club whispered about in music circles but rarely advertised.

Everyone in the know said The Diggout was where legends got their first shot, long before the land had heard of them. But that wasn't what made it special.

He stepped inside and descended a steep flight of narrow stairs, his paw trailing the rail. At the bottom, he followed a wider corridor packed with noise, movement, and creatures of every kind. He passed a porcupine with glow sticks, a group of young raccoons trading dance moves, and even a snake coiled around a badger's shoulder like a fashionable scarf. Everyone seemed to be having the time of their lives.

Then Moss entered the main room and stopped cold.

It was a large basement, hazy with stage lights and warm with energy. A jazz band was playing a fast, electric number, and the crowd was swaying and stomping to the beat. But what stunned Moss was the band itself.

Every member was of a different species.

A hefty owl with sequinned feathers and a velvet voice stood centre stage in a purple dress, her wings cutting the air with soulful gestures. Behind her, a hairy rat with bare shoulders pounded the drums fiercely. Two sweating trumpet players—a mellow pig and a wiry goat—took turns blasting brass flourishes.

And at the keys sat what looked like the oldest cat Moss had ever seen, wearing dark sunglasses and a cosmic grin. Despite her age—and the fact that she was blind—her paws danced over the keyboard with dizzying skill.

Moss's jaw slackened. He looked around to see if anyone else was as shocked as he was, but no one batted an eye. The music, not the species, enthralled the crowd. No rules. No barriers. Just pure, glorious sound.

So, this was it—the real music scene of Birdheights, the underground world where the old rules didn't apply and the best art was born from diversity.

As far as he could tell, the One Species Rule didn't exist in The Diggout.

A gentle tap landed on his shoulder, and he turned to see a familiar face.

"Hey, dawg," came a warm, gruff voice. "How you been keepin'? Good to see you."

"Rocko!" Moss grinned. "Great to see you too!"

His gaze returned to the stage. He couldn't ignore it.

"What's catching your eye, bro?" Rocko asked, folding his big arms. "You appreciating the music at The Diggout?"

Moss nodded slowly. "The band. They're . . . all mixed. How's this even possible? I thought it was . . . banned."

Rocko let out a quiet laugh. "Sure it is. Officially. But this here's the underground. The rules don't apply, man. Not for musicians. Not for artists. Music's got its own rules."

He thumped a paw against his chest. "The coolest beats come from the strangest mixes. That's just the truth, brother. You dig?"

Moss chuckled. "I've been playing in the Superband Competition—"

"Yeah? Good on you, man. That's something. But that's the mainstream circuit. Clean-cut. Tame. All surface, but no soul."

"They don't permit mixed. Too bad."

"Of course not," Rocko said, shrugging. "Anything cool, they wouldn't allow. As soon as it becomes official, it stops being raw and meaningful. That's the deal. But here?" He gestured around the club. "Here, the future's already happening."

"Maybe," Moss said softly. "But the future's still hiding in the shadows."

"Give it time," said Rocko, clapping him on the back. "Now, come meet the crew."

He led Moss to a side table where half a dozen dogs lounged around with bottles of fizzy soda and tubs of popcorn. The air smelled of cinnamon, sugar, and cheap bubbles.

"You want a drink, bro?" Rocko asked, already reaching for a bottle. "Try the caramel fizz. It'll knock your tail straight."

He handed it over. Moss took a sip and immediately smiled. It was frothy, weird, and delicious.

"So, how's the comp going?" Rocko asked. "We don't follow the mainstream stuff much. Seen it all before. Not enough heart."

"Well . . ." Moss exhaled. "Believe it or not, we've made it to the final. But now it's a tie, and we've been told to play again in the morning. One more performance to decide everything."

"Dang. That's a big deal."

"Maybe. Ruffa—our so-called manager—and this crocodile, Herbert, think we will win. But I'm not sure. Something feels off. The whole thing's a mess."

"Hey," Rocko said, raising an eyebrow. "Ain't you the lot with the twelve-piece dog band? Biggest bunch ever to hit Birdheights?"

Moss smirked. "Technically, yeah. That's us."

"They must dig your sound. Twelve mutts? That's practically a marching band."

Moss hesitated, the truth pressing up against the inside of his chest. Then it tumbled out.

"They're . . . not all dogs."

Rocko blinked. "Say what?"

Moss looked around nervously. No one was paying them any attention. He lowered his voice.

"They're not all dogs. Eight of them are cats. We've been disguising them. That's the real band. The honest truth."

Rocko stared at him for a long second. Then he leant back and laughed.

"Now we're talking! That's the best thing I've heard in months!"

Moss didn't laugh. "It's not funny, Rocko. It's serious. If the judges find out, we're finished. It's all been smoke and mirrors. Costumes. Lies. Even the cats' mothers were hypnotised to play along."

Rocko's smile faded. "Whoa. That's heavy."

"Yeah." Moss looked down at his soda bottle. "It's beyond heavy. And I don't know how to carry it much longer."

Rocko nodded slowly, his expression softening. "Well, you just bought yourself a listener, brother. And maybe . . . maybe an ally."

Moss looked up.

Rocko took a swig of soda and grinned. "Because now that you've seen what real music looks like . . . You ain't gonna unsee it."

"What are you saying, buddy?" Rocko asked, his brow furrowing. "I don't catch your drift."

"I can't explain it right now," Moss said, eyes flicking to the stage. "I shouldn't. At least not until this is over . . . Maybe when it's all done."

He nodded toward the band. "Hey, I like this singer. What's their name?"

"Molly and the Mops," Rocko replied, still studying Moss. "Yeah, she's a real gem. Got a voice like silk and gravel rolled into one. But listen—I've gotta tell you something. You probably don't wanna hear it."

"Tell me what?" Moss asked, uneasy now.

"This stays between us, agreed?"

They clinked their soda bottles in a silent pact. Moss nodded. He trusted Rocko, always had.

"I really shouldn't be talking to you about this," Rocko began, leaning closer. "But I heard something a few days ago from a good source. Someone who knows the ways of the city—works outta the mayor's office."

Moss sat up straighter. "Go on . . ."

Rocko lowered his voice. "The Superband Competition? It's another con, bro. All this hype and celebration about music and togetherness—it's a glossy distraction—a publicity stunt. Birdheights has been seeing a population slump for years. The birds don't wanna do the hard graft anymore, so they're trying to attract fresh blood— Animalians with dreams, ambition, energy. But the city's not offering what it promises. It's not delivering. That's the con."

Moss blinked. "You mean they're using the competition to . . . what? Fool people into moving here? Present them with a grandiose illusion? The good life?"

Rocko nodded solemnly. "Exactly. Make 'em believe Birdheights is the land of opportunity. And while that's happening—while the stage lights and jazz hands keep everyone excited—certain elites are busy securing their plans behind the scenes."

Moss narrowed his eyes. "What elites?"

"There's a tiger band in the final. Three of them. Supposed to be the rising stars of this show. But here's the issue—it's all rigged. They're going to win. It's been decided already."

Moss stiffened. "You're kidding?"

"I wish I were," Rocko said. "But I trust my source. The judges? They'll pretend that it was a tough call. They'll act like it was close. But no matter how good your band is, you're just a stepping stone. A necessary sacrifice to make the win look legitimate."

Moss stared into his drink. "This explains everything. Why couldn't the judges decide? Why do they suddenly want one more performance? It's not about the music—it's about keeping up appearances."

"You think you're playing for them. They're playing you!"

"So . . . what makes these tigers so special?" Moss asked, already suspecting the answer.

Rocko shrugged. "Simple. Boreme Kildare."

Moss looked up. "The merchant?"

"The richest, most powerful merchant in Birdheights," Rocko confirmed. "Owns half the businesses around here. Birds try to keep him in check, but they tolerate his antics because he brings in revenue—and immigrants. But he's outgrown their leash. Word is, he's eyeing a future mayoral run. And guess who's in the tiger band?"

Moss groaned. "Don't tell me . . . I don't think I want to know."

"His son. Larun Kildare. And if Larun wins, he's promised to join the family concern. It's all neatly contrived. A hero story to feed to the papers. 'Young prodigy wins first competition, joins father's empire to shape the city's future.' Truly inspiring. Beautifully staged."

Moss rubbed his forehead. "So, we never stood a chance."

"You were never meant to win," Rocko said quietly. "You were meant to impress just enough to make Larun's win look deserved. That's the playbook. But here's the worst part—"

He paused.

"They're planning to expose a scandal in the morning— some cheating allegation against one of the bands. Make an example out of them. A spectacle. Word is that it'll clear the path for the tigers."

Moss froze. "You think they're set to beat us?"

Rocko looked grave. "If you're the only real competition left . . . then yeah, I'd bet on it."

Moss sat back, stunned. "Then it was all a con. Right from the beginning."

"There must be something they can stick on you," Rocko said. "Something they can use against you guys. A reason to disqualify you and make it look justifiable. They need only the right excuse to get their way."

Moss's thoughts spiralled. The disguises. The secrecy. The hypnotised mothers. The missing bus. The constant delays. All of this. Played straight into their paws.

"Oh, no . . ." he muttered.

Rocko leant forward. "Whatever it is, Moss—you gotta be ready. And maybe think about whether it's time to take the power back. You dig?"

Moss didn't answer. He just stared at the bottle in his paw, watching the last bubbles fizz and fade.

Suddenly, Moss's eyes widened.

There, weaving through the crowd at the back of the club, was the same sly-looking photographer he'd seen near the competition stage. The flashbulb. The moment. The mask. It had all seemed too perfectly timed—and now Moss realised why.

A pit formed in his stomach.

He remembered what Kreamy had told him about the mask—how itchy and unbearable it had become. At the time, it seemed like a minor inconvenience. But now, everything clicked into place. What if someone had tampered with her mask? What if the discomfort had been intentional?

Then came the memory of Lizzalee. She had looked at Kreamy during that strange moment on stage, as if expecting something to happen. Not surprised—ready.

Oh, no . . .

None of it was a coincidence.

They'd all been set up.

Moss's thoughts raced. Lizzalee had surely informed her superiors all along. They had watched closely as the Dogwood Droopsters grew in popularity, carefully directing them to the finals—not because they supported them, but because it served their needs. They were after a big twist—a controversy.

Push the cats and dogs right to the edge of glory—then expose them.

Let a desperate photographer capture the perfect moment. Let a masked cat reveal her identity in front of the crowd.

He could almost hear the headlines:

"Fraud at the Finals: Disqualified for Deception!"

"Dog Band Found to Contain Hidden Cats!"

"Tigers Roar to Victory After Devious Competitors Unmasked!"

It was so purrfectly orchestrated. Kreamy's itchy mask . . . The eager lensman with his flash ready . . . And the fact that the mask just happened to come off at the most theatrical moment of their performance? It all stank.

Moss felt sick. He wouldn't be surprised if the judges themselves had leant toward voting for the Droopsters—until this "evidence" conveniently tipped the scale. After all, how could a dishonest band be crowned the winners?

This was how it worked in big cities. The bigger the spotlight, the longer the shadows. And in Birdheights there were always hidden paws pulling strings behind the curtain. Ruffa had played dirty, sure—but Ruffa was an amateur climbing the rungs of the success ladder. The real manipulators were leagues ahead—professionals in the art of fixing outcomes while smiling politely.

But Moss wasn't going to take it lying down.

No way.

Not this time.

His eyes burned with quiet fury. He wouldn't let the cats and dogs be humiliated, not by some rigged machine, some power-hungry bird council, and certainly not by a family of flashy tigers and their empire-building father.

Enough was enough.

"You alright, bro?" Rocko asked, studying his face. "You look like you just saw someone eat your lunch."

Moss turned slowly. "I'm fine. I'm good. But . . ." He paused, heart pounding. "I need to ask you something. It's small. No—it's quite a big favour. And I'll understand completely if it's too much. But I've got to ask."

Rocko leant in, serious now. "Shoot, bro. Whatever it is, if it matters to you, I've got you covered."

Moss nodded. He could feel the plan forming already.

He wasn't sure how this was all going to play out. But one thing was definite.

Tomorrow, someone in Birdheights was going to be very surprised.

And it wasn't going to be him.

<h1 style="text-align:center">CHAPTER 25</h1>

<h1 style="text-align:center">Night Birds</h1>

The Eight Cool Cats were fast asleep on the top floor of the bus when a strange noise echoed up from the lower level. KT blinked awake, ears twitching. He nudged Fangl, who groaned and nudged Sylvest in turn.

But before either of them could move, Tinki was already upright.

"Someone's lurking about downstairs," she whispered, eyes alert. "We ought to check it out."

It was too late to keep things quiet—most of the others were already stirring.

"Wait for me," Sylvest muttered as he rolled upright and shuffled after her.

"And me," Fangl added. "This could be dangerous."

But before they caught up to Tinki, Mimi and Purrsteph padded softly toward the stairs.

"Ladies first," Mimi said coolly, brushing past the boys.

"What's the big problem?" Kreamy groaned, rubbing her eyes. "It's not even morning yet. I've barely closed mine."

KT scowled. "I should go first. You girls could get attacked, and—"

"I heard it first, and I'm already halfway down," Tinki cut in without looking back.

"Shhh, all of you," Doubler hissed. "If someone is down there, they've heard us by now."

Then, frighteningly, two feet began ascending the stairs.

Tinki froze.

"Ohhh!" she gasped, stumbling back as a nervous-looking figure emerged from the shadows.

"Hey there! Stop—it's just me!" came a breathless voice.

It was Moss.

Tinki narrowed her eyes. "You startled me!"

"Hi," he said sheepishly, stepping into the light. "Didn't mean to spook anyone."

The tension eased. Tinki glanced back up the stairs. "It's okay. Just Moss. From the mutts."

"Oh, that Moss," Mimi muttered with a smirk. "The night creeper."

"I didn't mean to sneak up," Moss said, ears drooping. "I was trying to be quiet."

"Well, that went well," Purrsteph muttered dryly.

Moss climbed the last few steps as the group gathered to face him properly.

"Hey, Moss," KT said. "Did you get kicked out of your hotel room? You haunting our bus now?"

"Nah, I've got a room. I just . . . couldn't sleep. But that's not why I'm here."

Fangl groaned, pulling a blanket back over his head. "Please tell me this isn't going to take long."

"I wouldn't have woken you if it weren't serious," Moss replied. "I came to tell you something important. Really important."

"Well, go on then," said Tinki.

"Yeah, spit it out," added Purrsteph.

Moss looked around at the sleepy, curious faces.

"I'm afraid we're not going to win the Superband Competition," he said flatly. "No matter how well we play in the morning. The tigers are going to win. It's already been decided."

A stunned silence followed.

Moss took a breath. "It's worse than that . . ."

Fangl blinked. "Worse, how?"

Moss's voice dropped. "They've got a photo of Kreamy taking off her mask. They're planning to use it to expose us—to humiliate us. The whole band'll be disqualified. The tigers win by default."

A collective gasp went through the group.

Kreamy looked around wildly. "What? Oh, no . . . Are you serious? I'm to blame. I got us into this situation."

"It's not your fault," Moss said quickly. "I think someone tampered with your mask. Probably put some irritant in it. Forced your paw. It wasn't an accident, and it wasn't just you."

Purrsteph folded her arms. "Lizzalee. It had to be her. I knew something was up. I've been sneezing since I put mine on."

He stepped off his idling chopper, crossed the garage in five firm strides, and grabbed Herbert by the collar. He spun the croc around in one fluid motion.

"Whoa! What in the—" Herbert spluttered, thrown off balance.

Rocko raised a paw. For a moment, it looked like a punch was coming. But instead, he snatched something shiny from Herbert's waistcoat—the pocket watch.

"No!" Herbert cried, lunging for it.

But it was too late. Rocko hurled the watch onto the floor.

CRACK.

The delicate glass shattered instantly. Gears and springs were scattered across the concrete like frightened ants.

Herbert stared down in horror. "My watch," he whispered. "My precious watch . . ."

Then he burst into loud, dramatic sobs.

"I'll tell Ruffa!" he wailed. "You've ruined everything! You have no right!"

"You know something? We're busy," Rocko said flatly. "You should leave."

Herbert stood frozen, mouth quivering, as Rocko clenched his paw again with a silent warning. Herbert gulped, spun on his heel, and ran—his scaly tail swishing behind him as he disappeared into the night.

The cats slowly exhaled.

"Can someone please explain what just happened?" Kreamy muttered, rubbing her temples. "I wasn't listening. Everything's fuzzy when I haven't slept."

"We're getting out of here tonight," said Tinki. "That's all you need to know right now."

"About time," Kreamy replied, flopping back down. "At least give me a little nap first. A girl's got to rest."

"We can't," said Tinki. "We're leaving immediately, Kreamy."

Kreamy blinked at her. "Can't a girl get any beauty sleep in this madhouse?"

Fangl stepped forward, addressing the group. "In half an hour—maybe less—Herbert will be back. And he won't be alone. Ruffa will come with him. And when that happens . . . well, let's say it won't go our way. Nobody will believe us. Moss has warned us, and frankly, I believe him. We don't have time to second-guess it."

"I'd like to be gone before that happens," said Kreamy, now wide awake. "I'm tired of bad management and worse disguises. Let them win their crooked trophy. I want my peace back."

"I'm sorry to rush you all," KT said, "but we must move now. We can discuss it on the bikes if you must."

"Did you say bikes?" Kreamy asked, alarmed. She peered toward the rumbling noise below. "Are you kidding? Bikes? At night? That's crazy. Can't we take our bus?"

"We don't have the keys," said Sylvest. "And even if we did . . ."

"Even if we did," KT interrupted, "the bus isn't fixed. Ruffa hasn't paid the mechanic yet. They've been holding off. He's flat broke."

"And the only thing that is running," Moss added, "is our chance to get out of this place with our dignity."

Kreamy sighed and rolled her shoulders.

"Fine," she grumbled. "But I swear—if my fur gets wind-swept or I fall off a bike, someone will hear about it."

* * *

It wasn't long before the Eight Cool Cats were seated on the bikes, helmets fastened, and tails tucked tight. The roar of the engines filled the garage as Rocko raised his paw toward the exit.

That was when they appeared.

A dozen apes stormed in through the garage doors, their fists clenched, their brows furrowed, and their movements slow but deliberate.

"Oh no," Tinki whispered, her eyes wide. "Herbert must have reported us already! What now?"

The bikers and cats froze. Rocko narrowed his eyes. Moss stepped forward but quickly realised there was no way out without running straight through the apes.

Then, Doubler piped up from the back of the group, pointing at a battered truck sitting idle on a ramp.

"Hey, fellas!" he called. "Did you know this truck's packed full of ripe bananas? The door is not even locked. And if no one moves it soon, those bananas will rot. That's a lot of waste for a city like Birdheights."

Rocko caught on immediately.

"Tell you what," he added smoothly. "Why not let us quietly tell that slimy croc we weren't here? We won't say a thing . . . help yourselves to a few snacks. And trust me, Herbert and Ruffa are flat broke. You won't get credit for your troubles."

The lead ape, a hefty brute named Hunk, eyed them suspiciously.

"You think we can be bribed with a few bananas?" he scoffed. "What do you take us for—buffoons?"

Smackie stepped in, arms folded. "Just telling it straight. Our so-called managers? Can't afford a single bus repair. You think they'll pay you? You're being conned, just like the rest of us."

A tense silence settled in the garage.

Then a scrawny ape darted behind the truck and opened the cargo door. A moment later, he reappeared with a glowing yellow bunch in his hand.

"They're telling the truth, Hunk!" he shouted. "The whole truck's loaded!"

The garage went dead still.

"So, what's it gonna be?" Moss said calmly. "Bananas or a brawl?"

Hunk glared at him. Then—without a word—the apes turned and made for the truck. Moments later, they were howling with laughter and stuffing bananas into their mouths, crates flying open like party favours.

The Choppy Chomps didn't wait.

Engines revved. And one by one, the bikes peeled out of the garage and into the cool night, stars twinkling above as they roared down the moonlit road toward Dogwood.

Moss didn't join the convoy. He returned to the hotel, slipping quietly into his room and shaking Sniffer awake.

Sniffer groaned. "What—what's goin' on?"

Moss explained everything: the escape, the apes, the broken pocket watch, the tigers, and the fix.

Sniffer sat bolt upright, jaw slack. "They left? They left?"

"They had to," Moss said. "You'll understand when you see what comes next."

Moments later, they gathered in the next room with Smackie and Rommy. Rommy emerged from the bathroom, towel over her head, brushing her fur into place.

"Wait, no performance in the morning?" she asked. "You're serious?"

"No cats, no band," said Moss. "But we don't know what happens now. Ruffa and Herbert are going to go ballistic when they find out. And if we're not careful, we will get the blame."

"We should stay," said Sniffer, reluctantly. "We're stuck anyway; if we're here, we might learn more about their plans. We play dumb. Act surprised. Like we don't know a thing."

"Nonsense," snapped Smackie. "Why bother? I'm going back to Dogwood. They can keep their phony competition. This thing was a set-up from the start."

"I don't know . . ." Moss said slowly, half to himself. 'The judges might see through it. Maybe they'll realise something's wrong. And if the photo gets questioned, if it's challenged—maybe we still have a shot."

"You think so?" Sniffer frowned. "But you warned the cats! You blew the lid off everything. You want to undo that now?"

"I'm saying—who knows?" Moss replied. "Maybe it's not over."

"I think everyone's in on it," said Smackie grimly. "They're just waiting for the photo to make it official."

Rommy had heard enough. She tossed the towel aside. "I'm not playing one more note for Ruffa or that silly crocodile. I'll head back to Dogwood first—walk if that's the only option."

"But how?" asked Moss. "There's no public transport between here and Dogwood."

"Then we're kind of stuck," Sniffer groaned. "Until Ruffa coughs up the money for that bus repair."

"Alright," said Smackie, rubbing her face. "Then we sleep. And in the morning, we see what we're dealing with."

None of them wanted a confrontation. But none of them trusted this city anymore, either.

At least one thing had changed: the cats were free. When Ruffa and Herbert returned to the garage, the Eight Cool Cats were long gone. Also, likely they'd be taking their mommies with them, even if they had to drag them out kicking and meowing.

Maybe that would keep Ruffa distracted long enough to leave the dogs alone.

It had been a long, ridiculous, exhausting day. But somewhere deep in their thoughts, a quiet satisfaction began to take root. A little justice had been dished out tonight.

And with that thought, they finally surrendered to sleep, knowing that whatever tomorrow brought would have little to do with music.

CHAPTER 26

Mommies Rescue

To say that the journey late at night on bikes with the Choppy Chomps wasn't exhilarating would've been a flat-out lie. None of the Eight Cool Cats had been especially keen on the idea—at least not at first. But once they were seated on the back of those gleaming chrome machines and felt the wind zipping past their whiskers, it turned out to be one heck of a ride.

Still, their minds weren't on the scenery or the thrill. They had bigger things to worry about—namely, how they would rescue their mommies back at the compound.

The Choppy Chomps, cool and daring as they were, had made their terms clear: they'd deliver the cats to Dogwood, but the mission would end there. No interference, busting down doors, or getting caught by law enforcement. They might have been rebels on the road, but even rebels had to pick their battles.

As the bikes tore through the night and rumbled into the outskirts of Dogwood, KT, Fangl, and Sylvest exchanged hurried thoughts over the roaring engines.

"Herbert and Ruffa won't be far behind," KT muttered grimly. "We've got a small window of opportunity—maybe a couple of hours if we're lucky."

"Then we mustn't waste a single minute," Fangl said.

When the convoy pulled up to the familiar gates of Ruffa's compound, the bikers revved to a halt. Rocko threw a casual salute.

"End of the road, brothers and sisters. Hope you make it back without too much further aggro."

"Thanks, Rocko. You've done more than enough," said KT, his voice heavy with urgency.

They leapt off the bikes and sprinted toward the buildings. Herbert's lodge stood quiet, with a single light glowing inside. But otherwise, the structure lay in darkness.

Then Purrsteph's sharp eyes caught something. "There!" she pointed. A second building behind the lodge had some interior lights on.

The cats broke into a run.

As they approached, Fangl leant toward Sylvest. "Even if we get to them, how do we return to Purrville?"

Sylvest said nothing. He hadn't figured that part out.

"We'll take the Dogwood High bus," Tinki blurted, her voice catching with excitement.

"Good idea," Fangl replied. "But where's the key? And who knows how to drive it?"

"We'll deal with that after we get our mommies," said Sylvest.

They reached the lit building, panting. Mimi pressed her face to the window and gasped. "They're in here!"

The window creaked open, and Mrs Krusher peered out.

"Mimi! Oh, my little kitten! You're back!" Her eyes lit up. "How was it? Did you all do well? We were waiting for such exciting news!"

The other mommies crowded around the window, beaming and calling out affectionately to their children.

Mimi's face fell. "They're under Herbert's spell," she whispered. "They don't understand. They don't even know that they've been hypnotised."

"I'm hungry," one of the mommies said, glancing behind her. "Where's that Mikey? I wish he'd stop disappearing every morning. How am I supposed to get some breakfast?"

The cats slumped under the window.

"Please give us a moment," Purrsteph said gently, drawing the others to a quiet corner of the lodge.

They gathered.

"We need a workable plan," Tinki said. "Anything. I don't care how crazy."

"Just give up," Sylvest sighed. "They'll let us go, eventually. The show's over. We didn't win. It's finished."

"No way," said Doubler, eyes narrowing. "Since when did you become a wimp, Sylvest? You used to believe in yourself. In us."

Sylvest looked away.

"I think he's just exhausted," KT said. "We all are. But we can't stay here. We need to do something."

"We've got to take swift action," Fangl insisted. "We need a good idea."

A heavy silence settled.

The night air was still. The lights flickered from the windows. Somewhere inside, a mommy laughed.

"I've a silly idea."

All heads turned.

"You may not like this," she said, her voice low. "But it might be the only way."

There was a momentary lapse in their conversation. The Cool Cats glanced at one another, hoping this might offer them hope. No one wanted to admit defeat.

That was when Kreamy had a flash of inspiration.

"Maybe," she said slowly, "we can get hold of the ice-cream float."

The others turned to her.

"You know," she continued, "Ruffa's stupid ice-cream van. It must be around here somewhere. We could use it to take the mommies away. If we dress it up right, they'll think it's part of one of Ruffa's half-baked plans."

"YES! That could work, maybe," Doubler exclaimed. "Escaping in Ruffa's ice-cream van—how poetic! And the mommies might fall for it. Besides," he added with a disgusted sniff, "you won't catch me riding the stink-wagon that is the Dogwood school bus. That thing hasn't been cleaned since the day it was made."

Fangl suddenly perked up. "I think I know how to sell this to them. Follow me."

The kittens nodded and followed Fangl back toward the building.

Fangl took a breath and addressed the mommies at the window with a newfound flair. "Mrs Krusher, we've come to collect you for tomorrow's big performance. But not quite yet—we need to finalise your transport first."

He dropped his voice to a reassuring tone. "In the meantime, Ruffa has instructed us to ensure you freshen up for the big occasion. You'll be our front-row cheerleaders tomorrow, and we want you looking your radiant best!"

The mommies looked at each other in surprise. Mrs Krusher peered deeply into Fangl's eyes—so deeply that Fangl thought he saw a whole glittering galaxy spinning inside her pupils.

"Did Ruffa and Herbert send you to pick us up?" she asked, her voice floating with wonder.

Kreamy stepped in smoothly. "It was always the plan. The bus was too full earlier, so Ruffa sent us back to get you."

"How'd you get here without your transport?" Mrs Krusher asked.

"We hitched a ride," Kreamy replied. "A croc heading to Swamptown gave us a ride in his pickup."

Mrs Krusher gasped. "My poor kittens! Cramped in a pickup truck just to come back for us! Oh, I must thank Ruffa. He's such a thoughtful leader."

The kittens tried not to gag at the compliment, visibly

"So, we're leaving when the sun comes up?" Gilda asked, squinting. "With all of us? And no big bus?"

"The school bus is still being repaired in Birdheights," Doubler said, "but don't worry. The ice-cream van is more than roomy enough. I've done the math. It's . . . surprisingly spacious. Once we shift some of the ice-cream machinery."

The Eight Cool Cats nodded with the widest, most innocent grins they could muster.

Now, the mommies might have seen through the paper-thin logic on a regular day without hypnotic brain fog swirling around their heads. But not tonight. They were quickly on board and had no cause for concern.

"Oh, I'm SO excited!" one mommy squealed. "We'll see the performance and watch our darlings win the glorious Superband Competition!"

The mommies burst into gleeful clapping, swinging their heads like excited puppies.

Kreamy decided to seal the deal. "So go freshen up, and we'll bring the ice-cream van round in just a few minutes, alright?"

The mommies all grinned and nodded. Then Mrs Krusher closed the curtains, and excited chatter and rustling outfits began behind the glass.

The Cool Cats exhaled in relief.

"Alright," said KT, "now all we need to do is find that ridiculous van and figure out how to drive it."

"Piece of cake," said Sylvest. "All we need now is a miracle."

"I think I know where the ice-cream van is," Kreamy muttered, glancing over her shoulder like she half-expected someone to be eavesdropping. "I saw it parked the other day, near the old barn. They never used it for our trip to Birdheights, so it's probably still there."

"Show us," said KT, his tone firm.

Within minutes, KT and Kreamy were prying open a large barn door. It creaked as it swung outward. Inside was Ruffa's gloriously tacky ice-cream float, decked out in faded pastel colours and topped with a melted plastic cherry.

A rusty hook holding a single key was hanging right beside the doorframe, as if placed by fate itself.

"Seriously?" KT scoffed, grabbing it. "Not even locked. They didn't think anyone would be dumb—or desperate— enough to steal it."

They all stood silently around the van, blinking at it with mixed feelings. Could it possibly hold all eight of them, all their mommies? It looked unlikely.

KT hopped into the driver's seat and turned the key. The engine coughed twice, then roared to life with surprising gusto. "Okay, here we go. Let's do this!"

Kreamy leapt inside and opened the sliding door. "Uhhh . . . yeah. It's going to be a tight squeeze."

Still, there was no choice. They began hauling out half-empty crates, ice-cream tubs, stale cones, and a forgotten novelty horn shaped like a banana. After about twenty minutes of rearranging, stacking, and some mild arguing, they made as much space as possible.

Half an hour later, the float stopped outside the mommies' building. The mommies piled into the back one by one, cooing excitedly, oblivious that this was a full-blown prison break.

KT, Fangl, and Kreamy took the front seats. Fangl twisted around to check on the situation in the back. It was, in a word, chaos. Mommies on laps, fur in faces, tails in mouths—but everyone was grinning.

"They believe they're headed to the final," he whispered. "This looks like it's actually working."

To boost morale, Kreamy fired up the float's ice-cream machine. She'd filled it with milk earlier, and the refrigerated ingredients were now wonderfully chilled. Soon, cones were being passed around the back, sticky paws gleefully grabbing two, sometimes three at a time. The air was thick with the sweet smell of vanilla.

Even Kreamy helped herself to a cone. She gave a little sigh. Ruffa should've stuck with this, she thought. He'd have been a legend.

The van trundled out of the compound and soon passed the Dogwood sign at the town's edge. KT was laser-focused on the road. Not a single car in sight. The streets were still dead. It was all going too well.

Too well.

Then came the flashing blue lights in the mirror.

"Awww, no . . ." KT muttered. "Not now."

Behind them, a police cruiser rolled up, lights spinning but sirens off.

KT had no choice. He eased the float to a stop and cut the engine.

"Everyone stays quiet," Kreamy warned, quickly brushing stray cone crumbs off her dress.

The officer stepped out of the cruiser and walked toward the float, flashlight in hand. His name was Harold, a sleepy-eyed beagle with a limp and a reputation for being extremely by-the-book.

He approached the driver's window, blinding KT with his beam. KT shielded his face.

"Oh, sorry there, son," Harold said, flicking off the light. "Didn't mean to roast your eyeballs."

KT forced a polite smile and slowly rolled down the window.

"Evening," Harold said. "Nice night for an ice-cream run. Mind telling me what's going on in there?"

Behind him, the police cruiser's lights kept spinning. The Cool Cats held their breath.

Was their getaway foiled?

"What are you all doing out here so early in the morning?" Harold asked. His voice wasn't stern—just mildly baffled. "Are you heading back to Purrville? This road's usually empty until later in the day. Early start? It's not safe."

"I'm truly sorry, sir," Fangl replied with earnest politeness. "Ruffa's asked us to cover his morning ice-cream deliveries. He's . . . unwell and, uh, been detained in Birdheights."

Harold leant in through the driver's window, not bothering with the flashlight this time. He squinted at the van's interior, his nose twitching. His eyes widened when he spotted a van packed with kittens and mommies, all sitting quietly, blinking back at him with expressions like startled deer.

"I see," Harold said slowly. "Didn't know Ruffa had . . . friends. That's news to me. Herbert, there's that croc, but he's more of a hired claw than a friend."

"Well, you're not wrong," KT added. "It's a . . . business arrangement. We help him out now and then. He gives us the occasional feline treat."

Harold's brow furrowed. Something about this didn't add up. The kittens looked cagey. The mommies looked glazed. And everyone smelled faintly of fresh soft serve.

Then Mrs Krusher piped up with glee: "We're on our way to Birdheights to watch our children in the Superband Competition! It's all so exciting!"

Harold blinked. "You are, dear? But—"

"We're making a stop first," KT interrupted quickly. "Back home to collect our things. It's been tough lately, and the judges want us for a recall."

Harold was still trying to piece things together. Just as he was about to turn his flashlight back on, Mrs Krusher chirped, "Our kittens are going to win! Can you believe it, sir? Us and the Dogwood Droopster! Working in unison. The dream team has been created."

Harold scratched his chin. "Funny. I thought the Dogwood Droopsters were at the show. Didn't realise the Eight Cool Cats were involved in some way."

"They are, they are!" Mrs Krusher gushed. "It's so exciting!"

"Uh-huh . . ." Harold muttered.

"We're helping in the background," Mimi interjected, waving her paw theatrically. "Stage crew. Cheer squad. Artistic morale boosters. It's all very . . . collaborative. Ta-dah!"

Harold managed a half-smile. "Show business sure is a strange business." He took a step back from the window. "Look, I get it—kind of. But you really shouldn't be on these roads so late. I try to patrol the area to keep it safe, but I can't be everywhere. If someone breaks down or runs into trouble . . ."

He trailed off, still puzzled, when another thought struck him.

"I heard the Purrville school bus has gone missing. The mayor and chief of police are in a right flap about it. Do any of you know anything about that?"

KT, Kreamy, and Fangl shook their heads too fast. Behind them, the rest of the van went still, as if holding its breath.

Just then, a loud rustling came from the woods. Harold spun around and shone his light toward the trees. Something significant and swift had just darted across the clearing.

"Oh, my whiskers," KT whispered. "Was that a nasty grog?"

"Absolute nonsense, youngster," Harold muttered though his voice lacked conviction. "Those creatures don't exist—just forest stories. But either way, you'd best move along. No sense lingering around this patch of woods tonight. Go on—get to where you're going. I'll check this out."

Harold turned and immediately swept his flashlight across the trees, visibly uneasy.

KT didn't need telling twice. He fired up the engine and pulled the float back onto the road.

"What was that?" Tinki asked once they were moving again.

"Could've been a grog," Fangl said, eyes still fixed on the dark tree line. "I believe they do exist. This land is so strange."

"Just the wind," KT muttered. "And maybe a trick of the starlight. I had the high beams on for a moment—probably startled a deer."

"Let's not dwell on it," Sylvest said. "Chief Harold will spend the next hour hunting imaginary grogs and eventually go home for his cocoa. Meanwhile, we'll be home. Safely."

Behind them, Mrs Krusher still looked dreamy. "So tomorrow we're off to Birdheights, right? We'll see you perform?"

"All in good time, dear Mrs Krusher," Fangl said gently. "Just a little rest first. You'll see Birdheights soon enough."

An hour and a half later, the ice-cream float rolled quietly into Purrville. The van eased down sleepy streets, parking discreetly near KT's house, half-hidden beneath a row of trees.

One by one, the mommies were returned home with their children, all still enchanted by the fantasy that they'd be watching their beloved band perform again in the morning.

The Eight Cool Cats, however, knew otherwise.

They had made it home. But the story wasn't over yet.

Not by a long shot.

CHAPTER 27

Back . . . Finally

Smackie exited the bus and stepped onto the dusty gravel, blinking at the morning light. Her ears twitched as she took in the conversation. She looked from Harold to Ruffa to Herbert—her expression unreadable but her posture tense.

"Good morning, Officer Harold," she said, her voice as neutral as a politician's pawshake. "Is everything alright out here?"

"That depends," Harold replied, narrowing his eyes slightly. "Were you aware that your band managers sent a van full of kittens and their mothers back to Purrville in the middle of the night?"

"I wasn't," Smackie replied evenly, though her tail twitched with restrained irritation. "I can't say I'm surprised, though. They've been invaluable."

Ruffa cleared his throat. "We had to delegate urgent tasks, you see. Band logistics. Very normal in the industry."

"Oh yes, very normal," Herbert echoed, nodding eagerly. "Milk. Mommies. Music. It all goes together when you're . . . professional."

Harold raised an eyebrow. "Your tour bus went missing. Your ice-cream float went missing. Now your guests—who I understand were not fully themselves—have also disappeared. And no one thinks this is even a tiny bit odd?"

"It's a bit unusual, I'll grant you that," Ruffa admitted, adjusting his scarf and trying not to sweat. "But certainly not something criminal."

Just then, Rommy appeared at the top of the stairs inside the bus and called down, "Is it true the ice-cream van's gone?"

Harold looked up. "Yes. Driven off in the early hours, it would seem. With a cargo full of mommies."

Rommy whistled and turned to Sniffer, who joined her at the stairwell. "Well, that's that. Guess we're not going back to Birdheights."

"Maybe not," Sniffer muttered. "But I wouldn't mind seeing someone finally get Ruffa's tail in a knot."

Smackie turned to Harold. "Look, officer, we've had enough of this whole charade. The kittens weren't here of their own free will. Those mommies weren't either. Everyone's been manipulated and lied to. Hypnotised. It's all been smoke and mirrors from the start. You should investigate this mess."

"That's a serious claim," Harold said, his voice quieter now. "Do you have any proof of that?"

"Only what we've seen and lived through. The cats came back to rescue their mommies. That's all you need to know."

Herbert's eyes bulged. "She's starting a smear campaign! A slanderous ploy orchestrated by our jealous underlings!"

Harold held up a paw. "Enough."

He turned back to Ruffa, now visibly sweating beneath his shaggy fur coat.

"I will need a full account of where the ice-cream van went and under whose orders. And I'll be filing a report with the mayor of Dogwood—and possibly the mayor of Purrville too. There's something not quite right here."

"I can get you all the paperwork you want!" Ruffa said hastily. "A receipt! A waiver! We have . . . plenty of administrative documentation!"

"I'm sure you do," Harold replied dryly. "I'll be back tomorrow morning to get to the bottom of this. You'd better hope that van returns by then, and that every one of those mommies is safe, fed, and fully alert. We need to be kind to one another. Cats are our friends. We are theirs."

With that, Harold turned, stepped back into his pickup, and rumbled down the dirt track, his headlights still faintly glowing despite the rising sun.

Smackie stared after him, then turned to Ruffa and Herbert.

"You two are finished," she said. "Whether you know it yet or not. He knows the truth now."

And with that, she turned and walked back up the bus steps, her head held high.

Ruffa and Herbert stood silently in the dust, blinking.

Michelangelo slowly backed away behind a fence post, pretending to be invisible.

The Droopsters were falling apart. And the only ones not yet in full retreat were the ones who still believed they could bluff their way to victory no matter what.

But even they were starting to see the cracks taking shape.

***

Upstairs, Smackie had been nudged back onto the tour bus steps by Herbert, who behaved like a pushy bouncer at a shady nightclub.

"Keep your claws off me, Herbert," she snapped, shaking herself free. "You're such a mean bully. You know that?"

"Am I?" Herbert hissed through gritted teeth. "Well, I think you'll be safer up there until we've re-entered the compound."

"You mean until you've figured out the latest lie you plan to tell."

Herbert didn't reply. He just went back down the stairs and muttered something inaudible that sounded like "ungrateful talent."

Back upstairs, Moss was quick to bring Smackie up to speed. He told her about his biker friend Rocko, the getaway, and how, judging from the chaos below, the Eight Cool Cats had pulled off the impossible and taken their mommies home.

The other dogs on the bus blinked in disbelief.

"No way they actually pulled it off," said Sniffer. "With the ice-cream float? That thing's a rolling fridge. They must all be shivering."

"Looks like they did it," Moss replied, grinning. "And Herbert didn't even realise until Harold started poking around here."

Meanwhile, Ruffa was driving in silence, his grip on the wheel so tight that his knuckles were going pale beneath the fur. He was itching to speak about cowardly kittens running home to mommy, but he decided now wasn't the time to say anything. First, he had to fix things back to the way they were.

Back at the compound, Ruffa retired to his office alone. He sat on the edge of his velvet chaise lounge—the one he'd bought on store credit, believing it was only a matter of days until stardom. Now, in the silence, he stared at the wall and muttered bitterly.

"Life is unfair to me. Again. Always me."

He sniffed. "No matter how hard I try to do it right, I get swindled. And if I try to cheat like everyone else, they cheat me even more. I can't win."

Then he sobbed into his tail.

In the next room, Herbert was hunched over the accounts ledger like a gambler trying to convince himself he still had chips left.

He opened his purse for the seventh time, hoping the coins would magically reappear. Nothing. He sniffed and slammed the purse down. Tears began to stream down his cheeks—massive crocodile tears that landed on the ledger in gloppy puddles and smeared the ink.

Their dream of musical domination, fame and fortune, headlines, and screaming fans was all evaporating—all that scheming, all those "creative adjustments"—gone. What remained was a broken bus, a stolen float, zero credits, and a band on the edge of an all-out revolt.

But Herbert, ever the rationaliser, thought, *People will say we lied. We manipulated kittens and hypnotised their mothers. But they don't understand. We were innovators. Disruptors. Pioneers of performance. Geniuses.*

You had to cut corners to get ahead. Right?

Still, deep down—even Herbert couldn't escape one sobering truth:

The curtain was falling.

This act was over.

CHAPTER 28

Winners or Losers

The following day in Birdheights, the announcement was made: the three tigers had won the Superband Competition. Nothing more was said about the Dogwood Droopsters, who had finished a valiant second. They had given their all, made sacrifices, and performed with heart, but like so many, they came close yet walked away with nothing. And as often happens, the winner takes it all, while the runner-up fades into memory.

Strangely, no one mentioned the mysterious photograph taken by Snoop, the wandering freelance photographer. As far as anyone knew, Snoop was still hustling for a big break, dreaming of his photo making the front page.

But there was more to it.

Snoop had heard whispers—strange goings-on with the Dogwood Droopsters. Word on the street was that they'd been double-crossed, and Snoop had unwittingly been part of it. He wasn't there by coincidence; he'd been allowed in, placed in the right spot, and used as a pawn to serve powerful interests in Birdheights.

And one of those powerful interests was Kildare, the imposing tiger patriarch, who had rigged the outcome of the competition so that his son could win on his first attempt. But now, Kildare was having second thoughts. He'd overplayed his paw. Even the judges were annoyed because the Droopsters deserved to win and had been pushed back to second place.

On top of that, strange rumours were swirling around Birdheights about Ruffa and his band. Something wasn't adding up. So, Kildare summoned Lizzalee, the seasoned show manager, and pressed her for details. She'd seen it all, and knowing she could land herself in trouble if she lied, she told the truth—at least the parts she could confirm. Kildare listened attentively. It didn't take long for him to piece it together: Birdheights had been outfoxed by Ruffa.

But Lizzalee hadn't told everything. She'd also tipped off Snoop, letting him photograph the performance from a restricted vantage point. That photograph ended up in the hands of Brawl, editor of the *Dogwood Times*, whom Kildare quickly paid off. The photo vanished. One of Kildare's messenger birds literally flew it and delivered it directly to him.

With the competition concluded and his son set to retire from music and begin his proper business career, Kildare found himself free of any significant conflict of interest. He now had a new plan—a bigger one.

Despite their humiliating loss and his creditless return to the compound, Ruffa wasn't about to be a total loser. Kildare arrived at the compound with a lucrative proposition out of the blue a few weeks later. He wanted to form a strategic partnership between his business empire and Ruffa's newly infamous band, the Dogwood Droopsters, who had shown incredible potential even to make it to second place.

Kildare had plans for the following year's Superband Competition. It would be grander, glitzier, and far more lucrative, sponsored, televised, and monetised. He wanted the Dogwood Droopsters to train hard, purrfect their craft, and return to the stage to win and dominate. And then? A national tour. With the tigers—now semi-retired—as their opening act.

There was just one minor hiccup: Kildare didn't know the true identities of the band. Not until he saw the photograph of Kreamy that Snoop had taken.

Suddenly, it all clicked into place.

The Droopsters were something special. Different. Talented in a way that couldn't be bred from one species. They also had something the tigers didn't: heart.

Even though Herbert had stopped talking to Ruffa and threatened to leave for Birdheights permanently, Ruffa remained undeterred. With Kildare backing him, Ruffa believed anything was possible. All he needed now was a new plan.

But one unexpected twist unsettled him.

During his visit to the compound, Kildare had taken a liking to the food—and to Mikey Angels, Ruffa's quiet but competent chef. Kildare had known Mikey for years, albeit silently, and now decided to recruit him formally into his business. Mikey would cook, but more importantly, he'd serve as Kildare's eyes and ears.

Ruffa didn't love the idea of Mikey's defection, but he swallowed his pride. With so much promise on the horizon, he could afford to lose a chef.

And to keep things smooth, Kildare also made Herbert an offer he just couldn't refuse. Herbert stayed at the compound, tasked with developing the Droopsters' talents. Though he and Ruffa now barely tolerated each other, they agreed—for the time being—to coexist peacefully.

Because one thing was sure: the Dogwood Droopsters were not done.

CHAPTER 29

Night Bird Said

Word spread quickly through Purrville that something peculiar had happened involving the Eight Cool Cats—and, more bizarrely still, they had somehow been involved in the Dogwood Droopsters' Superband audition. Rumour had it that the dogs had asked for their help. Willingly.

This unsettled many of the good citizens of Purrville, none more so than Professor Fishtail. In a determined academic huff, he personally visited every mommy and kitten, wagging a paw and giving them all a thorough telling-off.

The school bus eventually reappeared, but it had been mysteriously painted entirely white, with no markings to show it had ever belonged to the school. A complete repaint was necessary and expensive, and the school's budget was already stretched to the breaking point.

Police Chief Kitty Smallpaws was relieved that everyone was safe, but she had a lingering sense that no one was being entirely honest with her. She questioned the mommies one by one, received vague, smiley responses, and finally gave up, filing the incident away in a thick, baffling report that she slipped into the "Unusual" drawer of her filing cabinet. She closed it with a sigh and a shrug.

No one had been hurt, and the bus still worked. That was something.

As for the repainting costs, a minor miracle occurred: Mrs Krusher—Mimi's mother—offered to pay for the whole thing herself. This unexpected generosity calmed Professor Fishtail down just enough for him to retreat to his classroom.

Life gradually returned to normal. The Eight Cool Cats returned to school and talked about how the competition had died down, and attention shifted toward the next big event: the school's annual nursery rhyme performance.

It took time for the Eight Cool Cats to process what had happened properly. For some, it felt like a blurry dream. For others, a full-blown nightmare. But their mommies were back to their usual selves—fully de-hypnotised, well-rested, and making breakfast again. Slowly, the kittens began to sing again and think ahead to lighting up Purrville with their next melodic nursery rhyme show.

They didn't expect to hear from the Dogwood Droopsters ever again. So, when Moss unexpectedly showed up in Purrville, they were surprised.

The Cool Cats were hanging out at Wimplebuns, eating Tracker's delicious plant burgers, when Moss appeared at the door with a grin and a handful of glittery invitations.

He went straight over and launched into a speech about the legendary underground music venue called The Diggout in the heart of Birdheights. "The Droopsters are on next week!" he boasted, inviting them each. "It'll be the first show following . . . all that happened."

The cats looked unsure of how to react.

"You'll come check us out, right?" Moss asked, with a glint in his eye.

"NO. No way!" Kreamy cried out. "I'm never going back to that city again! I don't like it one bit."

Everyone chuckled.

"Come on," said Moss, smiling. "It wasn't that bad."

"It was also everything else that happened," Kreamy muttered. "Try being crammed into an ice-cream van with your own hypnotised mommy and then smuggled out like a criminal."

Doubler raised a paw. "Uh . . . logistics? I doubt we can borrow the school bus again. Professor Fishtail keeps the key on a chain around his neck now. Rumour has it he sleeps with one eye open every night."

Moss waved the concern away. "Rocko and the Choppy Chomps will pick you up. They'll take you there, you'll crash at their place outside Birdheights for a few days, and then they'll bring you back safe and sound. Easy."

That got their attention. Biker travel? With Rocko? Suddenly, everyone was curious about this new adventure.

***

The sun was shining when the Choppy Chomps rolled into Purrville. The Eight Cool Cats climbed aboard the bikes with wide grins and sparkling eyes, the wind lifting their whiskers as they zoomed down the hills toward Birdheights. They passed the old bridge where they'd been stranded not long ago—this time flying over it like champions on wheels.

They liked the idea of visiting Rocko's hangout as it was a magnificent ranch house amid acres of farmland. The fields stretched out in every direction as far as the eye could see. The Choppy Chomps weren't merely bikers—they were also skilled farmers.

Rocko's crew supplied fresh produce to Birdheights and nearby towns, and their business thrived. The ranch sat just half an hour south of the city, with a handy bus stop outside the main gate. From there, a regular shuttle ran back and forth to Birdheights.

The Cool Cats liked it there.

"Rocko grows many different fruits," whispered KT. "I can get used to this."

They spent that afternoon relaxing in hammocks, sipping juice straight from coconuts, and watching bees drift lazily across the fields. Tomorrow they'd be in Birdheights.

The sun set over Rocko's ranch with a golden glow.

And for the first time in a while, everything felt cool again.

That evening, The Diggout was humming with energy, packed from wall to wall with music lovers and soda-poppers alike. The Eight Cool Cats stood near the back, thrilled to see the four original Dogwood Droopsters jamming joyfully on stage. Rommy gave them a cheeky wink mid-song while Moss, grinning widely behind his drum kit, pointed his sticks right at them between beats.

Rocko and his biker crew were in full swing too, knocking back bottle after bottle of fizzy soda pop as if determined to drink The Diggout dry.

The set ended with a roar of applause. Even though the Droopsters didn't sound quite as tight as they had during the Birdheights competition—when they'd unknowingly been playing with the Eight Cool Cats in disguise—they were still far better than in the old days when they were just four dogs lacking inspiration.

And best of all? There was no Ruffa. No Herbert. The band was flying solo.

Well, almost. Mikey Angels was there, quiet in the corner, sipping ginger soda with a watchful eye on everything.

Smackie stepped up to the microphone as the crowd settled again and cleared her throat.

"Good evening, gentlefolk," she said warmly. "Hope you're having a great time in one of my favourite places. We have a little surprise for you tonight: dogs, cats, birds, and all kinds of Animalians."

That got the crowd murmuring. A few whistles echoed, birds chirped excitedly, and two unfamiliar tigers chuckled to themselves somewhere near the bar—but mostly kept quiet.

Out of nowhere, a powerful presence strode onto the stage: Kildare, the business tycoon tiger himself. His arrival caused a stir. Every animal in the room knew him, even if only by reputation.

He stood centre stage, flanked by two apes hauling extra instruments and placing them neatly on upturned chairs. Additional microphones were arranged with mechanical precision.

Kildare raised a paw, commanding silence. "Tonight," he announced, "we don't just present the Dogwood Droopsters. Nor shall I allude to the mysterious band that once performed in disguise. Hearing is believing."

He paused, scanning the room.

"No," he said. "Tonight, we unveil something brand new. A band formed from one of the most remarkable musical collaborations ever seen in this land. Eight of the most remarkable Animalians. Straight out of Purrville. Talented, brave, and—for those in the know—already legendary."

The Eight Cool Cats exchanged wide-eyed glances.

Then Kildare made it official.

"Friends and creatures of The Diggout, I give you . . . The Woof Purrs!"

The crowd exploded. Cheers, howls, and whistles filled the air as Kildare approached the cats. "Let's welcome to the stage: Fangl! Sylvest! Mimi! Purrsteph! KT! Doubler! Kreamy! And Tinki!"

With mouths still open in disbelief, the Eight Cool Cats slowly rose from their table.

"Did he just say we were going on—" KT began.

"He did," Fangl confirmed, stunned.

They stepped onto the stage, greeted warmly by Smackie, Rommy, Sniffer, and Moss, who nodded with pride and pointed them to their places.

The lights dimmed slightly. The Diggout fell silent.

Even the two sniggering tigers had stopped. One of them, in fact, was Kildare's son, who wisely said nothing. His father's eyes were sharp, and he was watching them too.

Then, the beat began.

Moss set the tempo with a rhythmic tap, and one by one, the band joined in.

Rommy and Doubler took centre mic for vocals. Guitars twanged from Tinki and Rommy, with Sylvest and Sniffer grooving on bass. Mimi played a swooning violin. Kreamy joined in with her sweet, crisp flute. Smackie blew a bold trumpet line. Fangl stood tall with his dazzling double-neck guitar, and KT, beside Purrsteph with her shimmering cymbals, completed the layered percussion.

It was no ordinary band. It was a symphony.

The music swelled and surged. Rhythms soared, harmonies danced, and the crowd—at first frozen in awe—began to sway, then shuffle, then leap up and down to the music. Some could even flap their wings and hover.

A dancing fever took hold.

The Woof Purrs had arrived.

Kildare stood to the side, snapping claws to the rhythm, his striped shoulders bouncing joyfully. "Magnificent," he muttered, barely able to contain his pride.

Even Mikey Angels was seen hopping with excitement behind his corner soda pop. He raised his glass quietly to the stage.

It was a moment none of them were likely to forget.

And this was only the beginning.

Tucked away in a shadowy corner near the speaker stack, a tiny hummingbird hovered in place, her wings a faint blur against the warm light. Milly Tweety was scribbling furiously in a spiral-bound pad, humming softly to the beat and muttering to herself as the Woof Purrs played their hearts out on stage.

"Incredible," she whispered. "The real winners of the Superband Competition revealed at last. You'll never believe it! By your faithful field reporter, Milly Tweety . . ."

She grinned. The headline had already formed in her mind. She could practically see the print running hot off the presses. This was the one—her breakout story. Her legacy.

"What are you scribbling in your notepad?" asked a voice nearby.

She turned to see a tall, lanky brown bear with absurdly thick yellow glasses and the most vacant, drowsy eyes she'd ever seen.

"Oh, you'll find out soon enough, big guy," she said with a gleam in her eye. "It's something monumental! You were here for it—the night the land changed its tune, and a new age of music was born!"

The bear blinked slowly and turned back towards the stage, unsure what to make of her excitement.

Milly, meanwhile, was hardly able to contain herself. Her feathers fluffed with anticipation. In her jacket pocket was the photograph—Snoop's mysterious competition shot. It was gold. She had the proof. She had the words. She had the scoop of the decade.

But just as she reached down to scribble another explosive line, a figure appeared beside her.

Mikey Angels.

The crocodile stood silently for a beat, his wide eyes half-lidded and inscrutable. Then, with one claw, he gently shook his head. And with the other, he wagged a long finger, disapproving, ominous.

Before Milly could protest, Mikey moved like lightning. He plucked the notebook from her grasp and reached into her jacket with surprising precision, retrieving the photograph as if he'd known exactly where it was hidden.

Milly gasped, wings fluttering in protest—but then froze. She remembered where she was. This wasn't some back-of-the-building press room. This was The Diggout, filled with powerful Animalians, not all of whom respected the rule of the written word and her line of work.

She clenched her beak, swallowed her scream, and shrank into a quiet sulk. How dare that crocodile snatch her story, her moment, her destiny!

But deep inside, she knew there were forces in this room far bigger than bylines and exclusives. The rules had changed; she would not be silenced.

Mikey, stone-faced, turned and made his way across the club to the biker table. He leant over to Rocko and whispered, "I've got to talk to you. Now. We good?"

Rocko, unsure what this was about, but reading the seriousness in Mikey's eyes, nodded. They slipped out the side door into the back alley.

Under a dim flickering bulb, Mikey handed Rocko the photograph and the crumpled notepad.

"I just took this off that nosy little reporter over there," he said flatly. "If this gets printed, it'll ruin the show. The whole competition might fall apart. No more Superband. No more next year. Done."

Rocko examined the items in his paw, then looked back at Mikey.

"I'm giving this to you," Mikey continued. "Because even though I'm not exactly anyone's favourite croc, I still have a conscience. I'm not giving it to Ruffa. I'm not giving it to Herbert. They wouldn't know what to do with it, anyway. They always take things too far. They don't like to share."

He leant in, narrowing his gaze.

"This is now your problem."

With that, Mikey turned and walked off into the shadows, disappearing around the corner and leaving Rocko standing alone in the alley with the truth of the Superband Competition clutched in his paws.

For a long moment, Rocko stood still, the sounds of the club pulsing faintly behind him—music, laughter, stomping feet.

Inside, the Woof Purrs were playing their finest set yet.

He didn't know what to do with the photograph or the notes. Not yet.

But he knew one thing: he would let the music play on tonight.

And tomorrow perhaps as well.

CHAPTER 30

Big Reset

Later that evening, they all gathered at Rocko's ranch for a nightcap of milk—and something a bit stronger. The cats were more than content with the milk, but the dogs, particularly Rocko and his biker crew, preferred their drinks with a serious bite.

The mood was light enough—until Rocko casually produced the photograph and the scribbled notes for all to see.

Kreamy took one look and nearly spat out her drink. "Ack!" she shrieked. "That's me! That's when we . . . I mean—look at my face! I look so guilty!"

"Easy now," said PurrSteph, gently patting her back. "It's not like anyone's going to publish that thing. We've got the evidence, not them."

She nodded at the photo. "And even if Snoop wanted to run it, the powers that be in Birdheights would never let it see the light of day. They'd rather let the whole story vanish than risk the Superband Competition being exposed as a sham."

"That's right," Rocko agreed. "No one crosses Boreme Kildare. The editor of the *Dogwood Times* wouldn't dare go against him."

"Well," Doubler said suddenly, "what if we did?"

All heads turned.

"What are you saying?" Smackie asked, eyes narrowing.

"What if we published the truth directly?" Doubler said. "Let everyone know what happened. Purrville has its own little newspaper. We could take it there. Kildare might run Birdheights, but in Purrville, he's not so important."

"I wouldn't be so sure," said Smackie, folding her arms. "Messing with someone like Kildare could land all of us in serious trouble. He's got claws that reach far and deep."

Rocko nodded gravely. "Still. What you did—what we all did—it was real. That photograph proves it. You played your hearts out, and you deserve to be proud."

"I still don't get why Mikey gave it to us instead of to Ruffa or Kildare," Sylvest said.

"I do," Moss replied. "Because Ruffa and Herbert would only mess things up. They'd use it as leverage to suit their needs. Try to blackmail Kildare or cause some big stink. Mikey knew they'd ruin it no matter what—and maybe get themselves fried in the process."

A heavy pause settled over the group.

"There's nothing we can do with it," said Tinki. "We just have to accept that. Life's not always fair for the little Animalians. Some things aren't meant to be."

And just then, from the shadows, a voice muttered: "Some things aren't meant to be—but maybe some things are still possible."

They all jumped.

Out of the dark stepped Ruffa—ragged, smudged, and unmistakably Ruffa. A stubby cigar stuck out from the corner of his mouth, puffing a faint trail of smoke. He scanned the room with glassy eyes and a sly smile.

"Ruffa?" Rocko stood up sharply. "How did you get inside here?"

"Easy, brother. Don't get your hackles up," Ruffa said, holding his paws. "I'm not here to fight anyone. I sent Mikey the photo to give to you. He came back and told me he had. So, I followed you. Slipped in behind—very sloppy security. I just wanted to see how it was going."

"I don't believe you," KT snapped.

"You expect us to think you're on our side?" Sylvest added.

Ruffa sighed and took the cigar from his mouth.

"No," he admitted. "I'm not on your side. I'm on my side, like everyone else. But you know what? We've all been cheated by the big tiger in this room. That puts us—at least for now—on the same side."

There was silence. The cats exchanged uneasy looks.

"This crazy band thing is done," Tinki muttered. "Whatever it was . . . It's over. We'll never be a real band. Tonight was just a dream."

The room went silent. Even Ruffa looked lost in thought, scratching at his scruffy ears, the fire in his eyes dimmer than usual.

Maybe Tinki was right. Perhaps the experiment—the dream of a fusion band—had run its course. Maybe its number was up.

But maybe, just maybe, not quite yet.

Ruffa puffed once more on his stubby cigar before letting it droop from his mouth.

"What you say has truth to it," he admitted, his voice quieter now. "There's nothing we can do about our present situation. This time, we're beaten by the powers that be. But there's always next year, and the year after that. I can improve the costumes, train you better than I did before, and we can fool them again. We might've made it this time; we were close."

"Stop it!" Fangl burst out, his voice slicing through the air. "Just stop, Ruffa. You can't wait for things to happen magically. You can't keep lying to everyone. Taking us all for fools."

"I think I missed something," Sniffer said, blinking. "I thought we were no longer talking to each other. Especially with him."

"You're right, brother cat," Moss said. "Except, there's no such thing as winning or losing in the big scheme of things. That's just someone else's scoreboard. Believing you've lost means you've agreed to their game, rules, and terms. And if you cheat to win, you're still playing their game. Either way, they've got you."

He paused, the room now wrapped in his rhythm.

"But no rule is sacred. Nothing is set in stone. Every rule was made by someone no smarter than any one of us. The truth is, we don't have to follow any of them blindly. It's time we made some of our own rules. And if we make them smart enough, others will follow us."

Ruffa slumped into the empty armchair in the room, suddenly thoughtful, chewing over the words in his mind. He stared into the flickering light of the hearth, haunted by a growing realisation: maybe all those rules weren't written with dogs like him in mind. Perhaps they never had been.

"Well then . . ." he said at last. "Why don't you artists show me a way? Because I can't think of anything. Their rules still trap us. Rules written by someone we'll never meet. We lost, and we'll keep losing."

At that moment, Mimi Krusher set down her empty milk glass, stood tall, and drew a long, proud breath. Her eyes gleamed with a spark more dazzling than anyone had seen in her before.

"Well then," she said, waving her arms like a conductor of ideas, "it's lucky I happen to have a bold and audacious idea—something fiendishly clever that might change the whole game."

Ruffa raised an eyebrow. "Is that right? Well, go on then, smarty pants. We're all ears and wagging tails."

Mimi took centre floor with feline flair. "It's simple," she began. Then she launched into an idea so outlandish, so gloriously eccentric, that every creature in the room leant in, eyes wide, jaws slack. Even Ruffa, of all dogs, stared at her with genuine awe.

When she finished, the room fell into stunned silence.

They glanced at each other individually, trying to gauge whether everyone else had heard the same thing. Had she just come up with a way?

Finally, Rocko broke the silence, tail wagging ever so slightly. "To be purrfectly honest . . . it could work like a charm."

And that was it.

No one spoke another word.

The Eight Cool Cats, the Droopsters, Rocko and his mellow crew of biker-farmers, and even Ruffa—the dog no one liked but somehow couldn't shake—each stood up and quietly padded off to bed.

Because this fight wasn't over.

Tomorrow was another day.

And tomorrow might belong to them—if fortune, for once, favoured the foolish, the fearless, the smaller Animalians who walked this land—the almost forgotten.

CHAPTER 31

The Fix

The very next day, things began to change—quietly, but unmistakably—from the moment they got up.

They ate their breakfast in near silence, the weight of Mimi's audacious idea still fresh in their minds. Without much fanfare, they packed up their things and went their separate ways: Rocko and his biker gang reclaimed their ranch, the Droopsters returned to Dogwood with Ruffa and Herbert in tow, and the Eight Cool Cats were dropped back home in Purrville.

However, though their paths split, one idea now connected them all: Mimi's plan.

It was strange, almost laughable at first, but the more they thought about it, the more it began to take root. It would need precision, patience, and preparation if it were going to work. There would be no slip-ups, no shortcuts, and it had to be perfectly executed and timed just right.

Back in Purrville, the Eight Cool Cats knew they'd eventually have to explain to Professor Fishtail why the school bus had mysteriously gone missing again. The story would have to be vague enough to avoid scrutiny, but that was a problem for later. Right now, there was only one thing to focus on: the plan.

Fortunately, Ruffa and Herbert had already made progress. They'd discovered that Professor Fishtail sometimes forgot to take the key home and left it in his desk. On one such occasion, they seized the opportunity. The school bus was quietly borrowed—again—and driven back to the compound for secret modifications.

Herbert, still not fully in the loop but back on speaking terms with Ruffa, was put in charge of the bus adjustments. Meanwhile, Ruffa spoke quietly with Mikey Angels, who met in secret with Snoop.

The result? Mikey returned with precious material—footage and photos from the Eight Cool Cats' final Birdheights performance. The visuals came from a fanatical music lover with their camcorder, and Snoop had paid handsomely to acquire it, no questions asked.

Crucially, Mikey still didn't know what the footage would be used for. That was by design. His conscience—or worse, his loyalties—might get in the way if he knew too much.

In truth, neither Mikey nor Herbert knew Mimi's masterstroke. And the fewer who knew, the better.

Over the following weeks, preparations quietly accelerated. The Eight Cool Cats returned to Dogwood thrice, sneaking into Ruffa's compound for long, secret rehearsals with the Droopsters. Something incredible was happening.

The sound was richer. The rhythm was tighter. The connection felt real.

This wasn't a chaotic collision of cats and dogs anymore—it was something else. Something whole. The Woof Purrs were becoming more than a gimmick. They were becoming a band.

At Ruffa's remote compound, no one was listening but them—and that was exactly how they wanted it.

The weeks flew by, and suddenly, the day was upon them. The moment they'd all been striving toward. The event that would offer them a stage bigger than any they'd stood on before.

On this day, something fundamental would change— not just for them, but for all Animalians who believed in music, difference, and truth.

The land was about to hear the Woof Purrs.

And this time . . . they could not be ignored.

CHAPTER 32

Birdheights Parade

The Eight Cool Cats and the Dogwood Droopsters had seen the posters plastered across Birdheights during their last visit but paid them little attention. After all, the annual Birdheights Carnival Parade was just another city spectacle—a loud, flashy event winding through the metropolis's main street from mid-afternoon into the night.

Every year, Animalians from all over the land would dress up in flamboyant costumes, roll out extravagant floats representing their village traditions, and join the procession, bringing joy, music, and a little mayhem to the capital.

But Purrville had opted out long ago. The cats of that tidy town considered the whole affair vulgar—too loud, too chaotic, and far too public for their refined cultural values. A handful of curious cats would quietly attend as spectators, but they never spoke of it back home. The Purrville Newspawper rarely mentioned the event—unless a cat had been robbed or mildly insulted. It simply wasn't their thing.

Until now.

Purrville would have an unofficial entry this year—a float with live music provided by a most unusual band. Bands were allowed; music was always part of the parade. However, the rules stated that bands had to represent their village's culture and sound. There were no prizes, no formal recognition—just the spectacle.

The Droopsters themselves hadn't taken part for years. Nine years earlier, they had been banned after rumbling down the main street in a loud float that was deemed a public menace. The authorities barred them for five years; since then, Dogwood hadn't bothered to send anyone again. No one wanted another ban.

Some floats were pushed by brute physical force. Others were motorised, creeping slowly down the road. The speed limit was strictly enforced: no float could exceed five miles per hour. Anything faster earned another five-year ban—and parade officials were known to time each float with near-military precision.

On a bright, cloudless morning, Herbert pulled up at Ruffa's compound in the tour bus—except it wasn't just a bus anymore. It had been gloriously transformed. Rebranded as The Woof Purrs, the open-top float was a monument to everything they were about to reveal.

The now-infamous image of Kreamy removing her mask during the Superband Competition was placed on either side of the bus. The very photograph Snoop had taken, and Mikey Angels had quietly retrieved. And that wasn't all—on the back of the bus, a massive screen now played the grainy footage of the crowd going wild during the Droopsters' legendary performance, which had nearly stolen the show.

Earlier that morning, Ruffa had personally collected the Eight Cool Cats in his milk float and brought them to the compound. When they saw the bus, they were speechless.

It was magnificent.

They stared at the resurrected school bus, their instruments slung over their shoulders. The four Dogwood Droopsters proudly admired their ride.

Herbert stepped down and gave a wave. "Welcome back, everyone. It's so good to see you. Today's the day! We're going down the main street of Birdheights, and this time, the parade won't know what to expect."

"Are we sure this is going to make any difference?" Kreamy asked, a little sceptical as she climbed aboard— then promptly froze.

Inside, the bus had been completely gutted and reimagined. It was stunning. Velvet seats, gleaming surfaces, flashing lights, and an impressive array of brand new audio equipment. It looked like a professional mobile stage. There wasn't a hint left of its school bus past.

"Wait until they see the inside," Herbert muttered to Ruffa with a grin.

"I cut no corners this time. The slush fund has worked wonders."

"I still can't believe you used your entire life savings," Ruffa said, half-impressed, half-panicked. "I'm broke. You're broke. We're both broke."

"What does it matter?" Herbert shrugged. "If you're going down, you go down in style. Might as well make it unforgettable."

The band climbed upstairs, and gasps followed one by one. Massive speakers. Guitars on hooks. Glittering drums. A small lighting rig. It was a dream stage on wheels.

"It'd be wrong to change it back," Doubler sighed.

"Who said we were changing it back?" Sylvest said with a grin. "We keep it. Think of the possibilities."

"Yup. We're going for broke," Mimi added. "Literally. Poor Professor Fishtail . . . he might have to build a new one."

"I don't even want to know how they paid for this," Tinki whispered.

"Rumour is, it came from Herbert's hidden stash," Smackie said. "He has many pockets."

"Who knew that old croc had a soft spot for music?" Sniffer joked.

"He doesn't," Moss replied dryly. "But he had a well-stuffed wallet with extra folds. Although this may be the last of it."

"At least he's got good taste," Fangl smirked.

"And guts," Sylvest added. "Takes guts to bet it all on something unknown."

"Time to roll," Herbert called out. "We've got a schedule."

"One heck of a day ahead," Ruffa agreed.

"You're right about that," Herbert said, firing the engine.

And with that, the Woof Purrs pulled out of the compound and headed for Birdheights—ready to bring music, mischief, and maybe a little mayhem to the city streets.

***

Later that day, after an uneventful journey, the customised tour bus finally reached the outskirts of Birdheights.

As they approached the city, Herbert activated one of the Woof Purrs float's secret weapons—long, sweeping drapes rolled down over the sides and rear of the bus. In an instant, all the branding, the giant photo of Kreamy, and even the projection screen were all hidden from sight. To any outsider, the bus looked anonymous—just another curious, oddly shaped float from somewhere deep in the provinces.

Only those who had been at The Diggout gig might have recognised them—and even then, the name Woof Purrs meant little. It was still fresh. Still underground.

As the bus rolled toward the starting zone, the parade officials began their meticulous inspections. Floats had to comply with Birdheights regulations, including a strict five miles per hour speed limit. Violations meant instant bans, sometimes for years. They weren't taking chances.

But Herbert was ready.

Inside the tour bus, he'd installed a genius workaround: a heavy brick encased in metal lodged securely beneath the accelerator. Screwed into the vehicle's frame, the block ensured the pedal couldn't go down far enough to break the speed limit—not unless someone had a screwdriver and a lot of time. The design wasn't Herbert's own. It came from none other than Mikey Angels, who had once been something of a getaway artist. The croc had a colourful history of skirting rules in multiple cities—and had only avoided capture by disappearing just in time.

Now he was a senior assistant to none other than Boreme Kildare, the shadowy merchant mogul who practically owned half of Birdheights. No one dared cross Kildare unless they wanted their tail feathers clipped for good.

Parked in the float compound, the band helped themselves to cool drinks from a giant cooler onboard. Then they stepped beneath the central marquee, mingling with hundreds of other performers across the land.

The cats and dogs drew stares.

Mixed bands were rare. Cats and dogs? Together? In public? That was pushing it. Many Animalians hadn't seen such a pairing since the infamous Droopsters incident nine years prior, when the band had been banned for five years after creating a deafening uproar during the parade. Even now, few from Dogwood or Purrville ever bothered turning up again.

But this year . . . was different.

The parade's starting order was finalised by Pelican Joe Hightoes, a sharp-beaked stickler for order. When it came time to list the Woof Purrs, he paused.

"Dogwood and Purrville?" he muttered. "Shared float? Never heard of that before."

Still, there was no rule against it. He stamped their papers, and the line-up moved forward.

The floats rolled out of the lot and crept onto the main avenue one by one. The party had begun.

Birdheights' main street thrummed with energy. Music blared from every corner, and dancers twirled on floats and beside them. Confetti rained from above. Side barriers were removed as the public merged into the street, becoming part of the show. It was wild, glorious, and precisely what the Woof Purrs had planned.

The rules of safety were still enforced. No children under ten were allowed among the performers, and eagle-eyed police officers—literally—kept watch. Parrots barked orders. Crows shuffled documents. But the eagles, broad-shouldered and cold-eyed, radiated absolute authority. Each carried a baton at the ready. No nonsense today.

The Woof Purrs float remained hidden among the final ranks as the parade rolled along.

Then . . . it happened.

The drapes dropped.

Lights flicked on.

Music blasted from the speakers, so loud that the crowd jerked around in surprise. On either side of the bus, images of Kreamy removing her mask beamed proudly to the world. On the back screen, the footage played—raucous cheers, a standing ovation, the legendary moment the band had been denied.

And then, scrolling across the bus in vivid LED lights:

The Woof Purrs performed last month at this year's first Superband Competition. They were not allowed to win because the judges did not pick the best band.

"The winner was the band belonging to Boheme Kildare's son."

"Someone cheated badly."

"The Woof Purrs, a fusion of musicians from different clans, created a new sound . . . but were ignored."

"Today, we will be ignored no longer."

The message wrapped around the bus again. Then again. And again.

At first, the crowd thought it was a publicity stunt for next year's contest. But as the bold words repeated, something shifted. Heads turned. Conversations hushed. Onlookers leant forward. This wasn't a promotion. This was a revelation.

As the first track ended, a figure stepped up on top of the bus: Ruffa. With a mic in paw and a quiet confidence that stunned even his bandmates, he began to speak.

"Fellow Animalians! Citizens of Birdheights! Have you ever wondered why music never changes? Why don't artists mix? Why do new sounds never emerge?

"It's because those in charge—those who own the stages—fear to allow change to happen.

"But music belongs to everyone. To us all. There should be no walls between genres, no rules that forbid collaboration between clans. Music is, and always should be, universal."

A hush fell over the nearby crowd.

Then the next track began—louder, more defiant. It shook the pavement. Ruffa stepped down, calm as ever. And once again, when the music stopped, he repeated the message.

Twelve songs. Twelve speeches. One bus.

And a growing sense among the crowd that something bigger than a parade was happening right before their eyes.

The cats and dogs aboard the Woof Purrs float could feel it—something special was happening. Their sound had never been this tight, this alive, this fierce. Every beat, every chord, was laced with adrenaline and defiance. They were more than a band now. They were a message.

It didn't take long for word to reach the top.

Buck Cloudwings, the Chief of Police of Birdheights and a proud eagle of high reputation, received an urgent report: a mixed-species band was parading through the city, defying cultural norms and directly implicating Boreme Kildare himself. And they were doing it loudly without any restraint.

Buck's feathers ruffled at the report. He wasted no time notifying Deputy Mayor Muffat Flapwell, who, red-faced and panicked, immediately contacted Kildare. Within minutes, the tiger tycoon, flanked by his security team and Mikey Angels, appeared on the scene.

As Buck flew overhead, he could hear the music blasting from the Woof Purrs float. When he landed nearby, the crowd was thick, and the float's presence attracted lots of attention. The police were stuck—too many onlookers, too much excitement. Pushing through could cause a full-scale riot.

"This is outrageous!" Flapwell hissed. "They're stirring up trouble, mocking the system! I won't tolerate it."

"Arrest them all, now!" demanded Kildare, storming beside the chief. "That's an order."

Buck Cloudwings hesitated.

"If we move now, we'll light a fuse under this street," he warned. "Birdheights is already under too much pressure because of the rules we keep setting for others to follow. You want us to be the spark that sets it all off?"

Flapwell's face twitched nervously. Kildare growled.

"I don't care! These mutts and kittens are trying to ruin my good reputation."

"You mean . . . they're telling the truth?" Buck raised a feathered brow. "You want us to punish them for being honest?"

The two stared each other down.

Kildare's bodyguards shifted about uneasily, not sure what to do.

But Buck wouldn't budge. "My officers are going to stay out of it."

"Fine," Kildare growled. "Then I will handle this insult myself."

With that, he headed off through the crowd.

Atop the float, Ruffa was repeating his message through the speakers:

"Fellow Animalians! Are they denying us the right to create great music together? Why are we being told to obey the rules of those who fear things being done differently? Music should belong to all of us. It's time the rules were changed. Let music be set free!"

The crowd cheered. Down below, Boreme Kildare nudged his way forward.

"Move aside! Get out of my way!" he barked, pushing smaller animals out of the way.

From atop the float, Fangl peered down.

"He looks furious," she said.

"That's because we're telling the truth about him," Moss replied coolly. "Truth has claws."

The others chuckled as Kildare finally reached the front of the float.

"You filthy rascals!" he shouted, eyes blazing. "Nobody makes fun of me and gets away with it!"

He stood before the moving float, paw held out, forcing Herbert to slam on the brakes. The sudden jolt knocked a few musicians sideways, and Ruffa nearly toppled off his pedestal—until Smackie grabbed him just in time.

"Thanks," Ruffa muttered.

"Don't mention it," she smirked. "Good to have you back."

"I never left."

"You kind of did."

As the float halted, Kildare smacked a paw against the windscreen.

"You're going nowhere, you hear me? This charade ends now!"

But Rocko had other plans.

From the side of the street, Rocko and his biker gang silently rolled in. With practised ease, Rocko and a fellow rider cast a massive fishnet forward, looping it between their bikes and hauling it toward Kildare.

He didn't even see it coming.

The net hit him from behind, swept his feet off the ground, and flung him forward—until he landed, with a heavy thunk, stuck to the front of the bus like a disgruntled bug on a windshield.

The crowd exploded with laughter and applause.

Fangl and Sylvest darted downstairs to secure the net through the windows, tying it tightly from inside.

"How long do you reckon he'll be stuck there?" Fangl asked.

"Oh, for a good while." Rocko winked. "Parade's not even halfway through. Keep playing; this is fun."

The float began to roll again. Red-faced and growling, Kildare could do nothing as the music resumed behind him.

"Woof Purrs! Woof Purrs!" came the chant from the crowd.

Up top, the band kept playing. Down the street, the tempo kicked up a notch. A fiery blast of drums, shrieking guitars, and blazing brass sent shockwaves down the avenue. Rommy stepped forward and barked into the mic. The music surged.

Then—silence.

One gentle note from Fangl's keyboard.

Mimi leant in and sang in the softest, most unmistakable voice imaginable. The crowd hushed. Her tone was tender, like a lullaby wrapped in starlight. Rommy joined her, humming gently, the two voices melding into a soulful duet.

Another cymbal crash—and the music exploded again. Chaos, beauty, and pure energy whirled around the crowd. They weren't just watching the parade anymore. They were part of it.

On the front of the float, Kildare's face flattened against the glass.

Herbert glanced at him uncomfortably. Then, on impulse, he flicked on the windscreen wipers. They got stuck on Kildare's head.

"Oops," Herbert muttered.

Kildare growled, but nobody could hear him. The music was too loud.

Snoop was jogging alongside, snapping photo after photo. Milly, notepad in paw, was scribbling down what she saw as she tried to keep up. This was history in the making, and they were there on the front lines.

Behind them, the deputy mayor wiped sweat from his brow.

"Should we . . . free Mr Kildare?" a nervous officer asked.

Chief Buck Cloudwings smirked.

"Let him enjoy the view. He has the best seat in the house."

Mikey Angels strolled beside the float, laughing to himself. Ruffa gave him a wave. Herbert nodded. And Mikey, for once, said nothing. He knew this day would be written about for generations.

No one remembered who had won the Superband Competition.

But everyone remembered the day the Woof Purrs rewrote the rules in music.

And Boreme Kildare? His face said it all—squashed against the windscreen, eyes darting with fury, netted like a fish on display. The tiger, who once ruled the city, was now part of the act.

"Someone is going to pay dearly for this," he muttered through clenched teeth. "You'll see . . . all of you . . ."

But nobody heard him.

Because the music roared louder.

CHAPTER 33

Good to Be Back

That night, they had to make their way home. The Woof Purrs couldn't afford to stay at any Birdheights hotel, no matter how triumphant their performance.

Rocko offered them beds at his ranch, but they all agreed: it was best to head back. Each had their own home to return to.

As they drove into the night, Herbert remained on high alert. The brick and casing had been removed, but he still drove slowly due to poor visibility. Kildare had been untied near the end of the parade by a couple of his men, so at least the view through the windscreen was no longer quite so unnerving.

First, the Eight Cool Cats were dropped off at their homes in Purrville. Then Herbert took the Droopsters back to their abodes in Dogwood. Just as dawn painted the sky, the school bus returned to Ruffa's compound.

Herbert staggered into his house and fell into bed without even undressing. He was snoring in seconds. Ruffa wasn't far behind. Across Animalia, heads hit pillows, and sleep came fast.

Two days later . . .

Purrville was buzzing. Whispers spread about what had transpired in Birdheights, though nothing yet appeared in the Purrville Press. Its editor, Bigeyes Furrystone, refused to publish hearsay. It wasn't until two days later that a copy of the Birdheights Daily landed on his desk.

Furrystone read the front page: *"Woof Purrs Stun and Impress in Birdheights Parade."*

Beneath the headline were names—every member of the Eight Cool Cats, the Dogwood Droopsters, Ruffa, and Herbert. The deputy mayor had officially awarded them Outstanding Participation Certificates. A sidebar column revealed that the Superband Competition had, under public pressure, created a new accolade: the Audience Award for Most Outstanding Band. The inaugural winners? The Woof Purrs.

Back at home, Mrs Krusher read the article aloud three times. Each time, she grew prouder—and more suspicious of her daughter's ever-mounting adventures.

Boreme Kildare, meanwhile, was livid. He dialled Deputy Mayor Muffat Flapwell in a fury. Flapwell mumbled something about the mayor issuing a statement once his three-year sick leave ended. Everyone in Purrville knew that day wasn't coming anytime soon.

The Principal's Office

The Eight Cool Cats sat across from Professor Fishtail, glasses of warm milk in their paws. His desk was cluttered, his expression stern.

"What will I do with you lot?" he grumbled. "The school bus is missing. The old one's back in service, barely running. You cavorted with dogs! Dogs! And now you're town heroes? Preposterous."

Tinki raised her paw. "Sir, we were kittienapped—"

"Yes, yes. But to believe a crocodile hypnotised eight intelligent mommies! Preposterous! Are you hearing yourself?"

Fangl calmly replied, "We thought you might say that. So, we invited Herbert. He's outside. He can demonstrate how it happened."

"Demonstrate? Don't be absurd. A hypnotist crocodile—rubbish. Fine. Bring him in. I'll enjoy watching him make a fool of himself."

Ten minutes later...

Herbert stood in front of the professor, swinging a golden stopwatch.

"Repeat after me," Herbert said, his eyes locked on Fishtail's.

The professor's eyes glazed over.

"You love what the Eight Cool Cats have done with music."

"I love what the Eight Cool Cats have done with music."

"You will praise them."

"I will praise them."

"You won't punish them at all."

"I won't punish them at all. They are—remarkable musical heroes."

The cats smiled. Herbert had one final whisper for the professor, then pocketed the watch and shuffled out. The bus would be returned, eventually . . . maybe.

"Thank you for your time, sir," said Tinki.

"You're all excused. Do keep up the good work in music."

They bowed and left, still grinning.

EPILOGUE

The Purrville Performance

That evening, the Purrville High School auditorium was full to bursting. Word had spread, and every cat in the village wanted a glimpse of the mysterious, celebrated Woof Purrs.

Four dogs joined the Eight Cool Cats on stage when the curtain rose.

Silence. Utter silence.

Ruffa walked on, smiling broadly.

"You know your Eight Cool Cats," he announced. "Now, meet Rommy on vocals, Smackie on trumpet, Sniffer on bass, and Moss on drums. These four helped win the Audience Award. Together, they are the Woof Purrs!"

Silence.

He went on.

"They stunned Birdheights. They changed the musical landscape. Now they're here to perform for you!"

Still no response.

Then KT and Moss struck the drums. The stage lit up, and the secretly enhanced sound system blared with glorious, irresistible sound.

The audience, sceptical at first, couldn't resist the music. Paws tapped. Heads nodded. Then came the chorus.

By the end of the set, the entire hall erupted. Applause thundered. Cheers echoed for nearly ten minutes.

Professor Fishtail climbed on stage, dazed.

"Erm . . . why am I up here? Oh yes. Incredible. That's what this was."

He shuffled off, leaving Ruffa holding the mic. Ruffa turned to the twelve musicians on stage.

The audience stood—all of them.

Moss looked at KT. Kreamy at Rommy. Tinki at Sniffer.

They weren't two bands anymore.

They were one. They were incredible.

The Woof Purrs.

9 781919 287812